# The Puzzle

## A Novel

Susan Davis Sandberg

Cover design by John Sandberg

SusanDavisSandberg@gmail.com

ISBN-10: 0984992316
ISBN-13: 978-0-9849923-1-7

In memory of my typist Glenna Goulet
My first big fan

# Chapter 1

Harsh male voices in the hall woke her. Coral Svenson lifted her head up and blinked in the darkness.

She was alone. The voices moved past her door to the office adjacent to hers. The words were indistinct but the voices were familiar although she'd never heard Governor Whalen Atkins so angry.

Quickly Coral felt around for her glasses. Her fingers found them folded neatly just beyond where her folded arms had cradled her head. Slowly her memory was becoming less fuzzy.

She'd had a splitting headache and taken two of the aspirin she carried in her purse in case she felt a tightening in her chest again. Her mother had died of a heart attack at age sixty. Coral was fast approaching that milestone.

The throbbing had lingered and Coral had turned off her desk lamp because the glare hurt her eyes. Then she'd removed her glasses, laid her head on her arms and closed her eyes to wait for the throbbing to ease so she could drive home and crawl into bed.

Sleep will never come, was the last thought she remembered having. She was exhausted.

I should have gone with Tara was the first coherent thought that flashed into her mind once it cleared. She hated

1

to be in the office when Brian Harvath, the governor's right hand man, was on a rampage. The spillover bathed everyone nearby in its ugliness.

Tara's call from Southern California before the dinner party telling her that Sandy had taken Winners Dog on the first day of the two-day Specialty had warmed her.

"Why don't you fly down?" Tara had urged. "You can show Sandy in Breed while I show Banner. Come on. It'll be fun."

Coral had brushed her daughter off. "There's so much to do here."

"What?" her daughter countered. "For once you don't have a dog at home. With Biscuit being bred at Markham's, you're free."

"I have to go to this dinner. The governor's expecting some corporate execs from New York and Texas. There will be so many loose ends to tie up afterward."

"You work so he can play," Tara injected sarcastically.

"Tara!" her mother scolded.

"I'm not sorry, Mother. He takes advantage of you. Why doesn't his secretary pick up the pieces?"

"She doesn't work..."

"I know. She doesn't work weekends. For heaven's sake, Mother, you're a volunteer. Why should you? I know you think the sun rises and sets in the man, but I don't think he's worth a second of your time. You can bet your bottom dollar he wouldn't consider giving you a second of his."

The conversation with her daughter had nagged at her and she'd left the dinner party during desert and gone straight to the office. No one had noticed her departure just as no one had noticed her discomfiture when she was introduced to

Huxley Zurich, founder and president of LAITA, an organization she despised. His handsomeness surprised and irritated her.

When the outer door to the adjacent office opened, the words of the two men became distinct. Coral shrunk in her seat, uncertain whether to interrupt their angry exchange to apprise them that she was present or to simply sneak out.

The light was switched on and streamed through the door cutting a swath across Coral's desk. She cringed and automatically rolled her chair further back into the shadows.

Now is the time to speak, she told herself. To say 'You woke me.'

She rose from her chair and moved around her desk. The thick carpeting on the floor of the posh law offices in downtown Ardilla, offices that had been turned over to the governor for this campaign, softened Coral Svenson's footfall. She was still in the shadows when she heard Governor Atkins say, "I know what to do with this!"

Coral hesitated, forming her words in her mind.

The shadow of the tall, broad-shouldered man momentarily blocked out the light streaming in through the door. He turned toward the shredder standing just inside her office doorway and angrily shoved a large photograph and a paper into its revolving jaws. The strips of shiny colored paper fell into a waiting plastic bag. Already two plastic bags filled with interoffice memos, rough drafts of speeches and notes on strategies sat on the other side of the machine waiting to be picked up by the special service on Tuesday.

Coral Svenson stood breathless, her mouth dry, her palms sweaty. She took a small step forward.

"What the hell does Varrieur want?" Came the shout from the other room.

Coral withdrew her foot. Her heart beat wildly.

"To be the ambassador to France," came the terse response as Atkins spun on his heel and left the room.

Coral stood flat-footed, unable to react quickly enough to enter his field of vision.

"And what did you tell him?" Harvath growled. Coral imagined the square-jawed shorter man cocking an ear to catch the front door opening. His brow would be furrowed in consternation.

Atkins chuckled. "I told him to brush up on his French."

"The others will be here any minute," Harvath warned. "We've no time for jokes."

"Who's joking," the governor responded, his voice somber. "He's got the negatives."

"Who else knows?"

"You, me and him. That's it."

And me, Coral concluded silently. Only I don't know what I know.

"It can't happen again!" Harvath growled.

"It won't," Atkins promised.

"Shouldn't have happened this time." Harvath went on, his fury still simmering under the quiet of his tone.

"Make it go away, Brian," Atkins ordered in a flat voice.

"You know..." Harvath began.

Atkins interrupted the familiar spiel of his chief political advisor, the man whose rank in the party could mean the difference between victory and defeat, the man who had the stature to draw into Atkins' campaign the best strategists, lawyers and speechwriters in the political arena. "I know. I know. The American public does not elect a man who engages in aberrant..."

Harvath cut in. "Try loathsome, detestable, unconscionable, immoral, sacrilegious..."

Atkins blocked his charge with a defensive firing of his own, "No one was hurt. It's not even a felony."

Horvath's scorn exploded.

"What the hell are you saying? Because if you think that this addiction of yours is not serious we may as well stop right now. Because if you think that, you'll want to whet that appetite of yours again, and all will be lost. You must treat this with the seriousness it deserves."

Coral stood riveted, unable to even think.

The returning volley was almost weak by comparison. "It will never happen again."

"It better not," came the stern warning.

"You have my word."

"You can't even think about it. Dream about it. Or even let a fleeting remembrance of it cross your mind," Harvath warned.

The outside door opened and the hallway filled with the babble of excited voices.

"I said, 'You have my word,'" Atkins repeated as petulantly as a child eyeing a cookie jar, hoping to sneak out one more.

"Okay then, I'll take care of it," Harvath replied as the voices passed by Coral Svenson's door and floated into the lighted room. The older woman stepped back against the wall resting her gray hair on the linen wallpaper that rose from the wainscoting. She wiped her hands on her skirt and wished fervently that she was in Southern California with her daughter.

Governor Whalen Atkins' booming voice woke the gray-haired woman from her brief reverie. He was introducing everyone in the room to the visitor.

"You know Brian Harvath, of course," Atkins began.

Coral envisioned the visitor shaking Horvath's thick-fingered hand as he spoke, "Our former Secretary of Defense, of course." Huxley's voice carried his pleasure.

"Everett Cox, Frank Whiting," Atkins went on. "Careful what you say around these two."

"Lawyers, huh?" said the visitor mockingly.

Coral imagined Cox's dark brows coming together slightly. Every inch the picture of the erudite, corporate lawyer he once was, Everett Cox was at the same time sensitive enough to pick up the negative vibes hidden beneath the coating of the joke.

Coral pictured Frank Whiting running his fingers through the tangle of curls that bushed out above his ears in an effort to hide his annoyance at the slur. While Whiting had the slightly rumpled look of a college professor, he too had been a successful lawyer before joining the governor's team. His area of expertise had been civil rights and his clientele had forced him to hone his ability to read a man's bias swiftly and accurately.

"And Caleb Brinson accompanied you here," Atkins continued smoothly, "I'm sorry we didn't have much personal time at the dinner which is why I invited you here afterward."

Despite a slight curiosity as to which of the party guests was so honored, Coral's mind left the meeting and focused on how she could exit without being seen or heard.

The terseness in Everett Cox's tone brought Coral's focus back to the meeting. He'd interrupted the opening remarks of the speaker.

"Yes, Mr. Zurich, we know you run the League Against Inhumane Treatment of Animals. We recognize that LAITA is one of the most powerful animal rights groups in the country. Your tactics are at times suspect and that's because your organization has two agendas: the superficial money-raising agenda which paints you as a humane organization that cares about animals and is willing to wage a spirited war in their defense and the hidden agenda which is to control the animal industry. I assume that you are here because you have something to offer a potential presidential candidate and you need something from a winning candidate."

Coral's mouth dropped open. She'd long ago discontinued her considerable support from LAITA when they supervised the poisoning of twenty-two show dogs as a protest against dog showing. The tactic had galled her. Those poisoned had suffered needless agony. Such wanton cruelty in an agency purporting to be against the inhumane treatment of animals was made more insidious by the use of children to feed the dogs the poisoned treats.

Coral Svenson took two steps forward. That he had been a guest at the dinner had surprised but not alarmed her. The governor courted many groups. But that he should be treated with deference was shocking. Surely there was some mistake.

The next voice she heard was the governor's. "I see, Huxley, that you are surprised that my staff is aware of all your agendas. In a good working relationship, it is important that the partners be aware of each other's goals. Don't you agree?"

Before Huxley could take over the conversation, Whiting added, "We believe we can benefit one another."

He gave his unruly hair one last finger comb, before launching into his spiel. "Non-profits are notoriously disorganized as a group. They are all scrambling for available funds by trying to focus the attention of the public on their particular need. The United Way sprang up because people were sick of being bombarded by so many organizations that they welcomed the concept of one large gift that would take care of everyone. It didn't work out. Most groups didn't get enough to fill their needs. Some were left out altogether. Environmental groups and animal rights groups never even made it under the United Way umbrella."

Cox tag-teamed his associate, picking up the narrative and spinning it in a slightly different direction. It was done with subtlety and had the desired effect of keeping Huxley's attention. "Control of the animal industry provides leverage in the transportation, entertainment, farming, manufacturing, research, pharmaceutical, and retail industries. Currently, you personally are moving people into various organizations that deal with animals. For example, we know that you have infiltrated the Humane Society on national and local levels. We've watched you turn Animal Cruelty Prevention groups into militant organizations. But you go beyond that. LAITA opposes the use of animals to help people. This agenda you approach more subtly; for example, you pressure the Trustees of Helper Dogs for the Blind to put Will Groton in as CEO. I assume that your plan is to undermine the operation there, but I don't understand how one such placement will further your cause very much."

Coral remembered the negative changes that had taken place since Groton's arrival, the insertion of business professionals with no dog experience over dedicated staff. The new hires played with numbers and treated dogs like manufactured products. While Coral had chalked the changes up to growth, her daughter had insisted that there was more. Tara, currently a stringer writing feature articles for The Oakland Daily Journal, planned to approach the editor with a proposal to write an investigative piece.

Coral leaned closer to the door and strained to hear Zurich's mumbled response.

"He wasn't our only placement."

She heard the feigned surprise in Cox's voice. "There are others?"

Zurich's voice was suddenly smug. "That's because you think only in direct terms. Groton has been peppering key posts with inept people. When he retires in a couple of years, the place will fall apart."

"They could learn their jobs by then," Cox inserted.

"Maybe if they were bright or dedicated. They are neither. As soon as the disintegration begins, they'll use their titles to land other jobs in the animal industry leaving chaos in their wake. That, my friends, is how you bring down the enemy. You destroy him from within."

"How can your orchestrate this?" Cox asked. "You can't know people on every board of directors."

Zurich chortled. "You hold the key in that last statement. You think you're so smart. How do you think I do it?"

Everett Cox's hesitation was minute. Coral held her breath waiting. She liked this bright young man with the dark eyes and handsome even features and had hoped that Tara would find him attractive.

"I think you check out the Board members and single out one you can influence."

"How?" Huxley Zurich challenged.

"I imagine that you offer a favor; for example, you will steer the animal rights activists away from investigating the research activities of the major manufacturer upon whose board that particular trustee also sits. In exchange, your candidate is hired."

"Close," Zurich admitted. "So why am I here? Certainly not to put a bug in some board member's ear."

"You want what we want," Whalen Atkins said. "Money and power."

"I've got both," Zurich stated flatly.

"But not as much as you could have," Atkins replied.

"I don't need your help."

Atkins was quick to acknowledge the man's ego. "No, I don't suppose you do. But it wouldn't hurt your prestige any to be a personal friend of the President of the United States, would it?"

For several minutes not a word was spoken. Coral heard the clink of the decanter against a glass. Since the governor knew the preferences of all his associates, she guessed that he was looking at each with a bottle in one hand and a glass in the other and pouring the drink after an approving nod. He did his homework when it came to men he wanted to impress.

Coral felt sick and dizzy both. Her headache was returning. She closed her eyes as she slid to the floor.

The clink of glasses woke her. She glanced at the lighted hands on her watch. She'd only dozed a few minutes. She was surprised that she'd done so at all. She had to do something about this overwhelming fatigue. Something must be wrong with her.

If she fell asleep again, she most certainly would be found.

# Chapter 2

The glint from the metal edge of her purse stuck in the kneehole of the desk caught her eye. The conversation from the next room had taken a cheerier tone. Evidently, the business that drew them together was finished. It was Friday night. The bar was well stocked. Drivers were waiting by the limousines to take them home. There was no reason to stop partying.

Coral flipped over onto her knees, hiked up her skirt and crawled to the desk. She was behind the desk when the voice of Huxley Zurich entered the room.

"Hey, where's the light switch?" His words were slurred. "Never mind. I found it."

Coral tucked her slim legs close to her as the lights went on.

"This isn't the bathroom," he said. "Where the hell's the bathroom?"

"Go straight," Everett Cox called. His voice was clear. "It's..."

"Too late," came the mumble just before the retching began.

The stench hit Coral's nostrils instantly. She clapped her hand over her mouth and nose to block the smell out and the protest in.

The men in the other room were silent.

Cox's voice was soft when he spoke. "Come on. Let me show you where to wash up... No, turn around. We'll use another bathroom."

"Need any help?" Whiting asked.

"Catch the light," Cox replied.

Coral heard Whiting gasp, "Ugh! What a mess!" just before the light went out.

"Close the door," Whalen Atkins said.

Just like that Coral was bathed in darkness.

Slowly, she rose to her feet and moved around the desk. The stench rose to greet her.

She fished the miniature flashlight out of her purse and, pressing the tiny button, shone its light across the floor. She avoided the mess as she cautiously made her way to the shredder. Holding the flashlight between her teeth, she opened her purse and removed her bulky wallet and tucked it under her arm. She reached down and plucked a fistful of shredded paper from the top of the plastic bag fastened to a square metal holder. She quickly stuffed the paper into her purse. The light picked up a few stray colored strips so she grabbed a second fistful and scrunched them into her bag on top of the first. She turned off the flashlight, dropped it into her purse and snapped it shut. The wallet remained tucked under her arm.

"What're you doing?" Atkins voice boomed from the other room.

"Thought I might clean up a bit," Cox replied.

"Leave it."

"Coral will be upset."

"She'll call someone to clean it," Atkins explained. "Now shut the damn door."

As the stream of light narrowed, Coral skirted her desk and raced toward the door that led into the hall. She ran down the carpeted hallway to the stairway door that led down to the parking lot behind the office building. The last door was a fire door with a bar handle that opened from the inside and then locked itself automatically when it closed.

Coral knew that the limousines were parked out in front. It was expected that clients of the law offices would be ushered in the front. The lower level parking was for the staff. Coral was the only one who parked there so her white BMW was waiting next to the door.

She fished her key from her jacket pocket and slid behind the wheel. Without turning on the lights she eased herself out onto the back alleyway. She drove slowly past the Village Restaurant parking lot and onto the lane that led past the gas station on the corner. She rounded the corner, turned on her lights and entered the highway that threaded through the town.

She turned right again and looped back past the building where the law offices were. The lights were on in her office. A chill ran down her spine.

# Chapter 3

By the time Coral turned off the highway a quarter of a mile later onto Country Club Road which wound along the valley floor between the Club and the tree-studded hills, she knew someone would come after her.

Something had clued them into her presence. She guessed someone heard the car motor turn over and glanced out the office window. Her BMW was white. Even with its headlights off it was easy to spot.

It would take them a few minutes to discover that the shredded photo was missing. They'd want to get it back before she pieced it together so they'd move quickly.

Backroom shenanigans were not unusual. Deals were struck; promises made; support given. It was the nature of the political infrastructure. She'd heard it all before.

Only the photograph was different. And the threat it posed. The demand made had verified the seriousness of the problem. She didn't have much time.

She could almost hear Tara's voice telling her what to do. She'd raised a very bossy daughter.

"Get down here as fast as you can," she imagined Tara saying. "Two heads are better than one."

Tara liked using old cliché's when talking to her, the same cliché's Coral had used when rearing her only daughter.

Somehow it settled better when Tara did that. Coral's mind could handle the familiar easier than the new.

As Coral's gleaming white sedan turned into the hills surrounding the Ardilla Country Club and began its journey up the torturously winding, narrow road, past the stone and stucco, shake-roofed houses of the rich, hidden behind meticulously kept thick layers of landscaping, she dialed the local cab company and promised a ten dollar tip if the cabbie could make it to her house in fifteen minutes.

Even as she was making the offer, she realized that Atkins' men would beat the cab there.

She slowed to make a hairpin turn and realized that Atkins' men would turn up her driveway. If she were waiting around the bend, they wouldn't even see her. She had already started to give her address, "Twenty two... er sixty Hillside Circle. That's off Country Club Road."

Her address was twenty-two twenty. She had no idea if there was a twenty-two sixty.

"I'll be standing by the mailbox on the left side of the road," she added. It was eleven o'clock. The chance of another woman standing, bag in hand next to a mailbox, at such an hour was minute.

She turned and her lights shone on the aggregate stone driveway cut into large squares by rows of brick. Her husband had been very proud of his handiwork although he hadn't personally laid a single brick. It added an elegant touch to the uphill approach to the sprawling brick and wood house. From the drive a curving brick walkway cut through a carpet-like lawn to a raised brick entry area in front of a pair of polished oak doors flanked by stained glass windows. A small brass plaque fastened on the door frame gave the name of the security company guarding the property.

The garage door opened at the press of the remote button in Coral's hand and the light that automatically went on inside the garage showed her it was empty. She drove her car in, grabbed her cell phone, her purse, her wallet and her keys and began counting. She had five minutes.

The garage door hit the ground one minute later. Coral had already grabbed a cloth shopping bag from the shelf by the side door, shoved everything she was carrying inside and entered the kitchen. She tore Tara's taped copy of her itinerary off the kitchen cabinet and stuffed it into the bag as well.

One minute, ten seconds.

She ran into her bedroom, threw the cloth bag on the bed, threw open her closet doors and pulled the small soft leather suitcase from the shelf, threw it on the bed and opened it.

One minute, forty seconds.

She grabbed her travel kit and a pair of shoes from the floor of the closet and put them on the bottom.

Two minutes, ten seconds.

She removed her skirt from the closet and folded it and its hanger on top of the shoes. Her blouse and vest were next.

Three minutes, forty seconds.

A second blouse, a pair of slacks–both tossed hurriedly inside the case.

Four minutes even.

From the second drawer in her bureau, she grabbed a fistful of undergarments and pulling back the skirt, stuffed them on top of the shoes.

Four minutes, forty-five seconds.

She zipped the bag shut, grabbed it and the cloth bag and reaching into her closet snagged a second purse.

Five minutes. Time was up.

Coral went back into the kitchen, opened a bottom drawer and pulled out several plastic bags. Five minutes thirty seconds.

She ran through the living room into the den, opened the top drawer in her desk and grabbed the glue stick.

Six minutes. She'd used up her grace period.

She was out of time. On the way through the living room, she spotted the new puzzle she'd just bought and swooped it into her cloth shopping bag on top of the glue stick and the plastic bags. She didn't know why she grabbed it, but it was small and so she didn't stop to question her action.

At the front door, she opened the tiny cabinet imbedded in the wall behind the framed print, set the security alarm as well as the automatic timer on the lights. Behind her the bathroom light went on. When she was home, it was on all night, so the timer turned it on immediately.

Seven minutes, thirty seconds.

She was cutting it too close.

She saw the approaching headlights when she was only halfway down the driveway. They shone on the shrubbery across the road first but as the car swung around the corner, they'd shine directly on her.

Quickly she ran across the driveway and as the headlights lit up the bushes and shrubs to the right of the driveway, Coral ducked behind a pair of tall oleanders on the left.

The car pulled past her and parked with its headlights shining on the closed garage door. There were no windows in the large door. The only sign of life was the light in the back of the house.

Slowly Coral eased herself down toward the road behind the oleander hedge. She dare not miss the cab.

The men didn't leave the car immediately.

Coral waited at the edge of the driveway for the sound of a car door to slam. She dared not peek for fear that they would spot her. She stood rooted to the spot for over a minute, her panic rising as the tenths of a second flicked by. Once she crossed the driveway, she'd be pretty much out of sight. One couldn't see the road from the house, except through the opening cut by the driveway. Even if they didn't actually see her get in, they'd see the lighted sign on the top of the cab when it came to a standstill and guess that the passenger might be her. She had to reach her rendezvous point for her hastily sketched out plan to work.

Just as she was about to bolt and take her chances she heard a car door slam. She held her breath. A second slam.

They were announcing their presence to whoever was in the house.

Cautiously, she peeked about the foliage. She recognized Caleb Brinson walking to the front door. She poked her head out a bit further, just in time to catch Whiting heading around the garage toward the back. Their car blocked the garage. They had supposedly left her with no way out.

She ran across the driveway and up the road, her crepe-soled shoes making a soft crunching sound that the heavy growth of pyricantha that bordered the front of the property effectively muted. Fear spurred her on. Years of jogging up and down these hills made this short nighttime run manageable.

Twenty-two sixty was farther up the road than she thought, four houses instead of three. Every fifty feet the number changed; the house numbers were as widely spaced as the houses. This was one of the prime locations in a town which boasted seventy-five millionaires a quarter of a century ago and now had too many to count. A sliver of land and a shack near the highway sold for a quarter of a million and became a real estate office. The shack was tastefully renovated and continued to be affectionately termed 'the shack' despite its new cedar siding and colorful landscaping. It was home to Ardilla's landmark oak tree and when the new owners wanted to expand their parking facility, the city fathers persuaded them not to.

Coral had just begun to breathe heavily when she pulled up next to 2262. There was no 2260. She stood in front of the number on the mailbox and waved at the cab that rounded the corner less than a minute later.

The ten dollar bill was in the cabbie's hand before Coral opened the back door.

"This is a circle," she said. "Keep on going."

"It'd be faster if I turn around," he argued. He was a small man, with tattooed arms that were well-muscled.

"I'm a generous tipper," she reminded him.

He shrugged and continued forward.

Coral fished her cell phone out of her bag, dialed the police and reported a car at 2220 Hillside Circle. "Mrs. Svenson is on vacation," she added.

"Ain't that where you was?" the cabbie interjected. Coral saw him looking at her through the rearview mirror.

Coral hedged. "You picked me up at 2262."

A question from the dispatcher brought Coral's attention back to the phone. "Who am I? I'm a neighbor in a cab on my way to the airport. That's why I saw them. Will you check it out?"

"We'll send someone right over," the dispatcher said.

"Oakland Airport, please," she said as the cab sped along Country Club Road. "I need to catch a plane.

"The red-eye to New York?"

"To L.A.," she replied as she punched in another number. "Reservation desk, please...Darn! They put me on hold."

"Last plane for L.A. left an hour ago," Guado put in. He turned onto the highway that bisected downtown Ardilla.

"Are you sure?" Coral asked.

"Take it from me, Manuel; nobody wants to land in LA at 2 AM. You can't even rent a car after midnight. Believe me, I know. The wife and me took our kids to Disneyland. We fly into LAX. We was supposed to arrive there at eight. We get there at nine thirty. We wait for the shuttle for our rent-a-car place, and it don't come. We wait and we wait. Marie makes me call. And I get promises for an hour and a half and then nothing. The kids are really tired by now, and so's Marie. She's pregnant, you see. Then we don't see many shuttles and it's getting close to midnight and we're looking at spending the night on the bench outside the terminal. So I flag the next shuttle. I don't care which car place he's from. He takes us to his base and the lights are going out. They open back up and rent us a car. So you know if them guys close up it's because there ain't no more customers coming their way."

"Take the Warren. It's shorter. I don't want to miss a flight by seconds," Coral said as she punched in a new number on her cell phone.

"You got them numbers memorized?"

"I make a lot of travel reservations for people and I remember numbers."

"Then you gotta know about flight schedules."

Coral laughed good-naturedly as she waited for an answer. "All I know is how to make a reservation. I never paid any attention to times."

Suddenly, Coral got through. "Alaska Airlines? I need a reservation on the first plane that'll take me from Oakland to Granite County... Not until then...? What in the world am I going to do for seven hours...? No, I know it's not your problem. Book me a seat in first class... Marie Guado... I'll pick it up in half an hour."

She saw the cabbie startle when she said the name and as soon as she'd completed her conversation, she began speaking.

"Mr. Guado, I need your help. I am trying to get to my daughter who's in Southern California. The men at that house, the ones we reported to the police, were at my house. They are after me."

"Then the cops got them."

"There are others in the group."

"They weren't cops, were they?"

"No. Of course not. Why would I report them if they were police?" Coral's voice carried her surprise.

"To keep more of them busy."

"What a great idea!" Coral chuckled. "I'll remember that one."

Manuel Guado's mouth turned up slightly. This woman was something else. "So whatcha gonna do when they ask for identification?"

"Oh, didn't I tell you? You're going to buy the ticket and I'm going to buy it from you."

"Me? I ain't got that kind of money."

"I'm going to give you the money in advance."

"And I'm gonna leave you alone in my cab? No way." Suspicion coated his tone.

"You're going to take the keys."

"Then the meter will stop," he protested feebly, not daring to suggest that she could hot wire the car.

"So I pay when you leave and, when you come back, you can start it up again. I mean you do have down time, don't you?"

Manuel nodded but his dark brows were touching.

"Besides," Coral went on, "I'll pay you for buying the ticket."

This time the lips parted in a real smile. "You got a deal."

Coral again had her cell phone to her ear and Manuel turned onto the Warren Freeway north of Oakland. It wasn't faster at this time of night but the lady was going to get what she wanted.

Coral leaned back as she waited for Tara to pick up the phone. She hoped her daughter was there. She counted the rings as she thought about Tara's situation. The banquet would have been over long ago and the dogs would have been aired and crated for the night. Banner and Sandy would be tethered to separate bed legs on top of clean sheets spread out on the floor. The dog show committee had reserved a block of rooms on the seventh floor so the barking dogs wouldn't have much effect on the regular clientele. And even if Tara slept through the ring of the phone, Banner wouldn't. His barking would wake her.

All this went through Coral Svenson's mind as she let the phone ring. Banner must be barking up a storm.

Tara's voice was breathless when she answered.

"Where were you?" Coral asked.

"Mom? It's almost midnight!"

"I'm coming down. I'll be there in the morning. Where were you?"

"Next door talking. Banner started barking and when I came in to quiet him, I heard the phone," Tara replied. "So tell me, why the change of heart? You were so set on not coming."

"I wanted to share..."

"Mom, it's midnight. What's going on?"

"I came privy to some information by accident. It could destroy my friend whom you don't like."

"Where are you calling from?"

"A cab."

"You're coming down by cab?"

"Don't be silly! I'm flying out of Oakland on Alaska Airlines at six-thirty in the morning. I'll be arriving at Orange County airport..."

"You mean John Wayne International," Tara inserted. "Keep up with the times, Mom."

"...at eight," Coral Svenson finished, ignoring her daughter's remark. It was Tara's only annoying habit. It only appeared when Coral had made some denigrating remark but right now Coral couldn't think of what she'd said that had annoyed her daughter. Tara would remember though and tell her if she asked.

"Tara, I'm in serious trouble," Coral stated flatly.

Tara picked up the significance of her mother's statement at once. "Does he know?"

"I believe so." They were communicating in their mother-daughter shorthand.

"What'll he do?"

"He sent two men to the house five minutes after I left the office...actually seven minutes."

"You timed them?"

"I was timing me. Packing. Trying to get out before they came. I saw my office light go on when I was on the highway behind the office. They know I took the photo out of the shredder."

"Before or after?"

"I have the strips."

"And everyone knows you're a puzzle whiz," Tara commented, no trace of her former annoyance. "What are your plans?"

"I'm buying my ticket in someone else's name for starters."

"No good, Mom. You don't think they'll just call the airports and find out who bought tickets after midnight?"

"Can they do that?"

Tara raced on without answering.

"Make it a Mr. and Mrs. purchase. You also need to reserve a seat on Delta or United or whoever out of San Francisco to LAX in your own name. Use your credit card to guarantee it." Her suggestion was close to an order. "Where are you going to stay?"

"I was going to use Marie's name again and get a room near the airport."

"Red flag, Mom."

"Mr. and Mrs. again?"

"You don't register anywhere...wait. I take that back. You register at the Wayfarer Inn near the San Francisco Airport. You know; the one we always pass by on our way in."

"But that's so far away from Oakland," Coral protested.

"You're not staying there," Tara replied impatiently.

"Tara, I'm dead on my feet. I can't ride around in a cab all night. On top of that he has to keep checking in with his dispatcher."

"Change cabs."

"I'm using his wife's name. He's going to buy the tickets for me. If he goes back to Ardilla, I'm afraid they'll find him and find out about the tickets."

"Then keep him with you. Do you have money?"

"Enough."

"Then after he gets your two tickets, in Oakland, have him tell his dispatcher that you won't fly coach and so you're going to try to get a flight out of San Francisco and you want

26

him to take you there. These airport trips are a flat fee and big bucks. You won't get an argument."

"So I go to the San Francisco airport?"

"Not quite. You pull up at the Wayfarers Inn I mentioned and book a room."

"Then what?"

"You go to Becky's and get some rest."

"He has to call it in."

"Tell him you want to go somewhere near San Francisco State but you don't have the exact address."

"They were at the house," Coral said dully. Her head was spinning again. Maybe she could nap on the way to San Francisco as they crossed the Bay.

"What's that mean?"

She roused herself to respond.

"They could have my address book."

Tara fell silent for almost a minute. Her mother closed her eyes.

For just a second she told herself.

"Mother!" came the sharp voice. Coral was startled awake. She apologized as she straightened up.

"How sensitive is the stuff you have?"

"Very."

"He won't want it to pass through too many hands then."

"I wouldn't think so."

"If he has you arrested, the secret might spill out."

"I would guess he'd be afraid of that."

"Then he's going to limit the men involved," Tara said. "He's going to follow the cab trail. So all you have to do is have the cab wander up and down the streets for a nonexistent house while you take a nap at Becky's. Think he'll do that?"

"Why can't he just wait with me at Becky's?"

"Because his mileage has to check out."

"They might zero in on her house and wait there for me to show and find me."

"What other addresses do you have in your book?"

"There's Liz on James Street, Barbara on Stillman and Laura, you know, with the poodles, on Marina Boulevard."

"Where are they exactly?" Tara asked. "I don't have a map."

"Becky's house is practically across the street from San Francisco State except that 19th Avenue is between the college and the tracks, so..."

Tara cut her off. "In the southwest part of the city. Where's Barbara?"

"On Stillman which is a couple of blocks from McLaren Park right off 101."

"In the southwestern part. We want something farther away."

"Laura's on Marina Boulevard. That's as far north as you can get. And Liz is on Jones between the Embarcadero and the Presidio."

"Isn't Liz on that street that stands on its head?"

"The one you hate to drive down? Yes."

"Make that the destination. It's a crazy part of town."

"It's a good location," Coral protested lamely.

"A street so steep you take your life in your hands just to walk to the corner grocery store?"

"I'll misdirect them there," Coral promised.

"So I'll see you at the airport at eight."

"The governor has his own plane."

"You think he'll come here?" Tara asked worry creeping into her voice.

"He might. Go to the show with Joyce Webb. Set up next to her."

"Banner and Sandy will love that. Buffy's in season."

"There's safety in numbers," Coral finished. "I'll meet you there."

"You don't know your way around down here."

"The cabbies do."

# Chapter 4

Officer Shawn Gallaghan was the first to arrive at the Svenson house. He pulled his squad car across the driveway, effectively blocking the exit and waited for back-up.

Chief McLean had hammered that concept into the heads of his younger staff at every meeting which means Shawn had heard it at the start of every shift for the last four months. When McLean didn't say it one of his two assistants did. Lieutenant Greg Lim said it tersely, repeating the words as if they were law; Alex Caribou, also leftover from Chief Wrysinski's reign, drawled it slowly, but he always added something to make it stick.

At the beginning of this shift, Caribou had asked everyone, "Which is the greater number–two or one?" No one had answered. Everybody suspected a trick. It was too obvious a question. They were college graduates after all. He and Stephanie were both Berkeley grads and Drew had managed an AA degree from DVC.

Alex had retained his poker face and said simply, "Two is the right answer."

And he'd left them standing there dumbfounded.

"It's gotta be that mixed heritage of his," Drew, the tallest and thinnest of the threesome, commented as they left the squad room. "Maybe the Filipino part."

"I'd go for the Indian half," Stephanie put in. Her smile was attractive and she flashed it when she was annoyed.

Shawn voted for the Hawaiian quarter. It was their standing response to Lieutenant Caribou's ability to catch them off-guard.

Drew Manning and Stephanie Brandt had been baptized into police work under Chief Chattaway in Manzanita, the next town over. Drew's father was a local politician with strong Republican ties. Chief Chattaway was a politician's dream, but Drew wasn't like his father. He chafed under the incompetence running rampant through the force and did statistical analyses on his computer at night. He was just about ready to expose the department's ineptitude to someone–he hadn't figured out to whom–when two openings were posted for the Ardilla force.

Stephanie Brandt, who'd left the Manzanita force for Ardilla six months after Drew was hired, because, as she told Drew, she was tired of being a secretary, called him to let him know about the openings.

He'd discovered there were sixty applicants for the two spots and so he almost didn't apply. McLean told him later that his computer skills got him in.

Shawn, whose father was in the military, had grown up and gone to school in diverse locations. He found he had an ear for language and had learned both Japanese and German before he entered high school. There he picked up French and so he majored in languages in college, adding Russian and Spanish to his repertoire. He was being tutored in Vietnamese when McLean hired him. Shawn, blonde, curly-haired, handsome and muscular, didn't fit the standard perception of a student as Drew did; but, because he was, the two bonded quickly.

Drew figured that Stephanie might be long term. Stephanie's husband was a tax lawyer in Manzanita and she was locked into the area. Ardilla was the cream of the small city police forces in the area and McLean put her in a squad her first day. Drew felt that his lack of a four year degree made him less marketable than those who'd graduated with one. Silicon Valley was coming up with big money offers but he didn't want to be locked in at the lower levels. He saw his future as a computer expert on a large city police force and he saw Shawn, with his linguistic skills, gone within a year. How could McLean not see the long term?

Everyone at the station talked about the force expanding, and Drew was told he needed to shake all the bad habits he'd developed in Manzanita because the expansion was coming soon and, if he was ready, he'd move up.

He guessed that McLean was planning to swallow up Newell's force which was a mere five officers in all. That wasn't much of an expansion. And since none of the Newell force held a rank below sergeant, who was he going to outrank?

Stephanie Brandt arrived at the Svenson house only minutes after Drew Manning. She pulled her squad in front of the other two and got out quickly. "The security people are reporting a possible break-in," she informed Shawn and Drew. Her voice was low, her jaw square and her body stocky. Her experience gave her confidence.

"Ran the make on the car," Shawn said. "It belongs to Everett Cox of Sacramento."

"The governor's aide?" Drew queried. "What's he doing here?"

"Let's go ask him," Stephanie said, indicating to Drew that he should cover the back door. The rookie Shawn she'd keep with her.

The front door was ajar. Stephanie drew her gun and pushed it wider with her finger. The two stepped inside.

Shawn checked the dining room while Stephanie eased herself into the living room. The door from the garage opened and Drew stepped into the kitchen. Shawn passed him and disappeared into the bedroom wing while Stephanie eased toward the sound of voices in the den. Drew and she came around the archway from different directions with their guns drawn.

"Police," Stephanie said. "Hands up."

Caleb Brinson lifted his partly bald head and smiled in what he hoped was a disarming manner. "It's okay, Officers. We are just hunting for some papers Mrs. Svenson took home by mistake."

"Hands up!" Stephanie said firmly.

The younger man put down the paper he was holding and said something to the other man in Yiddish.

At that moment Shawn rounded the corner and took out his handcuffs.

Frank Whiting protested at once. "There's no need for those. We aren't criminals."

Despite both men attempting to interrupt, Stephanie recited the Miranda warning. Both finally gave up and let her finish before exploding.

"I am a lawyer," Frank Whiting said. "I know my rights. And we didn't do anything wrong. We are just here to pick up some papers the governor needs."

Caleb picked up the phrase he felt Frank hadn't emphasized enough. "We work for Governor Atkins."

Caleb paused. He saw recognition on the face of the gaunt, dark-haired member of the group. He looked him straight in the eye. "Our identifications are in our wallets."

Drew motioned Shawn to examine the ID's in the wallets.

"They're who they say they are," Shawn reported, signaling Drew with a wave of his hand.

Drew leaned over and whispered to Stephanie that he wanted to confer.

"Watch them," Stephanie said to Shawn and walked to the hallway with Drew. They heard the two men talking rapidly in a language neither could understand.

"What's up?" Stephanie asked.

"First off, Shawn wanted them to talk some more," Drew said.

"What language are they speaking?"

"My guess is Yiddish."

"I didn't know Shawn spoke Yiddish."

"I think he understands it. You know him and languages."

"You said, 'first off.' What's second?"

"These guys are with the governor. Things could get messy."

"This isn't Manzanita," Stephanie reminded her friend. "McLean plays it straight. They broke into the house..."

"Maybe they had a key."

"The alarm went off at the security office. If Mrs. Svenson had given them permission, she'd have told them about the alarm. Still, I'd better call McLean. This is too big for me."

"What about them?" Drew said.

"Tell them we're calling our chief. That'll keep them happy for a little while. No lawyer wants to be booked."

When Drew returned, the men were speaking English. Shawn nodded at Brinson. "He wants to make a phone call."

"I guess it'd..."

"No," Shawn said a bit loudly. "We're supposed to process them first."

"Boy, you are the go-by-the-rule boy tonight, aren't you?" Drew sneered, his thin cheeks coloring a bit. His father would dress him down for letting a junior officer decide his course of action. And there's no way he wasn't going to find out.

"We need to tell the governor where we are," Caleb Brinson urged, his slight nasal twang reminiscent of a whine. "He's waiting for those papers."

"We do have this rule," Drew apologized. "I'm new on the force and I sometimes forget. You get a phone call down at the station after you're booked."

Whiting objected, "But we don't want it to go that far."

Caleb picked up the plea, his twang causing Shawn to again cock his head as he tried to place the accent. "It would be best for everyone concerned that our little faux pas not become official. It could unnecessarily embarrass the governor. And he doesn't take kindly..."

"Let me interrupt you, Mr. Brinson," Drew said straightening up. "We don't take kindly to threats no matter how polite the words are. But before you get your hackles up, let me tell you that Officer Brandt is contacting our chief right now and we are waiting until he arrives before we go ahead."

Again a heated discussion in Yiddish took place between the two men. When it was over, Caleb Brinson said calmly, "That's fine. We'll wait."

When Chief Spencer McLean arrived, he had Lieutenant Lim in tow. Lim had his forensic kit with him. Stephanie Brandt met him in the hall and gave him a quick rundown on the situation.

"You were right to call me," he told the young woman, guessing she was worried that she'd acted timidly. "It's a delicate situation."

"Do we turn them loose?" she asked. Drew Manning, who had joined her, waited with baited breath. He knew what Chattaway would have done.

"Whatever for?" McLean said. "When they broke in, they tripped the alarm. It's the middle of the night. Who comes after papers at midnight? You caught them actually rifling through her desk. They didn't just break in to see if the lady was alright. Start with burglary. Add breaking and entering and hope there's not more. Drew, go with Lim. See if you can trace Mrs. Svenson's steps through the house. I want some assurance she's alive before I take another step."

"Does that mean we're going to let them go?" Drew whispered into Lim's.

"It means the chief will decide after we make our report."

The last sentence stuck in Drew's craw. He feared he'd jumped from one intolerable situation to another. The only difference was that this man caved in less conspicuously. As the two men entered the garage, Drew put his hand on the BMW and spouted, "They were talking Yiddish to each other. Shawn signaled me it was something big. They did it more than once."

"Stop that!" Lim scolded.

"Stop telling you something's going on?"

"Not that. You're putting your hands all over the car. You might destroy prints of whichever one came in this way."

"How do you know someone came in this way?" Manning asked.

"Garage light is on."

Drew stepped back from the car. "How do you know Mrs. Svenson didn't turn it on?"

"Look on the wall," Lim said. "She has an automatic garage door opener. It lights up the garage. She'd have no reason to turn on the light after she reached the door to the house."

"Suppose she needed to find something?"

"Then she'd have turned it off as she went into the house. The action would be automatic."

"So I dust the switches and back door."

"Not now. Now you follow me."

"Where are we going?"

"The woman who reported this said Mrs. Svenson was going on vacation, but we're going to assume nothing. Otherwise we might miss something."

"We're in the kitchen," Drew said. "There's nothing here."

"It's what's not here that's important."

"Not here?" Drew asked. "That makes no sense. If it's not here it'd be gone. How can you find what's gone?"

Lim pointed at the cabinet.

"She tore a piece of paper off the cabinet," Drew snapped. "So what?"

"Look around."

"I don't see anything. The kitchen is clean," Drew's words slowed. "Really, really clean. This woman wouldn't have torn the paper away from the tape holding it up, would she?"

"I'll make a forensic man out of you yet. Let's do the bedroom."

Drew stood just inside the doorway with Lim and viewed the room.

"What a mess!" Drew said. "Who would've thought it?"

"Look around again," Lim suggested.

Fancy bottles of perfume sat neatly arrayed on a dust-free glass tray on the dressing table. A silver brush, comb and mirror were neatly arranged on one side. Three red roses spread their leaves above a tall narrow-necked cut glass vase. One of the three blossoms drooped slightly. Drew guessed they had not been cut that morning.

He looked at the bed. The cover was tucked under the pillows in a straight line. The bottom of the spread was rumpled as if something had laid on it. On either side of the bed the nightstands stood, their surfaces shining under the lamps that graced them. On one was a black leather bound Bible and an empty cut glass dish. On the other was a digital clock and a small bud vase with a single yellow rose. The woman liked roses.

She was also neat.

"Looks like she packed in a hurry," Drew concluded aloud. "She didn't take time to put anything back."

"Not a search?" Lim asked.

"Uh uh. Just one drawer open. Not three or four. One pair of shoes missing. The others are still in a row. Clothes shoved sideways so she could remove a garment. She packed."

"Why the hurry?" Lim asked.

"Had a plane to catch?"

"Maybe," Lim said. "But if she had a reservation, why the scramble?"

"She misjudged her time?"

"Maybe," Lim said. "Take photos."

"We don't have a crime," Drew said. "I mean, it doesn't look like her things were pawed through. It looks like she packed in a hurry. Where's the crime in that?"

"Take pictures," Lim said. "There was a break-in. This room was disturbed, so take pictures. We can't rule out the possibility that we're being set up to think she packed and left."

"What are you going to do?"

"Look around some more," Lim said and left Manning with the bag. Drew opened it up and went to work. He had his orders. Computers and forensics. The two were wed. And Lim was quite the expert in the latter he'd learned.

Meanwhile, Chief McLean took Shawn Gallaghan to the far end of the dining room.

"As one Irishman to another, where'd you pick up Yiddish?"

"You're not Irish," Shawn protested. "McLean is Scottish."

"Sometimes an Irish lass falls for a handsome Scot. You do believe I had a mother, don't you?"

Embarrassed, Shawn ignored the question and went directly to the heart of the matter.

"It seems Mrs. Svenson took off with some shredded stuff—mostly a large, color photograph. They want to get it back before she pieces it together. Time is important to them. They saw a cab pass by just after they arrived. They think now that she took it."

"They think she went to a friend's house?"

"That's what they thought at first. That's why Whiting took the address book. But as they talked, they decided that she would've driven herself to a friend's house, so now they figure she is probably going to her daughter."

"Where is her daughter?"

"L.A. At some dog show. They figure Mrs. Svenson plans to fly there."

"Is that it?"

"Well, they think we're all dumb cops," Shawn said. "And considering my remark before, maybe they aren't too far off."

"Hey, my father things that the name makes me all Scot. My mother called me her little Irishman. The tag stuck. In my father's family, I'm called the Irishman," McLean replied, deftly taking Shawn Gallaghan off the hook. "Now, do these yokels know that you understand Yiddish?"

"No."

"Keep it that way. I'll explain later. Right now I have to deal with them."

And having said that Chief Spencer McLean strode through the living room and into the den where the two men, still handcuffed, were seated. He smiled pleasantly.

"Well, gentlemen," he said good-naturedly. "You've gotten yourself in a bit of a pickle. Didn't your mothers teach you that you never enter a house uninvited?"

His casualness disarmed the younger man, but Caleb Brinson had endured all the discomfort he planned to for one evening.

"I want these handcuffs removed," he demanded. "And I want to use the phone."

"Sorry," McLean said politely. "You've been arrested. The handcuffs stay on. And the phone call must be placed from the phone at police headquarters."

Frank Whiting, who was used to gesturing when he talked, was equally frustrated by the cuffs. He stood instead and used his shoulders to punctuate his remarks. "We didn't come here to steal anything. We came here to retrieve some of the governor's work papers that Mrs. Svenson accidentally took home with her. She wasn't here so we let ourselves in."

"With a key?" McLean asked as if it mattered.

"The door was open," Whiting claimed.

"Chief, come here," Lim called from the other room. "See what we found."

"Had she given you blanket permission to enter her house whenever you felt like it?" McLean pressed, then suddenly seemed to consider his lieutenant's call important and, before Whiting could reply, he said, "Excuse me a minute."

The Chief returned with an apologetic smile, "Sorry, what he found has nothing to do with you gentlemen and your search. Just some shredded paper. The bedroom just seemed such a strange place to find something like that, don't you agree?"

Whiting snapped at Caleb Brinson who had started to speak. He did so in Yiddish and Caleb fell silent.

McLean pretended not to consider the exchange important. He returned to his question. "Well, gentlemen, did she or didn't she?"

Both men looked at him blankly.

"Did she give you blanket permission to invade her premises whenever you felt like it?"

Whiting was beginning to be wary of this police chief. It was time to finish this.

"No, she didn't," he replied. "We assumed that it would be alright. I'm sure the judge will see it that way too."

"Careful," McLean chuckled. "You're playing lawyer-D.A. here and I'm not the D.A. I'm a cop. My power ends when the courtroom doors open."

"These charges are so spurious the D.A. won't even file them," Whiting charged, the ears beneath his bushy hair reddening.

"Don't count on it," McLean countered, his voice rising slightly. "He files what I tell him to file. I make my cases. My paperwork doesn't fall into cracks."

Brinson couldn't hold back his anger any longer. "You don't know who you're screwing with."

"I know exactly with whom I'm dealing," McLean responded his eyes steely, his jaw clenched. Whiting momentarily was taken aback by the sheer power of the man. It wasn't his height although he was well over six feet, or his build which was obviously athletic or even the piercing blue of his eyes or the resonance of his voice. It was none of those things and yet all of those things. The man exuded power. He was a leader of men. "I'm dealing with two men who just committed a burglary, have been arrested and are about to be booked."

"Book us?" Caleb exploded. "We don't have time to be booked! Look, what if we cooperate. Here let me empty all my pockets. You can see I didn't take anything."

McLean smiled. "Sorry. Not good enough. Mrs. Svenson is missing. You two are going to jail."

"She's gone on vacation."

"Where?"

Whiting interrupted. "We don't know."

"She took a cab," Brinson interjected, eager to be free.

McLean nodded at Stephanie who rushed off to check with the cab company.

"While she's doing that," Caleb said, "check out my pockets and let me go."

Gallaghan led the two men into the dining room where he uncuffed them and each emptied one pocket after another.

McLean plucked the address book from among Whiting's paraphernalia. Whiting noted that the chief was wearing thin plastic gloves.

"Yours?" McLean asked without flipping the pages.

"Yes. Of course," Whiting said. "My wife's, actually. It has a few numbers of people down here that she wanted me to call."

McLean motioned to the dark-haired officer passing by. He handed him the book. "Manning, dust this for prints, inside and out. My guess is that Mrs. Svenson's prints will be the only ones on the inside pages."

"Okay," Whiting said hastily. "It's hers. I picked it up to see if I could find a phone number we could call in order to locate her to tell her we'd come and taken the papers so she wouldn't worry and I must've slipped it into my pocket when the officers surprised us. I forgot it was there."

"You think fast on your feet," McLean commented. "Why lie?"

"You mean about it being mine?" Whiting said. "I just wanted to get out of here. The truth seemed so limp."

"The truth is never limp," McLean said sternly. Whiting saw the steel in the blue eyes bearing down on him. McLean's next words chilled him. "You're a lawyer Whiting. You know there's no such thing as negligent larceny. Gallaghan, book them."

The man was no fool.

Brinson protested immediately. "Why me? I didn't know he had the damned book."

"Didn't you?" McLean queried.

"No!" Brinson stated emphatically.

Stephanie stepped into the room. "No cab came here, but..."

"In the hall," McLean said. He moved Stephanie out of earshot then told her to continue.

"One stopped several doors up and the passenger asked to go to the Oakland airport," she reported.

"I need time to get hold of Mrs. Svenson," McLean said.

"I can make it a teaching exercise for Gallaghan," Brandt replied. "I'll have him process both men. That would take twice as long."

"That's what I like–creativity," McLean said heartily.

Officer Stephanie Brandt beamed. Her square face with its strong jaw was mannish until she smiled. Smiling softened her features and over the years she learned that and used her smile to disarm people.

At that moment one of the cell phones on the table rang.

"That's my phone," Brinson said. "It's probably the governor."

McLean stepped into the room. "Do you want me to answer it?"

"Well, yes..." Brinson began.

Whiting interrupted him with a shout. "No!"

Brinson stared at him. Quickly Whiting quietly explained in Yiddish that the governor might believe he was talking to one of them and say something that he shouldn't.

"Let it ring," Brinson said.

"Officer Gallaghan," McLean said. "Book them. Officer Brandt will oversee your processing. I want no mistakes on this one. If Officer Brandt needs to respond to another call, you will wait. Understood?"

Gallaghan had no idea what the chief was doing, but he was a man who followed orders to the letter. And it wasn't until he put the two men in his squad that he knew why the chief had set things up as he had.

In the back, the two conversed in Yiddish. And in the front seat, the handsome, blonde officer listened.

# Chapter 5

The leased law offices were located on the Country Club side of downtown Ardilla whose heart had been pierced as had those of all its neighbors by an eight-lane freeway coupled with an almost equally wide BART station and tracks. The needs of San Francisco whose professional core preferred to live beyond the Berkeley hills rose above local consideration. Thus Ardilla, like its neighbor, Manzanita were bisected by a highway system that grew fast and large to accommodate the rapidly accelerating cry for faster transportation into the heart of the city.

At the moment, however, Governor Whalen Atkins was not on the crowded BART train he'd fought to provide, but pacing up and down in his lushly furnished Ardilla office. Only Brian Harvath was with him. The polished Everett Cox was escorting Huxley Zurich back to his hotel to ease the abrupt end of the party that Coral Svenson's action had called forth.

Whalen Atkins, a former Stanford football running back, was pacing the floor, something he rarely did.

"There was no answer," he was muttering. "Why didn't Caleb pick up the goddamn phone?"

Harvath, who didn't dare sit in the presence of such anxiety, could think of only one reason but he dared not offer it. Instead he made a suggestion, "Perhaps it's time to call in our Special Forces unit."

Whalen gasped. "She's a friend!"

"They can track her faster than we can," Harvath said soothingly. "If we can get the material back still shredded, then she poses no threat. You can dispense with her services quietly."

"She has influence in this town. I need her on my side."

"We can hold her at bay with a threat."

"She's not afraid of dying."

"She told you that?"

"She and I talked about death back at Stanford. One of those deep philosophical group chats common then. Most of what was said I've forgotten, but not how she feels about dying. Of course, her daughter could be a problem. She's a reporter."

"A feature writer. She wouldn't know the first thing about digging up the real truth. And isn't Clayton Keyman her editor at the Oakland Daily Journal?"

Atkins' smile showed his even teeth and folded his cheeks into a wealth of lines that doubled the effect of his smile. That, along with his thick hair graying at the temples, his even features and his muscular build, evoked images of a fifty-year old Superman. In fact one cartoonist drew him complete with tiny cape flying behind his head. The imagery stuck and with it the illusion that Atkins was a hero.

"Then let's not get ahead of ourselves," the governor said.

Harvath had been waiting for him to calm down so they could map out a plan of action. "We need to stay one step ahead of her, however. And we need to be prepared to go all the way."

"I'm not sure Cox, Brinson and Whiting would go along with that last part," the governor said.

"That's why we need the special force. Let Cox, Brinson and Whiting go back to what we hired them to do–strategize your campaign."

"They know," Atkins reminded his chief advisor.

"They know nothing," the shorter man said. "Let me call in Eddie and Herb now. Let's get them on this thing from the start."

"Do we have to tell them?"

"That the photo is of you in a compromising sexual act, yes. The rest, no."

"Because I wouldn't want..."

"You should've thought of that earlier," Harvath quipped. "This can't happen again. I understand you slipped, but you can't let this happen again. In fact, if we don't contain this indiscretion, your campaign is finished. And Varrieur has to go."

Atkins flared up. "That's what I said before. Why is it okay when you say it but not when I say it?"

"Because I've weighed the repercussions. You hadn't."

Atkins stopped short. "Oh. You mean his friends."

Harvath allowed a grimace to appear. "His powerful friends. Friends who need him. Friends who would be upset if his death were not only a complete accident but an accident with a fall guy, someone in no way connected to you or anyone in this campaign."

"Where would we find such a person?"

"You won't find him at all," Harvath said. "That's what Guzman and Landecker will do. You'll read about the accident in the paper. It'll happen after the negative has been secured."

"And the list?"

"We can explain that away, but it won't come to that, believe me. It's just a list of contributors to your campaign fund who are completely unrelated. The photo is the problem."

"Bring in the team," Atkins said.

# Chapter 6

On the drive from the Oakland Airport to San Francisco, a light rain began to fall. It wouldn't be much of a shower. It was too early in the year for a cleansing rain. It would wet the dry dirt and leave a thin layer of slippery mud like frosting on the parched earth.

Coral Svenson had two first class tickets on Alaska Airlines in her purse. She had told Manuel Guado to keep the change and he'd pocketed forty-six dollars and a new determination to see this lady through the night.

Using her cell phone, Coral Svenson ordered a first class ticket out of San Francisco to LAX on United in her own name, guaranteeing it with her credit card. Then she ordered a second ticket on the Delta flight and a third on the American, all leaving in the morning, all flying to LAX. She hoped that her pursuers would believe this was a feeble attempt by her to confuse them and result in them concentrating their focus at the San Francisco airport. Hopefully they would be busy darting from one departing gate to another while she boarded her flight out of Oakland. The plan had flaws, but she was too tired to worry about them.

Manuel dropped her at the Wayfarers Inn. She paid for the room and took the elevator to the eighth floor. She splashed water on her face to wake herself up and then washed her hands. She was moving too slowly and she knew it. She deemed the stop necessary. She had to hide the shredded paper.

Manuel had said he wouldn't report their arrival at the Inn until she was back, but she knew that if his dispatcher called him, he might have to tell her he was still engaged. The men chasing her would know what that meant.

Quickly, she reached inside the cloth shopping bag, pulled out the two plastic bags, opened them and stuffed half the shredded paper from her purse in each. When her suitcase and purse would slide past the fluoroscope at the check-in, the shredded wad of paper might bring questions. On the other hand, she herself would only go through the metal detector.

She slid one plastic bag under each arm and tucked them inside her bra. She viewed herself in the mirror and adjusted them until the bulges were barely noticeable under her jacket. Then she took out her airline ticket and put it in the deep pocket in her skirt. In the other pocket went her flat leather card carrier with her credit cards and most of the large bills from her wallet. Her early years in the city had taught her that purses were a favorite target of thieves.

It was the middle of the night, a dangerous time in the city. She looked out the window and saw Manuel circling below as she'd requested. She didn't want to leave the room unless she was certain he was waiting.

His lights were flashing. Her puzzlement lasted only a second. He was warning her.

Had he seen something?

He'd been circling. How long had he been circling with his lights flashing?

Coral snatched up her purse, the shopping bag and the suitcase and hurried toward the door.

Opening it a slit she poked her head out and peered up and down the corridor. It was empty except for a room service cart outside one of the doors between her and the elevator. The cloth covering draped over both sides.

All that lay between her and the safety of the cab was the elevator and the main lobby. She had no weapon. Coral looked at the cart. She shoved her suitcase onto the lower shelf and pushed the cart to the elevator. If a man was on the elevator, she'd shove the cart at him and run for the stairs.

The elevator, however, was empty. She pushed the cart into the back corner and pressed the button for the ground floor.

The elevator stopped on the sixth floor and a portly man in a gray suit entered, pushed the third floor button and turned toward the door, scarcely looking at her. Coral stepped back and the back of her calves touched the cart. She gripped her cloth bag and purse tightly and prayed as she watched the floor level lights.

The elevator stopped at the third floor and the man stepped out into a seemingly empty corridor. Coral loosened her grip on her purse and stepped toward the door to push the button to close the door. Suddenly, the portly man turned, put his hand on the door and held it open. A second taller gray-suited man stepped in, moved quickly behind her and whispered harshly, "Your purse and bag, please."

She felt a sharp jab in her back and without a word handed over the bag and slipped the purse from her shoulder.

She felt his hand slip into her right jacket pocket and deftly remove the card key to her room. As quickly as he had entered, the man left.

The door closed slowly. Coral shrunk back and again stumbled into the serving cart. She was shivering.

Her hands clenched and unclenched as if trying to ascertain whether she was still holding her purse and bag. Her mind was numb. While she had prepared for this eventuality in the room, she hadn't truly thought it would happen.

She slipped her hand into her left jacket pocket. Her cell phone was still there. Should she call someone? She'd been robbed at gunpoint? Knife point? She didn't know. What did the men look like? They wore gray suits. And they looked like ordinary people. One was stockier than the other. The second man was taller. How tall? Taller than me. What color eyes? She hadn't seen their eyes. Hair? They both had hair. She couldn't remember more than that. Gray or light brown. Maybe dark brown. Not red. That's all she knew. Black or white? Caucasian she thought, although she couldn't be certain.

What was taken? My purse, a bag, my wallet, my driver's license. They got my driver's license. Well that doesn't matter; they got my car keys too.

Suddenly it struck her. In her purse was her house key. And in her wallet was a card with the security code on it. Talk about an invitation.

"Well, Lady, you coming out or you going back up?" The voice was harsh, the words slurred. Holding the door open with a pudgy hand was a short, fat, dark-bearded man who was obviously intoxicated.

Coral moved toward the door and her jacket dragged the cloth half off the cart. The sight of half-eaten food on the plates beneath made the man grab his mouth and run toward the washroom.

Coral picked up the cloth and roughly folded it on top of the cart. As she was doing so, she spotted her suitcase. She grabbed it off the shelf and hurried from the elevator.

I have to get it out of here, she thought irrationally. Her mind couldn't focus on the larger danger. It could handle moving to protect her remaining possession.

She hurried through the lobby, telling herself that the men would head to her room first. That meant they weren't on her tail, so she didn't have to run.

Manuel was waiting at the curb.

"Your timing is great," she said as she climbed into the cab.

"Glad you made it," he replied. "I was worried."

"I was robbed," she announced. It was easy to tell Manuel. He wouldn't ask her whether the robbers had blue eyes or brown, whether she was scared by a gun or a finger.

"What'd they get?" he asked. "You still got your bag. How'd they miss that?"

Coral smiled. "That's the good part of the story. Take me to Becky's house."

"Where does Becky live?" Manuel asked as he pulled away. He glanced in the rear view mirror. The woman was still shaking. He turned on the heater. The stale warm air filled the cab.

"In San Francisco," Coral said.

"It's a big city," Manuel commented.

"Go north."

"San Francisco is north of here. You got an address?"

"It's in my purse," Coral said without realizing what she was saying. "Wait I'll get it. It's off 19th."

"That'll do for starters," Manuel said picking up his mike. "Going into the city. Exact address unknown. It's off...

"Jones Street!" Coral said suddenly.

"Jones Street," Manuel repeated. He clicked off the mike. "That's way over by the Embarcadero. One of them streets that goes straight down to Hell."

"It sure does," Coral agreed. "Take Nineteenth."

"I won't be going nowhere near Jones if I take 19th unless your map of the city is different from mine."

"We're going to Marina Boulevard," Coral said.

"That's over by the Golden Gate Bridge," Manuel said. "That ain't where Jones Street is." He was worried. The woman wasn't making sense. He wondered if the robber had hit her on the head.

"Nineteenth goes right there."

"Right where?"

"Marina Boulevard, of course. I changed my mind."

Manuel glanced back through his rearview mirror. The lady had the phone to her ear and was telling the operator to put her through to the Wayfarers Inn.

"I was robbed in one of your elevators a few minutes ago... No, of course, I'm not there. Do you think I want it to happen again...? I'm calling to tell you they stole my key... No, I don't have the room number. It was on the eighth floor. My name's Coral Svenson... Of course, I'm paying for the room. I used it. But not the key... But that's not why I'm calling. They took my purse and a cloth shopping bag with another purse inside and I think they may dump the purses in the hotel. I've got my keys, my driver's license and my wallet in one of them. I need your security person to look on the third floor. That's where the man jumped in and took my purse. And in my room on the eighth floor... No I will not call you in the morning. They have my house keys and my address. I do not want my house robbed or my car stolen while I'm gone. I need to know what they took. I will call back in half an hour."

"There won't be no money left," Manuel commented. The woman was functioning again.

"They didn't get my money."

"They like credit cards just as much."

"They didn't get those either," Coral said. "Let me make one more call and then I'll tell you why they didn't get my suitcase."

This time the operator put her through to the Ardilla police. As soon as she identified herself, she was put on hold. She grumbled about it and Manuel offered a bit of advice.

"You gotta say it's an emergency."

"It's the middle of the night," Coral shot back. "What else would it be?"

"Chief Spencer McLean, Mrs. Svenson. How may I help you?"

"It's the middle of the night," Coral sputtered. "What are you doing up?"

"If the criminals would confine their activities to daylight hours, so would I," he replied pleasantly. "We did nab the two men who broke into your home. May I ask? Were all the doors locked?"

"Of course, they were and the alarm was set."

"Even the back door to the garage?"

"It was today. I locked up this morning before I went to the office. I knew I'd be home late."

"Did you give anyone permission to enter your home?"

"No one," Coral replied. "I know the men who broke in, but that doesn't mean I won't prosecute. I won't have my home invaded!"

"Did you call to see whether we'd answered your call? It was you who called from the cab, wasn't it?"

"Yes," Coral admitted, "but I didn't call to see if you did your job but rather to tell you I need you to do another. I was robbed at the Wayfarers Inn near the San Francisco Airport. I thought I could get a flight out tonight but I have to wait until morning, so I booked a room nearby. The robbers–there were two of them wearing gray suits–took my purse and in it was my driver's license with my home address, my house and car keys and the code to my alarm system."

"You're afraid they might rob you."

"If they were real robbers, the chances are good they'll try."

"I can put a man there," McLean said. "You should have your code changed and change the locks on your house."

"I can't do either of those things until Monday, but I don't want anyone in my house while I'm gone."

"I think there's more to this, Mrs. Svenson. Won't you please let me help?"

Coral Svenson was tempted. His voice was nice and she desperately wanted to lean on someone in authority.

"I have to check you out first," Coral blurted out and then hung up.

Spencer McLean stared at the dead phone in his hand and laughed. "Check me out? I'm the chief of police!"

"People watch too much TV," Lieutenant Alex Caribou said from the doorway.

"Mrs. Svenson was robbed in San Francisco."

"It's two in the morning," Alex replied, his broad, flat face devoid of expression.

"In the elevator at the Wayfarers Inn."

Alex's stoic Indian demeanor carried over into his voice. He called over his shoulder, "No interruptions."

"The robbers–two of them–wore gray suits."

Alex frowned slightly. "Well, people do dress up in the city."

"Check the airlines. I want to know what flight she's on."

"Meanwhile you want me to spread the word around here that you're a good guy."

"Who's she going to check with in the middle of the night?"

"Me."

"You?"

"I know her daughter. She likes me," Alex said.

"How come you know her daughter?" McLean probed lightly.

"She's a reporter for the Oakland Journal."

"Isn't the editor–Keyman I think his name is–tight with Atkins?"

Alex nodded. "I got her cell phone number."

"You've what?"

"In case a big story breaks out here."

"She'll be asleep," McLean worried aloud.

"Not after her mother's call."

"When she calls you, let me talk with her."

"She could call the paper," Alex said.

McLean picked up on the negative possibilities.

"Get me her number," he ordered. Alex gave it to him verbally.

McLean stared at him. "You have it memorized?"

"We're friends."

McLean punched in the number. "And it never dawned on you in all your conversations... Darn, it's busy...it never dawned on you to mention me in a good light. You know, my sterling character, how much you liked me, how her mother could trust me."

"Nope," Alex said as he ducked out the door.

McLean punched the redial button. The phone was still in use. He began to punch the button at regular intervals.

Alex poked his head back into the room. "She's holding on line two."

McLean looked up at his lieutenant. His predecessor had picked his men well. His eyebrows arched in a question.

"I went through the switchboard," Alex said.

"You know where she's staying?"

"I got her itinerary on my desk."

"You've what?"

"In case something happened to her mother."

McLean punched the button for line two and introduced himself. "Please don't call your paper and ask about me. I need to find your mother. I think she's in danger. Please tell her to trust me."

"Just a minute."

McLean heard soft noises after the phone was placed on the nightstand. He tapped his fingers on his desk. He hated holding.

"I'm back," the young voice said. "I told Mother to expect you. I assume you want to see her evidence."

McLean tried to harness in his surprise but it didn't work. "She's still got it?"

"Mother can be clever when she puts her mind to it."

"You told her she can trust me?"

"I told her Alex said you were okay."

"That's it?"

"Alex doesn't waste words."

McLean chuckled. "Oh, you've noticed that too."

"Alex has the address," Tara said, then added in a softer voice, "Please protect my mother."

There was something about that voice.

# Chapter 7

After a few wrong turns and double backs through the maze of streets fronting San Francisco State University, Alex Caribou pulled up in front of the small two story house on Denslowe. The driveway dipped down sharply into the garage which was half a story below street level. The second floor windows of the house faced the street; the first floor window overlooked the sloping lawn. In the rear, the land dropped away from the house. In the city, house sites were frequently located on the upside or downside of a hill. On Jones Street the houses sat on the hill sideways like a skier who's stopped himself on a slope. Here the houses faced the hill like a skier trudging up a slope.

It was a modest house and the door was opened by a spritely elderly woman with short straight dark hair that gave her a more youthful appearance than her age dictated. At her feet were three excited dachshunds.

"Dr. Griffin," Chief McLean opened with sincere deference, ignoring the low-slung dogs for a moment. "We would like to talk with your house guest. I'm Spencer McLean of the Ardilla Police and this gentleman is Lieutenant Alex Caribou."

Becky Griffin immediately took to the man towering over her. She especially liked his acknowledgement of her hard earned medical degree. The use of her title showed respect which wasn't always forthcoming lately. Her dogs sensing her approval of the man immediately leaped around his legs asking to be noticed.

She ushered them into the dining room where three mounds of shredded paper sat on the dining room table and a slender, attractive gray-haired woman was busy laying out the strips from one of the piles.

"The red one is Rufus," Becky Griffin said.

McLean looked puzzled. Two piles were white, the third, multicolored.

"And this one?" asked the voice behind him. "She's pretty."

"That's Lisa. And the wild boar is Anya," Becky said, her voice reflecting her pleasure that her dogs were being admired.

"Lisa is Rufus' mother and Rufus is Anya's father," she went on.

"Three generations," Alex mused aloud squatting down to pet Rufus. "Rough coat."

"They're wire-haired," Becky explained.

"What do they do?"

"You mean besides filling my house with love?"

Alex nodded and the doctor went on.

"They will go in a hole after a rat."

"That takes bravery," Alex said simply.

Dr. Griffin nodded. "It does indeed."

Meanwhile, McLean had been watching Coral Svenson piece together the multicolored strips.

"Why three piles?" he asked finally.

"Becky sorted them by feel. Her vision is clouded by cataracts. She's going to have one eye operated on next week."

"What are you looking for?"

"The reason a future president would promise an ambassadorship to France on the basis of a photo."

"Who is to be the recipient?"

"Somebody with a French sounding last name."

"So you don't know who's blackmailing him?"

"That's why we're going to piece together the white stuff," Coral explained without looking up. "He put two pieces of paper through the shredder, one after the other."

"Alex," McLean said. "Get started on one of these piles. I'll do the other. The first one done gets tomorrow off."

"I've already got it off," Alex said. It was the largest string of words he'd uttered since arriving.

McLean moved his pile to a clear space on the table, sat down and spread the strips of white paper out before him. Rufus immediately jumped in his lap and put his paws on the table.

"You planning to help?" McLean asked scratching the small red dog gently behind his ears.

Becky watched her dog closely. After a few moments she went over and picked up four strips.

"These are the edges," she said. "Rufus' nose says they have the most scent."

"Pretty one, come here," Alex said. Anya and Lisa both responded by jumping into his lap.

Becky Griffin laughed. "Anya doesn't like to be left out. Here, I'll take one. We'll work on yours together."

"No fair," McLean objected.

"You have Rufus," Becky countered.

McLean grumbled good-naturedly as he bent to his task.

"Pieces of numbers," Alex said turning toward Becky who was pulling out strips, bringing them close to one eye and separating the blank ones from those with printing on them. She pushed more toward him.

"Names," he announced.

"A piece of a letter," McLean announced a short time later. "It doesn't appear important."

Alex looked over. He raised one dark brow in silent query as his eyes fell on the narrow block of strips pieced together.

"I matched the letterhead," McLean announced. "I can extrapolate from the middle what it says on the sides."

"Last one," Becky said, handing Alex a strip. "What've you got?"

When Chief McLean pushed back his chair, Rufus jumped down. McLean leaned over Dr. Griffin's shoulder and began reading the names aloud. "Martin Deane, Naomi Lebowitz, Michael Pascual, Hirishi Sasaki, Fenway Chadwick..."

He paused.

"Mean anything to you?" he asked Coral Svenson.

"They could be contributors," Alex offered. "There's ten thousand dollars listed opposite each name."

McLean aimed his question at Coral Svenson. "Why shred such a list? What else do they have in common? Here let me read some more: Rolf Sandelin, Gloria Steinman, Angel Romero, Andrea Gilchrist, Mary Tagliaferri..."

"Maybe they're buried in the same cemetery," Dr. Griffin remarked dryly. "Fenway Chadwick, Mary Tagliaferri, and Rolf Sandelin are dead."

Chief McLean looked down at the top of the small woman's head. "You knew them?"

"Fenway Chadwick, I knew. He was an old hard-core, tight-fisted Democrat. He wouldn't give a red cent to a member of his own party. He certainly wouldn't give ten thousand to Atkins' campaign."

"What about Rolf Sandelin?"

"He was a councilman who died a couple of months ago."

"What party was he affiliated with?"

"None that I know of."

"And Mary Tagliaferri?"

"A sixteen-year-old girl, killed by a car a couple blocks from here."

"She wasn't old enough to vote even," McLean said. "Hardly your typical ten thousand dollar contributor. Alex, read the rest of the list."

He started where McLean had stopped. "Lillian Johnson, Carrie Collier, Sue..."

Coral Svenson gasped. "Carrie Collier?"

Alex backed up. "Yep."

"You know her?" McLean asked.

"She's dead," was all Coral could say. The blood rushed from her face. Her finger lay on top of the partially completed picture. It was tapping slowly.

McLean circled the table and looked over her shoulder. Three strips had been matched and showed the face of a young girl.

"Cee Cee," she murmured. "That's what her friends called her."

"Cee Cee for Carrie Collier?" McLean said fitting two pieces of the puzzle together in his head. He picked up a strip. "Let's finish this photo."

Coral Svenson let her thoughts spill out slowly, the monotone signaling her detachment from even her words as she spoke them. Her mind was unwilling to even consider the possibilities. "I bought a new puzzle. I put it in my suitcase. Tara and I like to work puzzles together when we talk. It's a picture of Cezanne's Le Lac D'Annecy. Are you familiar with it?"

McLean waited silently for her mind to assimilate the shock of what he could already see in the reassembled photo.

"It's an impressionist piece full of blues and yellows and I saw it on the internet with the color missing and all I could see were shadows and lines and I didn't know what I was looking at. I remember the impression of those shadows and lines and how I couldn't make out what I was seeing. I came across it by accident and it wasn't labeled and I remember a line in the center with a shadow falling from it. A strong shadow arched over the line like a dark gray rainbow. That's what this looks like to me. Only it's not, is it? It's Governor Atkins having sex with Cee Cee, isn't it? Her arm is hanging over the edge of the bed like that of a person completely relaxed. There's no tension in the fingers. None..."

Her voice faded. "Photos aren't always accurate," McLean cautioned.

"He accepted it as a true picture of what went on," Coral murmured.

"An indiscretion needn't mean the end of his career, especially since the girl is dead. She won't rise up to haunt him except in his dreams."

"She won't do that," Coral said. "Whalen didn't think it was serious. His main political advisor is the one who went berserk. Brian Harvath yelled about this being immoral..."

"It is," McLean said. "Atkins is married."

"And loathsome..."

"A bit strong for this act, but it could be considered such."

"Detestable..."

"From the wife's point of view."

"Sacrilegious..."

"That Harvath fellow did use some strong words, didn't he?" McLean said. "I gather he was making a point and the governor wasn't listening."

Coral looked up. "Yes, Harvath was and, you're right, the governor was ignoring him. That probably explains his choice of words and his anger. Harvath hates being ignored."

While Coral was speaking, Alex leaned over and whispered something to Dr. Griffin. She shook her head and he immediately left the table.

"Where are you going?" McLean asked the retreating figure.

"Computer," Alex replied as he opened the front door.

He came back with a laptop. A short muscular man with tattoos on his arms followed him in. He doffed his cabbie's cap.

"He said it was okay," Manuel said timidly.

"Did you report your location?" McLean asked.

Manuel nodded.

"We haven't much time," McLean said. "Let's get to it."

"We haven't any time," Coral announced. "Atkins' men are in San Francisco. They might have even followed Manuel."

Before McLean could stop her she reached for a discarded plastic bag, scrunched the photo strips together and jammed them into it.

"What'd you do that for?" the chief asked in dismay. "We weren't done studying it."

"Study?" Coral spat back, derision coating her words. "Study? Is that what you call it?"

Spencer McLean swallowed his anger at the implied accusation and replied calmly. "There was something wrong with the picture. The girl was too relaxed."

"I don't want to discuss it," Coral replied primly. "I need to think about this. I'm not ready to be a whistle-blower. A lot of people could get hurt. Cee Cee has a family. They were very proud of their daughter and this... this...liaison would distress them. And the photo, if it were published, would devastate them. It would destroy her reputation and tarnish theirs. The governor's indiscretion was just that. It was stupid, especially in an election year, but every candidate has a few skeletons in his closet. Let him who is without sin cast the first stone."

"I'm a policeman," Spencer McLean said levelly. "I don't judge. I don't convict. I don't sentence. I merely arrest those who've broken the law. I don't even determine the law. The people do that. If Governor Atkins has committed no crime, then I am not going to arrest him."

"Even an investigation could ruin him."

"I can be discreet."

"You'd be in a good position to run for office yourself if you..."

"Alex, gather up the rest of the paper, take it to the station and piece together what you can."

Coral Svenson burst in.

"Can you do that? I mean is it legal?"

"Your home was broken into, you were robbed in an elevator and you're fleeing in fear. I want to know why?"

"But is it legal for you to piece together shredded paper from someone's office?"

"Not if I take it without a warrant or if I suggest that you take it, but, in this case, you took it and gave it to me."

"That makes me a thief, doesn't it?"

"It's a tricky point. A man's garbage is no longer sacred once the garbage collector picks it up, but you plucked a handful of shredded paper out of a basket inside the office."

"Are you going to arrest me?"

"If Governor Atkins presses charges, then the shredded paper becomes evidence."

"He won't want that," Coral concluded, relieved.

Dr. Griffin, who had disappeared during the conversation, reappeared with a roll of tape and with one swift move, tore off a long strip and laid it across the list of names and numbers.

"No sense having to start from scratch," she said decisively.

"We gotta go now," Manuel said.

"He's right," Coral said. "If my stop here appears to be brief, then maybe the men after me won't know that we've pieced together the shreds."

Coral then excused herself and disappeared into the bathroom with the plastic bag containing the photo strips.

"She's not going to flush the photo down the toilet, is she, Dr. Griffin?" McLean worried aloud.

Becky Griffin looked up into the worried blue eyes of the man towering over her.

"No," she replied. "It would clog up my toilet."

"Does she know that?" he whispered bending slightly.

Dr. Griffin raised her voice. "She knows that the men following her want the photo back and destroying it is not the answer."

McLean walked over to his lieutenant.

When Coral emerged from the bathroom, both Lieutenant Caribou and Manuel Guado were nowhere in sight.

"Where's my cabbie?" Coral asked.

"Gone," McLean said. "There's been a change of plan."

# Chapter 8

As the cab pulled away from the curb, the downstairs lights in the house went out. Neither of the two men in the cab looked back.

Manuel Guado slowed for a stop sign while radioing his dispatcher. Lieutenant Caribou set the plastic bag of shredded papers beside him on the back seat and picked up his hand held police radio.

Coming up the cross street, a dark sedan turned onto Denslowe. Its headlights swept the cab and the men inside the sedan saw the mike in the driver's hand. The cabbie was checking in. As the sedan passed the cab, Alex put his radio to his ear.

"A police handset," Eddie Landecker announced.

"She couldn't know we're on her tail," Herb Guzman argued. "And she didn't have time to put the stuff together in the cab."

"Maybe she did," Eddie suggested sticking a cigarette in his mouth and lighting it. The glow from the lighter accentuated his long face.

"Just what the hell do you think you're doing?"

"Afraid someone'll see me?" Eddie joshed. "We're in a car with headlights on for chrissake."

"Put it out!" Herb ordered angrily. "You're lighting up your damn face. Damn you! Now I'm going to have to open a window in order to breathe."

Eddie took a long drag, then pulled out the ashtray and crushed the cigarette into it.

"There's the house. It's dark," Eddie said. "You better turn and follow the cab."

"She didn't suddenly turn into a cop with a police radio," Herb reminded him.

"Don't matter," Eddie argued. "She ain't here. She's gone. All we got is the cab."

"There's a car in the drive," Herb remarked as he began a three-point turn on the city street narrowed by the cars parked along the curb. "The other drives are empty."

"So what!" Eddie said, not following the direction of Herb's finger but instead peering down the street where the cab's brake lights showed that it had stopped at a second stop sign. He looked back at the car parked on the sloping driveway. "Dumb thing to do to brakes, parking like that."

"It's probably the car the cop came in," Herb stated flatly.

"It ain't a squad."

"Detective grade or higher would be my guess," Herb said. "Maybe we're supposed to follow the cab."

"Well, while you're guessing, that cab's rolling. I say we chase it, catch it and if the stuff ain't there, we come back here."

"Suppose she still has it," Herb postulated. "And somehow she found out we know about the cab and she's just waiting for us to leave so she can split."

"Too much supposing," Eddie remarked as Herb completed his three-point turn on the narrow city street.

"Gun it!" Eddie demanded. "She'll be here. She don't know about us. She ain't going nowhere until morning. It's that cab that's a now-or-never deal."

The sedan leaped alive as if Eddie's words were the pressure on the accelerator. It bounced down the dip at the first intersection and took the second dip also without stopping. At the third, Herb looked left in time to see their target turn right two blocks down. He didn't turn. Instead, he stepped on the gas and raced through the next three stop signs without even a moment's hesitation.

At the third sign, Herb flipped off his lights and accelerated as he turned left. His tires screeched in protest. His engine roared as he depressed the gas pedal.

Without lights, the black car sped down the two blocks into the intersection just as the cab was crossing it. At the last second, Herb swerved and caught the rear of the cab. The impact spun the cab sideways.

The radio flew from Alex's hand it he fell onto the floor under the driver's seat. Alex's head hit the side door with a solid thump. The plastic bag hit the back of the passenger's seat and dropped at Alex's feet.

Manuel's head hit the back of his headrest as he flipped his foot off the accelerator and jammed it down on the brake. The car continued its spiral and did another full loop before its front fender hit a lamp post which crunched through the metal as if it were paper and inserted itself between the wheel and the axle.

The air bag exploded in Manuel's face.

The sedan screeched to a halt and two men leaped out and ran over to the cab.   Herb checked out the driver. Manuel lay unconscious in the front seat.   Eddie circled around the cab to the rear door on the opposite side of the cab.

Alex, still lying prone on the back seat, lifted his head and looked toward the back door as it opened.   The man's features were a blur.   A flashlight blinded him.

Alex raised his arm to ward off the light.   Three rounds were fired.   Two hit his forearm; the third, his shoulder.   He fell backward.

"It's here," Alex heard the shooter cry.

"Grab it and let's go," the second man shouted.

"I gotta check..."

"I'm leaving."   The voice was harsh and determined.

Alex heard the sound of one set of footsteps running. The shooter was still hovering in the doorway.   Quickly, Alex jerked his body.   He let his uninjured arm drop to the floor, dropped his jaw and rolled his eyes sideways.   His injured forearm stayed draped over his forehead.   He resisted the urge to blink or breathe.   Maybe he'd get lucky.

The bullet hit him in the chest.   He jerked reflexively and then lay still.

The running footsteps told him his assailant had fled.

"Officer down," he whispered into the open radio on the floor before he lost consciousness.

# Chapter 9

Lieutenant Greg Lim moved quickly, notifying the San Francisco police first then calling his chief.

The shock drained Chief McLean's face. The two women didn't see his reaction because the lights were still off. Rufus was the first to sense the change in the man. His bark alerted Becky Griffin who turned on the light when Lisa joined in.

"Is he dead?" Chief McLean asked.

Coral whispered to Becky that they should get ready to run.

"I'm not going anywhere," Becky Griffin said. "I'm not leaving my dogs."

"We'll take them," Coral assured her. "You can't stay here."

"Why can't I?" the old woman asked. "If anyone comes around, I'll call the police."

"They could cut your phone wire," Coral suggested. "If they killed Lieutenant Caribou, they won't hesitate killing you."

As Coral argued with her friend, Chief McLean finished issuing instructions to his lieutenant.

"I'm not afraid!" Dr. Griffin said with a strength of conviction that would brook no challenge.

"This is not up for debate," McLean said. "Those men will come back here."

"You two go," Becky Griffin said. "Don't worry about me. I can handle myself."

"Where are the leashes?" Coral hurried into the kitchen and returned with three leashes.

She then called Rufus to her and snapped a leash on his collar. Anya rushed over and pawed at the loose lead draped over Coral's bent leg.

"What are you doing?" Becky asked angrily. "I said I was staying here!"

Coral snapped a lead on Anya and then handed the two to McLean. "My suitcase is by the door."

McLean tucked the laptop under his arm, held the leashes for both dogs in one hand, snatched up Coral's small suitcase and went out the door.

"Lisa, come here," Coral called. The little brown and tan dog ran up and stood waiting for her leash to be snapped on. Once that was done Coral stood up.

"You can stay here and get shot if you want, but I'm not letting your dogs get hurt," Coral said sternly. "Or didn't it occur to you that these men might beat them to death one by one in front of you just for the hell of it?"

Silence fell as Dr. Rebecca Griffin let her imagination take hold of the scene.

"Let me get my coat and purse," she said.

"Skip the purse," Coral said moving out the door. "I'll pay your cab fare back."

The old woman reappeared, her coat on and her purse in hand. "You'll do no such thing. Besides I can't unlock my door without a key, now can I?"

Coral took Lisa out to the car where the other two dogs were waiting.

As Coral entered the car, she saw headlights turning the corner.

"Hurry!" she shouted back at her friend. "Someone's coming."

Becky stayed at the door. Coral held the excited dogs inside the car. They began to strain to jump out through the open back door.

"What's wrong?" Coral called.

"Key's stuck," Becky called back.

"Leave it," Coral said.

"I have to lock up," the old woman said stubbornly.

"Come quick!" Coral shouted. "Rufus got away from me."

The old woman spun around and sprinted down the stairs calling her dog's name.

An answering bark from inside the car brought Becky up short. "Rufus is in the car. Who's missing?"

"You," Coral said holding the door open. "Get in. The only thing on this property that's irreplaceable is you and your dogs."

Dr. Griffin hastily climbed in and sat down. "Well, what are we waiting for? Let's move out!" she said.

The headlights passed behind them and as they did so a garage door opened. Light flooded the driveway and showed a single driver. The car slid down the driveway and the garage door closed behind it. The street was again dark.

"That was scary!" Coral breathed.

"Now can I get my key?" Becky asked her hand on the car door handle.

"No!" her companions chorused. McLean shoved into reverse and backed out of the driveway. The dogs scrambled onto the laps of the two women, put their paws on the window ledge and pressed their noses against the glass. Riding with people was a new idea. Usually they rode on the flattened rear section of Becky's station wagon which was complete with non-skid carpeting near the front and three open crates to curl up in lined along the back door.

"I have to check on Alex first," Chief McLean announced as he headed east. The women agreed aloud that Alex's wellbeing was the first order of business.

McLean flicked on the flasher located on the dash and sped through the darkened intersections with only a slight pause. His car was ushered to the front.

"Stay," he ordered the two women and the three dogs as he leaped from the car, identified himself and rushed forward.

The paramedics had just loaded Alex onto their gurney when McLean stepped up, identified himself, took Alex's hand and asked the paramedic how he was.

"Miracle he's with us," one said. "Four bullets, one in the shoulder, one in the chest, two in the arm. His assailant was out to do him in."

"Now, if you'll move back, Sir," said the other paramedic. His manner and voice were impatient.

McLean didn't budge. "Alex, squeeze my hand if the answer is yes. Did they get the evidence?"

One squeeze told him Alex understood. McLean had assumed that they had.

"Two of them?"

One squeeze.

"Sir, you have to let go."

"Did you see the shooter's face?"

No response.

The paramedic grabbed McLean's wrist and tried to pull his hand away. "You've got to let go. We're trying to save this man's life."

"So am I," McLean said. "Just keep moving. I have only one more question."

The paramedic separated the two hands and his partner pushed the gurney hard. "You're done."

They slid the gurney into the ambulance and McLean said. "Take his hand for one second."

"We're busy."

"I can identify his assailant if he answers the next question. Just take his hand. One second."

Alex lifted his good arm and grabbed the paramedic's forearm.

"Was he wearing a suit?" McLean shouted as the back door was slammed shut.

The driver hurried around to the front and McLean followed him. "Well?"

The voice from the back said, "He squeezed my arm."

The ambulance took off with the siren screaming.

McLean was on the radio to Lim before the wailing was distant enough so he could hear. "Send two men over to St. Mark's to guard Alex. They will try again."

"Won't the city police guard him?"

"I want our men inside the room with him."

"Can he identify them?"

"No, but they may think he can and that may scare them into trying again," McLean said. "Have Manning do some computer searches for us. They got the list but the women with me may remember some of the names on it. I'll radio them to you as soon as I get them."

"Where will you be?"

"At the hospital as soon as I drop the ladies somewhere safe."

"I got the shooter's voice on tape," Lim said.

"How'd you do that?"

"Alex was going to give me some names from the list and I set up to record them. I got two before the accident. Then I got the crash, three shots and the voice yelling that he got it. There was another voice but I couldn't make it out. The shooter argued with him and then shot Alex again."

"See what you can do to enhance the voice in the background. Good work, Lim."

McLean strode over to the man peering inside the wrecked cab who appeared to be in charge, identified himself and said, "I have with me a person who can give you a partial description of the shooter."

Detective Mark Volatis stood up. He was a tall man who liked peering down his long nose at people. This time he found himself eyeball to eyeball with the speaker.

"Was your guy here?" His words came out sloppily. The large teeth were crowded along a jaw too small to hold them.

"No, she wasn't," McLean started, "but..."

"Then I'm not interested." He turned away.

Startled, McLean sputtered slightly. "The man was the same one that robbed her earlier."

"And you know that for a fact?" Volatis asked.

"We have reason to believe..."

"You're the sheriff of Ardilla..."

"Actually, I'm the Chief of Police."

"Whatever," Volatis sneered. "What I'm trying to say is that this is the big time. Don't interfere."

"I need my man guarded."

"He'll be safe enough. We don't have killers roaming the halls of our hospitals."

"If he's killed on your watch," McLean said his tone ominous, "I will hold you personally responsible."

"Look, much as you might have little crime waves in your burg that ties into a single perp, here we have multiple perps. Your friend was robbed. Have her file a report. Your deputy was shot but not robbed, so we've got two different MO's here, and so two different perps."

"He was robbed," McLean said. "So was the lady. In both cases, the perps were after the same incriminating evidence."

"Evidence of a crime committed here?"

"No, one committed in Ardilla, but not by these men personally, which is why I'm here."

"Let me get this straight," Detective Volatis said. "A crime was committed in Ardilla and the lady snagged the evidence and raced into San Francisco and someone tried to rob her and failed. Then you found her and took the evidence away and these same robbers followed a cop who was riding home in a cab and shot him and got the evidence which did not exonerate them of any crime."

"When you put it that way, it sounds a bit crazy," McLean admitted good-naturedly.

"You're over complicating the whole thing," Volatis said. "Go home. Let us do our job."

"You're looking for two men in gray suits," McLean said.

"This is San Francisco," Volatis commented. "Half the town wears gray suits. Go home."

"I'm sending men to the hospital to guard my man."

"It's your budget, not mine," Volatis said, turning away.

A shouting match brought both men around the cab to a bus bench from which Manuel was rising.

"It happened on your damned street," he yelled. "I ain't paying nothing. I didn't do nothing. Some maniac hits me and I gotta pay towing? No way."

Detective Volatis walked up and by his presence took over. He looked down his long nose at the short, dark-haired man and said with authority, "You can't leave your disabled vehicle in the middle of the street."

"It ain't mine. I ain't paying."

"Your company must have towing insurance."

"Yeah, for local hauls. And we got a garage too. But this is a tow clear across the Bay Bridge and through the Caldecott Tunnel. Our garage is way the hell on the other side."

"So you pay and the company reimburses you," Volatis spat out impatiently.

"Fat chance!" Manuel exploded. "Why don't you catch the guy what done this instead of leaning on me?"

"You give me any more lip and I'll lock you up." Volatis' voice was harsh. The threat was real.

"What the hell for?"

"Reckless driving. Speeding. I can come up with others."

McLean spoke up. "The cab was deliberately broadsided."

Volatis scowled. "How do you figure that?"

"No skid marks."

"And no lights on that car that rammed me," Guado added. "I looked both ways. I ain't fool enough to jump in front of a speeding car when I got a cop in the back seat."

Detective Volatis frowned. He hated being one-upped by an out-of-town yokel in front of the men he outranked.

"You're the driver. You're responsible," he decided.

"Don't you need to impound this car and have forensics go over it?" McLean asked without criticism.

"Big, big waste of time," Volatis said peevishly. "Your man wasn't shot up close. No tattooing, soot smudge or burn on the victim or his clothes. The shooter stood outside. He didn't leave any clues. Besides this is a cab. Hundreds of people have touched the edges of the door and climbed inside. We'd be following down leads from here to eternity if we had to follow up on all of them."

"The car would have a crushed fender," McLean added.

"So we stop everyone with a ding in his car?" Volatis sneered.

"Did you get the plates on that car at the Wayfarers?" McLean asked.

Manuel reached into his pocket. "Yeah."

He handed McLean a slip of paper. Detective Volatis reached for it, but McLean deftly avoided the outstretched hand and read the numbers aloud. Then he pocketed the paper.

"Now you have the license number of the car that hit this one. Find it and you'll have your shooter," McLean said. "And if you don't want to impound this cab, I do."

McLean then motioned to Manuel Guado to follow him. Manuel ran to catch up with McLean whose long strides distanced him from the center of the melee quickly.

"Just where the hell do you think you're taking him?" Volatis stormed, hurrying after them. He noticed two of his men on either side of the unmarked car. His step became determined. He was in control.

McLean smiled at the two officers and instructed Manuel to get in the front seat then he turned. "Didn't I tell you? Manuel's a material witness to a burglary at a home in Ardilla. We need his statement. I suggest you call the cab company about the vehicle. Tell them it's being impounded by the Ardilla Police. I'm going to tell them that you have the license plate number of the vehicle that struck their cab deliberately. And if you don't follow through on it, you'll answer to the cab company and their insurance carrier. And if you think Manuel made a fuss, try going up against one of them."

The officers stepped away from the car as McLean folded his large frame into the driver's seat.

Volatis saw two small dog heads poking through the back window. The sight rendered him speechless long enough for McLean to start backing up.

"They've got the cutest dogs," one cop commented.

"Shut up!" Volatis snapped.

Spencer McLean picked up his radio mike. "Lim, we have a make on the plate."

# Chapter 10

"They got the bag of shredded paper," McLean said as soon as he had threaded his way through the crowd of curious onlookers and the maze of police and fire vehicles.

"We thought as much," Dr. Griffin said, "so we made a new list. All we need is for you to tell us what names you remember."

"Where are we going?" McLean asked.

"To Virginia's house."

"Where's that?"

"North of Golden Gate Park."

"I'm going the wrong way," McLean said.

"Well, then, turn around," Becky said completely unruffled.

"You couldn't have told me sooner?" the chief asked, a bit disconcerted.

"You didn't ask sooner. How was I supposed to know that was our next stop?"

McLean spotted the edge in Becky's voice and immediately apologized. A grunt from the back seat told him she was considering his apology.

"While I'm at it," he said in a placating tone, "please let me apologize about the key. I will see that it is recovered and delivered to you. I couldn't do it at the crash site. The timing was wrong."

"For you, maybe," Dr. Griffin replied. "One of the young officers who stopped to pet my dogs promised to recover it and deliver it to me."

"You two have been busy," Chief McLean commented with a smile. "Now for the names. Do you have Zhang Jun?"

A negative response prompted him to go on. "How about Tony Biglin?"

"Keep going," they urged in unison.

"Michael Chin, Fenway Chadwick and something Johnson. That's it, ladies. I hope you remembered more."

"We did," Dr. Griffin said. "Only one of those you remembered was on our list–Fenway Chadwick."

"How many do we have?"

"Twenty-three," Becky Griffin said proudly.

McLean whistled. "That's over half."

He handed them the radio, instructed them how to work it and told them to call in the list. Manuel concentrated on directing the chief to the park, happy to be of use to the man who'd extracted him from a sticky situation.

"You tell your boss, we'll pay the fare from San Francisco to Ardilla," McLean said as they rode along. The women were busy with the radio and McLean spoke softly so as not to disturb them. "That should tell him that we know you weren't at fault."

Manuel nodded. He'd be fired anyway, but it was nice to have a police chief say he'd done a good job.

McLean noticed the sadness following the nod. It wasn't the look on the Mexican's face but the slight slump in his shoulders.

"Is your record clean?" he asked abruptly.

Manuel looked over. McLean sensed his surprise.

"I ain't never been arrested," he answered proudly.

"Ever think of becoming a cop?"

"I got four kids," he replied.

"So how well does a cabbie's take home pay feed them?"

"We make do," Manuel said.

"I can offer you better."

Manuel gasped. "Me?"

"You don't think you could be a better cop than that jerk you were up against on the streets back there?"

"Hell, he weren't no good. He wouldn't listen."

"So then, why not?"

"My English ain't so good."

"I know that. What else?"

"Barely made it outta high school."

"So you aren't a student."

"I don't know nothing about being a cop.

"We've got a training program. Some of my hires have no police experience."

"But they got college, right?"

"Most of them have some."

"Cops gotta be smart."

"You speak two languages. Not everyone can do that. Besides there are other things cops gotta be. They've gotta have heart and loyalty. You put yourself on the line tonight."

"Me? I didn't do nothing."

"You could've split at the Wayfarers but you didn't. When you saw my car in front of Dr. Griffins' house, you still came to the door. And just now, when I told you to follow me, you didn't hesitate. I measure a man by his actions."

"Hey," Manuel protested, "she was paying good. There weren't no noble motive behind that first part. And you was saving my ass."

Spencer McLean laughed heartily. "And honest to boot."

"Hell, you just need a cop who can speak Spanish," Manuel concluded. "A token Mex."

"I've already got a cop that can speak Spanish. And Russian. And Japanese. And French. And German. And is learning another language which at the moment I can't remember and I don't need a token anything."

"What've I got you want?"

"You mean besides courage and integrity?"

"Yeah, besides them two." Manuel's voice revealed a tinge of pride behind the argumentative front.

"You can read people. It's a talent. I want you on my police force, rough edges and all."

Manuel's mind processed the possibilities with lightning speed. "When do I start?"

"Right now," McLean said. "Alex is lost to me for a while. So I need a man I can trust."

"Do I get a gun?"

"Your training on firearm safety starts Monday," McLean said. "We'll teach you how to shoot safely and then you get a gun."

"Cops need guns."

"You're a trainee. You didn't just sit in a car and drive. You practiced first, right?"

"So I get to drive a squad car because I've practiced, right?"

McLean laughed. "You got me there."

Manuel Guado sat temporarily speechless reviewing his decision. A better job with training. He wondered if he should drop the class he was taking in computers. He decided to ask later. Maybe they'd want him to keep it. He'd probably still be working nights. Day shifts always came with seniority.

It'll be safe, he'd tell Marie. Ardilla cops don't get killed. Alex was shot in San Francisco not Ardilla. But most important, he'd be respected.

A warm glow settled over Manuel and he nestled inside it. Busy with such thoughts, Manuel only half-aware of his surroundings, McLean was on the radio telling Lim that he'd just hired a new man.

"Emergency hire," McLean said. "Temporary for three months. Starting time is now. Trainee status. He'll come in tomorrow morning to fill out the paperwork."

Manuel's bubble burst. He opened his mouth, but Dr. Griffin shouted over his worry.

"There's the house!"

McLean pulled over, turned to Manuel and said, "I'm bypassing our usual hiring procedures."

Manuel choked out one word as a question, "Temporary?"

"It's the first step," McLean explained. "Not the whole staircase. Everyone's on probation the first three months. Everyone. Is that clear?"

Manuel nodded numbly.

"I keep my promises," McLean said. "I mean what I say. The reason you're on my team is because I trust you. With so giant a conspiracy going on, I can't afford to take on a new man I don't really know. A plant could undermine us."

"Suppose I make a big mistake?" Manuel said envisioning himself as a fall guy.

"If you have any questions about anything, check it out. Anything. No matter how small. Got it?"

Manuel's acknowledgement was interrupted by an altercation in the back seat.

"You're dead tired," Becky Griffin was saying her voice raised several decibels. "You've got to rest."

"I'll sleep in the car and on the plane," Coral argued.

"We'll be hours at the hospital," McLean interjected as he pulled up in front of the house. "Stay here. Manuel will come back and pick you up in time to make your flight."

"See, he agrees with me," Becky added, placing her hand on the door handle. The front door of the house opened and a white- haired woman appeared.

"Chief, we're safe now, right?" Coral began. "I mean, we weren't followed, right?"

"Go on," McLean said.

"So Becky is safe here now. If you come back to get me, you could be followed."

McLean looked at Dr. Griffin. In the dim light, he could see she looked frail and tired. Her involvement had to end now.

"Mrs. Svenson will stay with us," McLean decided. "We will see she rests."

90

"Here's the list," Dr. Griffin said. "I thought up two more partial names so I wrote them down. Lydia or Linda or Lila De Mars and something Knitting or Kmitted or something like that."

"There was no Lila," McLean said. "But there was a Lalley. All those 'L' names reminded me."

"The Lalley was a woman," Coral added.

"We'll call you for more," McLean promised as Dr. Griffin threw open the rear door. The three dachshunds scrambled out and ran toward the lighted doorway, their leashes trailing behind them. They heard the woman in the doorway chuckle as she greeted them. They ran past her. In the open doorway behind her was a small white poodle.

Twenty minutes later, at the hospital, Chief McLean introduced Manuel as an undercover officer and asked for the use of a private room for several hours. The ER receptionist flatly refused, stating that the hospital was not a motel.

Rather than argue, Spencer McLean simply asked her where the waiting room was and the cafeteria. Then, to Manuel's surprise, he stepped quietly away from the desk and headed toward the cafeteria.

Manuel could feel the eyes of the receptionist boring into their backs. The cafeteria was straight down the corridor and McLean punched through the double doors and straight up to the counter where he ordered coffee.

At his urging Coral and Manuel each selected wrapped sandwiches to go with their coffee which he suggested they have capped.

"I'm tired, not hungry," Coral said.

"This is for when you wake up," McLean said.

"I'm going to sleep on a metal chair in a cafeteria?"

"You're going to sleep in a bed, as soon as I find one. Follow me."

When they left the cafeteria, the receptionist was nowhere in sight. The threesome ducked down the first corridor to the left off the main hall. McLean stopped in front of a door marked "Blood Donors".

"Let's hope this is empty," he said as he opened the door. Four white-sheeted beds sat in a row on the left. On the far wall behind the glass doors of a large cabinet sat boxes of syringes, cotton, Band-Aids and plastic gloves.

McLean's eyes swept past those to the desk and the white cap perched on a slicked down head of black hair that was curled just below the ears.

The round-faced, dark-skinned nurse looked up from her paperwork. "Yes?"

"Could we trouble you...?" McLean began without stepping inside.

Coral interrupted him. "We're here to donate blood for our friend who was shot." She gently pushed past the tall chief. "I assume I can stay here until I recover. I've lost a lot of sleep and it might take a while."

"You can stay as long as you need to, Honey," the nurse said, a broad smile lighting up her dark face as she reached for a clipboard. "Just need to get some information."

Manuel stepped in behind her. "Me too. He was a cop. I'm a cop." He said this proudly.

"Sit over there," the nurse said waving a hand toward a row of straight chairs lining the wall opposite the beds.

The nurse looked up at the tall man and raised a brow in query.

"Take care of these two. I'm going to check on Alex first," he said.

Then turning to Manuel, he said, "Stay here until I return. While you're lying there, have Mrs. Svenson give you a full description of the men who robbed her. Write it all down."

Manuel nodded eagerly. He'd just received his first assignment. And it was an important one.

# Chapter 11

Several miles from the crash site and the swarm of uniformed officers, a dark sedan with a crumpled right front fender had pulled into an alley and parked between two darkened commercial buildings. The two men inside were examining the plastic packet of shredded paper under the light below the dash.

"Just white paper," Eddie said his long fingers combing through the shreds. "Some of it is stuck together."

He pulled out a dozen long strips held together near the top by a single piece of scotch tape. He leaned over. The light from below accentuated the hollowness of his cheeks, giving him the appearance of a gaunt ghost until he stuck a cigarette in his mouth.

Herb started the car and accelerated fast out of the alley. "They separated them. They've put them both together."

"It's just a little bit of tape on a dozen strips," Eddie said leaving the unlit cigarette dangling from his thin lips. Not a word had been spoken about the shooting. It was all part of the job.

"No witnesses" was their code.

A siren wail sounded in the distance and Herb squeezed the steering wheel and stepped on the gas. The ambulance had arrived. Maybe the cop wasn't dead. Herb didn't know whether to consider that good or bad.

"Did he get a look at you?" Herb asked as he turned the corner onto Denslowe.

"Who?" Eddie asked, his mind still on the taped strips in his hand.

"Put that away," Herb growled. "We got work to do."

Eddie looked up and surveyed the street.

"Car's gone," Eddie announced, still fingering the strip.

"I can see that!" Herb barked. "You think I don't have eyes?"

"House is dark," Eddie added as Herb turned the car around. "That's funny."

Herb slowed. "What?"

"I'd swear that I saw a bunch of keys hanging from the front door lock."

Herb stopped in front of the driveway.

"You think the photo's in there?" Eddie asked hopefully.

"Not a chance!" Herb replied. "But what is in there is an address book. Find it."

Eddie hopped out of the car. When he reached the door, he tried to pull the key out but couldn't. He gripped the knob with one hand and twisted the key with the other. The key didn't turn, but the knob did and the door opened.

Eddie's search was fast and efficient. The desk was on one side of the living room. The address book was in the second drawer. He pulled the front door closed behind him and left the key in place. His last action was to wipe his prints off the doorknob.

Herb pulled away quickly and Eddie flipped through the pages in the book.

"Lots of numbers in here," Eddie said. "It'll take us days to track them all down." He threw the book onto the back seat.

"Any addresses with just first names?" Herb asked, aware that Eddie would have to scramble to retrieve the book. He smiled inwardly. Served him right. He didn't have to shoot that cop. He had the light shining into the man's eyes the whole time.

Eddie found six, and Herb pulled over so he could study a map of the city and plan his route. They checked all six houses. No sign of the woman. Herb decided to double back.

As he was approaching the first house on the list, his cell phone rang.

"What the hell!" he exclaimed angrily. "Hasn't he got any sense at all?"

"Don't answer it," Eddie said.

"I have to," Herb grumbled.

"There's a light on," Eddie pointed out. "There wasn't when we were here before."

Herb pulled over and instructed Eddie to check out the house. Herb reached for the ringing phone as Eddie swung his long legs out the car door.

"What the hell are you doing?" Herb growled into the mouth piece.

"Calling from a pay phone," came the sharp reply. "She called us."

Stunned at the news, Herb Guzman could only choke out a repetition of the words spoken. His mind whirled with possibilities. The first thought that bubbled to the top was that she saw Eddie pump four rounds into the cop. If Eddie went down, so would he. He could feel the sweat forming on his bald pate. He pulled out a handkerchief and wiped his brow and ran the linen cloth all the way to the fringe of hair just above his neck.

He heard little of what Brian Harvath said next because the man was ranting about the shooting of a cop and the publicity that would draw. By the time Herb finished his wipe, he'd calmed himself.

"Where'd this shooting take place?" Guzman asked calmly.

"In San Francisco," Harvath sputtered. "You aren't going to claim you know nothing about it."

"I'm going to claim just that," Guzman said.

"She said some of the shredded paper was gone from the cab after the accident. Who else would take it?"

Herb looked at the plastic bag of paper on the seat beside him. "Well, we don't have it. We followed the cab for a couple of blocks before we realized that she wasn't inside so we turned around and went back to the house. By the time we got there, everyone was gone. The door was ajar so we went in and looked around. The shredded paper wasn't there, not that we thought it would be. We found some leads though."

He watched as Eddie disappeared around the side of the house.

"You don't have the paper?" Harvath pressed.

"That's what I said," Herb said impatiently.

"She said it was taken from the cab," Harvath repeated, his mind still grappling with the new picture Herb Guzman had just painted.

"You called me to tell me this?" Herb asked peevishly. "If we had it, don't you think we would have called you?"

"Yes, I suppose so," Brian Harvath wavered, his voice thick with lingering suspicion.

"So all she said was taken was shredded paper. Does that mean that all we need to worry about is the photo?" Guzman pressed. He was winning this one. He had to hurry. He saw Eddie at the far side of the house.

Harvath roused himself to the original purpose of his call. "She called the governor and told him she's going to give it back because she didn't want the girl's reputation ruined."

Across the street Eddie had broken into a full run.

Herb had to finish this before Eddie got into the car and interrupted with some foolish remark that would wreck Herb's carefully crafted story.

"And you believe her?" Herb asked as he pressed the power lock down.

"Actually, I do," Harvath admitted slowly. "But it doesn't matter."

Eddie's hand was on the door handle. He jiggled it, then bent down and motioned to Herb to unlock the door.

Harvath's voice was firm. "Continue as planned."

Herb flipped the door lock switch as he spoke. His words hurried one on top of the other. "I need three men to cover SFO."

"Move it!" Eddie shouted as he opened the door. "The dogs barked."

"And Oakland?" Harvath queried as Herb started the car.

"The rest is mine. Don't get in my way," Herb responded gruffly.

Before Eddie had closed his door, Herb took off.

"Didn't see her," Eddie blurted out before Guzman managed to break the cell phone connection. Herb glanced into the rear view mirror and saw two old ladies and five dogs pour out the front door. She wasn't in the crowd. So Eddie hadn't missed her.

Guzman turned at the next intersection. The police would be told they turned west. After a few blocks he turned again and then one more time.

Just before he reached the Bay Bridge, he pulled into an alleyway behind one of the old brick buildings near the bay and stopped. He took the shredded paper out of its plastic bag and set fire to it. He watched it burn, then climbed back in the car and headed for the Oakland Airport.

# Chapter 12

While Guzman and Landecker surveyed the Oakland airport terminal building which was but a single story glass-walled building serviced by a road sandwiched between it and the parking lot, Spencer McLean was lying on a hospital bed talking to his assistant on his radio while blood was being siphoned from his arm into a bag hung discreetly below his line of sight.

"Frank Whiting and Caleb Brinson made bail," Lim reported.

"Bet they never even made it to their cells."

"They never even got to their phone call. There was nothing we could do."

"Don't worry about it, Lim. By the way, I told Alex earlier. I figured he'd tell you when he got back. I'm going to LA with Mrs. Svenson."

"Is she in danger still?"

"That's right," McLean replied, looking over at Coral who was dozing in the bed next to his. "I'm going to see my first dog show."

"Should I send back-up?"

"No, this is a holiday."

"There is much to do here," Lim protested.

"You can handle things," McLean said with confidence. "Manuel will be bringing my car back to the station. He has Mrs. Svenson's description of the men who robbed her. Put Gallaghan on. He can type the report."

"Why Gallaghan?"

"Manuel wrote it all out in Spanish. He said it was faster that way," McLean said. With Manuel sitting on one of the nearby chairs, munching on his sandwich, McLean didn't elaborate.

"You are not alone, are you?" Lim asked.

"That's right," McLean replied as if Lim had repeated his instructions, which was something Lim rarely did.

"I am to assume you perceive Mrs. Svenson to be in peril," Lim said. "And that you believe her attackers will follow her to Los Angeles because she is a key element in this case."

After McLean affirmed his conclusion, Lim walked out of his office and into the computer room where Stephanie Brandt and Shawn Gallaghan were watching Drew clue John Hong on the placement of the tiny camera attached to the laptop computer tucked in the drawer in the stand next to the hospital bed that Alex was destined to occupy.

"Gallaghan," Lim said quietly. The curly, blond head whipped around.

"Sir?" Gallaghan said standing upright. While he wasn't as tall as McLean, he was considerably taller than Lim who appreciated the military snap to.

"Get our new man, Manuel Guado on the chief's radio and have him read his report to you. I understand it's in Spanish."

Gallaghan raised his eyebrows. "He doesn't speak English?"

"Not as well as Spanish," Lim replied. "The witness is still there, in case he overlooked something."

"The witness speaks Spanish?"

"English," Lim replied with finality that forbade further questioning.

Gallaghan picked up a headset, put it on and sat down at a computer to type in the report as it was given.

Lim moved on to Drew Manning. "What about the names on the list?"

"All dead," Manning replied. His eyes stayed focused on the screen in front of him.

"What else?"

"So far nothing," Drew replied, pausing to communicate briefly with Hong. "Nothing relevant, that is, except for the fact that all those I've done have died within the last six months. Causes of death vary. Ages vary. No racial pattern. A couple of things stand out though."

Lim waited.

"This part of a name–Kmitted or Knitting. There is a Scott Knittel that died within the last six months. If he's on the list, he's the fifth one from Manzanita out of a little over twenty total. What are the odds of that?"

"Strange," Lim mused.

"You want something even stranger. The first name on the list, one of the two Alex read onto the tape, Martin Deane, he's not local. He died here. An accident. I punched up the Bay Area Times for the date after his donation and he's from Texas. What's he doing on a list of local donors?"

Gallaghan's laughter interrupted them.

"Do you mean duck, like in quack, quack?" he asked into the headset. He typed in the word. "That's an odd thing to notice... I see... By the way, Manuel, we need to know where the list came from... We know that... Before that..."

All three officers in the room turned toward Shawn Gallaghan. They had assumed the list had been generated in the campaign office. The men they had arrested kept referring to the shredded paper as the governor's property.

"A Frenchman?" Shawn repeated so the others could hear. "A funeral director. Thanks, Man."

"Quiet Rest Funeral Home," Stephanie Brandt put in. "Andre Varrieur is the owner. He has a string of them."

"Maybe that's the connection," Manning said as he moved to a computer and his long, thin fingers flew across the keys.

As Manning pulled up information files, Gallaghan popped in with an observation. "When they were talking in the back of the patrol car in Yiddish, the one kept moaning about the first name on the list, and the other one kept saying there was no way a connection could be made. No way at all."

"Who was first on the list?" Stephanie asked.

"The Texan," Drew replied, his face drawn as he searched the file in front of him.

"Was he buried here?"

"No," Drew put in. "He was shipped home and buried there."

"There goes that connection." A quick flash of a nervous smile signaled her disappointment.

Drew leaned back and grinned. "Guess which funeral director handled the shipping of the body."

103

"Start with the Texan," Lim said tersely and left the room.

# Chapter 13

When Manuel Guado came around the horseshoe-shaped access road that divided the airport's short term parking lot from the terminal, he didn't glance sideways or he could have seen a black Cadillac with a dented right front fender. However, had he noticed it, he probably would have assumed that the man sitting behind the wheel smoking a cigarette was waiting for an arriving passenger to fetch his luggage.

Manuel was busy listening to last minute instructions from his new chief. He stopped the chief's light blue sedan opposite one of the large glass entry doors.

The man in the parking lot snubbed out his cigarette and punched a number on his cell phone.

Spencer McLean left the car and carried a small suitcase into the terminal building. Then, the car, its female passenger still seated inside, pulled away.

The Cadillac headed for the parking lot exit. A second man climbed in while the driver was waiting for his change at the exit booth.

Herb puffed as he settled into the passenger seat. Eddie accelerated quickly. The lights of the departing car were still visible at the far end of the long access road. It was dark and no other cars were on the road. Following their prey would be easy.

Surprisingly, the car in front of them moved slowly. The Cadillac quickly closed the gap. Suddenly, the light blue sedan turned right into the parking lot of the five-story Oakland Airport Lodge.

Herb rubbed his hands together. This was going to be easy.

Eddie flicked off the headlights and the black Cadillac crept around the building.

"Where'd he go?" Eddie asked as the two men surveyed the parking lot.

"Give them a minute to get out of the car," Herb said. He peered at the row of darkened autos neatly parked in long rows across from the back entrance. Both men realized simultaneously that they'd been duped.

Meanwhile Manuel was travelling back up the access road without lights. He turned them on when he neared the end of the horseshoe. Spencer McLean stood in the doorway to the building. Coral Svenson left the car and ran toward him.

The Cadillac rounded the corner in time to see the two meet and walk hastily toward the departure gates. Herb jumped out and Eddie sped away from the building after the lone driver in the blue sedan.

Spencer McLean hurried Coral Svenson across the open area in front of the ticket counter toward the waiting areas outside the terminals. Before they went through the check point, he ushered her through a small door to one side marked "Security" and quickly identified himself. It only took a few minutes for Chief McLean to arrange a special boarding.

Outside, after a brief search, Herb Guzman figured out where the two had holed up. He studied the scheduling board and then bought a ticket on the first flight to Orange County. Afterward, he went to the coffee shop, ordered a cup of coffee and contacted Eddie.

"As soon as you're done, take the next flight to Orange County and call me when you get there," Herb instructed.

Eddie was winding through the streets of Oakland following a cabbie who was determined to shake him.

"He isn't taking the freeway," Eddie reported.

"He will," Herb predicted. "Pick your spot."

As he finished his call, Eddie drew close enough to see the cabbie's cap. Suddenly Manuel made a sharp turn off High onto Sixth and roared up a hill. Caught off guard Eddie swung the big Caddy left but he overshot the turn and the blue sedan was over the crest of the hill and out of sight before Eddie recovered.

Once over the brow of the hill, Manuel turned right, onto Crestview, pulled over and shut off his lights. The Cadillac sailed past him on Sixth. Two blocks later Eddie realized what had happened. He turned around and retraced his route.

By then Manuel had already returned to High Street and was speeding toward the freeway ramp. He entered the merging traffic on the freeway with no tail.

Eddie guessed what the cabbie had done and entered the freeway at the next on-ramp. He sped down the divided highway and soon had the chief's sedan in his sights.

Manuel spotted the single headlight in his rear view mirror. Looking down at the switches on the dash, Manuel remembered Chief McLean's parting words. The siren was for emergency use only.

The dark Cadillac was bearing down on him, its lone headlight reminding him that the Cadillac was a bigger, faster car. This lightweight car of the chief's was no match for it.

He moved into the left lane and switched on the siren and the flasher. The cars faded to the right as he approached, then fell in behind him. The Cadillac, however, caught up to him and hung on his tail.

Manuel's hand trembled slightly as he threw the radio switch.

"I need help," he said without preamble.

The call came into the station. Within seconds Lieutenant Greg Lim came on the line. "Where are you?"

"On the Warren heading north. I got a Caddy on my tail and he's gonna take me out any second."

"Same one?"

Manuel liked a man of few words.

"Yeah," he said.

"Stay out of his path until the first turnoff after the tunnel."

"Old Miners Road?"

"We'll meet you," Lim said.

"Yeah," Manuel mumbled. "If I even make it to the tunnel."

"Outdrive him," Lim ordered.

Manuel mulled over Lim's last words as he raced down the Warren. How does one outdrive a car with twice the speed?

Would he live to tell his kids how he'd evaded pursuit on the city streets? There were no streets to turn onto along the freeway. The rising hillside on the right crowded the road barely leaving a narrow pull over lane for emergencies. The steel barrier on the left kept cars from tumbling over the drop onto the other half of the freeway.

Suddenly, Manuel was jolted. His head whipped forward and back. He pressed the accelerator to the floor and swore he heard laughter from the man in the car hugging his rear.

His mind raced. The only thing his car could do better was turn in a tight space. Taking an off ramp was out. The Cadillac would negotiate the turn better than he would.

Briefly, he considered turning up the small access road on-ramp a quarter of a mile further down the road. The Cadillac would never make the turn. But then he'd be stuck on a road that literally went nowhere.

A few hundred yards ahead, the freeway split. The right merged onto the freeway going east through the tunnel to Ardilla, the left faded down into the heart of Berkeley.

He took the left hand fork with the Cadillac sniffing his rear bumper and, at the last possible second, veered right, bumped over a mound of dirt and onto the road going west. The Cadillac followed, its weight making it possible for it to bump over the dirt obstacle without turning over.

The maneuver, however, put space between the two cars. Thus Manuel entered the freeway a dozen car lengths ahead of the Cadillac. Because it was a couple hours before dawn, the lanes were devoid of traffic.

Manuel turned off his siren and flasher. He knew Eddie wouldn't think twice as to why.

Manuel slowed almost imperceptibly as he moved into the far left lane. The Cadillac matched his moves, gaining ground every second. Suddenly, Manuel made a wide sweeping turn and headed for the access road on-ramp on the far right.

Eddie chuckled as he swung the Caddy around behind the smaller car. What a dumb move!

Manuel switched off his lights and Eddie laughed out loud as he completed his turn and straightened his wheel.

The little blue car spun around in front of him and Eddie nicked its rear fender as it completed its turn and sped by him down the slope back onto the freeway.

Eddie screeched to a halt and backed down the access road onto the freeway, straightened his wheels and gunned his engine. The little shit wasn't getting away with this. The taillights up ahead disappeared inside the tunnel. It was just a matter of minutes and he'd be next to him again. This time he was taking him out.

As Eddie emerged from the tunnel, he searched the well-lit freeway in front of him.

Nothing.

That little car wasn't that fast. A green and white sign announced the Old Miners Road exit in a quarter of a mile. Eddie swung off the freeway. He spotted red rear taillights disappearing around a bend in the road and he raced after them.

As he rounded the bend, the flashing lights of two police cars parked across the road a hundred yards ahead made him slam on his brakes. The deep ditches on the side of the road told him his only chance was to back up the way he came.

He screeched to a halt, shifted into reverse, put one hand on the back of the front seat and turned to back away. Two squads, lights flashing, were approaching from behind, side by side.

## The Puzzle

As he turned again, he saw two rifles leveled at his head. He put his hands up.

# Chapter 14

Coral phoned her daughter from the security office in the terminal after Chief Spencer McLean received an update from his second in command.

"Tara, your friend Alex Caribou, was shot this morning. Four times."

Coral heard her daughter gasp and she went on quickly. "He's going to live. I can't explain all this right now. The Ardilla police caught the shooter, but the shooting happened in San Francisco and a second attack occurred in Oakland. I need names of policemen in those cities who don't like the governor."

Tara laughed. "My friends, you mean."

"Exactly," her mother replied good-naturedly.

"That's easy. Sergeant Lamont Hale in Oakland. He and I went to Berkeley together. We dated a couple times. He's very handsome, very smart and black."

Coral was not shocked by this revelation; only mildly surprised and a bit pleased.

"Who else?" Coral probed.

"You're determined to be unflappable, aren't you?" Tara accused.

"We'll argue later when I get to the show. Right now, give me the names."

"In San Francisco I was in a criminal law class with Kathy Riley and Devin Simonton. They're both sergeants on the San Francisco force."

"Do you know them well?"

"Kathy's mother is Korean and Devin's mother is Vietnamese; his father is black. They're my link to the Asian community in the city. Actually to the Asian minority, the Chinese community being so prevalent. And to answer your question, they're friends I see frequently."

"Tara, I love you!" Coral exclaimed. "Chief McLean and I will see you in a couple of hours."

She handed the slip of paper with the three names to McLean and told him they were trustworthy. McLean passed the information along to Lim.

Meanwhile Tara put in a call to the San Francisco police and asked for Sergeant Kathy Riley. Her second call was to her editor.

Her mother held the key. If cops were being attacked, it was something big.

# Chapter 15

Herb Guzman sported a thick dark brown wig, a matching well-trimmed beard and prince nez glasses pinched on his nose, making his eyes appear closer together. His stocky frame was dressed in brown pants and a dark green jacket. His black, pointed-toe shoes had been replaced by brown loafers. This transformation had taken place in the airport's men's room in the predawn hours.

She might recognize him. Or if not him, his attire. He'd put his gun in the case with his gray suit and checked it through when he'd bought a ticket to Orange County. Then, he'd gone to the waiting area, grabbed a discarded newspaper and watched the gathering group of early morning departees.

He'd chosen the last seat by the window in coach assuming she'd be in one of the seats in front of him.

He scanned the passengers' faces in first class before passing through the kitchen area into coach. He moved slowly, affecting a limp so the people behind him wouldn't become impatient. When he reached his seat, he swung in quickly and eyed the group in the aisle behind him. There were no new faces.

The passengers settled into their seats and, for the first time, Guzman feared he'd made a mistake. She'd outfoxed him. He shook the idea from his thinking.

Then, as the steward prepared to close the door, two more passengers slipped in. He immediately stood up and moved into the aisle to get a clear view. He opened the overhead compartment and pulled out a pillow and sat down.

He'd seen enough.

She was on board. He opened up his cell phone and made two calls.

Then he sat back and closed his eyes.

Everything was set.

# Chapter 16

Tara Svenson looked at the two Labs pacing about the hotel room uncertain why their mistress was active before dawn, but ready to accompany her wherever she was going even if it meant another elevator ride of which they were not fond.

"Your mom's coming down, Banner," she informed the black one who stopped, sat and cocked his head. His name meant something was going to happen. His eyebrows rose and fell as he asked what that something was.

"Not Biscuit," she went on. Her nervousness playing itself out as she talked. "Biscuit is at Dorothy Markham's house being bred to Stuffy. I know you think she should have been yours, Banner. You've thought that every time she's come in season since you were five months old. You were a stud even then." She laughed at the memory. "The same explanation holds now as then. She's your mother."

Banner's eyes stayed focused on her face. He perked his ears. He liked being talked to.

Tara couldn't resist squatting down and rubbing him behind the ears. "It's not as if you have never been used. You've had your turn."

The younger dog came over and nuzzled against Tara begging for a share of attention.

Tara scratched him along his back as he rubbed against her. "Sandy is proof of that. I know you didn't want him, but I did. And that's what matters. And because he won yesterday, your dance card is going to be full again. Siring a Specialty winner is the ticket to more breedings. Believe me; you're going to be glad we kept Sandy."

Both dogs moved closer simultaneously and knocked Tara backwards. As she lay on the floor, each apologized by licking her face.

She waved them away. "Now I need a shower."

Accordingly, she padded into the bathroom and turned on the water. She turned around and laughed when she saw both dogs hiding on the other side of the bed.

"I said I needed a shower. Not you."

The water was warm and, as she let it cascade down her slim young body and darkened her auburn hair, she let her worries follow the water down the drain.

The man had been caught. He was in jail. Her mother was safe. Tomorrow they'd be together at the show. She wouldn't let her mother out of her sight again.

Her editor had not wanted to give her the story.

"You're too close to it," Clayton Keyman had argued. He hated going up against Tara. Redheads were unpredictable when they argued.

"You mean I might come up with some real dirt on your buddy," she'd countered.

"I have reporters who aren't as ready to lop off Atkins' head as you are."

"Haig Palmer?" Tara had rejoined scathingly. "He doesn't have the sense to know the truth if it stands up and waves its arms."

"Haig is a good reporter."

"Maybe for obits. He can't mess those up. The man died. He was stabbed, shot or poisoned. That's as far as he goes. This story demands more. I have the inside track."

The pregnant pause told Tara she'd crashed the hard shell and was about to draw out the succulent meat.

"No innuendos."

"None. Facts only. Provable facts," Tara promised.

"You'll keep me informed about how the investigation's going?" he said.

"Only if it's more than supposition," Tara hedged. Keyman was tight with Atkins.

"I want even those," Keyman insisted. "I want everything. I want to know what leads you're following."

"Come on," Tara urged. "You and I are on opposite sides of the fence here. I'm not going to give you that so you can spill it into the governor's camp so they can put a lid on it."

"Haig Palmer has the story," Keyman declared. "He won't play games with me."

"And when Governor Atkins is hung out to dry by the San Francisco Chronicle, you'll be out of the newspaper business."

"Atkins is a friend of our publisher too, you know," Keyman pronounced. It was rumored that in exchange for the paper's backing, its editor was going to be offered a position on the White House staff.

"The paper has its money on the wrong horse," Tara stated flatly. "This one isn't going to make it to the White House."

"If it's petty," Keyman warned, "I'll quash it."

"This is not petty, believe me," Tara said. "This is why we're reporters. To..."

Keyman cut in. "Spare me the soliloquy. Besides, you're not here."

Keyman thought he'd trumped her ace. Tara's response was quick.

"I don't need to be. My mother and the Ardilla Chief of Police are flying down here."

"I need someone up here."

"Okay, let Palmer do his stuff. Mine will be better," Tara replied. "I get a by-line."

"If I run it," Keyman hedged.

"This story's big," Tara said with finality. "I'm sure the Chronicle will love it."

"Damn you!" Keyman exploded and Tara knew she'd won it all. The story was hers with a by-line.

Now all she needed was for the Ardilla Chief of Police to cooperate. She knew from Alex that he was an up-front guy. The question that remained was did he like reporters?

She'd soon find out.

She stepped out of the shower and, as she toweled herself dry, the two Labs emerged from their hiding place.

"It's only a job, guys," she said. "It's only my whole life."

# Chapter 17

Tara Svenson was on edge. Alone in her hotel room hours before dawn with the lights on, nothing to read and no one to talk with, she turned on the television set and flipped through one infomercial after the other.

She guessed that people up at that hour were desperate and would watch anything. She was desperate; but after ten minutes of instruction on how to make a million in real estate, she turned off the set.

It was too dark to walk the dogs. Too early for breakfast. Too soon to go to the airport and wait for her mother's flight to arrive. It was also too early in the investigation to expect her police friends to have any information other than what she already had.

She decided to write a side-bar on Alex. She knew him well enough. She picked up her computer and logged into the paper's morgue. She'd written a feature on him when she first started. It was one of a series of profiles of bi-racial policemen.

She reread her article, took a few notes and then made a phone call. Her mother had said he'd been shot four times. It wasn't accidental.

The hospital confirmed his presence but the person on the switchboard would give out no information on his condition.

"Give me his room, please," Tara said.

"He is not receiving calls," the woman replied coolly.

Before the operator disconnected, Tara quickly inserted her alternative request, "I want to talk to Sergeant Bill Radanovich or Detective Langston Brooks. They should be in his room."

Tara was put on hold. The operator was back in half a second. "Who is calling please?"

"Tara Svenson. My mother was with Alex Caribou earlier."

Another thirty second wait took place.

"Sergeant Radanovich speaking," came the cool voice over the phone.

"My mother called me from the airport and told me Alex had been shot four times. How is he?" Tara hoped the answer to her query would confirm the number of shots as well as give her an update on his condition.

The voice that responded was warmer. She was in the loop. "We've been told he's going to pull through. He's in recovery."

"When Mother left, he was still in surgery," Tara said. "It sounded bad."

"He deflected the two aimed at his head with his arm," Radanovich explained. "One hit the bone; the other just tore through the flesh and grazed his ear. One round hit him in the shoulder and one that should have gone straight into his heart was deflected by his shield."

"His wife made him put the shield in his breast pocket," Tara murmured. "I wrote about that when I did a story on him."

"You doing another one?"

"Yes," Tara said.

There was a pause, and then Tara said, "It was my idea that Chief McLean meet my mother in San Francisco."

The sergeant responded to the worry in Tara's tone.

"What happened wasn't your fault. The taxi was broadsided."

"Mom didn't give me details," Tara confessed. "What was Alex doing in a taxi?"

"He had some evidence he was transporting."

"And was the evidence recovered?"

"It's still missing."

"My mom wasn't with him?"

"She and the chief were in the chief's car," Bill Radanovich said. He began to realize he was being a bit too talkative. "I think maybe I've said too much."

"Next question won't be about the investigation," Tara promised. She needed one more piece of information. "Can I call on people to donate blood in his name?"

Bill Radanovich was taken slightly aback. "Yeah. Sure. They've got a blood donor room on the first floor."

"If I call for blood," Tara said disarmingly, "I won't be putting Alex in any danger, will I? I mean you guys are going to guard him even though the shooter has been arrested?"

Again she surprised Radanovich. "There were two men," he blurted out.

"So your orders to guard him are ongoing?" Tara asked, and then quickly added. "Don't answer that. I can ask Chief McLean when he gets here."

She heard the man breathe a soft curse. She responded with an assurance that she had most of the information already. "Blame my mother," she said in parting. "It works for me."

Radanovich chuckled and Tara closed with a thank you.

During the next forty minutes, she wrote the first article under her by-line and e-mailed it to her editor. What he did with it would determine their future.

Keyman read it. She had facts that Palmer hadn't dug up and she'd fleshed out the victim as only she could. It was a good piece. And it contained not a single innuendo. He ran it unedited.

# Chapter 18

Tara arrived at the airport fifteen minutes before the Alaska Airlines flight was due to land. The dogs were in their crates behind the middle seat. The crate doors faced the rear gate of her 1995 Plymouth Voyager. A cooler with cold drinks, sandwiches and cooked liver to bait the dogs in the ring took up half the middle seat. Two canvas-backed folding chairs with padded arms were crowded between the driver's seat and the middle seat. A large bag of dog food sat on the floor by the door and pans were tucked under the front seat. Leashes and towels were tucked between the front seats and a jug of water from home sat beside the chairs. Next to that sat a bag with grooming brushes, scissors, nail files, cooling coats, small water bottles, folding water dishes, plastic bags and show collars and leashes, black for Banner, tan for Sandy. If the chief was large, her mother would have to squeeze onto the small section of seat she'd cleared and the chief would get the front seat. His legs would straddle the giant, round can of dog biscuits.

As she pulled around the line of cabs, she noticed the cab at the front of the line had his hood up. She circled around the parking lot and passed along the front of the terminal building again. Some people parked in short term parking and walked inside to meet passengers as they deplaned. Tara didn't consider that option. While the dogs were usually safe in their crates when she stopped to eat on her travels, she rarely left them.

So she continued to circle. She planned to wait at the end of the cab line once the passengers began pouring through the door. The loading zone was a space four car lengths long. You could see the baggage carousel on the other side of the glass wall.

Cars passed her and tried to spend their time waiting there, only to be waved away by the traffic cop if their stay was longer than two minutes. Only those actually loading luggage and passengers earned the coveted spaces. Tara decided to continue circling until her mother actually exited the building.

As more and more people poured through the doors, the number of cars coming up the road swelled. More tried to squeeze into the loading zone than there was room for. Cabbies, their back seats full, pulled out and thrust themselves into the tangled mess. The traffic officer slowly sorted them out and kept the line moving.

Tara drove around the circle hoping she'd timed her arrival well. As she inched along behind an SUV, a minivan nosed part way out of his space in the loading zone. The SUV turned into the space while in the outside lane directly in front of the SUV, a sedan stopped and the driver jumped out and ran toward a woman exiting the building.

Tara saw her mother come through the doors behind that woman. She opened her door and stepped on the running board and shouted.

As she did so the cabbie five car-lengths away, at the front of the line slammed down his hood and shouted at

Coral, "Hey, lady. I'm ready to go. I can get you outta here fast."

Tara shouted again and the tall man with her mother turned. Tara waved at him.

As Captain McLean hesitated, Coral hurriedly entered the door being held open for her by a plump, bearded stranger. The cabbie slipped behind the wheel and started the engine.

The tall man turned back toward his charge and shouted, "Wait!"

The plump man slammed the door shut and slapped the top of the cab. The driver took off.

Spencer McLean ran after it expecting it to slow down and stop for him. Instead it sped up. He slowed and stared after it dumbfounded.

His brain processed what had happened quickly. He raced back to the traffic officer, explained that there had been a kidnapping, gave him a partial plate and the identifying logo on the side of the cab then hastily slipped into the driver's seat of the open sedan blocking the left hand lane. He shoved the gear in drive, bounced the car over the curb onto the grassy strip alongside the road and nudged a palm tree. A man ran toward him shouting his protests.

"Ticket him," McLean yelled at the cop as he climbed out of the sedan and waved the minivan through. Tara slid up next to him and stopped.

Once McLean had one foot inside the door, Tara sped down the road. McLean glanced sideways at a younger version of Coral Svenson. Trim, attractive and with a cap of red hair. He wasn't expecting the latter. And while the red was mixed with enough brown to mute the red into auburn,

Tara Svenson was nonetheless a redhead. He was in for a wild ride.

Tara swung right and slid through a yellow light at the intersection.

"There he is," she shouted. "He must've had a long wait at the intersection. Why didn't Mom get out?"

McLean didn't answer. He was on his cell phone.

"Lim, Mrs. Svenson's been kidnapped. I'm only three cars behind the cab she's in. I need help. Tara, give me a location."

"East of the Orange County airport on Flyaway Drive. We're coming up on Hydrangea."

Tara inserted her minivan in front of a white sports car in the right lane. His tires screeched. His horn blast announced his fury at being cut off. She passed the cars behind the cab then swung back into left lane sharply. Again a horn sounded.

The cab sailed through the intersection on the yellow; Tara stayed on its tail. She saw her mother look back through the rear view mirror. Her face was drawn.

Tara waved.

McLean was still talking to Lim. He read him the plate number and then told him that the cops should be looking for a cab with a dark green minivan on its tail.

"We need to get her out of there," Tara said. "We're coming up on a red light. I can pull alongside in the left turn lane. You'll only have seconds."

McLean's' answer was to unbuckle his seat belt, reach back, unlock the side door and push it open as the two cars slowed down for the light.

McLean thrust his legs out.  Suddenly, he leaned sideways.  A gun had appeared in the driver's hand.  The chief spun around as his feet hit the ground.  He reached inside the side door and grabbed the forty pound sack of dog food.  It was still two thirds full.  His long arms swung the heavy green sack at the driver's window as it was being powered down.

The gun discharged into the sack as it smashed the remaining glass and knocked the driver sideways.  A second shot was fired.  It whizzed past McLean's ear as he threw open the cab door and dove at the driver.

"Get out!" Tara yelled at her mother.

"I can't," Coral screamed.  "No handles."

The driver, pinned under the dog food bag and the muscular frame of the tall police chief, lifted his foot off the brake and raised it to kick his opponent.  The cab lurched forward and rammed the car in front.  The impact jarred the struggling men.  McLean's grip on the driver's left hand gave way and the man reached down and pulled out his knife.  McLean grabbed the wrist of the hand holding the knife.

The gun in the driver's right hand went off again and the car in front of the cab took off.

This time the bullet sailed through the open front door of the minivan and sliced through the forearm of the woman gripping the wheel.  Tara screeched.

The sudden sharp pain catapulted her out the door and around the side of the van.  She ran to the cab's rear door and grabbed the handle.  It didn't open.  She tried again to no avail.

McLean pushed the knife hand over the driver's head with one hand while the other grappled for the gun.

Tara searched the front panel for a knob that would open the glass partition dividing the front and back section of the cab.

The driver's knee came up and hit McLean in the groin. The chief momentarily lost his ability to withstand the pressure exerted simultaneously by both the driver's hands. The gun in the right hand turned toward the woman in the back seat while the knife in the left descended straight toward the neck of the man pinning him down.

Tara yelled at her mother to duck. Then she flung herself on top of the two men and reached for the knife which was scraping McLean's neck. As she landed on McLean's back, the gun discharged, but the sudden weight of her body changed its trajectory. The bullet drilled through the glass behind the driver's section and smashed into the steel roof above Coral's head.

Tara dug her fingernails into the driver's wrist. McLean pushed the knife away. The double pressure loosened the driver's grasp on the knife. Tara grabbed it and pressing it against his throat told him to drop the gun.

While most men don't believe a woman capable of following through with such a threat, the driver heard the steel in Tara's voice. The knife dug into the flesh of his neck and his fingers opened. The gun slipped to the floor.

"You can get off now," McLean grunted as police sirens filled the air.

Tara, however, was frozen in place. He could still grab the gun. He still had at least one bullet in it. Someone could still get shot.

"You can get out now, Ma'am," said a voice from behind. "We've got the situation under control."

"Not until you get that gun," she said, not moving. "He can still reach it. I don't want to get shot again."

The door on the other side of the cab opened and the gun was retrieved from the floor. Tara scrambled backwards, still holding the knife which she dropped on the ground as soon as she looked around and saw several guns leveled at her.

"That's her!" a woman shouted. "Those two just jumped out of their car and attacked that cab driver."

McLean backed out slowly. "We did indeed," he said in a strong voice. "To rescue the lady he'd kidnapped."

McLean held both his hands up. This would be straightened out quickly enough.

One of the officers pulled the dog food bag off the driver who then climbed out protesting that he'd been attacked by two maniacs.

An officer leaned over and peered in through the back window. "You can get out now, Ma'am," he said.

"I can't," Coral shouted. "The door has no handles. And don't you dare hurt my daughter."

The officer tried to open the door from the outside. The cabbie, meanwhile, had moved slowly backwards as if to distance himself from his attackers.

"He was kidnapping me," Coral shouted.

An officer on the other side, tried to open the door on his side.

"It's locked," he announced.

"Hey! Let go!" came a shout.

They all turned.

A man with a long fuzzy white beard and tattoos on each muscular arm stepped out of the crowd, the cab driver's arm firmly gripped in his hand. "He was slipping away. Didn't you guys have some questions for him?"

# Chapter 19

Tara, a towel wrapped around her forearm, was typing on her laptop which was perched on her knees. Spencer McLean was in the driver's seat following a squad car to the hospital.

Suddenly, Tara shoved the laptop at her mother who was seated behind her.

"It hurts too much to type," she announced. "I didn't know one used muscles in the forearm to type."

"Then don't," Coral replied.

"You do it." Tara demanded.

"Do what?"

"Type out my story."

"This is no time..."

"He gave me a by-line, Mother," Tara said testily. "He's upset because I'm here and not there. This story will square things."

"You're on vacation," Coral replied. "So stay on it."

"Type, Mother!" Tara ordered.

Spencer McLean grinned. They were a perfect match.

"What's this headline?"

Tara smiled as she repeated it, "Cop, Reporter Shot in Daring Rescue."

"It's a bit much," Coral admonished.

"It's a grabber," Tara countered.

"Sounds like I was hanging off a cliff."

"He had a gun and a knife," Tara exclaimed. "You just type."

"I can't believe you got them to give up that dog food bag. We can't use it. It probably has glass inside."

"And a bullet," Tara announced.

Chief McLean started.

Tara caught the ripple of shock her statement had caused and hurried to explain that the bullet might match some unsolved homicides in the Bay Area. She knew several cops who would check it out.

McLean protested that it was evidence in this investigation and would have to be turned over to the police here.

"They'll have the bullet in my arm," Tara said. "That's the one they need to make their case. Who cares if a dog food bag got shot?"

McLean laughed. "You're right there. What I don't understand is why does your arm hurt so much now that you can't type but didn't hurt when you were wrestling with that cabbie for the knife."

"He was going to kill you and my mother," Tara replied. "My brain has a good sense of priority. Which is why Mother has to stop interrupting me and just type what I tell her. I have to get this out of my head so I can concentrate on the dog show."

"You're not going to make it," McLean said sadly.

"Maybe not to watch the bitches," Coral put in, "but we'll be there for the Breed. We'll both see to that, believe me."

And McLean did.

By the time they pulled up in front of the Emergency Entrance, Tara had dictated most of the article. As McLean parked, Tara reached over and pressed the lift gate release.

"What are you doing?" McLean asked.

"We're going to put Banner up front to guard the van. I don't want anyone driving off with our dogs while we're inside."

Coral hopped out, lifted the back gate and released Banner from his crate. As the big black Lab jumped down, Sandy stood up in his crate and wagged his tail.

Coral couldn't resist his pleading. She released him as well. After all there were two front seats.

The windows were lowered halfway and Banner poked his head out the driver's side window and watched his two mistresses disappear into the big building. Sandy sat upright, staring through the windshield. They were on duty. Neither would stir until Tara or Coral returned.

As the threesome walked toward the building, the man sitting in a car two rows away saw the moving of the dogs to the front and decided that the pack of shredded paper had probably been left in the car. Then he saw Coral race back to the car and retrieve a bundle of clothes and what looked like a small computer and doubt assailed him.

Still, he took out his gun and attached the silencer. The dogs would be no match for his gun.

# Chapter 20

As they walked into the hospital, Tara looked at her mother. "What in the world are you doing with all those clothes?"

"I thought that after you got patched up, you'd want to get rid of that bloody shirt. I brought the matching skirt," Coral said holding out the set.

"We could go back to the hotel," Tara said. Her annoyance was obvious.

"There may not be time," Coral said.

"Mother, there's plenty of time before Breed," Tara snapped. "Time to eat. Time to change. Time to settle in before we need to show."

"What's wrong?" Coral asked.

"The colors," Tara said. "You're showing Banner; I'm showing Sandy. I need dark brown not cream."

"Take my dark brown skirt," Coral offered, "I'll wear the cream."

"It's longer than I like," Tara complained. "And what about the shirt?"

"I have a print blouse that will go with either," Coral said. Seeing the distress on her daughter's face, she added, "If there's time, we can go back to the hotel and change again."

"That would be foolish," Tara grumbled. "We'll do it your way."

"What's really wrong?" Coral probed.

"I want to mention the reason you were kidnapped in the article and I know you'll object."

"Can't it just be left unsaid? I'm rich enough."

"That would be misleading," Tara responded stiffly. "And my reports are going to have a thread running through them."

"I'm returning the photograph," Coral announced. "I've already told the governor and that's where it will end."

Suddenly Tara's brown eyes blazed and her lower lip trembled. "Are you crazy, Mother? He had you kidnapped."

"Wires got crossed," Coral replied calmly. "It was a mistake."

"Tell her, Spencer," Tara called as an orderly led her into an examination room. "I got shot. Tell her."

Coral turned away from the tall man who was hovering nearby and walked toward the admissions desk and asked for the admittance form. She told the nurse that her daughter was covered by insurance at the paper where she worked and hurried into the room where Tara lay and grabbed her purse.

"A local," Tara was telling the doctor. "I need to be wide awake this afternoon when I go into the ring."

"You box?" Joked the intern.

"Dog show ring," Tara said. "Mother, back me up."

"She hasn't finished her news story," Coral said. "Don't dope her up."

"Mother, you write the last paragraph," Tara said. "Read it to me when they're done patching me up if I'm awake. We've got a deadline to make."

Coral walked out into the hall and sat down. She laid the clothes on a chair and opened up the laptop. Spencer McLean sat beside her.

"He had time to call it off," he said quietly. "The man who opened the cab door for you was on the plane with us."

Coral looked at him with disbelief.

"You're mistaken."

"He banged on the top to signal the cabbie to take off. He knew we were together."

"The man simply made a mistake," Coral argued. "He thought we were going separate ways."

"Your daughter's right. It's not over."

"But I told Whalen I'd keep his secret," Coral protested. "I told him I'd return the photo if no one else was hurt."

"Your daughter was shot."

"Accidentally, I'm sure," Coral insisted. "She wasn't a target."

"No one is so blind as he who will not see," McLean said. His blue eyes bore into the questioning brown ones of the gray-haired woman staring at him from the chair beside him. "Is your daughter as stubborn as you?"

"Worse," Coral said and smiled slightly. "We are both fiercely loyal which makes us great friends. Unfortunately, we are as loyal to our ideas as well as to people which is the other side of the coin."

"Loyalty can be betrayed. Judas betrayed Jesus who loved him totally," McLean said.

"Now you're bringing out the heavy artillery."

"Your loyalty is misplaced," McLean said. "Your offering is seen as a weakness by these men. They now want more than the photograph returned. They want you dead."

"But why?"

Before he could answer, his cell phone rang.

Coral looked at the computer screen as McLean stood up and walked away. Tara would expect a factual report. She began typing.

McLean meanwhile wandered down the hall, listening intently to Lim's report as he stared at the floor tiles. He was standing near the entrance when loud barking brought his head up. Phone still in hand, he rushed toward the entrance doors.

The cop standing in front of the treatment room reacted by following him, unsnapping his holster as he did so.

"What are you doing?" McLean shouted as he cleared the door.

Herb Guzman jumped. He quickly tucked his gun beneath his jacket, turned, saw the cop behind the Ardilla police chief and backed away.

"Nothing," he said. "I was just gonna pet the dogs."

"Stay right there," McLean ordered as he walked toward him. His face reflected his recognition of the man who'd ushered Coral into the cab.

Herb continued his back up. His car had been moved close, the door left ajar, the key in the ignition, the motor running.

"He's got a gun!" Herb shouted and when McLean turned, he dashed sideways, slipped into the driver's seat, shoved the gear shift into drive, slammed his foot down on the accelerator and raced away.

"He's one of the kidnappers," McLean shouted at the cop. "Go after him."

Within seconds the squad car was in pursuit siren screaming, lights flashing. McLean walked up to the car. Neither dog barked at him.

He reached over and petted Banner's broad black head. The tail thumped against the seat back.

McLean walked around the car and Sandy turned sideways to face him. McLean reached in and stroked his yellow head and while he did so, he noticed the small case Coral had been carrying was lying open on the backseat. Coral had removed most of the clothing from it, but the travel kit was not only closed, but highly visible.

It appeared to be a perfect place to hide a shredded photograph. If the man wasn't caught, he'd be back. McLean hurried back inside.

Coral looked up from her task. "Come and tell me whether Tara will go for this."

Spencer McLean hesitated and then sat down. These women didn't need to be more frightened than they already were. He decided not to tell them about the man's visit.

He took the laptop from her and read the words:

"While the kidnapper remains mute about the motive for the kidnapping, Mrs. Coral Svenson told the police that she possessed certain politically sensitive documents, the nature of which she would not reveal, and that it was these documents that the kidnapper was after. She stated that she was making arrangements for the safe return of these documents to their owner."

"It's good to a point," McLean said. "It doesn't indicate whether the documents are merely campaign strategies or something more dire. That part is good. The last sentence needs to be changed."

"Changed how?"

"Write: 'Mrs. Svenson has turned the documents over to the Ardilla Chief of Police for safekeeping'."

"Why say that? I already told the governor I'd give the shredded photo back to him."

"First of all, he probably suspects that I've seen it. Your friend Becky taped the list of names together. He's got to believe you did the same thing with the photo."

"And second?"

"The woman in the photo wasn't murdered. I'll hand the photo, still shredded, back to the governor. He isn't the first politician to slip over the line when a pretty woman crosses his path. I don't need to even deal with the photo. The names on the list are enough. And once he has the photo as well as the list back in his hands, he'll believe he's home free. He knows we saw a list of contributors' names. He has no idea we suspect anything. If it weren't for Dr. Griffin, we wouldn't have."

"He'll never be right in my book," Coral said firmly. "He shot Alex; he shot Tara; he kidnapped me–all because he was embarrassed by a silly photo."

"He's running for the Presidency. He can't afford a scandal," McLean commented sagely.

"I told him I'd return it and not tell anyone. I'm an honorable woman, I keep my word."

"He wouldn't understand that."

"I'll give you the photo when we go out to eat tonight."

"Why wait?"

"We can't eat before we show," Coral said purposely misunderstanding his question. "Our stomachs are tied up in knots."

McLean decided not to pursue it. He switched to her tack. "I thought you two had been doing this for years."

"We have."

"And you still get nervous?"

"That doesn't change," Coral said glancing at her watch. "Tara needs to send this now to make the deadline."

"Do you know where to send it?"

"Tara has the e-mail address in the computer," Coral said. "Do you think it's finished?"

McLean looked over her shoulder as she scrolled up to the start of the article and then read it with her.

"It needs a close," he announced. "A piece of information less important than the rest. All reporters end that way. When I read an article that's how I know the editor hasn't cut it."

"I don't know how to do that."

"She says that we were shot but she doesn't mention how seriously. Say that my injury was minor and that I was treated and released and that Tara underwent an operation to remove a bullet from her arm and is expected to be released later," McLean said.

"That's important," Coral said as she typed in the new paragraph.

"Yes, it is," McLean agreed, "however, it's less important."

"Maybe it should go higher up."

"Tara wanted the motive next," McLean said. "She would have ended it this way."

"Done," Coral said as she brought up the address list. "Look, she's listed the San Francisco Chronicle and The Bay Area Times as well."

"Send it to them too. The Chronicle will put it out on the wire. My guess is that Keyman won't."

"Why not?"

"He's an Atkins' supporter. He knows who you are. This smacks of trouble in the ranks."

"I don't want to bring the governor down," Coral protested checking off the other two addresses as well.

McLean eyed her solemnly. "Don't you?"

Coral punched the send key.

# Chapter 21

Frank Whiting charged into the governor's office in Ardilla and Brian Harvath scowled his disapproval at the interruption. Frank slid his fingers through the bushy hair below his receding hairline, a gesture he engaged in when he sensed he'd upset his boss.

"What is it?" Caleb Brinson barked.

None of the three men seated asked Whiting to sit. At the moment he was an intruder.

"Bad news," Whiting replied, his voice rising. "Keyman just called. There's going to be a piece in the afternoon's edition about a shooting in Orange County that alludes to a connection with the governor."

"Alludes to?" Harvath queried. His square jaw was set. His eyes never wavered from Whiting's face. Even his voice betrayed not a whiff of panic. "How?"

Caleb Brinson added a second question, "Who was shot?" He ducked his head as if apologizing for asking. He wasn't. It was a mannerism.

"The Ardilla Police Chief for one," Whiting replied, eyeing the empty chair. If he sat, he'd feel less like he was being reprimanded.

"What was he doing down there?" Whalen Atkins burst out.

Harvath answered the governor as if the question was merely one of fact. "He went down with Coral Svenson. I might have forgotten to mention that. But, then, I didn't know he was going to get shot."

"No one knew," Brinson said dipping his head further down so that his short black beard lay on his chest and his words emerged a mumble.

Whiting brushed his fingers through his hair again. He was beginning to understand what type of men Harvath had set on Coral's trail. He pushed on. "The other one was Tara Svenson, Coral's daughter."

"They shot her daughter!" Whalen Atkins exclaimed. "I know they look alike, but come on. Coral has gray hair. Her daughter's almost a redhead."

Whiting went on. "Coral was locked in the back seat of the cab. There were no door handles. It seems our esteemed police chief and Coral's daughter attempted a rescue and got shot. It's not serious. But they did manage to keep the kidnapper there for the police."

"Guzman?" Atkins asked Harvath.

"No," Whiting replied. "That wasn't the name."

"Then how come I'm implicated?" Atkins demanded.

"Coral's daughter is jumping to conclusions," Harvath replied. "I heard from Guzman ten minutes ago. He's still on the trail of the photo. He says he thinks it's in a case in her luggage in their car. He plans to get it this afternoon when the dogs are out of the car. He has help down there but he and Landecker are the only two that can be tied to us and Landecker is in jail here and not saying a damned word."

"So we tell Keyman to kill the story," Governor Atkins said.

144

Whiting shifted from one foot to the other. "The thing is, Sir, Keyman says she copied the story to the Bay Area Times and the San Francisco Chronicle."

"I thought she worked for the Oakland Journal," Atkins put in.

"Keyman was puzzled by that too. She's never done it before."

Atkins rose angrily. "Tell Keyman to fire her ass!"

"Er, Sir," Caleb Brinson insisted quietly. "That would be a mistake." His head went down again as he spoke. This time it was an apologetic gesture.

"Caleb's right," Harvath said. "Keyman can exert some influence if she's working for him. He will lose it if she's at the Chronicle."

"What influence?" Atkins charged pacing the carpeted floor behind his desk. "She copied every paper up here. The wire service will pick it up and it'll be all over the state. We need damage control. Is there nothing we can do?"

"We can tell Keyman to run the story," Caleb said, his eyes on the governor. "We can act as if we have nothing to hide."

"We need someone to talk to Varrieur," Brian Harvath said.

"So I tell Keyman it's okay to print the story?" Whiting asked, dancing toward the door.

Harvath nodded and continued with his new train of thought. "Who's our best litigator?"

"Cox," Whiting said, his hand on the knob.

"Get him in here," Harvath ordered.

When Whiting left, Caleb Brinson turned to Harvath, "How much are we going to tell Cox?"

"Just that the photo showed a sexual act."

"Suppose Varrieur tells him the whole truth?" Atkins asked.

"He won't," Harvath said.

"What's our approach?" Caleb asked.

Harvath responded. "Cox'll tell him that the governor will withdraw from the Presidential race and have him prosecuted for blackmail and..."

Atkins interrupted. "Won't the photo become public then?"

Harvath shook his head. "We use the same reasoning Coral Svenson used. We don't want to tarnish the reputation of a young lady who is deceased."

"Why do I have to withdraw from the race?" Atkins whined. His voice was like a child's, not the distinguished gentleman who wooed the ladies with his deep voice and brilliant smile.

"To save your face and ours," Harvath said. His brow furrowed and his eyes glinted coldly.

The governor folded into a petulant pout. He knew better than to display anger at his chief of staff.

Harvath softened his tone. "It's not going to come to that. Varrieur wants the ambassadorship. He can't be ambassador if you're not the president."

Atkins slowed his pacing. His face cleared. "That's true."

"And he has people he's in bed with who would not take kindly to his little blackmail scheme interfering with their plans."

Whalen Atkins stopped his pacing altogether and the birth of a smile of triumph got as far as the initial upturn of the outer corner of his mouth when Frank Whiting again burst into the room. Edward Cox followed on his heels.

"Andre Varrieur was hit by a car this morning," Whiting announced. "He was jogging along Country Club Road here in Ardilla."

"He doesn't live here," Atkins protested inanely.

Edward Cox spoke up.

"He stayed over after the party. He was too drunk to drive home," he explained. "I suggested it last night."

"Good God!" Atkins burst out. "He'll think it was us."

"Why would he think that?" Cox asked.

"Sit down, Everett," Harvath said grimly. "We have a job for you to do."

# Chapter 22

Tara's eyes spotted the clock on the wall beyond the curtained cubicle that was just one of many in the huge area that served as a prep room as well as a recovery room for outpatients. She tried to tell the time but her mind refused to translate the position of the hands into a meaningful answer. She had floated in and out of consciousness the whole gurney trip back. She could scarcely remember being transferred to the bed.

"They gave me drugs," she grumbled as her mother stepped around the curtain carrying an armload of clothes.

"I'm sure they didn't," Coral assured her daughter. She laid the clothes on the chair along with the computer. "You asked them not to."

"I'm disoriented. I can't tell time," Tara snapped.

"You're in shock," Coral said. "A body doesn't take kindly to the invasion of a bullet, no matter how minor, and your wound wasn't minor."

"It wasn't major," Tara protested. "If I wasn't drugged why can't I tell time?"

"Your mind is still reeling from the experience," Coral replied calmly. "It's ten-thirty. The operation went quickly and while there's a hole in the muscle, the damaged nerve..."

"What damaged nerve?"

148

"The bullet stopped at the bone and nudged a nerve."

Tara's face brightened. "So that's what caused the numbness. I thought I was having a stroke."

"You're too young for a stroke," Coral stated flatly.

"Young women have strokes," Tara argued.

"Not if they're my daughter they don't," Coral shot back. The idea obviously was untenable.

"If the bullet hit a nerve in my arm, why did my thumb feel funny?"

"When the bullet pressed against the nerve, it cut the flow of sensation to your thumb and little finger."

"How do you know?"

"The doctor told me."

"We have to hurry," Tara said suddenly. "We're going to miss the whole show. Is Chief McLean still here?"

"He's outside. It seems that the man at the airport who closed the cab door showed up here and tried to get into our car. Chief McLean wasn't going to tell me but I overheard a bit of his conversation with Lieutenant Lim. He said the dogs scared him off but I overheard him telling Lim the man had a gun."

Tara sat bolt upright. A spell of dizziness knocked her back on her pillow. "You have to go to them, Mother. We can't let them get shot."

The vision of her beloved dogs being shot caused the blood to drain from her face. Coral laid a gentle hand on her daughter's arm. "Don't worry. They're being guarded. If they weren't, do you think I'd be standing here so calmly?"

Tara managed a weak smile. "I guess not."

"You need to rest now."

Again Tara rose, but this time more slowly, using her good elbow as a prop. "We've got to go. We'll miss the show."

"There'll be others."

"Mom, I won yesterday. Sandy has to go back in!" Tara protested.

"I'll take him in," Coral said. "You rest. We have time."

"I want to do it," Tara insisted. "Besides, there's Banner."

"He can sit this one out," Coral decided. Tara spotted the regret in her voice.

"He has a chance to win," Tara argued rising to a full sit, then stiffening her good arm and using it as a prop to steady herself.

"You can't even sit up," Coral observed.

"Mom, we've dreamed of this. You and I showing two generations of our breeding. We thought we'd do it after they were both champions but this is even better. Banner has a chance to win the Breed at the same show where his son took Winner's. If you think I'm not going to go for it just because I got shot, you don't know me."

Coral grinned. "Lay back for thirty minutes and then I'll help you dress."

"Why wait?"

"Because it's private here," Coral said pulling over the food tray. "And you said you wanted to see the photo."

She reached down inside her blouse and pulled out the plastic bag with the shredded photo. The prospect calmed Tara.

Together mother and daughter separated the strips, smoothed them out and bit by bit pieced them together.

When they finished, Tara stared at the photo a long time. The sling hampered the movement of Tara's right arm so she asked her mother to smooth out the face of the girl.

Tara gazed at it for several minutes. Finally, she laid back and sighed heavily.

"It's Cee Cee alright," she admitted reluctantly. "It's just impossible to believe."

"People–even good people–have affairs," Coral suggested softly.

"Not Cee Cee," Tara said. "She was a virgin and she intended to...besides she was engaged...why would she...it just can't be." She turned her head away as if by doing so she could erase the factual evidence that lay on the metal tray. "Cee Cee and Kenny were a twosome since high school. She never cheated on him before he gave her the ring so why would she..."

Coral interrupted and pointed at the dangling hand. "There's no ring on her finger."

"That's her right hand, Mother," Tara quipped.

"We can't see her left hand," Coral observed, puzzled. "So how do you know this was taken after they became engaged?"

"It's her hair, Mom," Tara said more softly. "She cut it after he gave her the ring. Kenny likes short hair. It was her engagement present to him."

Tara sat up again and leaned over and studied the photo again. She straightened up slowly, a bewildered frown wrinkling her brow. There are no rings on her fingers," Tara said. "Cee Cee loved rings. She never wore less than two on each hand. Her sister Debbie told me that Kenny joked about his ring getting lost in the crowd."

In response, her mother moved her hands up to the portion of the photo depicting the face. "Look at this."

"No earrings," Tara observed. "She had two holes in each ear. She liked to wear non-matching pins and loops. She thought it gave her a more interesting look."

"Not that," Tara's mother said impatiently. "The expression on her face."

"What expression?"

"That's it. There is none. That's why McLean and I figured it wasn't rape."

"I'm more interested in why she wasn't wearing any jewelry," Tara said. "She wouldn't remove her earrings to have sex."

"She looks as if she's unconscious," Coral said. "By the way I have your watch and your earrings."

"That's it!" she exclaimed. "She was in the hospital."

"No wonder she looks so pale," Coral commented.

"Pale?" Tara queried, focusing again on the photo. "You're right. She's pale as a ghost. Sex doesn't do that."

"A hospital is a strange place to have an affair," her mother remarked absently. Her mind wanted to erase the image seared into her memory.

"She wasn't having an affair," Tara concluded vociferously. "She was drugged. That's why she looks so strange. She wasn't cooperating or resisting. She couldn't do either."

"Drugged?" Coral queried, pulling her mind back into focus.

The silence between them lasted for several minutes.

It was the older of the two that broke the silence. "It couldn't be rape."

"What else could it be?" Tara countered angrily. "It happened when she was in the hospital fighting for her life which makes it even more despicable. She was at the top of the heart transplant list but..."

Coral interrupted her daughter.

"It didn't happen at the hospital.""

"But the rings..."

"There is no monitor, no IV, no breathing apparatus— nothing. If she was in a hospital room, there'd be all that."

"It looks like a hospital room. Just a white sheet on the bed," Tara observed aloud. Suddenly, she stopped as the truth struck her.

"Rape is a felony," Coral offered nudging her daughter's memory of her repetition of the conversation she'd overheard between the Governor and Harvath.

"No rings means..." Tara began.

Her mother completed the thought, "It happened after they took away her jewelry which they always do when you enter a hospital and which they don't return until you leave unless..."

"Are you sure we aren't missing something?" Tara asked quietly.

"A misdemeanor, he said," Coral reiterated, also not wanting to draw the only conclusion left.

"But when she left the hospital..." Tara's voice faded as the truth hit her.

Together they stared at the photo.

It all fit. Governor Atkins was a necrophiliac.

It was Coral who broke the silence.

"We're in real danger," Coral concluded. "This photo could cost him the Presidency."

"You can't return the photo," Tara decided.

"I gave my word."

"Without a caveat?"

"Well," Coral hesitated. She could see where her daughter was heading. "I did say there were to be no more attacks."

"So you're free of your promise."

"This attack might not have been orchestrated by him," Coral said. "Why kidnap me to get a photo I was planning on returning?"

"Because he figured you might piece it all together. It wasn't a kidnapping. You were going to be killed."

"But then it would all come out," Coral protested.

"Would it? They'd have the photo. You'd be dead and so would your explanation. There'd be nothing left but speculation."

"Well, it won't happen again, thanks to my quote in the Bay Area Times and the Chronicle," Coral smirked.

"What quote?"

"We finished your article and sent it to your editor."

"I work for the Oakland Journal."

"I know. We copied the other papers just in case your editor messed around with my quote."

"What did you say?"

"That I had some politically sensitive papers in my possession and that was the motive for the kidnapping."

"You can't say that in a newspaper article," Tara snapped.

"You can if it's a quote and you believe the person you're quoting can back it up."

"It implicates him. You do know that, don't you? The editors all know you're spearheading the campaign for funds in the East Bay," Tara rattled on ignoring the knowing look on her mother's countenance. Suddenly, she added, "You planned it that way."

"Let's just say I'm a mother."

"What's that got to do with it?"

"Everything."

# Chapter 23

In the waiting room outside the recovery area, Chief Spencer McLean had finished answering Sheriff Andy Tolliver's questions and promised that both women would come down and make statements after the dog show. The Sheriff had protested that this was more important than a dog show to which McLean had replied that, while he didn't understand the hobby, to those involved in it, this show was terribly important. He added that the two women were on a winning streak and a person in that situation doesn't think of anything but the bigger win that's almost within his grasp.

Finally, the Sheriff left with the bullet extracted from Tara's arm sealed in a plastic bag and McLean's promise that he'd bring the two women to his office by five o'clock.

McLean checked the clock on the wall and did some mental calculations. He had time to check on the progress in Ardilla. He looked around. The waiting room was empty. Behind the desk the nurse had left to check out something behind the partition beyond which lay the outpatient receiving and recovery room, a huge square room partitioned into small cubicles by hanging drapes. He had seen such a room in one of the larger hospitals in the Bay Area. This hospital was built in the same era. It felt familiar.

He picked up his phone and called Lim.

"I know I put you in charge," he said with a hint of apology in his tone, "but I need to be in the loop."

"I'm pleased that you called. Much has happened. I am handling it, but please let me inform you about it," Lim replied. Years of working in a casual atmosphere had done little to dull the edge of Lim's formality.

"Talk to me," McLean said.

"They have lost the bullets," Lim announced. "They have lost the three bullets that were removed from Alex's body."

For a second McLean saw Alex as a corpse. He shook off the vision.

"Go on."

"San Francisco denied our request to send over the two officers you requested. They sent only Kathy Riley. Sergeant Mark Volatis had been assigned the case and they refused to remove him. He was upset that you tried to bypass him. You might remember him from last night. He came and I allowed him access to the prisoner. The suspect had said nothing to that point. He talked to Volatis.

"They were alone during the interview. He stationed Kathy in the observation room and told her to knock on the glass when anyone came in. I considered this suspicious and so I refused to release the prisoner to him. I told him we had arrested Eddie Landecker on a concealed weapon charge and we were holding him pending arraignment. Many words were spoken that were uncomplimentary. I also kept the gun."

"How did the bullets get lost?"

"Sergeant Riley does not know. She went to the hospital after she found that the bullets weren't in the evidence room.

She said the hospital spokesperson claimed to have already given them to a policeman. She described Sergeant Volatis but was told that the officer who picked up the bullets was not six three but a short, stout man."

As McLean listened, his lieutenant continued to tell him about the events that had occurred, leaving out nothing. McLean never wanted the short version.

"Sergeant Kathy Riley is upset with the way the investigation is going. Not only are the bullets missing, but Sergeant Volatis believes Eddie Landecker's version of what happened. Landecker claims that his car hit the cab but when gunfire erupted, he fled the scene. He wants to plead guilty to leaving the scene of an accident and Sergeant Volatis plans to recommend that the D.A. go with it. Sergeant Riley's argument that more investigation is called for has fallen on deaf ears.

"Volatis claims that without the bullets, there is nothing solid to tie Landecker to the shooting. Before talking to Landecker, Volatis and Riley interviewed Alex at the hospital. Volatis said Alex saw only the outline of the shooter. The flashlight shining in his eyes blinded him so he didn't see the man's face. Alex said that the shooter was tall. But Volatis argues that when a man is lying down, everyone towers over him. Alex smelled smoke on his clothes. Volatis said that not only does Landecker smoke, so does Guado. His money is still on the cabbie.

"Sergeant Kathy Riley told Stephanie that the time frame was wrong in Landecker's story. She said that Alex said he was shot immediately after the crash before he even had a chance to right himself. She said that Alex heard two voices. Then he was shot. The car left after that.

158

"When she pointed this out to Volatis, he argued that Alex could have been temporarily knocked out and lost a few minutes in time."

McLean interrupted Lim's recitation. "Where's the fourth bullet?"

"Sergeant Riley tried to locate it earlier to take a look at it. The cab wasn't impounded by the San Francisco police."

"I forgot to tell you last night. Volatis wanted the cab company to retrieve it."

"That is not standard procedure, Sir," Lim stated firmly. "A man was shot in that cab. It should have been impounded."

"Volatis was all for making a quick arrest and Manuel was his target. I told him he could ship it across the Bay to the Sage County impound lot and I'd foot the towing, so I guess that's what he did."

"What do you want me to do?"

"Hold up on the forensic work-up of the cab until I have a chance to negotiate with Captain Scoma. We need Volatis out of the loop."

"There is more to report, Sir," Lim said hastily. "Andre Varrieur was struck by an automobile on Country Club Road early this morning while jogging. It was a felony hit and run. The car swerved in order to hit him."

"Dead?"

"Close to it. He is in a coma. He is not expected to live."

"Who did the work-up?"

"Stephanie Brandt. She said she got a good print of the tire in the mud. Good photos showing no skid marks after the car veered off the road."

"Send her to the hospital. I want her in that room. She is not to leave. You understand?"

"It's been done."

"You're stretched pretty thin."

"We will manage."

"Let me get Sergeant Volatis out of your hair," McLean said. "Give me his captain's name and number."

As McLean was jotting down the number, a nurse appeared behind the desk and called to him, "Are you Spencer McLean?"

He nodded and quickly approached the desk. A janitor and a nurse entered the waiting area and moved past the desk into the large room behind it.

"Your niece is asking for you," the nurse said. "Last curtained area on the left down the aisle."

McLean looked where her finger was pointing. He hesitated.

"It's okay. She's decent," the nurse said. "She said it was important."

Phone in hand, Spencer McLean walked past rows of curtained cubicles and slowed before making the last turn.

Coral's head popped out. "There you are. We have some important news for you. We know why this photo is so important."

Tara sat forward, her tousled auburn hair framing a face alight with excitement. McLean felt his heart skip a beat.

"It depicts aberrant sexual behavior that would completely ruin him," Tara said.

"What did I miss?"

Tara pointed to the neatly arranged photo strips lying on her food tray. "This photo was taken after Cee Cee died."

160

McLean turned the table toward him and stared while the two women alternately explained their reasoning. When they finished, he said not a word. Instead he moved away into an empty cubicle across the aisle way and dialed the number Lim had given him.

"Captain Scoma," McLean said as soon as the husky voice answered the phone. "Spencer McLean here, Ardilla Chief of Police. My assistant requested two specific officers be sent to coordinate our investigation with yours. I want to reiterate that request. And let me tell you why. Our investigation is bigger than yours. The attempted murder of two police officers is only a part of the conspiracy we're investigating. Your Sergeant Volatis is making serious mistakes that could be detrimental to our investigation. You send me the people I requested and I will see that you share in whatever positive news coverage results. Just a moment."

McLean walked across the room and handed the phone to Tara Svenson. "Ask him about the missing bullets."

Tara took the phone. "This is Tara Svenson. I'm a reporter with the Oakland Journal. What's this about missing bullets?"

She grinned as she handed the phone back to Spencer McLean. The foul language was the first words to greet his ear.

McLean charged in. "Well, Volatis lost the damn things... I don't care whether he picked them up or someone else did... He was in charge of the case and the bullets are missing. I think he should find them... Not later! Now!"

McLean paused and held the phone away from his ear so the two women heard the shout. "What the hell are you doing calling me with a reporter in the room?"

McLean put the phone back to his ear. "Captain Scoma, that reporter and I were shot this morning.  We are in the hospital...  You may, of course, leave Sergeant Volatis in place and we will work around him and you.  Or you can work with us.  It's your choice.  Good day, Sir."

He clapped the cell phone shut.  "One thing at a time."

He looked at the two women.  "Any chance there is any fingerprints on those shreds besides yours?"

# Chapter 24

Lieutenant Greg Lim picked up the phone on the first ring, "Yes, Chief."

"Captain Scoma here. Put Sergeant Volatis on."

Lim poked his head out his office door and called the sergeant into his office. He closed the door and left the man alone in the room. Some things should be said in private.

He walked over to Sergeant Kathy Riley and told her he was going to send her and Shawn Gallaghan back to interview Eddie Landecker.

"Begin by telling Landecker you are taping your interview. Then Mirandize him again. He is to respond to you with words. This is very important. Then tell him all you want is for him to repeat what he told Sergeant Volatis. It is most important that you two do not question him. Let him do all the talking."

"I don't understand," Kathy Riley said, her voice as soft as her expression.

"What's up, Lieutenant?" Shawn added.

"Sergeant Volatis is talking with Captain Scoma. He is being replaced. I want Sergeant Riley unable to be disturbed during the transition," Lim explained.

"How do you know...?" Kathy began.

Shawn interrupted her. "Believe me, if he says 'it's happening,' it's happening."

"All investigation of the shooting will be suspended until you are done with your interview," Lim promised. He glanced through the glass window to his office in time to see Volatis slam down the receiver. "Go now!"

Shawn hurried Kathy into the interview room while Sergeant Harper fetched the prisoner.

"I'll take charge of the tape recorder. You do the talking," Shawn said with appropriate deference. Kathy nodded and smiled. Volatis wouldn't think of letting her take charge.

Lieutenant Lim turned to face Sergeant Volatis.

"We've been ordered back to the city," Volatis said through gritted teeth. "This was your doing."

"I wish I had such powers of persuasion," Lim said politely.

"The captain wants us to look for the missing bullets," he explained.

"Both of you?" Lim asked arching his brows in surprise.

"We're partners. Where I go she goes."

"Perhaps Captain Scoma plans to send a replacement. She can go back with him."

"He didn't tell me about no replacement," Volatis claimed. "Where is Sergeant Riley?"

"She's interviewing the prisoner."

"She's what?" Volatis burst out. "Who told her to do that?"

"I did," Lim replied calmly. "We have a tape of the shooter's voice. We will compare the tape she is making with one we have. So you see it is a very important interview."

Anger reddened Volatis' countenance. He clenched his fists but kept them at his side.

"You held out on me!" he charged. Then muttered just loud enough for Tom Kimber to hear, "A sneaky Jap trick. Better watch yourself."

Kimber grinned as he called out, "Hey Lieutenant. We're short a man. The sergeant here thinks we need a Japanese officer."

"Doesn't Alex have Japanese in his background? He has everything else," Lim commented wryly, his formality succumbing to his attempt at humor.

Kimber chuckled appreciatively. "I think you're right. Sorry, Volatis, our Japanese officer hasn't been in today to pull the fast one you're referencing."

"Cut the crap!" Volatis exploded. "You deliberately withheld information from me."

"I remember the lieutenant wanting to bring you up to speed and your reply. You said something about us staying the hell out of your way as I recall."

"That doesn't mean you don't tell me what you got!" Volatis raged. He hung his six foot three frame over the shorter Kimber and his spittle showered the young officer. Kimber took a step back and wiped his forehead with his hand.

Volatis took Kimber's step back as a sign of retreat and stepped up and again crowded him. "You know I'm right."

Kimber shoved his face forward. "You spit on me again and I'll arrest you."

Volatis' spittle flew out with his protest. "You wouldn't dare!"

"Why don't you just go back to whatever rattlesnake den you crawled out of and stop hissing at us," Kimber shouted.

Volatis spun on his heel and headed for the hall leading to the interview room. Kimber was faster and he blocked the passageway with outstretched arms. "Lay one hand on me and I'll arrest you."

Volatis pushed Kimber's arm aside and managed one long stride before he was flung sideways and his arm was locked behind his back.

"Take him to his car," Lieutenant Lim said quietly.

Dewey Harper stepped forward and took Volatis' other arm.

"Get your goddam black hands off me," Volatis spat. "No nigger is gonna tell me..."

Kimber interrupted harshly. "I'm not a nigger and neither is Sergeant Johnson. You owe us both an apology."

Mark Volatis realized immediately that he'd stepped over the line. He shrugged off the grips of both men angrily. "I'm going. I'm going. Don't make a federal case outta this. So the damned word slipped out. It happens. But just remember this. You guys disrespected me first."

As Volatis drove away, Harper turned to Kimber. "I'm glad he spit in your face. If he had spit in mine, that tiny jaw of his would be hurting for a month."

"Hey man," Kimber said. "He's gonna be hurting for longer than that after we write him up."

The two exchanged high fives and walked jauntily into the building.

"He's on his way back to the city," Kimber announced.

166

But they were wrong.

Volatis headed straight for the Sage County impound yard where the cab was parked. He identified himself, signed in and was shown to the cab. The man on duty hung around and watched as he opened the left rear cab door and searched it.

Volatis found the bullet imbedded in the fabric. The nose had been flattened by its impact with one of the steel bracing bars. He slipped it into a plastic bag.

He knew that forensics would find blood and cloth fibers on its surface, but that the bullet would not be traceable to the gun taken off Eddie Landecker. It would verify that the Ardilla policeman had been shot in the back of the cab, already an undisputed fact; but, it wouldn't prove that Eddie Landecker shot him. This bullet could be turned in.

The tape was another matter.

That would have to disappear later.

Right now, his job was done.

# Chapter 25

Sergeant Mark Volatis was not a particularly creative man. Nor was he especially clever. He did, however, have a finely honed sense of self-preservation. The person he accepted regular bonuses from expected certain things, among which was that he keep his job.

The bullets disappearing on his watch had been stupid. The captain held him accountable. While he thought he'd been clever using a snitch dressed as a cop, now he wasn't so sure.

He drove away from the impound lot, but, before he'd gone two blocks, he turned up a short side street crowded with car repair shops. He had to think.

Seeing all that dried blood on the back seat of the cab had given him an idea. He rolled it around in his mind.

He couldn't turn in the bullets taken from Alex's arm, shoulder and chest. They were his insurance. Later, he'd find a better place for them, but right now, they were safe. He pulled over and parked.

He fished out the gun taped under the dash and opened the chamber. There they were. The last three in the barrel.

After a few minutes he left the curb and drove down a lot alongside a body shop that was crowded with cars with smashed fenders, caved in doors and crushed grills until he found one missing a side window. Volatis pulled in front of it, got out, went to the rear of his car, pulled out a greasy blanket and opened the rear door of the wrecked car.

He bunched the blanket up into a wad, pushed the gun into its bowels and fired off three rounds. The bullets pierced the blanket and buried themselves deep in the thick upholstery in the upper portion of the rear seat. Volatis had aimed the gun so that the bullets would travel along the length of the seat back and using his fingers found their stopping place. With his knife, he sliced an entrance hole and extracted the first bullet. He studied it. Perfect.

It might be traced to a bullet in another homicide but he doubted it. If it were, he wouldn't be connected with it. It hadn't been one of his cases.

Quickly, he extracted the other two bullets and pocketed them. He looked around. The din from the car shops had masked the sound of the muffled gunfire enough so that it sounded like a car backfiring, a common occurrence on this street.

Volatis folded his lanky frame inside his car and backed out of the lot. He drove back to the impound lot and told the attendant that he'd forgotten to take pictures.

He left his car parked at the entrance and taking his camera strode to the cab where he had extracted the bullet. He opened the right rear door and shot a picture across the seat. The man was watching from his station.

He closed the door, walked around the cab and opened the other door, bent down and shot a picture. He looked sideways and noticed that the caretaker was out of sight. He leaned forward, scooped the three bullets from his pocket and rolled them across the seat through the dried blood. He brushed them into a plastic bag with his hands, rolled and pocketed the bag. He then stood up, closed the cab door and left the lot.

He'd tell his captain that he'd tracked down the bullets on a hunch. How was he sure they were the missing bullets? The captain would ask and he'd answer that he wasn't, but forensics could check for blood, couldn't they? If even a small particle was found, that'd prove they came from the lieutenant's body, wouldn't it?

Someone had snatched them to sell as souvenirs. That's what he'd say. And he'd promised not to charge the souvenir hunter if he'd give up the bullets. After all, the bullets themselves were what mattered, not who stole them. Besides without the bullets all he had to go on was suspicion. The guy should be given something for cooperating.

As he drove across the Bay Bridge into San Francisco, he went over his fabricated story several times. He couldn't see a single flaw in it.

It was perfect.

# Chapter 26

The call from Captain Scoma came in while Sergeant Devin Simonton, newly arrived from the city, was sitting with Kathy Riley and Shawn Gallaghan listening to the original tape. They were watching Lim pick out segments from the interview tape to use as a match. Drew had told Shawn earlier that there was no area in forensics in which Lim was not an expert.

"The man's a verifiable genius," Drew had reported. He had a more earthy term he wanted to use but his new goal in life was to stump the linguist with a word he didn't know.

Lieutenant Lim tore himself away to speak with Captain Scoma. He assumed that the captain was merely checking on his officers. He was wrong.

Scoma announced, with some glee, that Volatis had done his job and recovered all four bullets.

"Four?" Lim queried puzzled.

"He recovered three that had been stolen by some souvenir hunter. Our forensic lab is testing them now for traces of the victim's blood since we don't have a clear chain of evidence. The fourth he dug out of the cab door before he left."

"We were sending over a forensic team, to do the cab," Lim announced, piqued.

"My man took some initiative. He saw your team. He said they'd muck it up."

"He was wrong," Lim replied stoically. "Thank you for the information."

"We need the gun," Captain Scoma said. "You can send it back with my men."

"I will send you what you need," Lim promised, hanging up quickly before the captain could put any time constraints on him. He reported the conversation to the group.

"You're giving him the gun?" Shawn Gallaghan asked.

"I am sending him the ballistics report. That is all he needs at present."

"So I guess I'm going back," Sergeant Simonton said with a sigh. "It was fun while it lasted."

"Not right away," Lim said. "First, you, Sergeant Riley and Sergeant Harper are going out to do a workup on the cab."

"The bullet's gone," Simonton said. "What are we doing?"

"We must determine exactly what happened. I want a full forensic workup."

"Alex told us what happened," Kathy Riley said.

"Prove it," Lim replied.

"Yes, Sir," Simonton and Harper chorused.

# Chapter 27

Back in the Recovery Room in the Granite County Hospital, the two women stared at Chief Spencer after he asked if they thought there were any prints on the photo besides theirs.

It was Coral who broke the silence with a question. "Why on earth is that important? I know where I got the photo and I saw who put it in the shredder."

"And the man who gave the photo to the governor had a French-sounding name?" McLean reiterated.

Before Coral could answer, a buxom middle-aged nurse came around the curtain carrying a bag of clothes and a pair of shoes.

"I hear you're anxious to get out of here," she said cheerfully, "although I can't understand why. A little extra rest never hurt anyone. You'll feel much better in a couple hours."

She bustled around the cubicle, setting the clothes on the bed, moving the tray with the photo strips aside and setting the shoes on the floor. She drew the curtains and bid the two visitors to wait outside.

As Tara began dressing, the nurse fussed with various items in the room. She moved the chair back out of the way and then helped Tara remove her gown and handed her the shirt she asked for. The nurse rolled the gown into a ball and set it on a chair. She checked the nightstand as Tara buttoned her blouse. She picked up the wastebasket and swept the photo strips into it and set it down near the edge of the curtain next to the nightstand. She nudged it through a split in the curtain and a hand pushed an identical wastebasket back.

The nurse handed Tara the fresh cream-colored skirt and Tara told her that her mother and she were going to exchange skirts. The nurse slipped through the curtain and signaled to Coral to join her daughter.

Coral immediately spotted the fact that the photo was not on the tray.

"Where's the photo?"

Tara turned around. Her gasp of dismay was unmistakable.

"It was all torn up," the nurse said hastily as she lifted the plastic lining from the basket and set it on the tray. "But don't worry, it didn't go anywhere. It's all here in the bag."

The nurse picked up the rolled hospital gown and looked around the room as if to make sure everything was in order and then slipped through a slit in the curtain.

They heard her tell Spencer, "The ladies are exchanging clothes. They'll tell you when they are ready."

She walked swiftly straight down the aisle toward the dressing room, tossing the gown in the hamper on the way. She was gone in half a minute.

Tara and Coral exchanged skirts quickly and Coral helped Tara tie her shoes. Then she opened the plastic liner on the tray and looked inside.

"I don't see my plastic bag," she commented. "I can't use the liner. It's too big."

"Maybe now's a good time to give it to Chief McLean, Mother," Tara suggested, folding her blood-stained clothes. She turned to look at her mother. "What are you doing?"

"I thought maybe it was on the bottom and I could just scoot my hand..."

"Well, there go whatever fingerprints..."

Coral interrupted her. "This isn't our photo."

"What do you mean?" Tara shot back. "Who else's would it be?"

Coral pulled out a strip. "Look at the colors."

Tara pushed back the curtain and spoke directly to Chief McLean. "I don't know how she did it, but that nurse switched photos."

McLean took off down the corridor and turned in the direction he'd seen her go. He glanced at the people in the beds as he passed by.

He traversed every aisle before returning and announcing that she wasn't in the Outpatient section.

"I don't think she had it," he decided. "I saw her come out. She only had the rolled up gown and she tossed that."

"It could have been in the gown," Coral suggested without much surety.

"I don't think so," Tara said. "I would have seen her carry something over to the gown."

"You didn't see her toss the photo away," her mother pointed out testily.

"The wastebasket was behind me. The gown was always in my sight," Tara explained.

"I wanted to be rid of the damn thing, but I didn't want it stolen. If she didn't carry it out of here, who did?"

"There must have been someone in the cubicle behind me," Tara concluded aloud. "The baskets were switched. This was planned. Both are long gone."

"If you two will hang on, I'll ask about the nurse at the front desk," McLean said.

When he left, Tara said, "Let's look at it this way, Mom. It's gone. Maybe we'll be left alone now."

"But now we have no proof," Coral sighed.

"There's always the negative," Tara said. "But I thought you wanted to give it back and forget about it."

"I did before you were shot," Coral admitted. "And before I put that quote in the paper. Now what have I got to bargain with?"

"Bargain? For what?"

"Our lives, my dear child. Our lives."

# Chapter 28

The parking lot at the show site was crowded when the Svensons and Chief McLean arrived. After a brief squabble, Tara agreed to take the lightweight canvas chairs and find their friends while Coral and Spencer McLean parked and unloaded.

Because they were late, they were forced to park the minivan at the end of a long row of cars on the quiet access road. The sun was high in the sky and Coral announced that the dogs had to come with them.

"It's too hot to leave them in the car," she explained. "And I won't leave the back gate open considering what happened earlier."

"I'm surprised you let Tara go," McLean commented wryly.

"I don't really think we're in danger anymore," Coral replied loosening the bungee holding the rolling cart. Coral yanked it off the crate top and set it on the ground.

"I'm not certain being here is wise," McLean said stepping forward.

"Why on earth not?" Coral asked. Her eyebrows arched in surprise. She opened the crate door and released Banner and snapped the lead on his collar. She held out a second leash and McLean released Sandy.

"By the way," Chief McLean said, as he fastened the leash to Sandy's collar, "call me Spencer. I'd like to look like a casual observer."

Coral laughed. "You won't pass for that. You're wearing a coat."

"I have..." Spencer began.

Coral's laughter cut him short. "You look like a handler. Don't be surprised if someone asks you to take a dog in the ring."

"What do I do if someone does?"

"Just say this is your first dog show. That should scare off even the rawest novice."

"That's the truth," McLean said with a touch of surprise in his voice.

"The truth works," Coral grinned. "Especially if you're undercover."

McLean protested immediately. "I'm not undercover exactly. I'm on vacation."

"Let's give these dogs a chance to air while we have a chance."

"Air?"

"Relieve themselves," Coral explained. "Walk with me. The grassy ditch is perfect for our purposes although we need a tree. These are dogs and not bitches, after all, so let's walk down to that one."

Coral pointed out a tree ten yards up the road away from the row of cars.

"Won't Tara worry?" McLean asked.

"She'll figure out that I took time for this. She's an experienced show person."

"Don't you need to see how far along the show is?"

"I know where it is. Somewhere in the middle of the bitch classes," Coral explained. "Judges judge twenty-six dogs an hour and the show started at nine. The puppy classes alone took up most of the morning. The lunch break will probably come after the Bred-By class. I'd rather not miss that one, but some things take precedent."

"What needs to be unpacked?" McLean asked as he paused so Sandy could sniff the tree.

The air was warm, the sun bright, the wild grass a golden brown from a summer in the sun. McLean stood under the shade of an old oak and felt his tensions drain away. Surely, they were in a safe place.

"The crates and the cooler and the show bag." Coral replied, "That's it. We keep everything in the show bag."

"What about the dog food?"

"We don't feed the dogs until after the show."

"Then give me the car keys and take the dogs. Sandy's done."

Coral hesitated.

"It's tricky loading all that stuff."

"I'll make two trips if I can't figure it out," McLean smiled. "Go on. I won't be far behind."

When Coral joined her daughter, Tara asked where McLean was. Coral told her Spencer was unloading the crates.

"Mother, he'll forget something," Tara snapped. "He won't know how to do a final check."

"Leave the dogs here with me then and go," Coral replied evenly. "Spencer will welcome the company."

Coral smiled as she sat down and put one dog on either side of her chair. Sandy watched Tara leave with longing eyes. She was the liver dispenser.

Banner settled down at Coral's feet. Experience had taught Banner that one slept when one could at a dog show. Sandy hadn't learned this yet. His attention had been diverted from Tara to the bitches in the ring. He stood stiffly upright, wagging his tail.

As Coral's eyes wandered along the row of bitches standing in the ring waiting to be judged, they spotted a pair of feet toed outward. A chill ran down her spine.

She lifted her eyes and studied the man who was apparently not interested in her. He didn't glance in her direction once. His hair was dark and thick with a decided wave. His sunglasses were sporty and his nose, which was large, sported a white blob of sunscreen on it. His shirt was a tasteful light blue golf shirt; his pants, dark blue Dockers; his shoes, navy running shoes. His thick fingers sported multiple rings and he had two earrings in one ear. His attire sent mixed messages and Coral shook off the feeling that she'd met this man before.

There has to be more than one man in the world whose toes turn out, she told herself. Besides what would he be doing here? He already had the photo.

She picked up the catalog Tara had left on her chair and turned to the list of Bred-By bitches. Her friend Joyce Webb was in the ring with Muffy.

As Coral relaxed into her chair, Spencer McLean saw Tara approaching the minivan. He waved at her and asked her how many questions she'd fielded on having her arm in a sling.

"Some," she replied. "People about to go into the ring are concentrating on their dogs. They'll ask later."

"Do you have a camera?" he asked. "I'd be glad to take pictures of you and your mother in the ring together."

"It's in the canvas bag you're stuffing in the dog crate."

McLean reached inside and pulled out the camera and slung the strap over his shoulder.

"Extra film?" McLean queried. He planned to take some crowd shots for himself.

"In the glove compartment," Tara answered. "But I have a new roll in the camera."

"Mind if I take a shot of you to get a feel for the camera?" he asked opening the glove compartment and pocketing two rolls of film. He unsnapped the case and held up the camera as Tara was leaning over checking out the car.

She heard a click and backed out so fast she bumped her head. "What was that all about?" she said rubbing the sore spot with her free hand.

"I couldn't resist," he said grinning.

"Chief McLean," she began with a scolding tone.

He held up his hand. "No more. I promise. And call me Spencer. Now will you pose?"

"You had your one shot," she said tartly. "And you wasted it."

The camera which he was holding casually shoulder high clicked.

"You weren't looking through the viewer," she complained sticking her free arm on her hip in disgust.

He bent over and squinted. "Aimed it just right," he said. "You might come out sideways, but a frame'll fix that."

Tara opened up the glove compartment and handed him another roll of film. "You're gonna need this."

As they walked toward the ring, Tara said casually, "You're not married, are you?"

"Nope!"

"I knew it. Mother has that look in her eyes."

"What look?"

"That matchmaking look."

"Your mother does that too?" McLean chuckled. "We better never let our mothers meet."

"You're absolutely right. The only hope two single people have is to take on only one matchmaking parent at a time."

"I think we found something we agree on," Spencer McLean said. "That and the fact that your mother is a wonderful woman and you have two fantastic dogs."

Tara reddened as she beamed. She sped up her pace so he wouldn't notice her discomfiture.

He didn't hurry to catch up. She was attractive from all angles.

# Chapter 29

Chief Spencer McLean spotted Herb Guzman a few minutes after unloading the cart when he walked over to the hospitality table, downed a tiny can of orange juice, selected a plain donut from the scattering left in the large pastry box and set a Styrofoam cup under the coffee urn spigot. He took two shots of the man as he was putting away his camera.

The F-stop and shutter speed he'd pre-selected for the dappled shade under the trees lining two sides of the ring. Most of the exhibitors had crowded into the shaded area. The day was going to be a long one. An hour, even two, in the sun was pleasant. Seven hours wasn't.

The man stood out. He'd mixed dog showing up with either horse racing or a sailboat regatta and was dressed for both. Actually, he was poorly dressed for either. He was dressed so that he looked like a nerd and people would remember what they noticed first–the large nose with sunblock dabbed on it, the black sporty sunglasses and the earrings in one ear.

Guzman would have preferred a less conspicuous disguise but the lady had already seen him twice–once as a businessman, once as a professor-type. Both those times he looked older, more sedate. He needed to shock those images from her head. The rings and earrings were incongruous with sunblock and focused attention, the features that weren't his, particularly, the bulbous nose and the shock of black wavy hair.

He was sitting in a seat that was behind those at ringside and, when he peeked around the heavy-set woman in front of him, he had a camera to his eye. Spencer McLean's focus centered on him early.

He debated telling Tara and her mother since they were relaxed and enjoying themselves.

He decided that the man wouldn't try anything blatant. He could have taken out Tara and Coral in the hospital, but he hadn't. McLean decided that the attack would be subtle and against only one.

If the three were killed, the newspaper article would point a finger at the governor. It had to be an accident. Spencer McLean was at a loss to figure out what kind of accident could befall a woman seated in front of a show ring with scores of spectators.

He decided to watch the show. The man was directly across from him. He'd notice if he moved.

Tara and Coral were caught up in the excitement of the moment.

McLean leaned over and asked Tara, "What's happening?"

"The judge is making her selection," Tara whispered. "Her first walk down the line was to check expression."

"She put her hand on some backs."

"Double checking shoulder layback. She has fourteen bitches in the class. Usually the judge notes the outstanding ones when they enter the ring and she doesn't lose track of them. This is an English judge. She will critique all the dogs later."

"Critique?"

"Point out what's good. The English don't center on faults as we do. A dog has a good coat, another dog has a better one, the winner has a superior coat; that sort of thing. They find something to praise in each dog and the one with the most outstanding attributes is the winner. Sometimes they will say that one dog lacked the coat or the shoulder layback or the expression of another but they don't even hint that it was a fault."

"It sounds complicated–critiquing that way. Why not just point out the faults?"

"Because the dog show world is small. The judges' comments would be repeated. His faults would hang like a tag around his neck," Tara explained. "Each judge looks for a different combination of attributes and as long as no judge red tags a fault, any dog is free to win at the next show."

"Who are we rooting for?"

"Joyce, the third from the back. She bred Biscuit."

"Who's Biscuit?"

"Our champion bitch."

"Where is she? She wasn't at the house."

"She's being bred," Tara said and then squealed softly. "Oh, look, she's stopping in front of Muffy."

"That's good?"

"If she moves her, it is."

"Moves her?"

"Has her run across the ring and back so she can see her move."

"She didn't do it," McLean noted. "Is that bad?"

"Not necessarily. English judges aren't as hip on movement as American judges," Tara replied.

"I have another question," McLean said.

"Ask me in a minute," Tara replied. "Get a picture of the line, will you?"

McLean hoisted his camera and snapped two shots. Then he used the zoom and took a picture of Muffy. When he lifted his head he noticed that the man across from him was completely hidden behind the heavy set woman.

"Boy, you are camera shy," he thought. "Something's going down."

The judge had the group circle the ring once and then stop. When they did so, she pointed her finger at Muffy first and a whoop went up from the gallery. Joyce had many friends.

"She won," McLean said. "Does that make her a champion?"

"She won her class," Tara explained. "We have more classes to go. The winners of all the classes are then judged against each other and the winner of that group gets the points."

"There were over a dozen in this class alone," McLean commented in awe.

"That's more than there are at most shows," Tara replied. "On top of that, this was the Bred-By class, a class reserved for breeders showing the dogs they bred. It's a very prestigious win. The cream of the crop is in this class."

"Then she'll win over the dogs in the other classes."

"Not necessarily. Lots of breeders buy good show prospects from other breeders. Those pups are scattered throughout the classes. We bought Biscuit from Joyce.

Because Biscuit is owned by us and not Joyce, she couldn't be shown in Bred-By even when Joyce was at the show. Biscuit won her points out of the Open class. Most of the points are won out of Open."

"Then why would anyone show in any other class?"

"Each class tells the judge something. The puppy classes are divided by age; the Novice class says the dog is new in the ring; American Bred is for young dogs, dogs older than puppies, but not yet fully mature and you just saw Bred-By where the breeders show their line."

"So what class did Sandy show in yesterday?"

"Open Yellow."

"I thought Banner was his father."

"He is, but a person isn't the breeder unless she owns the bitch," Tara said. "You had a question."

McLean looked puzzled for a minute. "Oh yes, this fault thing. What if a dog wins at some shows and then a judge points out a fault?"

"Same result," Tara said. "We had a champion Lab once who had won Best in Show twice before one judge who was watching said he'd never put up a Lab with a tail that curled over its back. The handler heard about the comment and the dog was immediately retired from showing. The comment had a short life span. The dog left the breed world a winner."

A beaming Joyce Webb joined the group, "The judge is consistent," she said. "Hope she stays that way."

"Consistent?" McLean queried of his mentor.

Tara smiled happily. Her voice had an excited lilt. "Sandy and Muffy are from the same lines. The judge evidently likes the line. That is good news for all of us.

Joyce is showing Biscuit's sister Sweetie in Veterans and Sweetie's son Talker in the Best of Bred later."

"Against you?" McLean asked.

"Yep," Tara replied, her eyes dancing. "Cousin against cousin. Should be exciting. It'll come down to handling."

"You against Joyce?"

"A handler will take Talker in. Joyce will handle Sweetie if she wins unless Muffy wins in which case she'll take in Muffy and get a handler for Sweetie."

"So if you come with three dogs, you better be three people."

Tara laughed and nodded. "You catch on quick."

The camera was resting on McLean's knee when out of the corner of his eye he saw the man in the dark glasses stand up and stretch, taking off his glasses in the process.

His camera clicked.

Tara noticed. "There's no one in the ring. What are you taking a picture of?"

"Oh, did I press the button?" he inquired with seeming innocence as he looked down at the camera. The shutter clicked again. "I guess I'd better put it away."

"Check the film first," Tara said. "At the rate you're going you don't have any left."

McLean turned away from the ring and looked at the counter. "Two left," he said, swinging the camera up and snapping a picture of Tara. He stepped back and took one from the group. As he did so, he saw a woman turn and walk away.

He'd seen that walk before, but he couldn't remember where.

After he got his shot, he opened the camera and replaced the film. The woman turned again and walked past the group. He glanced up at her. Their eyes met.

She nodded and smiled. It was the smile that did it. The hair was short and curled; the buxom look was gone; but the smile was that of the nurse that he'd tried to find.

He nodded and immediately dropped his head had locked the camera shut. He put the roll of film in his pocket, leaned over and whispered to Tara.

"I want you to take the film out of my right hand pocket without anyone seeing you and put it in the cooler."

"What's going on?"

"Just do it," McLean said. "Please. We're being watched."

Tara refrained from looking around and Spencer McLean felt his respect take another leap. This woman could think on her feet.

She slipped the roll from his pocket and palmed it. He transferred a fresh roll from the left to the right hand pocket. If there were more on the grounds than these two, they were in trouble.

Tara opened the cooler and took out a sandwich and handed it to Spencer. "Don't get fussy," she hissed. "I need the plastic."

McLean obligingly peeled off the plastic and took a big bite of the sandwich and murmured his appreciation as he offered her the plastic wrap.

"Stop!" Tara hissed.

McLean, his mouth full, paused and wrinkled his brow in query. With his mouth full of peanut butter, he couldn't speak.

Tara snatched the sandwich from his hand. "This is mine."

McLean swallowed quickly. "It's what you gave me."

"I know what I gave you. Didn't you have enough sense to object? No one eats peanut butter."

Dizzied by her reasoning and her turnaround of exactly whose fault it was he bit into the sandwich, McLean mutely handed back the sandwich. To his amazement, she took it.

"Here's your sandwich. Roast beef," she announced coolly. "I can't believe you ate mine."

McLean saw Tara's mother watching the exchange with a twinkle in her eyes. He looked at her pleadingly.

"Tara," her mother said gently. "He really didn't know."

Tara's stubborn posture remained unbent.

"He should have," she insisted.

Coral grinned at Spencer McLean. "She gets that from her father."

"I do not!" Tara objected. "I get it from you and you know it!"

"I only provided half your genes. Your father supplied the rest. Being dead doesn't mean what he passed on doesn't still live in you," Coral argued. "You're more hardheaded than I am. He's got to take some of the blame."

McLean chuckled. "Why not just hand it all over to Tara. She can choose what she wants to do, genes or no genes. I think she likes being stubborn."

"I do not!" Tara exclaimed. "What a terrible thing to say."

"Well, it beats having to be reasonable and say you're wrong," McLean commented. "I'd do it except I can't afford to."

"And I can?" Tara said, her voice rising.

Her mother interrupted. "Tara, take a walk and cool off."

Angrily, Tara wrapped the plastic around the half-eaten sandwich and the roll of film she'd palmed and stuck it back into the cooler film side down.

"No one touch my sandwich," she warned as she strode off.

Coral leaned over. "You can go after her. The ring has broken for lunch. Nothing will happen for thirty minutes."

"Maybe I should just let her be."

"That never helps," Coral said. "She can't stand making a mistake. It's not that she doesn't like roast beef, it's that she finds peanut butter settles better on show days."

"Should I take her the other half?"

"She's too nervous to eat. That's why she acted as she did."

"You're calm," McLean observed.

"I just got here. And I wasn't planning to be here. And I'm so grateful to just have made it here alive that I'm satisfied," Coral said. "Tara was in competition yesterday and her competitive juices were at a higher level when she sat down. Give me another hour and I'll be hard to talk to as well."

McLean glanced around the area.

"Promise me you won't wander off," he said. "If you need to go to the Ladies Room, don't go alone."

Coral raised an eyebrow.

"The nurse from the hospital—she's here."

Unlike Tara, Coral looked around.

"There she is," McLean said aloud, thus giving the impression that Coral was looking for her daughter. "I'll be back."

As he hurried off, Coral's eyes followed him. During that moment, she realized that she'd been indiscreet.

"Lover's quarrel?" Joyce Webb asked and Coral laughed. "They just met. I think she likes him."

"She has a funny way of showing it," Joyce said and Coral put the presence of the nurse out of her mind. Maybe it was coincidence. Maybe the chief was mistaken. What could happen to her here?

# Chapter 30

An hour after he'd sent the team to the Sage County impound lot, Lieutenant Greg Lim faxed the ballistics report to Captain Scoma. The captain was expecting his officers to walk through the door with the gun and he immediately picked up the phone and dialed Lim.

"I got the report," he said bluntly. "Where are my men and where is the gun?"

"Your men are doing a forensic workup on the cab."

"What the hell for?"

"To verify Lieutenant Caribou's account of the shooting."

"They aren't forensic experts," Scoma protested.

"The man they are with is. He needs help and I'm stretched pretty thin over here."

"So you're wasting my manpower?" Scoma charged.

"No," Lim replied solemnly. "I am not. It is your case. The cab is here not there where it should be. Your men are here..."

"That's another thing. I want that tape."

"We will send you a copy," Lim said and then quickly finished his previous argument. "Your men will return with first-hand knowledge of what we are doing and duplicates of everything."

"We get the originals," Scoma protested.

"My chief will make that decision," Lim said politely, "meanwhile; the copies will help you decide your next step."

"When is McLean coming back?" Scoma asked petulantly. "It is a hellava time to take a vacation day. What kind of captain does that?"

"One that recognizes a danger to a member in his community. The safety of our citizens is our number one priority."

"Cut the crap. Send me my officers and the gun," Scoma ordered belligerently. "And the damned tape."

"I am sorry to refuse, but the beginning portion of the tape is relevant to another investigation. The best I can do is to send you a copy of the relevant portion. I will, however, have both of your officers present when I make the copy. Meanwhile please send me the ballistic report on the four bullets."

"I need my men back here," Scoma shouted.

"When all the evidence is over here?" Lim queried politely. "I will get back to you shortly."

Scoma cursed as he hung up. He turned to Volatis. "It's your dammed screw-ups that caused all these problems in the first place."

"He can't keep you from ordering the men back," Volatis said.

"Except that he's right. They've got the perp, the gun, the tape and the cab over there. I may hate his inscrutable guts, but he's got me by the balls. I need my men over there."

"So what do you want me to do?"

"Get forensics to move on those bullets. There's a reporter out there with half the story," Scoma said handing the fax to Volatis.

Volatis hurried away. By now the forensics team would surely have found traces of dried blood on one of the bullets. Or if not on the bullets, then in the bag. He'd let slip a worry that they'd been handled so much whatever bits of blood on them might have fallen off into the bag.

He'd been assured that they would consider that.

# Chapter 31

Drew Manning emerged from the computer room at Ardilla's small police headquarters which faced Newell Road on the south side of town. The land had been cheaper there and the backside of the acreage was an up sloping open space area so there'd been no hue and cry when the site was chosen. Much as the citizens wanted a good police facility in their town, no one wanted one in their neighborhood. There were no houses on the stretch of land between the busy access road through Ardilla to its closest neighbor on the south, the town of Newell.

A garden nursery stretched out over two hundred yards to the north and a real estate office had renovated the old white clapboard house standing a hundred yards south of the police parking lot.

Drew Manning liked the location. He liked the chief. He liked the way things were done. It was a far cry from the Manzanita Station House located on a tiny triangular piece of land where two main roads met. There had been no room to breathe there. The air inside the station had been as soul-scorching as the heat radiating from the concrete that surrounded the brick building. The Manzanita chief of police had been in everyone's pocket. Drew wondered how he kept his loyalties straight he had so many of them.

Drew had picked up some bad habits there and sometimes he wasn't sure where the lines were. His former chief had demanded information and hadn't cared how he came up with it. This chief might care.

He stretched and exited the building for a walk to the back of the building through the gate, locked only at night, more to keep the deer out than people, and slowly climbed the roughly carved steps in the hillside to a natural plateau under a hundred-year-old oak tree whose span shaded a redwood picnic table and several redwood lounge chairs. The natural patio was kept scrupulously clean by the men who used it. It was a place to renew one's soul.

Drew sat down, leaned back and studied the sky. He was certain he was on the track of something big, but he wasn't certain he had come by the information legally. And if he shared what he'd discovered he might taint the whole investigative procedure.

He gazed up at the clear blue sky wishing there were clouds for his imagination to play with.

The death records had told him that there was no foul play connected with the deaths. Martin Deane had indeed died accidentally. His rental car had been broadsided by a drunk driver who had a series of DUI's and was driving without a license.

Deane's body had been handled by one of Varrieur's funeral homes. That was his only connection with the others at first glance.

Drew Manning had already begun to unearth facts about some of the names on the list when he was told to center his attention on the Texan.

Golda Steinman, for example, a seventy-six year old Manzanita resident, had died of a stroke. Drew Manning knew how to enter the Mountain Valley Hospital records. He'd done it for Captain Chattaway several times while the pot-bellied, cigar smoking chief had hovered over him in a room cleared of all on-lookers.

"This information is strictly confidential," the captain would always say. "Don't disgrace your daddy now by blabbing and making me have to fire your ass."

When Drew had punched up the hospital records for Golda Steinman, he found nothing unusual. She'd had a stroke, languished in a comatose state for four days and then died.

Drew hadn't stopped there. Suspecting check fraud, he'd pulled up her bank records, another little service he performed repeatedly for his former police chief.

Once he tried to tell his dad what was going on, but his father brushed his concerns away with a comment about trusting the man you work with and learning from him. He pointed out that the chief kept things under control so they could all sleep at night. How he did it was immaterial.

Drew Manning guessed correctly that Golda Steinman would bank at the town's oldest bank. Her records showed enormous amounts in her checking and savings accounts. The lady could well afford a ten thousand dollar contribution. The puzzle was that that amount had never been debited from her checking account or withdrawn from her savings account. According to the bank, Golda Steinman had never made a ten thousand dollar contribution to anyone's campaign fund.

Who would write a check and give her the credit? And why?

When he was assigned to concentrate his efforts on Martin Deane, he again accessed the hospital records. Deane had died without ever regaining consciousness. The body had been flown back to Texas after a wire transfer of funds from a Texas bank to Varrieur's business account in Manzanita.

Drew Manning accessed Martin Deane's checking account. There was no ten thousand dollar withdrawal during the three months prior to his death. Drew, being the son of a politician in the governor's party knew exactly when the war chest was open to receive gifts. The Texan had not personally donated to the governor's campaign.

He rose from the chair, stretched and walked back to the building. He would dig a bit deeper. There had to be a connection somewhere. Meanwhile he'd say nothing.

# Chapter 32

When Spencer McLean saw Herb Guzman head for the parking lot in the middle of the Open class, he was immediately suspicious. He told Tara that he was going to follow the man.

"Leave the camera," she said. "I want some pictures of the winner. I can't believe you're going to leave now. This is the most exciting part."

"Gotta go," he said.

Hurriedly, Spencer slipped the camera strap off his neck and handed over the camera. He rushed away toward the minivan. The idea of a bomb being planted in the car scared him. Now would be the time to plant one–when everyone's attention is glued to what's happening in the ring.

I'm jumping at shadows, he told himself as he took long swift strides. These people had an opportunity at the hospital. Why not do it there?

The answer came to him almost as fast as he asked the question. They had to know they had the right photo in hand.

Now all three of them were dispensable. In fact, their deaths were imperative. They had to be taken out before they returned to the Bay Area. What better, faster, surer way than a car bomb?

As he hurried along, his eye on the disappearing figure of the man in the black wig, he bumped into a man emerging from the parking lot on the run.

"So sorry," the man said. "Are you hurt?"

"No, I'm fine," McLean assured him, anxious to catch up with his prey. He scarcely glanced at the man except to note that he was dark-haired and slender.

The man rushed off toward the ring where the final contest for the five championship points was being decided while McLean hurried toward the last place he'd seen the black-wigged man.

McLean's thorough search of the parking lot was fruitless. The man was nowhere to be found.

When he returned, Tara asked, "Where have you been? He came back right away."

Spencer McLean glanced across the ring. He was there alright.

"You missed Winners Bitch," Tara announced. "Muffy took Reserve."

"What does that mean?"

"No points," Tara said with a sigh of resignation. "Being second out of one hundred twenty-one bitches doesn't count."

"It's something," McLean commented. He looked for Joyce Webb to congratulate her.

Tara saw him look for her. "She's in the ring in Veteran's with Sweetie. You almost missed it."

"I wasn't gone that long," the tall, blonde man said.

"Winner's goes faster," Tara snapped. "And to answer your next question. The reason a Reserve Winner is chosen is just in case there is a problem with the Winner's entry."

"A problem?"

"Say the winner was entered in the wrong class, you know, too old for the 9 to 12 class or born in Canada and therefore not eligible to compete in American Bred. People make mistakes."

"That wasn't my next question," McLean put in with a pleasant smile. "I was going to ask you if you wanted me to take over shooting pictures. Aren't you up next?"

Tara handed him the camera. "There aren't many shots left. Be sure you change the film before the end of our class. You'll need lots of film for that. At least, I hope you will."

McLean grinned as he nodded. She was a bossy one. He wondered if she ever stopped issuing orders. He doubted it. He recalled the other occasions when she was her bossiest. It seemed that the more nervous she got, the bossier she got. It was a good barometer of her feelings. His discovery of that fact pleased him. The grin stayed in place.

It disconcerted Tara. "Well, have you got another roll of film or do I have to give you my spare?"

McLean patted his pocket and realized his last fresh roll was gone. True, he'd put it there as a decoy so he'd planned that it be taken; however, it took him by surprise that it had happened without him being aware of it.

"Usually there's a decoy," he mumbled.

"Here in the park? Why would anyone place a duck decoy on a lake in a park?" Tara asked.

"The film's gone. The new roll."

Tara shrugged off the apparent non-sequiter response. "That's okay. I have one in the show bag. I always carry a spare in there."

"Good," McLean said deciding not to remind her of the decoy film. The timing was wrong. "Isn't that your friend the judge is asking to run her dog?"

Tara turned.

McLean shot a picture of Joyce returning to the judge. The judge moved down the line moving one dog after the other. McLean turned and took a picture of Tara getting Sandy out of his crate. In the background, Coral was slipping Banner's thick metal collar off his neck and replacing it with a light weight black nylon show collar. The leash she attached to it was short and made of thin black leather.

Sandy's heavier collar was replaced with a tan nylon choke and Tara snapped a thin tan leather lead to it.

Coral reached into the cooler and opened a fresh can of soda and took a swallow. Spencer took a picture of her standing, soda can in hand, staring into the ring, her black dog standing quietly beside her waiting for orders.

It was a classic shot, McLean concluded. Coral would like it.

Tara bent over and pulled out the plastic container of liver and the box of film and set them on the crate top. Coral set her can on what she had designated as her corner of the crate and scooped liver chunks from the container into her pockets.

Tara saw McLean watching her mother.

"Try one," she urged. "They're baked with garlic. Quite tasty."

He shook his head at her offering and she popped it into her mouth and backed up. Sandy followed her and stood erect with his ears perked and his tail wagging in anticipation. Tara reached into her mouth and took out the liver and threw it at the waiting dog. Her hand hampered by the sling threw the tidbit sideways. Sandy eyed the tidbit but didn't break his pose.

"See you spit it out," McLean gloated.

Tara grinned. "He only got half. I ate the rest. I like the stuff."

McLean took two steps back as she started talking so that he had both her and Sandy in the frame. He snapped it while she was still talking.

Another classic, he told himself.

The judge had finished moving the dogs. The two women were simultaneously drawn to the events in the ring. Sandy scooped up the liver when Tara's attention was diverted. He hadn't lost sight of its whereabouts.

Tara heard McLean's camera shutter click and assumed he was shooting the final lineup. What McLean had done was frame the heads of mother and daughter watching the show.

"Another classic," he murmured.

Then he turned toward the ring and focused on the black bitch on the other side of the ring.

Her black coat was lustrous; her pose, picture perfect; her sparkling personality, evident to everyone at ringside. Sweetie loved being shown. She didn't need incentive. Joyce's hand never went to her pocket. She simply stood and smiled at her old bitch and her old bitch dropped her jaw slightly, panted lightly and smiled back.

There was never any doubt about who was going to take the class.

McLean swung his camera up to take a shot of Joyce receiving the ribbon and spotted the dark-haired man walking behind the group. He took two shots in quick succession, the first studiously aimed at Joyce and Sweetie, the second snapped when his eye was away from the view finder and the camera was being lowered.

"Now it's your turn," he said flipping open the camera back surreptitiously as he lowered himself into a chair. He quickly palmed the exposed film, closed the camera and set it on top of the crate.

"Not quite yet," Tara explained. "First they award the Obedience prizes. It gives us all a chance to get ready."

"Isn't it something to watch?" McLean asked a touch of disapproval in his tone.

"It is," Tara said. "A lot of people skip Veterans to get ready, but we couldn't. We had a friend showing."

"I see," McLean replied and Tara smiled. He did indeed understand. He was quick. One could love a man like that.

Coral picked up her can and took another swig. She set her can down on the back corner of Banner's crate. Spencer used the top of Sandy's crate, while Tara used the front half of both crates. She had water, root beer and coffee lined up. The sun had warmed the water but not the coffee. A fly was stuck on the surface of the brown liquid. The root beer, having just been pulled from the cooler, already had beads of moisture dotting its brown can. It looked inviting.

"Got another root beer?" McLean asked. The run through the parking lot had given him a hankering for something cold and wet.

"Take a look," Tara said upending her can and taking a huge gulp. "We have to air the dogs."

As Tara and her mother walked the dogs toward the exercise area, McLean opened the cooler, dug down to the bottom and pulled out a can of lemon-lime soda. He snagged the large bag of chips lying on top. He unrolled the bag, reached in and grabbed a couple of chips while simultaneously dropping the exposed film roll inside. The outside case might get greasy and have sprinkles of salt clinging to it, but the film wouldn't be harmed.

Stretching his long legs in front of him, McLean leaned back in his chair and stuck the open chip bag in his lap. The unopened film box lay in full view on top of Sandy's crate.

He picked up the camera once and took a picture. There was no film in the camera. He continued to take an occasional picture as Coral slipped the arm band up Tara's left arm.

"You're not going in?" Joyce exclaimed when she saw Tara with her armband on. "Muffy didn't win so my handler's assistant could take in Sandy."

Tara smiled. "We've been looking forward to this, Mom and I. Sandy will behave. Besides, the hand that holds the lead works just fine."

"But baiting and stacking takes two hands," Joyce commented. "Really, think about it. His assistant would do a good job for you."

"Sandy will just have to self-stack," Tara said and then added. "I'd go nuts watching."

Joyce broke away and walked toward the ring a wet towel hanging from Sweetie's back like a saddle blanket. The September sun was warm and Sweetie was an old dog. The towel would be taken at the last minute by the handler's assistant who would hold it outside the ring until the bitches were separated from the dogs and sent to stand in the shade in the corner. Then Joyce would have her bitch lie down and drape the towel over her. Together they would rest until the judge had finished evaluating the dog portion of the class. Her review would take an hour. There were twenty-five males.

Spencer McLean took a few shots with the empty camera before setting it down. He opened the tiny yellow box and took out the new film roll. He removed it from its miniature can and opened the camera back. Ostensibly he removed the old film and stuck it in the tiny can which he then pocketed. The opened box lay on the crate top.

The judging was a slow process for a man who didn't know quite what to look for. Tara had pointed out a few attributes a winner should have. He could see the level tail set, the hock angle and the depth of brisket, but the rest eluded him. He settled down to finding the ones he thought were the most handsome. He numbered both Coral's and Tara's dogs among them.

McLean had his eye on a striking yellow Lab that seemed to have everything and he was surprised when the judge excused that particular dog when making his first cut. Both Banner and Sandy remained in the ring along with Joyce's dog, Talker. Curious, McLean set the chip bag on the crate, got up and walked around to where a man with a sport coat and tie was handing the leash to a short plump woman with fuzzy hair. He walked up to the pair.

"Excuse me," he said quietly. "I couldn't help but notice your dog in the ring. I think he's a very handsome dog."

"Thank you," the plump lady replied, beaming.

"This is my first show, but I don't understand why he isn't still in the running," McLean queried pleasantly reaching down to gently stroke the broad head. "He looks like a winner to me."

"The judge counts teeth," the woman said simply.

On the opposite side of the ring, a buxom woman left her seat and walked to the side of the ring and stopped behind Banner's crate.

McLean's forehead wrinkled in query. "Literally?"

"Missing teeth is a fault, a major or minor one depending on which teeth and how many," the coated handler explained. "This dog is only missing one minor tooth. Most judges overlook it. All dogs have minor faults."

The buxom woman standing on the far side behind Banner's crate stared at the page in her catalog and slowly uncapped her thick black pen as she ostensibly watched the bitches come out of the shade and line up. The males took their place under the canopy.

"Only one tooth!" McLean exclaimed. "That's such a little thing."

"This is a Specialty," the handler said. "All the dogs are good. Every judge has some faults he dislikes more than others. Another day. Another judge. Another verdict."

A nod came from the black-wigged man seated so that he could see not only both Svenson women but their tall, blonde bodyguard as well. The buxom woman set her catalog on the crate to turn the page. Simultaneously, she passed the pen over the open drink can on Banner's crate, pausing just long enough to pour the contents into the can.

Then the woman moved away, recapped her pen and slipped it into her pocket.

Tara and Coral were watching Spencer McLean as he talked to the plump lady and the handler. They didn't dare discuss it with so many ears so near. Coral worried aloud about Tara standing so long and Tara immediately folded her legs and sat down. Coral joined her. Both dogs followed suit. There were fifteen bitches in the ring, three of whom the judge had seen before—the winner of the points, the veteran class winner, and the hunting class winner. Thirty minutes of judging lay before them.

Spencer McLean was back in his seat, the chip bag in his lap before the judge had finished judging two bitches. He finished his lemon lime soda and eyed the open cans on top of the crate. He looked over at the two women on the grass and pointed at them. Tara shook her head vigorously.

McLean was puzzled. Surely, she would prefer a fresh cold drink on her return. He decided she thought he was asking if she wanted a drink.

He picked up her can and catching her eye lifted it up and pointed to himself. Again a vigorous head shake was his answer.

He decided Coral might be more reasonable than her daughter and he reached over and picked up her can. Again Tara shook her head.

McLean set the can down. Rolling up the chip bag, he opened the cooler. He squatted in front of it and studied the contents: three bottles of water and two cans of grape soda. When he looked up he saw a young boy approach the hospitality table, hand over a dollar bill and come away with two cans of soda.

He immediately stuffed the chip bag into the cooler, slammed down the lid, rose and strode quickly toward the table selling soft drinks.

He spotted the men's restroom as he was handing over the money for the drinks and setting the four cans on the corner, he told the woman he had to wash his hands but he'd be right back. She nodded. Business was at a standstill. He and the young boy had been the only two customers in the past hour.

He entered the restroom and was standing alone in front of the urinal staring at the cement block wall as he relieved himself when a voice spoke from behind.

"Don't turn around," the voice said. "Don't reach for your gun. Mine has a silencer. All I want is the camera and that film in your pocket."

Spencer McLean had been caught off-guard. From the sound of the man's voice, McLean judged him to be near the door. Even if he pulled his gun, the man would be able to duck before he could turn and fire it.

Maybe when the man stepped forward for the camera, he'd have a chance to wrest the gun away. McLean assumed it was either the portly dark-wigged man with the sunglasses or the slender dark-haired man. Either one would physically be no match for him. McLean not only possessed an athletic build but the quick reflexes to go with it.

"I know you're planning something," the voice added as if the man with the gun had read the police chief's mind. "Don't. My partner has a bead on those two animals lying down next to the ladies. He's given me thirty seconds to emerge alone, camera in hand. First, though, take the film out of your pocket and toss it backwards toward the door."

"He wouldn't shoot into the crowd," McLean said reaching into his pocket. "He'd be caught."

McLean tossed the film box toward the door.

"Maybe. If he were using a gun," the voice replied. "Now the camera."

McLean slid the camera off his shoulder keeping his hands in plain sight. His movements were very slow and deliberate. The man didn't want to shoot him. If he had, he would have done so and grabbed the camera and film. McLean guessed that the group didn't want a scene. They weren't planning a bombing. They were planning something more subtle.

If he tackled the man when he reached for the camera, he'd throw a monkey wrench into the works. He laid the camera on the floor and gave a kick with his foot. It slid halfway across the floor.

"Ever hear of a blow gun shaped like a pen?" the voice inquired. "It is very accurate at ten feet. Death will be instantaneous. I'll bet my leaving here against your stopping me that not only can I shoot you before you can grab me, but my partner can hit both dogs and be gone before anyone notices anything."

The blonde curly head bowed as both hands were raised slowly and placed flat on the washroom wall.

"Five minutes," the man said as he grabbed the camera's shoulder strap and yanked it toward him.

McLean envisioned the man squatting down keeping the gun trained at his back. As he had repeatedly told his men, when in a tight spot, living is the number one objective. He didn't go into the exceptions.

For once he took his own advice.

He heard the scuffle of the shoes as the man ran out.

Quickly, he put himself together and leaped up the concrete wall. His fingertips curled around the sill of the open air slit located just under the roof overhang. He brought his eyes up to sill level and peered down at the man who had stopped just a few feet away to bury his gun in a holster under his armpit.

McLean almost lost his grip.

The man must have been carrying three hundred pounds. McLean looked down at thick straight black hair with strands of gray neatly combed to one side. The cheeks were heavy and the nose small. He couldn't see the eyes and he guessed the full beard, while neatly trimmed, was false.

The man, having holstered his weapon, shouldered the camera and walked toward the parking lot across the field behind the show site. McLean studied his walk. The tan polyester trousers bunched between his legs as he waddled. His dark brown sport coat covered his gun well as his body swayed with each step.

"Turn around," McLean whispered, his fingers tiring. The rough stone cut into their tips, sandpapering them into rawness. Then, as if he heard the man hanging by his fingertips, the fat man turned and glanced back.

Even the best can't keep himself from checking, Spencer thought.

Glasses, McLean noted. Small eyes. And three gold rings in his right ear. The hand swinging at his side wore a pinky ring that glinted in the sun.

He briefly considered chasing him; but, decided against it. Drawing him away could be part of a plan to leave the two women defenseless.

He lowered himself to the floor, washed his hands as he kept track of the time and then exited. He paused at the hospitality table long enough to pick up his four cans. Their smooth, cold surface soothed his raw fingertips. When he put them into the cooler, he dipped his hands in the half inch layer of ice water at the bottom. The resulting numbness stopped the burning sensation. Relieved, he folded himself back into his seat, wrapped his hands around one of the cold cans of root beer and settled in to watch the show.

He scanned the group on the far side of the ring. There was an empty space at ringside. A woman was hastily unfolding a chair in the space recently vacated.

McLean at first kicked himself for not checking sooner, but then consoled himself with the thought that whoever had been seated there would be on the roll of film safely hidden in the cooler. On top of that the clear and present danger was past.

Interesting, he mused. The man hadn't threatened the women; only the dogs. Briefly, he puzzled over it.

Four bitches were selected from the group. The rest left the ring. McLean felt naked without his camera. It was an uncomfortable feeling. He opened his root beer and sipped it. His fingers were demanding he not drink away their succor, so he held the can between his hands and saw Coral take a position in the back by her daughter who was standing near the end of the line.

The judge pulled his two class winners out of the line and moved them individually.

Tara sailed around the ring with Sandy, her dark skirt making a perfect background for her smooth running dog as he stretched his legs to equal her speed.

The bitch was next. When the judge ran the two together, both dog and bitch put their feet down with drum-like precision, but Sandy pulled away from the bitch. The dog had more reach. He covered more ground with the same number of strides. Part of it was because he was slightly taller but when the judge pulled out Talker and Banner and ran them against Sweetie, the old bitch could not be outdone.

It seemed obvious to McLean, even as a novice, that the winner was going to come from one of the five standing in a line in the center of the ring. He had his money on Sandy. The big yellow dog was showing beautifully.

Then the judge left the five standing in the middle of the ring and went back down the line of dogs he had not pulled out. Carefully he studied each face.

All waited for a nod to join the elite group in the center of the ring. The chocolate dog who had won the hunting class was given the nod. The group now numbered six. Chief was his name and immediately after he was pulled into the line the four males were asked to go around the ring together.

All four moved smoothly. Two blacks, a yellow and a chocolate. McLean cursed the loss of the camera. He could see no difference between them. He stuck with Sandy as his pick out of loyalty to Tara.

The judge then pulled a yellow bitch out of the line in back and put her in front of the Winners Bitch. Thus, Sweetie wound up last in line. The judge signaled the three to circle the ring. Joyce gave the other two a bit of a head start and then eased Sweetie into a fast smooth run. Sweetie felt she needed to catch up which was exactly what Joyce was counting on. The black feet flew, narrowing the distance between her and her two yellow competitors. As Joyce was finishing the run the judge waved her to the front of the line.

Sweetie stopped in front of the stout woman judge, her eyes merry because she'd obviously won the race. Her tail wagged furiously as she looked into the judge's face. The judge put a hand on Sweetie's head and ran it down her back.

Joyce beamed. Sweetie's thick coat was one of her best features. Sweetie stood stock still her eyes watching every nuance of movement in Joyce's face. Joyce's smile was a radiant one and it enlivened the old dog. She leaned forward slightly in anticipation.

Behind Sweetie, her son, Talker seeing his mother's excitement mount, came up on his toes in anticipation. When the judge stepped back to look at them, she saw a perfectly matched pair. Her glance down the line was perfunctory. She had her winners.

She pointed to Sweetie.

"Best of Breed," she said and Joyce responded with a whoop of joy.

The judge's finger pointed at Talker and upon learning that he'd won Best Opposite, Joyce's joy exploded into tears. Her handler hugged her and congratulated her.

Then Sandy took Best of Winners and Coral burst into tears.

"Don't be sad, my dear," the judge said. "It was very close. You also have a fine dog."

"I'm not sad," Coral choked as she brushed away her tears. "Sandy is my dog too. And her handler is my daughter."

"Well, having good dogs runs in your family," the judge said handing Coral a large green rosette. Coral hugged the rosette and she and Tara embraced as the judge awarded a second green rosette to the chocolate dog.

After a multitude of congratulations all around, Coral and Tara wound up back at the crates breathless. They offered the dogs water and Coral picked up her can of root beer.

"Mother!" Tara yelled. "You know better than that."

She grabbed the can from her mother's hand and with a quick turn of the wrist, she upended it and the brown liquid poured onto the grass.

"What are you doing?" Coral protested.

"You remember the rule you taught me. If you leave your drink unattended, get a new one."

"Tara, be reasonable," her mother scolded, embarrassed. "This isn't that kind of scene."

"This is exactly that kind of scene," Tara said firmly. She picked up her drink and poured it out as well. "There's grape soda in the cooler."

"There's more root beer," Spencer McLean said. "I bought some."

"Spencer, tell her she's overreacting," Coral urged, her face still flushed.

"I would if she were, but date rape drugs are so easy to come by and Liquid G can be lethal."

Coral tucked a finger into the can and tasted the drop of liquid that clung to it.

"Not salty," Coral announced.

Tara was quick to checkmate her mother's move. "Roofies are odorless and tasteless."

"Tastes funny," Coral added, "But considering the fact that I've been handling liver cooked with garlic, that's probably all it is."

McLean cut in. "A funny taste?"

"I explained..." Coral began.

"I want the can," McLean said firmly. Coral handed it to him.

"It's only root beer, I assure you," Coral said. "Tara's reaction has encouraged you to overreact."

"We need to get out of here," McLean said urgently, looking around. The man in the black wig was nowhere in sight. The crowd at ringside had thinned considerably. Part of that was due to the mass of people standing at ringside ready to enter the ring.

"I'm ready!" said a cheerful young voice. "Were you waiting?"

"Singer looks great," Coral said. "We're ready."

"Ready?" McLean burst out. "For what? We need to go."

"Stud dog class," Tara said lightly. "Come on Paula. Don't mind Spencer. It's his first show and he's ready for a steak dinner."

"It's almost five o'clock," Spencer said tapping his watch.

"Change the reservation," Tara said walking away. "By the way, Paula, congratulations on second place in your class. Sorry we missed it."

"What happened to your arm anyway?"

"Tell you later," Tara promised. "Just remember to relax. You've already won. And we've already won."

"This is so exciting," Paula squealed as the two moved out of hearing range.

"Spencer, be sure to get a picture," Coral called as she ran to catch up with the two young women, any possibility of a brush with death cast aside.

Spencer walked away from the ring and dialed the number of the sheriff's office. He apologized at once, explained that the women were still in the ring, said he had been robbed at gun point and he had a drink can he thought someone had dropped some Liquid G into that he'd like their forensic team to test.

He didn't mention the film.

Four people had been working this tiny show. The network must be huge.

He didn't know who was trustworthy down here.

He needed to get home–fast.

# Chapter 33

The excitement level in the car was as high all the way to the sheriff's office as it had been at the show's end an hour before when the two women lined up for the professional photographer.

Coral told McLean he didn't need to take any more pictures. This was the time for the pro to take over. McLean couldn't squeeze in even a sentence to tell them their camera had been stolen. He decided to wait. The camera was gone and there was nothing anyone could do to get it back.

McLean sipped a second can of root beer and ate the last sandwich in the cooler. He didn't count the half-eaten peanut butter one Tara had staked a claim on.

His eyes continually searched the group to see if he could spot anyone not attached to a dog somehow. There was no one. The spectators had left. The rest were packing up. The winners were in the ring being photographed.

First Joyce Webb went into the ring with her two winners. While Tara held their place in line, Coral ran back to the campsite where McLean was still sitting and fetched Joyce's yellow bitch Muffy and her ribbon. She hurriedly told him to keep an eye on their stuff and he chuckled as he nodded. Not often does a police chief get told to keep an eye on stuff.

Joyce had pictures taken separately and then in combination. McLean thought this was excessive until it was Tara's turn.

First, Sandy was posed alone with all his trophies. Then a pose with Banner with his green rosette and Sandy with his blue and white one. Finally Paula and Singer joined the group. One pose was taken with only Banner's blue ribbon from the stud dog class and Banner and his get, a second with all the ribbons and trophies won that day. Then Paula had a picture taken of her young bitch and its red ribbon. It was her first win.

By the time they returned, Spencer McLean was anxious. He needed to leave.

On his last call to Lim, the lieutenant had told him that Drew Manning had an idea what was going on and that it was big but he was afraid he'd discovered the truth by breaking some laws. Lim said that he hadn't asked Manning to explain.

"Good call," McLean said. "Tell him to talk to no one, then have someone start with where you had him start and monitor every move. I think Drew has been going over the line in Manzanita so long that the line has become blurry and he doesn't know whether he's walking on it or stepping over it. I'll be home as soon as possible."

That promise had been made over an hour ago and now the women were discussing feeding the dogs before moving on. The problem was Joyce didn't feed the same kind of food.

"Dog's don't care," McLean put in.

"Their mouths don't care," Tara informed him sharply. "But their stomachs do, especially when you're talking high performance food. Changing too fast could give them blow-out diarrhea."

McLean looked down at the two dogs that were watching Tara's hands move while she talked. Banner was drooling. Evidently, they recognized the word food.

"We could forgo feeding them," Coral suggested looking askance at the protester.

"Go find the food," McLean said. "I'll pack up."

"They've got boxes for the trophies," Coral said. "We need those. Grab the ribbons Tara. I'll take the trophies."

Tara handed McLean the car keys and he began loading the flat, metal cart. He stacked the crates first.

"We'll feed the dogs while we're at it," Tara called back. McLean paused a second and watched them leave. It had been a good day for them. One needed good days. They'd be safe enough with their dogs by their sides.

He shoved the cooler in the lower crate and the show bag in the top crate along with the root beer can the meager contents of which he was going to have analyzed. He set it upright and pushed the cloth bag against it to hold it in place. Next he dumped the water out of the stainless steel water dish and set it inside the crate. He looked around. Except for the folding chairs, Tara had scooped all the odds and ends into the tote bag.

He secured the crates with a bungee cord, tucked the canvas folding chairs under his arm and started for the minivan. The grass tugged at the wheels as he moved. It seemed heavier than the last time. Of course, then he had had company and been excited about seeing his first dog show. Now the lack of sleep and the long hours in the canvas chair had caught up with him. A steak dinner sounded inviting.

He trudged toward the minivan which sat all alone far up the access road. The cars parked near it had gone. He decided that after he finished packing, if the women weren't back, he'd move the van closer and hunt them down.

So busy was he with his plans, he didn't notice that he was being observed. He unloaded the crates, setting the cooler on the seat and the chairs on the floor leaning against it. He shoved the tote bag on the floor in back and climbed into the front passenger seat.

He opened the glove compartment and took out the tiny film canisters. Two were full. He held the two empty ones in his hand. He had planned to put his film in them and stick them in the glove compartment; but, he began to worry lest they get mixed up with Tara's rolls, so he decided against it. He pocketed the empty containers and went back to unloading.

When he set the crate back in its spot, the water dish inside rattled to the back of the empty crate and hit the metal root beer can.

Quickly he reached into the crate and rescued the can. He set the dish on top of the crate and, when he did so, he asked himself, "What are they putting the dog food in?"

Picking up the pan and the empty soda can, McLean slammed down the rear gate, threw the cart in front of the middle seat, tucked the root beer can beside the tote bag, slammed shut the side door and backed down the road toward the parking lot.

Two men in a car had watched his every move. They ducked down when he passed them. McLean, concentrating on driving backwards, didn't notice the quick movement inside the dark car parked on the side of the road.

He didn't even turn the car around to park but simply backed into a triple space and leaped from the car. As he hurried across the lot toward a group of motor homes and vans, he glanced sideways toward the rings. One man was busy dismantling the ring while another was carrying an armload of folding chairs to a white truck whose rear doors were open.

McLean skirted around the truck and when he did that the green car backed up into the space next to the minivan and the two men jumped out. One try told the first man, a lean dark- haired man, that McLean had forgotten to lock up. He leaned in the side opening and handed the tote bag back to the stouter, black-wigged man to search.

Herb Guzman opened the front door and dumped the contents of the tote bag on the passenger seat. As Guzman pawed through the contents of the tote bag, his companion spotted the empty can of root beer on the floor and after shaking it, tossed it out of the car. The lean dark-haired man then opened the cooler while Herb Guzman angrily swept the contents of the tote bag on the floor.

"Look in the glove compartment," the lean man suggested as he picked up each can of soft drink and shook it.

Herb opened the glove compartment and shouted, "Got 'em."

"Make sure they're exposed this time," the dark-haired man suggested. He rattled the potato chip bag and heard the sound of chips hitting the sides. He reached for the half-eaten peanut butter sandwich.

"These people save everything," he muttered.

"The film's exposed," Guzman announced. "Plant the bugs and let's get out of here."

The dark-haired man dropped the half eaten sandwich back on the melting ice. It landed film side down.

The two left the car doors open.

# Chapter 34

"What were they looking for?" Coral asked, dismayed at the wreckage.

Banner nudged the root beer can and it rolled across the asphalt. McLean picked it up, checked out the floor behind the seat and put it back.

Tara, meanwhile, repacked the tote bag. "I thought we were safe here."

"I told you..." McLean started.

Tara interrupted him with a tremor in her voice. "So many people. So many friends. I thought they'd just tail us from here."

"So you figured the longer you stayed..." McLean started beginning to understand the endless delays.

Again Tara interrupted. "Is that so hard to swallow? What could happen? You had them in your sights."

"Not all of them," McLean admitted. "And not every minute."

Tara stopped her task and turned. Her raised eyebrows asked her question.

"Your camera was stolen. And the film."

"From the cooler?"

"No, not those," McLean said. "At least I don't think so. He stepped over the rubble and climbed onto the back seat to check out the cooler. He pulled out the sandwich and turned it over.

He breathed a sigh of relief.

"I'm starving," Tara said. "Can I have my sandwich now?"

McLean handed it to her.

"We're all hungry," her mother remarked with a tone of disapproval.

Tara's defenses rose.

"You two had lunch," she countered. "My sandwich was guarding the film."

"If you had asked me..." McLean said as he unrolled the potato chip bag and reached inside.

"I know you would have, but we had hidden it so cleverly and I wasn't hungry then."

McLean held up the second roll. "Well, it worked."

"Let's go," Coral said. "Spencer, you drive. I'll sit in back."

"Sheriff Tolliver is expecting us," McLean said as he drove down the access road.

"I'm starving," Tara put in. "Let's eat first."

"There's an In-And-Out Burger place only a couple of miles from here," Coral announced. "Have you ever had one, Spencer?"

"Can't say that I have," McLean replied. He was ready to eat a horse, saddle and all.

"Everything's freshly made," Coral said. "It's quite unique. My stomach likes it better than most fast foods. We can eat on the way."

"The lines are long," Tara objected.

"I think we can manage a long line," the police chief said affably. "We need to eat."

The line to the take out window was long. McLean phoned the sheriff and told him about their detour. When he hung up, he was smiling.

"What's up?" Tara asked.

"Got a pen?" he replied. "They gave me their orders."

"Double their order. Cops are always hungry at night." Coral put in, "I'll pay. We need some goodwill down here."

"Think we're being followed?" Tara asked.

"Well, if they're behind us, we'll be at the station before they get their order," McLean chuckled. "It's always a long line there."

"Are you going to get the film developed at the sheriff's office?" Tara asked.

"I need to get back home as soon as possible. Waiting for that would delay us."

"But it makes sense," Tara argued. "We're here now. They might know the guys. Besides, I'd like my camera back."

"You're dragging your feet again," McLean observed.

"I am not!" Tara protested. "I'm just not willing to run so quickly into the unknown."

"Now you're being a bit paranoid."

"And you're not paranoid enough!" Tara shot back. "You don't think they'll anticipate our heading north and be waiting for us?"

"That's pretty hit and miss," McLean said. "On the other hand, it would be smarter to get the film developed here. I can fax the photos to my men and they can get a head start."

"And Mom can rest," Tara said relieved.

"You, too, Tara," Coral said.

Tara shook her head. "I can't drive. You two are the drivers. I'll stand watch."

"Stand watch?" Spencer chuckled. "You are paranoid."

"Events have made that a reasonable stance," Tara claimed. "And the only reason you keep accusing me of that is because you are too and you just don't want to admit it."

McLean let her have the last word.

She was right. His problem was how to guard against it.

# Chapter 35

Forty-five minutes later, Tara was walking out of the sheriff's office with Sandy and Banner in tow.

"I told them not to give in to you two," she muttered as she walked across the asphalt toward the gate. "I told them they'd have to walk you if they did. Nobody listened to me. Nobody. Mom said she needs to rest. McLean said it might be his only chance for hours. Sheriff Tolliver said he had to check on the film processing. Everyone else had an excuse. They all got busy when it came time to venture across the street to the empty field so you two could unload. I tried getting them to have pity on me because I have an injured arm and then Mom tells everyone I walk both of you on my left so I don't need my right hand at all. A lot of help she was. She was grinning the whole time too. Just because I argued with her about my flying home. Such a stupid idea. I'm feeling fine. So this is her revenge."

Tara paused at the edge of the sidewalk. The street was a quiet one, four lanes wide. It wasn't dark yet although the sun had set. The parking lanes in front of the Sheriff's office were empty.

Tara saw no car in either direction. She thought she heard an engine start up, but considering the number of patrol cars behind her, the sound didn't frighten her.

She stepped into the street with the two dogs. Then she heard a sound that did startle her.

It was the hiss of a cat. Sandy thought cats were for chasing. Tara looped the lead around her hand. Neither dog moved. Both ears, however, came forward.

There was a second hiss. It came from a different direction than the first.

Two cats, Tara concluded.

As a pair the two dogs stepped forward, their ears pricked, their bodies lowered. They were stalking their prey.

The sound of the oncoming car caught Tara's attention at the last minute. She stepped back and pulled on the leads.

At that exact moment, a cat leaped across an open space in the field in front of them. As the two cats met, the dogs bolted toward them. With the thick leather leashes wound around her wrist, Tara was yanked forward as the sedan charged toward her.

The cats met and exchanged swipes. Suddenly, they saw the dogs charging. Each flew in a different direction. The dogs gave chase and Tara scrambled to stay on her feet. She tripped on the curb on the opposite side of the street and crashed down on the hard dirt of the dry field.

The car swerved and missed.

Her scream brought her dogs to a halt. That and her abrupt fall which had the same effect as a dropped anchor. Still, they dragged her for a foot before stopping and returning to her side.

She had twisted away from her injured arm and thus scraped her entire left arm on the stone dotted edge of the field. Her legs fared better because she was still wearing her mother's long skirt.

The dogs stood over her licking her ear and neck. They were apologizing.

The brakes didn't screech, she realized. The tires didn't squeal. In fact, she remembered the engine revving up.

She rose and slowly assessed her injuries. Her arm smarted, her shoulder muscles screamed at her, her cheek stung. One knee sent shocks of pain straight to her eyeballs when she tried to use it to rise. Using the backs of her dogs, she eased herself into a wobbling stand.

She undid the leashes of both dogs and waved them into the field. "Hurry up!"

The command was given in a normal tone. Tara wanted to hug her two saviors but she knew that they'd assume she liked being yanked off her feet. Being angry with them wasn't possible.

"I heard the cats," she said as Banner circled behind a small, scrubby bush and squatted. Sandy roamed a bit further, his nose tracking the cat scent. Tara called him back and again urged him to hurry. Suddenly, she was feeling vulnerable.

Sheriff Tolliver was the first to see her come through the door. Her disheveled appearance brought him up short. "What happened?"

"The dogs saw a cat fight," Tara replied.

"I'll wake your mother," he offered.

"Let her sleep," Tara said. "We got any bits of hamburger left?"

"Maybe you should wash up first."

"For the dogs," Tara said quietly. "They saved my life."

Sheriff Tolliver smiled wryly, "Looks more like they tried to take it."

"A car tried to run me down. If they hadn't bolted when they did..." her voice trailed off and she began to tremble.

Sheriff Tolliver eased her into a nearby chair, brought her a glass of water and pried the whole story from her. Slowly, he questioned her, pulling out information she didn't even know she had. He possessed a skill for interrogation.

When she was done, the sheriff himself helped her clean and apply a soothing ointment to her arm and face.

"What about your knee?" the sheriff asked.

"It'll have to wait," Tara said. "Right now I need to write my story while I can still type."

Sheriff Tolliver sent a deputy to the minivan to fetch Tara's computer and cleared a desk in the outer office where she could work.

A deputy came in with the photographs from the film.

"What I don't get," Tara said as she looked over the spread, "is how they knew we were here."

"I'm not certain they did," Tolliver suggested as he separated the blow-ups McLean had ordered from the smaller shots.

"You believe me, don't you?" Tara gasped. How could he deny her story?

"Oh, I believe you were almost run over," Tolliver said soothingly. "The thing is it's a game among the kids around here. Speed past the sheriff's office without getting caught. It happens a lot."

"And my being there was an accident?"

"Something like that," the sheriff said.

"Can you blow this one up?" Tara asked, swallowing her anger.

The sheriff looked at the photo, "Why?"

"Chief McLean couldn't have guessed that the corner of his camera would have caught her, but see that hand near the crate across the ring at the edge of this shot of my mother and me. See if he can get more. Sometimes there's a bit more on the negative that gets cropped."

Sheriff Tolliver handed the photo to the deputy who headed for the lab. He hoped his compliance would appease her.

"What was in the root beer can?" Tara asked keeping her anger in check.

"Digitalis," the sheriff said.

"It was put in my mother's drink," Tara said.

"It would have looked like a heart attack," the sheriff said then added, "We also lifted a good set of prints."

Tara brushed their importance aside with a grunt. Her anger was subsiding, however.

"McLean asked for them."

"He did?"

"He thought one of the men might have touched the can. Everything else was wiped clean."

"So, do you have identification?" Tara asked.

"We're running them. It could take days for the results to come in."

"We don't have days."

"How long are you going to be here?"

"Until I finish my news story," Tara said a bit testily. Not being believed was still stuck in her craw.

She busied herself looking over the photographs. She selected four. One was a crooked picture of the black-wigged man who'd removed his sunglasses to clean them; a second was blow-up of a fat man with black hair and a full beard standing at ringside; the third, another crooked shot, this time of a slender dark-haired man; the fourth, a profile shot of the nurse from the hospital. Considering how many shots McLean took of these four, Tara decided they were his prime suspects.

She took the four photos to the small room behind the larger office. Sandy rose from his spot and followed her. She faxed the photos with a cover letter to her editor. When she reread her caption–Wanted in connection with conspiracy to commit murder, kidnapping, assault, attempted murder and armed robbery of two Ardilla residents and the Ardilla Chief of Police–Tara felt a sudden chill. She looked down at Sandy who was lying quietly at her feet and realized she was currently safe. Impulsively, she decided to send a copy of everything to the editor of the Bay Area Times and to her friend Sergeant Kathy Riley. Tara would have sent a copy to the Ardilla Police Department but she didn't have their fax number and she didn't want to wake McLean.

"I'm being too paranoid," she told herself. "Maybe the sheriff is right. Maybe it was just kids."

Tara returned to the desk and began writing her story. Sandy returned with her and settled down at her feet.

Banner, whose head was resting on the sheriff's lap as he looked through the pictures, lifted his broad black head momentarily, and then put it back where it had been. Sheriff Tolliver's hand stroked the soft fur lightly.

The phone rang and the sheriff went into his office to answer it. Banner followed him but when the sheriff didn't sit down; the big black dog ambled back to Tara's chair and settled down on the other side of it. Tara briefly stroked his head when he returned without taking her eyes off the script on the screen in front of her.

The sheriff trotted down the stairs to the lower level where the dark room was situated alongside the forensics lab and the evidence room.

Tara looked up when he returned carrying a photo in his hand. She waited for him to share it but he passed by her and headed for his office. As he did so, she dropped her eyes and a photo in the spread before her caught her eye. It was one of her and her mother standing side by side watching Joyce in the ring.

What a great photograph, she thought. The need to share it with a friend swelled inside her. She sorted through the other photos and came up with three more she viewed with excitement. One was of her and Sandy; one showed her mother and Banner and the last of the three showed Joyce and Sweetie in Veterans in the picture perfect pose that won them the class. Hastily, Tara scrawled a cover letter to Kathy explaining the last picture as being what had caused such a rapturous look on their faces in the first.

She hesitated before rising and reread the news article on her computer screen. She pressed the send key.

At that moment Sandy rose and his hackles came up. Tara looked around. The office was nearly empty. Sheriff Tolliver was at his desk studying the photograph; her mother and McLean were in the lounge sleeping. One deputy was at a desk near the front; another, seated toward the back.

She looked at Banner. He too had risen.

Tara picked up her photos and the cover sheet and headed for the office with the fax machine. The dogs followed her. They hesitated at the doorway. Both were facing the stairway. The deputy near the back was still writing. He hadn't heard anything.

Tara, knowing that the lab man was still downstairs, concluded that Banner and Sandy had heard him moving around.

"He's cleaning up, guys," she murmured. "Come in here with me."

The two dogs obeyed and she shut the door.

She taped the photos to blank paper and programmed the fax machine. The two dogs stood facing the door.

When the cover letter was accepted and began rolling through the fax machine, the dogs whined briefly.

Tara said soothingly, "It's just the..."

A single shot cut her sentence in two. The remainder of her words fell away soundlessly. They would not have been heard anyway. The two dogs barked vociferously and pawed frantically at the door.

Running footsteps told her that others had heard the shot and were responding. Behind her, she heard the hum of the fax machine as it accepted the first photograph.

She opened the door a crack to peek out and Sandy shoved his nose through. Tara, her right arm useless, her left knee refusing to support the right leg which was jammed against the door holding it in place, found herself losing the battle. Sandy succeeded in shoving the door open and both dogs ran toward the stairs.

Tara stumbled out behind them, planted her feet and shouted, "Here!"

Only Banner spun around and ran back toward her. But before he reached her, the front door opened and two hooded men entered guns drawn. Banner charged at the hooded men.

The taller, leaner man lowered his gun and fired a warning shot. Such a shot might stop a breed unused to gunshots, but field trained Labradors do not have a fear of the sound of gunfire.

Tara who had spun as her dog passed her saw the bullet dig into the tile in front of Banner.

"Here!" Tara shouted fiercely. Her voice almost cracked from the force behind it.

Banner spun in place like a skater on ice. His return was instantaneous. He spun to her left and sat smartly. Tara's mind was filled with gratitude that Banner was alive at her side.

That moment was short-lived. Sandy raced past them both and headed straight for the approaching duo.

"No!" Tara screeched. It was as if she had a leash attached to his collar and Sandy had hit the end of it. He spun part way around and looked at her. She followed her admonition with a command to heel.

Sandy hesitated. He still had the men in his field of vision. And they were moving.

The taller one leveled his gun.

Tara saw her dog caught between his instinct to protect her and his desire to obey.

Pushing the fear from her throat, she called up her sternest voice, and scolded him. "You get your yellow butt back here!"

The reprimand woke him from his fixation on the men and he took two hesitant steps toward her before stopping.

The men continued to approach.

Tara had two visions pop into her head. One involved Sandy being shot dead; the other, the man taking her hostage.

She stepped backward, and then forced herself to turn and walk away. Banner rose.

"Come on, Sandy," she said with forced cheerfulness. "Let's go. You too Banner. Cookie time."

She walked swiftly toward the lounge.

Neither dog moved. Both stood rigid, blocking the men from approaching their mistress. Both men raised their guns as they drew near to the desk. Each had a dog in his sight.

Banner's growl was distinctive. Tara knew instinctively that he was about to attack.

She whirled around. Banner's lip was drawn back. His growl increased in volume. Almost as an answer, Sandy's hackles rose and his lips curled. A growl came from his throat. Sandy was taking his cue from Banner. They would attack together. A pack of two.

She saw the men take aim.

"Stay!" she shouted.

The men looked startled, but held their fire.

Neither dog moved.

The shorter, stockier man approached the desk warily. Still neither dog moved. As the ring bedecked hand swept across the desk, from between Tara's lips emerged a soft hissing sound of warning to her dogs. They were not to move.

A dog was no match for a gun. Banner and Sandy didn't know that. But Tara did. She also knew that if either man shot her, the dogs would attack.

The hooded men knew this.

And they also knew that if they shot the dogs or her, the sheriff and his men would emerge from the stairwell and shoot them. Both had seen a head encased in a helmet poke around the corner. With Tara and the dogs between them neither side had a clear shot.

The ringed fingers dropped a photo on the floor and it landed face up. The man glanced down at it stuck his foot on it and slid it across the floor toward Tara.

"A keepsake," he chortled as he backed away.

His companion followed suit keeping a watchful eye on the dogs, neither of whom moved a foot. The lips, however, stayed curled, baring a set of strong teeth. The growling was ceaseless. The tails were high; the hackles raised; the muscles, tense.

Tara didn't release the dogs until the door closed behind the men and the deputies in riot gear rushed forward.

Chief McLean, gun drawn, burst forth from the lounge and nearly collided with the sheriff.

Tara immediately summoned her dogs to her and ran toward the lounge where she and her mother embraced their dogs, then praised them and wept.

"Keep the dogs here," Tara said after a few minutes.

"Where are you going?" Coral asked.

"To gather the photographs he missed before anything happens to them."

"We have the negatives," her mother said.

"I don't think so," Tara said. "That was their first stop."

# Chapter 36

Sheriff Tolliver was furious. His headquarters had been invaded. Evidence had been stolen while he was on duty. The gunfire had drawn them downstairs. Nothing else would have been so effective.

But probably most galling was the fact that he had not heeded the warning presented to him via Tara Svenson's near miss.

McLean had assured Tolliver that he hadn't been followed and Tolliver had therefore not believed Tara earlier when she claimed that the car incident was part of the conspiracy. He believed it now.

Photos were taken of the dusty footprint stomped on the single photo that lay on the floor. The photo was then dusted for fingerprints.

While in the sheriff's office, Coral studied the four photos of the show that had been in the fax machine when the melee started and the blow-up of the woman standing by the crate that was on the sheriff's desk, Tara was busy typing an update for her newspaper. Immediately after the attack, Tara had called her editor, told him what happened and accused him of setting her up. He had denied it, admitting only that he'd told the governor that she had promised pictures of the perpetrators and that Governor Atkins had considered that excellent news.

"Promised?" Tara had exclaimed. "You mean you didn't get them?"

"I got the cover letter but no pictures," Clayton Keyman had replied.

Tara had moaned loudly. "They're lost."

"Did you send a copy to the Ardilla police?" Keyman asked.

"No," Tara had replied thinking at first that he was anxious to recover them. "I didn't have their fax number and McLean was asleep. Besides I thought he might want to send them all."

"So no one has any photos?" Keyman pressed.

Suddenly, Tara was suspicious. "You double-checked your machine?"

"I got four blank pages," Keyman said. "Are you sure you loaded the fax machine correctly?"

"I thought you said you only got the cover letter?" Tara probed.

Keyman stumbled slightly. "Whatever. The point is I didn't get copies of the photos."

"I don't believe you," Tara retorted bluntly. "It's too bad you don't have them. I sent a copy to the Bay Area Times and it looks as if they're going to scoop you on the pictures."

"If they got them," Keyman bluffed. "And are you forgetting who pays your salary?"

"I'm not certain. Is it you or the governor?"

"I resent that!"

"If my story makes the front page intact, maybe I'll believe you."

The minute Tara hung up she called the editor of the Bay Area Times. The line was busy. She was transferred to the assistant editor who began to tell her they'd received the photos and the story when the line went dead.

When Tara called back, her call was transferred to the assistant editor's voice mail. She left her number. Then she called her friend, Sergeant Kathy Riley at home. Kathy listened to Tara's suspicions and promised that she'd go right down to the precinct station and retrieve the faxes. Then she added a startling bit of news.

"Did you know that the bullets turned in by Sergeant Volatis don't match the gun taken off the suspect, Eddie Landecker?"

"That makes no sense," Tara said. "McLean was told that his voice marched the voice on the tape."

"I know," Kathy replied. "I was there when they ran the tapes through the Spectrograph. The match was perfect."

"Then the bullets handed in were phonies," Tara declared.

"They had bits of Alex's blood on them. That's pretty compelling evidence that they're the real ones," Kathy stated. "But even if the real ones were found now, Landecker's attorney would claim they weren't the ones taken from Alex's body."

"There must be some clue on those bullets. You've got to prove they're phony somehow."

"I'll call Devin," Kathy said. "If he's ready to work on it, so am I. But please don't say anything to anyone. I don't want Captain Scoma to know what we're doing."

"I promise I'll sit on it." Tara finished. "Now get going to the station and call me as soon as you have them or even if you don't."

While she waited to hear from Kathy, Tara typed an update to her story and e-mailed it to her editor. Before she copied the Bay Area Times she put in a call to its editor. She was shunted off to the assistant again.

"Lynn," she said, "Donahue never called me back."

"He didn't?" Lynn asked with what Tara read as mock surprise. "Well, Jack is very busy."

"This is a big story," Tara said. "And it's local."

"You really need to talk to Jack," Lynn said.

"I've been waiting for his phone call."

"I'll give him the message again," the assistant said.

Tara slammed down the receiver. "He got to them too."

McLean called from the office where he'd been looking over Coral's shoulder. "What's happening?"

"The Bay Area Times. That's what. They're giving me the run-around."

"What about Sergeant Riley?"

"No word yet."

"So we wait," McLean said calmly.

"Look at this," Coral said.

The three crowded around the desk where Coral was pointing at a thick pen in the hand of a woman standing next to the dog crate.

"It might not be a real pen," McLean commented.

"It looks real enough," Tolliver said.

"It puts her beside the crate," Coral said.

"Puts who? The woman's head isn't in the picture," the sheriff observed.

"But her blouse is," Coral said. "An unusual print, wouldn't you say, Tara?"

Tara looked closely. "Most unusual."

"Put that together with an unusually thick pen on a buxom lady with a large ring on her right hand and you don't need a face," Coral said. "However, we have one in this shot of Joyce and Sweetie. Isn't that her standing off to the left?"

Coral held out the magnifying glass through which she'd been studying the pictures.

"I see only part of a face," Tolliver said. "There could be a hundred blouses like that one."

"And a hundred buxom ladies wearing them to a Specialty show which has maybe two hundred in attendance."

"So the odds are against there being two," Tolliver countered. "It still leaves room for doubt."

"Don't forget that I saw her there," McLean said. "I recognized her from the hospital. She's part of the conspiracy and she may be our best lead."

"What I could really get excited about is some clue as to who the men were who invaded my station," Tolliver said.

"Someone drove their car," McLean observed. "Whoever it was sat outside in the front and kept the motor running. Why do we assume the driver was a man?"

Tolliver protested. "But she's a nurse. Why would she get involved in such a risky deal?"

"Some of the pictures were of her," McLean replied. "And her part involved minimal risk."

"It could have been the fat man," Tolliver said.

"My money's on her," McLean countered. "The fat man has no idea I actually saw him well enough to match him up with a face in the group photographed at ringside."

"They were told," Tolliver countered.

"Maybe not," Tara insisted thoughtfully. "My editor says he just told the governor I'd sent pictures. My guess is he didn't supply details."

"Your editor was told to lose the pictures," Sheriff Tolliver reminded her. "He must have been given some idea whose pictures they were."

Tara's mother cleared her throat.

"I don't think Governor Atkins has any personal knowledge who these men are. Brian Harvath might know and a call from him is like a call from the governor himself. Besides, if the fat man believed that McLean didn't get a good look at him, he would never take such a risk to recover a photo of himself enjoying a dog show."

"You win," the sheriff said. "We'll start our search with the lady. I've called in our identification expert and maybe you three can help him create a likeness using our computer."

McLean sighed heavily because he was anxious to head home; but he nodded his acquiescence.

Tara noticed his reluctance to stay and correctly read it as worry over their safety. A quick departure might catch their pursuers off guard. She glanced at her watch. Thirty minutes had already passed since the robbery.

Time was fast fading as a friend. And she was out of ideas as to how to elude their pursuers except by simply driving north as fast as they could.

Tara was certain that their enemies would know exactly when they left and would follow them.

It was while she was helping the computer artist compile the nurse's facial characteristics that she conceived a plan that would net the sheriff one or more of his suspects and guarantee their safe entrance onto the major freeway that went over the Grapevine Pass leaving the LA basin and dropping down into the desert region surrounding Bakersfield. The road through the Grapevine was four to six lanes wide, a long slow upgrade that climbed several thousand feet, taxing car cooling systems to their limit. On the other side, the descent onto the valley floor had several downgrades that so strained the braking systems of the huge semi's that there were off-ramps of deep sand strategically placed to accept and stop runaway trucks.

It was a run fraught with danger. There were sheer rock walls to be jammed into and steep drops into deep ravines whose rocks would break a car into too many pieces to count.

It was not a place to be chased.

# Chapter 37

The call from Sergeant Kathy Riley that the faxed photos were in her hands, cheered everyone. Kathy, at Tara's suggestion, faxed copies to the Ardilla Police and to the Oakland Journal as well as back to the Granite County Sheriff's office.

Tara called her editor and told him that she would send the story and the photos to the Chronicle if he claimed he didn't receive them. She hung up the phone with a satisfied smirk.

"Why are you dealing with him?" her mother asked. "Why not just ignore him and go straight to the Chronicle?"

"He pays my salary," Tara said. "Besides he promised me a by-line."

"You're giving our enemies a heads-up," Coral commented. "Now they know..."

Tara cut in. "Know what? That we have faxes of the photos? That's not the real problem. The real problem is that we can identify them. The real problem is that we know too much. As long as we're alive, we're a threat."

"Then why didn't they kill us at the show?" her mother pressed.

"That was tried, remember?" Tara snapped.

"Oh, yes," Coral admitted a bit sheepishly, remembering the drug in her root beer.

"But now they've gotten more desperate. I believe the plan was for each of us to die individually—you from a heart attack, me from an accident of some sort, McLean probably in a staged shoot-out. But this failed attempt has only made us more dangerous, because now we know we're on to something. I'm convinced the clue to what's going on lies back in the Bay Area. This is why I'm feeding these stories to the press. I want someone to suspect murder if we all die in an accident on the way home."

"What a dreadful thought!" Coral exclaimed, lines of worry creasing her forehead.

"We not only have to make it home," Tara pressed on. "We have to uncover the truth before we're eliminated one by one."

"Can't we just hide?"

"Sorry, Mom. This won't go away. We've already disturbed too much ground."

"Surely, we can leave the investigation in the hands of the police," Coral suggested hopefully.

"This is my big story!" Tara exclaimed. "Surely, you don't expect me to run from it?"

"I expect you to stay alive for my sake," Coral said with decided firmness. It was as close to an order as she could come with Tara.

Tara looked at her mother with a rare display of sympathy and said softly, "We will watch each other's backs, Mother. And, with God's help, we will survive."

The conversation ended when Coral bowed her head in prayer. Tara, guessing what her mother was requesting, added her request to it.

Chief Spencer McLean came upon the two women with their heads bowed in prayer and swallowed his announcement until both heads were raised. When Tara's eyes met McLean's, she announced, "I need a camera."

"We're ready to spring the trap," he said. "We can't stop at a store and buy a camera."

"Borrow one," Tara said. "A reporter needs a camera."

Within minutes the dogs were loaded into their crates and Coral had positioned herself in the back seat wedged between the cooler and the dog food bag. Tara pulled out the cooler and handed it to Sheriff Tolliver.

"Mother needs to lie down. Trade you this cooler half filled with melted ice for a blanket," Tara said with a grin. "I'll even throw in this dog food bag with a bullet hole, bits of glass from the cab imbedded in the sack itself and buried deep inside an undamaged bullet from the cabbie's gun."

"That's worth two blankets and a pillow," the sheriff said signaling his deputy to fetch the requested items.

"Did McLean tell you what else I needed?"

The sheriff dangled a camera by the strap of its carrying case. "Fully loaded."

Tara studied the camera while McLean strapped the canvas folding chairs on top of the crate and then lined up the trophy boxes, suitcases, tote bags and dog biscuit can on the rear floor behind the front seats. A blanket was laid across the entire assemblage. Coral surveyed the completed project and declared it quiet acceptable, almost bed-like.

"At least I won't fall on the floor if we stop suddenly," she added as she climbed in.

Tara tucked the camera beside her purse which was between her feet as McLean drove out of the sheriff's parking lot onto the road and turned west.

"It's so dark," Coral remarked as she settled down. "How can they tell we're being followed?"

"The sheriff has cars parked at certain intersections, waiting."

"Go to sleep, Mom," Tara said. "There are two of us watching the road which is practically empty."

Coral closed her eyes.

Twenty minutes later, a call came in over McLean's radio. "Got them both, but neither driver is one of our original suspects."

"Two cars with only one in each?" McLean asked.

"Yeah," the sheriff replied. "I don't like it either."

One freeway led to another and the smooth turning of the wheels and the slight vibration of the minivan as it sped along soothed Tara. She closed her eyes without knowing it. Her head lolled to one side and came to rest on the window frame.

"I thought you were going to help me watch," McLean's voice said quietly.

Tara's head jerked up. "Did I fall asleep? Where are we?"

"Approaching the Grapevine. I need some coffee and Tolliver gave us a thermos but it's next to your leg."

Tara went to rub her eyes but the pain in her right arm reminded her that she should treat it with respect. She yelped lightly.

"It'll take me a minute to do this," she apologized.

"I can't believe you could sleep against the door with that arm," McLean commented. "Why not see if your mother's awake enough to handle pouring the coffee?"

Tara scrunched around in her seat and looked back at her mother. Her eye caught the three sets of headlights bearing down on them. The sets in the lanes on the right and left of them belonged to semis. A multitude of lights outlining the tops and sides of the huge trucks identified them.

A semi in the third lane from the right was unusual, especially since the van between them was rapidly passing both trucks. Why did the truck in the far left lane move out to pass a faster vehicle?

"How fast are we going?" Tara asked, still staring at the entourage behind them.

"The speed limit," McLean said. "I am a cop after all. Did you know that more tickets are written on the Grapevine than anywhere else in California?"

"Even so," Tara remarked. "They're really barreling. All three of them."

McLean glanced in his rear view mirror.

"They'll fall back as soon as we hit the grade."

Tara nodded. A five percent grade for five miles would take its toll on truck speed.

"Why don't we just let them pass," she suggested as she turned back around.

"I would if I could, but this car in the right lane is matching my speed," McLean said. "I think he's playing a game with me."

Tara glanced at the car to her right. The driver was a blonde wearing a jeans jacket. Seated beside him was a dark-haired man whose features she couldn't see. All she could see was that his hair was cropped short. Both were strangers.

"What happens if you speed up?" she asked.

McLean pressed down the accelerator and as the speed of the Plymouth Voyager increased, so did that of the sedan to their right.

"That car has more power, doesn't it?" Tara said, her stomach beginning to feel queasy. "I mean you can't win in a race, can you?"

"Nope."

"And what happens if you slow down?"

"He slows down," McLean said.

"Why does he want to keep us out of the right lane?" Tara wondered aloud.

"Who knows?" McLean replied with no hint of concern. The rumble from the approaching trucks blasted in through the two inch openings of the rear minivan windows. The noise was deafening. Fear clutched Tara's stomach. She doubled over.

"Get off the road," she yelled. "I'm going to throw up!"

A quick look around told McLean he had only one option. He jammed his foot on the accelerator and cut left in front of the outlying truck, sped across the left lanes of the wide highway and pulled onto the left shoulder.

Coral bolted into a sitting position and stared at the huge rusty rock hauler that roared past as Tara threw open her door and stumbled to the back of the car where she leaned over.

To the driver of the two bin rock hauler that roared past, Tara appeared to be vomiting.

McLean came around the car and solicitously asked her if she was alright. Tara raised her head.

"It was the only thing I could think of to say. I'm okay."

McLean straightened up and put his hands on his hips. His face was stern.

"I wouldn't cry 'Wolf' too often," he warned.

"There wasn't time to argue," Tara said defensively. "I had this vision of being trapped between two semi's and somehow being crushed to death."

"You're letting that paranoia of yours loose again," McLean said. "But if it makes you feel any better, this stop of ours will put them miles ahead of us. We're no longer even on the same road."

Suddenly, Tara was ashamed of her trickery.

"Sorry," she said sheepishly.

"Hold in your gut," Spencer McLean said roughly. "We need to travel as much by night as we can."

When they returned to their seats, Tara's mother offered the chief a cup of steaming coffee.

"That group should be reported," Coral said. "Racing on a freeway. Where are the police when you need them? I'm glad you got out of their way. We could have gotten hurt. Why did you pull over anyway?"

"Your daughter felt sick," McLean said.

"Tara?" Coral exclaimed. "Nonsense. Tara has the constitution of a rhinoceros."

"A rhinoceros?" Tara gasped. She frowned and disapproval coated her words. "A horse or elephant, Mother, but not a rhinoceros."

Coral didn't respond, but smiled a little smile as she settled back down to sleep.

"A rhinoceros, Mom?" Tara pressed on, still obviously upset. "Why a rhinoceros?"

Spencer McLean allowed himself a small smile too. He felt vindicated for some unexplained reason. He didn't attempt to analyze the cause. He simply enjoyed the warmth.

Of course, it could have been the coffee.

At Castaic, two semi's, a sedan and a van took the off-ramp and pulled into the parking lot of the coffee shop. The drivers congregated around the van where a stocky, balding man was watching a small radar screen.

There were forty-five miles of the Grapevine left.

# Chapter 38

Just after Castaic, Spencer McLean moved left to pass a string of trucks in the right lane. As he did so, one of the trucks cut in front of him. The sedan behind him simultaneously pulled out and began to pass him on the left.

McLean waited for the sedan's tail to clear so he could move in behind him and get around the truck in front of him. The upgrade slowed everyone down.

The rumble of the truck string on the right woke Coral who peered through the window at the truck that was pulling alongside on the right.

"I thought he'd passed us," Coral said.

"Different truck," Tara replied, her attention drawn to the truck just ahead of them in the right hand lane.

Her mother protested, "No, I'm sure it's the same one."

"This one has pictures of food on its side," Tara said. Her eyes then returned to the sedan on their left. She was beginning to feel claustrophobic again. When the sedan moved forward and a space on the left appeared to be opening up, Tara's claustrophobic fears began to dissipate.

"Not that one," her mother persisted. "The big rock hauler behind him, the one pulling up next to us."

Tara glanced back. "What's so unusual about it?"

"The huge dent in the side of the back bin."

The truck in front of them began to gain on the food truck. McLean drew opposite the rear axle of the long white truck. Tara stared at the cornucopia of overblown, painted vegetables spilling along its white side.

"When did you see its side?" Tara asked mentally urging the truck in front of them to go faster.

"When it passed, while you were running around the back to throw up. Our headlights lit up the dent in the back bin," Coral replied calmly. "What I don't understand is how we got ahead of it?"

Suddenly, Tara's mind took a quantum leap.

Without warning, she yelled, "It's happening again!"

McLean glanced into the rear view mirror. The headlights of the rock hauler were moving into his lane. He was flat against the middle of the food truck trailer. The truck in front of him was no longer gaining on the food truck. And the sedan to his left was matching his speed.

Without warning McLean hit his brakes. He dropped back a car length before the car on his left had time to adjust. Then McLean turned left sharply and jammed his foot down on the accelerator.

The right front bumper of the minivan dove into the rear fender of the sedan throwing it sideways. The impact spun both vehicles out of their pathways. Both drivers fought to regain control.

The driver of the sedan lightly scraped the rear fender of the truck in the lane to his right but the truck's speed took it out of the equation quickly and the sedan driver was able to stop his spin given the extra lane.

The Voyager, however, had spun directly into the path of the rock hauler that was fast moving directly toward its midsection. McLean's foot, which had left the accelerator upon impact with the sedan, punched the accelerator to the floor. The Voyager leaped forward as the rock hauler accelerated toward it. The reinforced steel bumper of the huge truck tore off the Voyager's rear taillight and the dark green paint around it as it roared past. The minivan spun around by the collision barely avoided a second encounter with the rear bin of the long truck.

McLean's engine stalled. The spin slowed and stopped. Before the passengers could breathe a sigh of relief, a loud blast from the horn of a semi bearing down on them told them that their ordeal wasn't yet over.

Tara's mind jumped into high gear. Head on, sideways, at a diagonal or from the rear–it made no difference. The semi would crush them and then drag what was left down the road as bits and pieces of their vehicle and their bodies fell under its double wheels. That they were its prey there was no question. He was coming straight toward them. And they were dead in the water.

Tara closed her eyes and prayed.

McLean concentrated on starting the car. The engine sputtered alive.

Tara opened her eyes as the rumble of the truck shook the minivan. It had moved over and was passing them. It wasn't until it passed that she heard the siren and saw the flashing lights. The police car slowed in back of them, its lights effectively moving the traffic around them.

"Where was it going, I wonder?" Coral asked no one in particular.

"To the accident," McLean replied slowly turning the dark green Voyager toward the right shoulder of the road where he stopped.

"What accident?"

"Ours. One of the trucks called it in is my guess," McLean said.

"They reported themselves?" Coral queried puzzled.

"They weren't all part of the scheme," Tara interjected.

"I think I broke my finger," Coral announced abruptly.

McLean turned on the inside light. Coral showed him her injured hand. The highway patrol car pulled up beside them.

"Anyone hurt?" a deep male voice called through his open window.

"You got a first aid kit?" McLean asked. "I could use some adhesive tape."

Tara hissed at him. "You don't know who you're talking to."

"I wouldn't worry," McLean said as he stepped out of the car. "He scared them off."

He walked forward and identified himself to the highway patrolman.

Together the two men fashioned a splint using pencils Tara dug out of her purse and adhesive tape. The last step was to fasten Coral's little finger to its partner.

"I can't move either finger," Coral announced.

"You'll just have to give up check writing," McLean said with a half grin.

Coral looked at her makeshift splint. "It could be worse."

The officer who had stepped in back of the minivan and was focusing on the damage to the rear agreed. "I think you can drive it."

Together the two circled the car assessing the damage.

A glint of red caught McLean's eye. He bent over and retrieved the first of two electronic tracking devices. McLean handed the highway patrolman the two devices and asked him to deliver them to the Granite County Sheriff. He explained that Sheriff Tolliver was working on a case with him and he might be able to track them.

As the cop was bagging the devices, he said, "I need to file a report."

"Of course, you do," McLean said, moving toward the rear. "And we're at your disposal, but, I'm afraid I don't have much to give you. It all happened so fast."

Tara exchanged glances with her mother.

"He was in a hurry a few minutes ago," Tara said.

"I'm hungry. I wish I had something to eat," her mother responded.

"We have a can of dog biscuits," Tara teased.

Suddenly, both poured out of the car and ran to the back where the two men were standing.

"We have to check on the dogs," Tara said.

"You can't let them out," the highway patrolman said. "It's against the law."

"They're in dog crates," Tara explained.

Permission was granted and McLean unlocked the rear gate. Both dogs stood up and tentatively wagged their tails.

"Don't open the crates," McLean warned.

"We need to check them out," Tara insisted. "They're upset."

259

"We'll stop at Gorman," McLean promised.

"How far is that?" Tara asked.

"About twenty-five miles," the CHP cop replied.

"That's too long," Tara wailed. "We need to check them now."

McLean shined his light into each crate. "No blood. And they're standing. They can wait."

"Dog biscuits," Coral suggested.

Tara ran to fetch the can.

While Chief McLean answered questions, Tara and her mother broke the large biscuits into small bits and shoved the pieces through the slim metal bars. The middle of the night treat enlivened the dogs whose tails were soon thumping against the sides of the crates in their usual staccato beat. Each dog managed to con three biscuits from its guilt-ridden owner. The usual was one.

"They're going to be thirsty," Tara observed.

"We'll water them at Gorman."

"Suppose..." Tara began and then stopped. The presence of the highway patrolman prevented her from voicing her fear.

"One worry at a time," Coral cautioned her daughter.

But Tara's gut told her the attacks weren't over yet.

Even after McLean climbed back into the driver's seat and they pulled out behind the patrol car, Tara didn't relax.

"He wants to look around there," McLean explained. "There's a rest area just beyond the town. You can let the dogs out there."

Coral was quick to realize the upside. "It'll be safe. The tracking devices will be in the patrol car in Gorman, but we won't be."

## The Puzzle

Her daughter's stomach, however, still churned.

# Chapter 39

"What I don't completely understand, Mother," Tara said as she sat in the front seat staring at the taillights of the patrol car, "is why the pursuit of us has accelerated so rapidly. The governor now has the list and the photograph. Why not stop there? Without the photo, you would have no proof. On top of that you indicated that you wouldn't say anything because you wished to preserve Cee Cee's good name."

"I guess the men around the governor don't trust me."

"So they attempted to kill you," Tara continued without acknowledging her mother's insertion. Her mind was on a roll. "And then they held up a sheriff's office to recover photographs."

"Your story incited them?"

"They got the photographs," Tara plowed on. "And now they've tried twice to kill us all. What do we know?"

"We know who were at the show," Coral said.

"Petty stuff. The digitalis may not have been intended to kill you outright," Tara mused aloud. "Maybe they merely wanted to prevent us from getting home. Put you in the hospital and we'd both be stuck here."

"I don't think those big trucks were a delaying tactic," Coral countered.

"Actually, neither do I. You must know something."

The chief cleared his throat. It was obvious he was about to step into the discussion.

"What was your position in the campaign?" Spencer McLean asked.

"Fund raiser. I arranged parties, dinners, luncheons– anything that would generate cash. People are more generous when they've met the candidate. Social gatherings are a pleasant way to accomplish that."

"Did all the contributions you handled come from these parties?" McLean asked.

"No, of course not. Checks poured into the office daily."

"And you handled them?"

"My staff did," Coral explained. "I was concerned with the arrangements mostly."

"Who set up the guest list?"

"I did."

Tara's face lit up. An idea hit her.

"You said that funeral director what's his name…"

"Andre Varrieur," McLean inserted.

"Yes, Andre Varrieur. You said that he was at the party the governor attended that night. Atkins got a packet from him. Why was Varrieur there? He doesn't live in Ardilla. I thought your parties were mostly for local people."

"Not always," Coral said. "He's an avid supporter of Governor Atkins."

"Why would he be invited to multiple fund raisers?" Tara probed.

"To give his support, I suppose," Coral said. "The governor often asks me to include him."

"He likes him?"

Susan Davis Sandberg

"Oh, no. He can't stand the man," Coral replied. "He says he's unctuous. I imagine that's why Varrieur's demand to be made Ambassador to France galled Whalen so."

"Does he contribute a lot of money?"

"Him, personally?" Coral queried for clarification.

Tara nodded.

"No, but he does seem to be a link to a wide circle of investors," Coral said.

"The names on the list?" Tara asked.

"It's possible."

"Why do you believe he's a link?" McLean probed.

"A few comments dropped now and again," Coral said, "nothing specific. And the fact that the governor keeps putting him on the guest list. The man likes parties and his presence is a quiet advertisement for his business. He makes a good first impression and people remember him when they need to arrange a funeral service. In fact, at his very first party, there was another man there who died in an accident the next day. He was from Texas and Varrieur handled shipping the body back."

"Do you remember the man's name?" McLean asked.

"It would be in my memory file, but I can't get to that now," Coral said. "It was a fluke. He wasn't local."

"So how does Varrieur fit in?" Tara pressed.

"He doesn't," Coral said. "That is, he doesn't politically. He engages people in conversation about their hobbies. Actually, I suppose that is a function. I just never realized it before."

"So do people hand over checks at these parties?"

"Sometimes."

"And you are in charge of them?" McLean asked.

"Initially, yes. But I have a staff that logs them in and banks them."

"Does Varrieur ever hand the governor checks at these parties?"

"No," Coral said.

"What about cash?" Tara asked.

"Sometimes the next morning Harvath will hand me a brown packet with cash contributions and a list of donors. They are generally not people who were at the party."

"A list?" McLean interjected. "Like the one we taped together?"

"Well, yes, now that you mention it, exactly like that," Coral said. "But why would the governor shred the list that came with the photograph? And where was the cash?"

"Good questions," McLean said.

"Maybe Varrieur absconded with the money," Tara suggested. "A monetary down payment on his blackmail demands."

"Whalen only mentioned the ambassadorship. He didn't say anything about money," Coral replied. "Why shred the list? With it he could demand Varrieur return the money."

"And announce the fact that he was being blackmailed? I don't think so," Tara countered. "Didn't you tell me once they had a nickname for Varrieur?"

"Caleb used to refer to him as the grave robber," Coral replied. "I called him on it once. He said that funeral directors were like the grave robbers of old in that they rob the dead."

"What else?"

"I told him they provide a service to the dead and it's not the same thing at all. By the way did I tell you to cremate me?"

"Only a dozen times, Mother," Tara replied, an edge to her voice.

"He laughed and said I didn't know the half of it," Coral said, "so I asked him why, if he despised the man so, did he go over to see him so much?"

"And?"

"Because he has connections was his reply."

"What kind of connections?"

"Why with some organization of funeral directors I guess," Coral said raising an eyebrow in surprise that Tara would question the obvious."

"You didn't ask?" Tara pressed.

"It wasn't necessary," Coral explained. "Governor Atkins habitually selects one or two influential people connected with a group and persuades them to join his team, and they become his liaison to that group. Take Friday night. Whalen was buddying up to the head of LAITA. I planned to tell him to steer clear of the man, but then I wound up on the run."

McLean's strong voice cut in. "When Caleb went to see Varrieur, did he always return with money?"

"No. Only once. I remember it was the day we argued. He slapped the envelope on my desk and said something about my recording the exact date of each donation. I told him I always did. And then he made some snide reference to my calling Varrieur a grave robber and I told him that I never said that he was. I told him that that was his term. Then he said he didn't want me to use it again."

266

As Coral was relating the incident her anger was rising.

McLean interrupted its buildup. "If you had to use the date the donation was supposedly given and not the date it was received, wouldn't that mess up your bookkeeping? I'm surprised it didn't arouse your suspicion at the time."

"Harvath said we were to follow the pattern the credit card companies use. They post the transaction date and the posting date. We post the donation date after the posting date. I was curious as to why we were doing it that way. It wasn't as if political contributions were tax deductible and therefore had to be posted before the fiscal year ended; but since it didn't mess up the bookkeeping, I didn't see any harm in it."

"What happened to that list, the one Harvath said was from Varrieur..."

Coral cut him off. "Whoa. He never actually said Varrieur gave him the money. I made that assumption based on our conversation and his innuendo. As for the list, it's filed with the others."

"What I don't get is the amounts," Tara inserted. "Why ten thousand. Is it a magic number that earns one special recognition of some sort?"

"Not that I'm aware of," her mother replied.

"According to Becky, one donor was a teenager. That doesn't fit. She can't even vote," Tara went on after a short pause. "You know that's a lot of money."

"I agree on that," Coral said. "Ten thousand is..."

Tara cut in. "Not her ten thousand. I was just figuring how much money the governor's campaign would get if Varrieur wrangled that amount out of each of the people he buried. I mean, think about it, Mother. He has what two, maybe three, funerals a week..."

"More," Coral insisted.

"We'll stick with the minimum–two. How many homes does he run? Six? Eight? Ten?"

"Close to a dozen," Coral replied.

"Take ten thousand per body and two bodies in each home and multiply that by fifty-two weeks in a year and you have over half a million dollars per funeral home. Eight homes translates into four million a year."

"Everybody doesn't donate," Coral countered unable to assimilate the magnitude of the suggestion.

"What if nobody does?" Tara said.

"Don't be foolish. Of course, people donate. I..."

Tara interrupted. "Where did Cee Cee come up with ten thousand dollars to donate to any campaign?"

"She had a trust fund," Coral replied.

"Mother, Cee Cee was a Democrat like her parents," Tara pointed out. "So why wouldn't her parents say something to you once they found out about the donation? I'll tell you what I think. I think they never said anything because they never discovered it. Because it never happened. Because Cee Cee didn't put ten thousand dollars in the governor's coffers. Someone else did and borrowed her name to do it. And that someone is borrowing other names as well."

"Varrieur?" Coral queried.

"He's rich," Tara replied, "but not that rich. I think he's the go-between."

"If so, why attack him?" Coral questioned. "Whalen would never cut off a link to millions. Not before the election."

"Nor would the men trying to buy into the governor's circle," Tara added.

"Someone else has thrown his hat in the ring," Coral decided aloud.

"Well, now," McLean inserted, "it seems you two have it all worked out. Are you going to consider any other possibilities?"

"No," they both chorused.

McLean laughed heartily, announced that they were approaching Gorman and then he said soberly, "You can pull the teeth of a bear, but he can still crush you."

"What's that supposed to mean?" Tara charged.

"You two are the puzzle experts," McLean replied. "You work it out."

# Chapter 40

While Tara and Coral Svenson were walking their dogs on a tiny plot of uncut weeds at the back of the coffee shop parking lot and shining their flashlights on the uneven ground checking for tiny particles of glass, at the San Francisco Police Department Forensic Lab, Sergeant Kathy Riley and her partner, Sergeant Devin Simonton were hovering over Stormy Callen who was examining a bit of fabric from the jacket Alex Caribou had been wearing when he was shot. Alex's shirt was next.

Drew Manning from the Ardilla Police arrived as Stormy announced that none of the threads from the pieces of clothing matched the bit of thread found adhering to one of the bullets.

"I've got a sample from the door, the seat and the floor," Drew announced. "Actually, I cut a piece of the seat fabric away because it seemed to be woven with more than one thread."

"Good! Good!" Stormy responded, taking the group of bags. "But what I don't understand, is why no one got me some threads from the doctor's gown?"

"We were too late," Kathy said. "The gowns are at the laundry."

Stormy's grunt spoke volumes, that and his black visage clouded by annoyance. "Even the type might have helped. But let's get on with what you do have."

Drew handed him the square of seat fabric first and the three onlookers held their breath as he extracted a bit of thread, prepared it for examination and then studied it. He shook his head after a few minutes and pulled out another thread and went through the same procedure with the same results.

After the third try Stormy looked into the anxious faces of the officers surrounding him, and said in a softer tone, "Fabric on seats in cabs is made not to shed particles."

An hour passed and all the threads from the seat cushion came up negative as well as the bits of fabric from the door and the floor carpet.

"I was so sure that's where Volatis got Alex's blood," Kathy said.

"I brought our photos," Drew offered. "Maybe if we compare them with his we'll see something."

Drew pulled out a blow-up of the seat of the cab and pointed to an area with dried blood stains on it. "See this slight depression? Lim figured that Volatis might have rolled the bullets here. He had me scrape the blood from here."

Simonton pulled Volatis' photos from the packet and laid them alongside those Drew brought.

Drew's finger rested on the largest blood stain pictured by both cameras. Something had indeed been pressed into it between the shots.

"And I suppose you want me to waste another hour on your bogus theory," Stormy snapped. "And find some foreign particle in both samples."

"Would you?" Kathy asked quietly, her soft almond shaped eyes carrying her plea to the next level. "We need to disprove this theory completely."

"And this will be the last I'll hear of it?"

"I won't bother you again," Kathy promised, lowering her eyes. It was a natural gesture of deference she'd picked up from her mother. She found that men responded to it. Stormy was no exception.

He took the plastic bag from Drew's outstretched hand. "Don't be breathing down my neck on this one."

Kathy and Drew stepped back. Devin, tied to Stormy by race, stayed put.

"The thread had to come from somewhere," Kathy remarked quietly.

"Stormy already proved it didn't come from Alex's jacket or shirt so the bullet didn't carry it into the body," Devin offered.

"Was there anyone in the cab with Alex?" Kathy asked.

"There were passengers before him," Drew said. "The thread could have been left by one of them."

"There's no way to know if it was," Kathy moaned.

"Unless Stormy finds a match in the samples of the dried blood I brought," Drew said.

"There's another way," Devin suggested. "We prove it didn't come from the other possible sources."

"You mean like the hospital gowns or the paramedic's clothes?" Kathy queried.

Devin nodded.

"Let's go!" Kathy said. The two rushed out leaving Drew alone with the taciturn forensic investigator.

# Chapter 41

Officer Stephanie Brandt rose from her chair opposite the bed where Andre Varrieur lay pale-faced under a white sheet, an IV in one arm slowly dripping sustenance into the comatose body. The stocky police woman was approaching thirty. She was armed with the confidence her Peace Corps experience gave her and the fact that her marksmanship equaled that of the best on the force. She was also wearing a vest. But she was wary.

A young, blonde nurse came in, smiled and offered her a cup of coffee. "Your partner asked me to give this to you. He said he might not be back for a while. Something about an upset stomach."

"Thank you," Stephanie said, setting the cup down.

With one eye on the nurse, Stephanie called her partner on her radio. Her message was automatically relayed to the station in Ardilla.

"Zack," she said without preamble. "If you're sick, maybe you should go home."

Stephanie saw a small smile appear on the face of the comely nurse.

"You know that my son catches everything I drag home, so do me a favor and don't bring it in here. The nurse told me..."

Stephanie leaned over and smiled. "What's your name, by the way?"

The fraction of a second hesitation was barely perceptible, "My friends call me Bunny."

"Well, Bunny," Stephanie said, "thanks for the coffee. How about checking on Zack for me? Tell him if he's not coming back he should call for back-up." Stephanie reached for the cup. "Meanwhile this coffee'll keep me awake."

When Bunny left the room, Stephanie was tempted to barricade the door, but she opted for another plan. Instead she picked up the coffee cup, walked over to the adjacent bathroom and set the cup down inside the shower. Then she flushed the toilet and ran water in the basin. She left the water running, left the bathroom and closed the door behind her. She moved to a corner behind the door leading into the room, upholstered her gun and waited.

She didn't have to wait long.

The man who entered the room had a hospital mask on his face. His hair was covered by a cloth cap. He looked at the empty chair to his right and glanced toward the bathroom on his left. Light was shining into the darkened room from under the door and the sound of running water was unmistakable.

Swiftly he moved toward the bed.

Stephanie slid across the wall and set herself in front of the door leading into the hallway.

The man slipped one gloved hand into the pocket of his lab coat and withdrew a syringe. He uncapped the needle and picked up the IV tube.

"Freeze!" Stephanie ordered. "You're under arrest."

The man turned his head slowly, the syringe in his hand suspended just above the tubing. "I'm a nurse," the man said calmly. "It's time for this patient's medication. Check the chart if you don't believe me."

"Lay the needle on the bed and put your hands on your head," Stephanie ordered.

"After I give him his medication, you can question me all you want," the man said decisively. He jabbed the needle into the tubing. Before he pushed the plunger Stephanie squeezed the trigger.

The shot reverberated down the third floor corridor. Inside the room the man grabbed his thigh and collapsed. Blood flowed between his fingers.

He pressed down hard on his wound.

A nurse rushed into the room. She saw a uniformed police officer holding a man at gunpoint.

"Quick," Stephanie shouted. "Remove the IV."

The nurse stood transfixed. Stephanie leaped across the room and with her eyes fixed on the man scrambling to rise, his hands grasping his leg, she yanked the IV tube out of Varrieur's arm. Her action brought the nurse awake and she rushed forward.

"Stand back!" Stephanie shouted as more heads appeared in the doorway.

With her gun leveled at the man on the floor, Stephanie moved around the bed so she could see both the door and the man on the floor.

"No one moves until my backup arrives," she said.

"But he's been shot!" the first nurse objected. "He needs medical attention."

A tall, thin faced man rushed into the room. "I'm a doctor. Let me attend to this man."

"Stand back!" Stephanie commanded sternly. "It's a leg wound. He can wait."

"It looks as if you nicked an artery," the thin faced doctor said, bending his head and looking at her over his half glasses. "He could bleed to death."

"You," she said to the man on the floor. "Put out your hands."

She threw her handcuffs to the doctor who missed catching them and bent over to pick them up. At the same time the wounded man objected strenuously. "I'm putting pressure on the wound. I can't move them."

The doctor scooped up the cuffs and moved forward.

Stephanie shouted at him to stop. He hesitated for a brief moment.

"You're overreacting," he stated and started forward again.

"One more step and I'll shoot," she warned.

His derisive grunt was followed immediately by the sound of a second gunshot.

He jumped back.

"Are you crazy?" he bellowed as he grabbed his arm.

"Back away!" Stephanie ordered. "This is an extreme situation and I will not be disobeyed."

"You shot me!" the doctor yelled his fury unabated. He was holding his injured arm as if to quell the pain. "You could have killed me!"

"I could have killed you if I'd wanted to. I also could have crippled you. I chose to do neither," the young stocky policewoman stated matter-of-factly. "That man is dangerous. He has already tried to kill one man. I'm not giving him the chance to kill another."

"She's a lunatic!" the man on the floor screamed. "I was just giving the guy his medication. Hey, you, Nurse, check the chart."

The young blonde nurse he indicated with a nod of his head stepped back into the room.

Stephanie didn't take her eyes off the man on the floor when she spoke. "No one come any closer."

The nurse hesitated. Stephanie tipped her head sideways and the nurse stepped back.

Stephanie spoke into the radio mike attached to her shoulder strap. "Sergeant, could you put on your siren. These people need to know you're coming."

The wail of several sirens pierced the thin window glass despite the fact that the room was on the third floor.

The man on the floor moved a hand and Stephanie glared at him.

"Going for one in the chest, are you?" she said coldly.

He looked into her eyes. There was no fear there. Where had she learned that?

His moving hand rejoined its fellow. The group stood in silence until two uniformed officers cleared a path for a man in plainclothes.

Stephanie didn't relinquish control despite the fact that the one in street clothes was Lieutenant Greg Lim.

Stephanie nodded at the bleeding man, "Sergeant Chang, search him, cuff him and stay with him while the doctor takes care of him."

"Al," Lieutenant Lim added, "Go with Chang."

Two more officers appeared. They were sent to find Zack Stevenson.

While a nurse set up a new IV for Varrieur, Stephanie told Lim what had happened.

"Why didn't you believe him when he said he was a nurse?" Lim asked.

"He didn't check the chart first," Stephanie replied.

"Why shoot him?"

"I had to disable him so I could pull out the IV."

"There'll be an investigation."

"Am I suspended?" Stephanie asked.

"No," Lim said. "I need you."

It was a simple statement of fact but Stephanie felt as if she'd been praised.

"If Zack is down, we're going to be really short," she said.

"Before he left for Granite County," Lim reported, "Chief McLean arranged for Sheriff Hobbs of Sage County to work with us. We will turn over the syringe and coffee to his lab for analysis."

"And my collar?" Stephanie asked.

"He is still your collar," Lim said. "Sheriff Hobbs will send a deputy over to relieve you."

"Suppose Varrieur wakes up?" Stephanie queried. "Don't we want someone here? And shouldn't there be two? He is the key to the whole mystery. He had visitors earlier. He'll have more. I'm sure of it."

Lim grew thoughtful. Stephanie Brandt waited for him to speak. His silence meant he was weighing what she said.

"I will send Chang up," Lim announced. "There should be two."

"Tell him to stay away from the hospital's coffee," Stephanie joshed. "I hear it's murder on the stomach."

# Chapter 42

The four men that had gathered around the governor's desk in the Ardilla campaign headquarters were tired and edgy. Saturday night had come and gone and they were now eating up the early hours of Sunday morning. None had slept since the shredded paper crisis exploded in their faces.

Everett Cox reported first. Despite having been at the hospital most of the day, he appeared unwrinkled and clean-shaven. He had waited hours, hoping for a moment of lucid conversation with Varrieur, but the injured man had not regained consciousness. He'd left when Varrieur had slipped into an even deeper coma and the chances were nearly nil that he'd ever open his eyes again.

Governor Atkins said that he'd called the group Varrieur's represented and been told they had hired a private investigator and that he had discovered that police had evidence that the car that struck Varrieur had swerved over onto the grassy shoulder and there was no evidence that brakes had been applied.

Atkins finished his input by telling the group he'd called Captain Dick Chattaway and asked for his help.

"That old fart?" Cox objected. "His brains left with his hair."

Caleb ran his hand across his thinning crop before he cut in. He dipped his chin and said quietly, "Captain Chattaway has always been cooperative."

"Don't you want the would-be-killer found?" Cox charged. "Because if you do, Chattaway will bungle it."

Brian Harvath intervened. "It's not his case. What we want from him is access to Varrieur's place of business in Manzanita."

"Oh," Cox said in the voice of a small boy.

"Why the Manzanita Home?" Frank Whiting asked, his rumpled brow matching his suit, "He has others."

"We figure that's where the negatives are," Harvath replied.

"Why not at his home?"

"And have his wife stumble on them?" Harvath shot back. "The photo was taken in Manzanita. It was delivered to the governor at a fund raiser here in Ardilla. We think the negatives are in the area."

His forehead deeply wrinkled with concern, Cox pursued the matter. "And you want the Manzanita Police to search for them?"

"Don't be stupid!" Atkins exploded. "We don't want Chattaway to investigate."

"Then why..."

"Chattaway's got this rivalry going with Chief McLean of Ardilla," Atkins explained in a calmer tone after a warning glance from Harvath, "I've heard rumors that McLean is ambitious. He wants a unified force working Ardilla, Newell and Manzanita. Chattaway is depending on his political connections to keep this from happening."

"What's he going to be able to do? It's not his case."

"Pave the way for the private investigator to search Varrieur's establishment in Manzanita."

"Without a warrant?"

"Chattaway is a master at that sort of shenanigans," Harvath put in.

"He'll mess up the investigation."

"The private investigator isn't going to mess up anything," Atkins responded hotly. "Neither the people Varrieur represents nor anyone on my staff had anything to do with this attack, but Varrieur has certain records..."

Harvath cut in sharply, "Photographs, you mean, Sir. Not records, but a photograph or maybe even several photographs of your indiscretion. That's all the P.I. is going there to find. Discovery of copies of the photograph and the negatives that would point a finger in the governor's direction. If that happened, it would cost us the election."

"But, by our asking Captain Chattaway for help, aren't we, in effect, pointing at ourselves?" Cox persisted, his mind racing through all the negatives.

"We told him we're doing a favor for a close friend of Varrieur. We told him the governor would consider it a personal favor."

"And he bought it?" Cox asked, his dark eyebrows rising slightly.

Harvath smiled and his square face lost its stern appearance. "As I said, he believes he's going to need a favor."

"And did he find anything?" Cox asked.

"He's there right now," Harvath said.

"Why did he wait?"

"There was a funeral at three and two rooms were set up for viewing until ten," Harvath explained. "It was a matter of discretion."

"He'll be turning lights on," Cox said.

Harvath smiled again. "Happens all the time." Frank Whiting combed his bushy hair with his hands and leaned forward. He was anxious to proceed. He had good news.

When Cox leaned back, Whiting jumped in. "The bullets don't match. But, then, you know that. The Ardilla Police still refuse to release the original tape."

"They can't refuse," Cox said.

"Landecker hasn't been arraigned yet," Whiting added.

"I thought we had clout in San Francisco," Cox put in.

"Ardilla is pushing to have him arraigned in Oakland first," Whiting said. "Assault on a police officer. He rammed an Ardilla squad car in Oakland. It's a delaying tactic, but it won't work. Oakland is willing to cooperate. They want the press to stay camped on San Francisco's doorstep."

"Why's Ardilla delaying the arraignment?" Cox asked.

"Because the DA in San Francisco is planning to take a plea and the Ardilla police are pissed," Whiting replied. "Landecker will plead guilty to misdemeanor hit and run. He says the two people were okay when he checked. He's sticking to his story that gunshots scared him off. The evidence the cop was supposedly transporting wasn't found in Landecker's car. As for his gun having been fired recently, Landecker claims that, when he heard gunshots, he fired his weapon as a warning and that someone else, as he put it, 'pumped lead into the cop'."

"And you believe him?" Cox asked incredulously.

"I think he's got a pretty good argument," Whiting said. "The bullets bear him out."

"And the tape?"

"Landecker's attorney says it's ambiguous. He thinks he may even get it excluded."

"On what grounds?"

"It might prejudice the jury."

Cox fell back in his chair aghast. He knew what had happened without really knowing a thing. This whole affair was becoming distasteful. A little sexual indiscretion he could forgive. It tarnished the governor's image in his eyes, but no man is without fault. But the group appeared to be overreacting to this whole thing. You don't shoot a cop over something like this.

Harvath noticed Cox's distressed look and turned to Whiting. "What did Landecker say about ramming the police car in Oakland?"

"He claims it was an accident and he was trying to catch up to him to explain and the cop ran away."

"He chased him though, didn't he?" Harvath asked, anticipating Cox's question.

"He says he was worried about being arrested later and figured he'd better clear things up right away," Whiting replied.

"So what do you see him ending up with?" Harvath pressed.

"All tolled–reckless driving, leaving the scene of an accident and discharging a firearm within city limits."

Everett Cox's beeper beeped and he excused himself to answer it. When he was out of earshot, Harvath said to Whiting. "Your friend appears a bit shaken."

"He'll be okay. It'll just take him a while to get used to the idea that politics gets its toes muddy. I think the articles in the Oakland Journal..."

Cox burst into the room. "Someone tried to kill Varrieur at the hospital. They've arrested the man."

"Cox," Harvath said. "Go down and monitor the situation."

"As his lawyer?" Cox asked pointedly. His brow was again smooth, his tone, however, carried a touch of sarcasm.

Harvath's response was immediate, "Hell, no! He's not one of ours. We just need to know where the cops are in their investigation."

"I can tell you where they are," Whiting interjected. "With this second attempt the case moves from hit and run to attempted murder. They'll head for Varrieur's office to look for a motive."

"Should we warn the P.I.?" Cox asked.

"No need," Harvath replied calmly. "He's with the Manzanita Police Chief. He's covered."

"Suppose he hasn't found what he's looking for?" Cox persisted, his negative vibes overwhelming him.

"Then there's nothing there to be found," Harvath assured the nervous young lawyer and with him the governor who'd begun pacing.

Cox inserted one last thought. "Suppose he overlooked it?"

"Then so will the police," Harvath replied with confidence. He turned to Whiting. "Frank, go with him. It may take two of you to keep tabs on this one."

As soon as the younger men were out of earshot Atkins turned to his chief political advisor. "What about the three thorns in my side?"

"The second attempt failed."

"I thought those men were pros."

"McLean is too."

"Tell me the men doing this know how to get around McLean."

"The car is bugged. He hasn't found the bug yet."

"And they have another plan?"

"They do."

"They know it has to be an accident."

"It has to appear to be an accident," Harvath corrected. "And it's probably taking place right now."

# Chapter 43

Banner and Sandy, being uncut males, each sprayed the same two-foot-high leafless twigs jutting out from the rock strewn earth and then marked separate rocks at the outer corners of the small patch of unpaved earth deemed safe by their handlers. When the dogs were done, they drew close and wagged their tails.

At Coral's suggestion, the two dogs were put in the front to guard the car while Tara used the rest room and Coral went up to the counter to buy an ice pack for her finger which was throbbing.

It's probably too late, Coral told herself, but still she urged the counter person to make up a pack for her. She laid a large bill on the counter and ordered five sandwiches to go and three cups of coffee.

Tara joined her as the sandwiches were placed on the counter. "Who's not getting two?"

"Me," Coral replied. "Or maybe you. It depends."

The counterman capped the coffee.

"Give me one more sandwich," Tara said. "I know you, Mother. You'll eat mine."

He called an order back to the cook.

"I can't eat two!" Coral protested and the counterman looked at Tara questioningly. Tara motioned to him that they wanted one more sandwich.

"Spencer can probably manage them all. He's big enough," Tara grinned. "If not, I know a couple of dogs who'd love to share a sandwich."

Spencer poked his head inside the coffee shop door. "We have to go."

Tara handed him two wrapped sandwiches and a cup of coffee. "We're waiting..."

"Now!" he said holding open the door with his foot.

Tara scooped up the other three sandwiches with her good hand and tucked them into her sling. Coral handed her one of the two cups of coffee and shouted at the counterman to keep the change, then grabbed her ice pack with her splinted hand and wrapped the fingers of her good hand around the remaining Styrofoam container of coffee.

"What about your other sandwich?" the man shouted as Coral exited.

"It's yours," McLean shouted as he pulled out his foot and let the door close.

"Why the rush?" Tara asked.

"The cop is leaving. We need to be right behind him so they'll follow him when he turns off the road up ahead."

"We have to move the dogs into their crates," Tara said.

"No time!" McLean said as he hurried around to the driver's side and fearlessly scooted Banner out of his seat and into the back. Tara climbed in simultaneously and Sandy was also shooed into the back.

As McLean turned the key in the ignition, the counterman rushed up and waved the wrapped sandwich at him. McLean lowered his window and reached for it. The car began to move forward.

"Your change," the counterman said digging into his pocket.

"Keep it!" McLean yelled as he passed the sandwich to Tara who was struggling to fasten her seat belt.

All three heard his shout of thanks.

By the time the minivan caught up to the patrol car, the Styrofoam cups were firmly entrenched in their holders, the seat belts were fastened and the dogs had been ordered to lay down and had done so. Together the two vehicles pulled onto the frontage road and from there onto the freeway.

The night air was fresh and McLean found that it revived him. He decided to leave the window open until someone asked him to close it.

The dogs sat up and Banner tucked his head next to McLean's left shoulder and let the wind blow his ears back. Sandy tried to squeeze in beside him, but Banner wouldn't let him so Sandy rested his yellow head on McLean's other shoulder and contented himself with staring out the windshield.

Before Spencer McLean could complain, Coral unwrapped her sandwich, and Sandy's head came off Spencer's shoulder and lowered onto Coral's arm. There it stayed with his eyes fixed on every movement of her hand to her mouth.

Tara unwrapped a sandwich and handed half of it to McLean, and he eagerly chomped down on it. Banner's tongue crept around McLean's ear and gently licked his cheek. After two more bites, McLean slipped the remains into the mouth of the dog drooling on his left shoulder.

Sandy immediately knew that Banner had been fed. He scrambled to the other shoulder of the food dispenser and waited for his portion. Coral tugged on his leash and scolded him.

"You can't bother the driver," she said speaking to Sandy as if he understood. "Especially now."

The downgrade was long and winding. A roadside sign announced a runaway truck off-ramp five miles ahead. The off- ramp was a wide road of sand deep enough to stop a huge, hurtling mass without killing the driver. It was not uncommon to see a truck buried in the middle of the sand pit.

Too much weight, too steep a descent and too long a downgrade were murder on brakes. While cars overheated going up, brakes on trucks failed coming down.

Coral glanced around. There were no trucks in sight. In fact, the road behind them was empty save for one lone set of headlights that appeared to be gaining on them. Just one.

She settled back into her seat and took another bite out of her sandwich.

The mood inside the minivan was relaxed. Conversation was minimal. All three were busy eating. It had been hours since any of them had had anything but coffee. Their stomachs had long since forgotten the burgers and fries they'd shared at the Sheriff's office.

They had escaped two narrow brushes with death. The resulting emotional roller coaster had drained them all of energy. They were hungry.

The minivan's headlights shone against the shiny steel rails at the shoulder's edge. The moonlight told Coral that they were rounding the side of one of the mountains in Tehachapi range and that they were closer to the top of it than the bottom. The moonlight outlined its companion in dark gray against a darker gray sky. Between the road they were on and the nearest mountain top was a black void. Only the steel rails separated the road from the void.

She wondered briefly how strong the wooden posts holding the lengths of corrugated steel were. Could a car pierce the barricade? Could a truck? What if a minivan hit one? Would it crumble as if it had hit a solid brick wall? Would it break in half and the weight of the top half carry the bottom over the edge to the chasm below? Or would it tear the rail in two as a runner tears a tape at the finish line?

Sandy nudged Coral's elbow and pushed one hand into the other.

A small yip escaped from Coral's lips. It was followed quickly by a sharp scold and the two in the front who had begun to turn at the sound, straightened themselves out.

Tara turned a few seconds later at the sound of Sandy smacking his lips. She began to scold her mother as McLean flicked his rear view mirror up to avoid the glare of the bright beams of the car approaching from the rear.

"Mother, you didn't reward him!"

Coral came back instantly in defense of her action.

"I did it right. I made him wait."

"For two seconds!" Tara said sharply.

The headlights disappeared as the white paneled truck moved around to the left to pass. McLean held up his arm to shield his eyes from the reflection in his side mirror.

Banner turned and sniffed Coral's hand as he straddled Sandy who was lying with his head in Coral's lap.

"Stop that!" Coral ordered. "Go back and stick your head out the window."

As she said that, the truck pulled even with the minivan and through the open front window of the truck, Coral saw a gun barrel pointed at McLean.

"Gun!" she shouted. Her hands reached out toward her dogs as two shots were fired. She pulled the dogs toward her and fell across them.

McLean grabbed his arm. The Voyager swerved and its rear end sideswiped the paneled truck.

Moving quickly to the left, the truck sped away.

The jarring as the two vehicles collided brought Coral's head up. She squinted her eyes trying to get a license plate number.

Meanwhile, the Voyager headed toward the steel barrier and the blackness beyond. Tara bent over to unsnap her camera case. She was confident McLean would be able to handle things despite being shot. After all, she had. What they needed was a picture of the van that rammed them.

McLean fought the wheel as his foot pumped the brake. The car didn't slow down at all. In fact it seemed to accelerate. The Voyager careened across four lanes before McLean, with the tires screeching, navigated a change in direction away from the sheer rock wall that lined the left side of the highway. He struggled to keep the minivan in the center lane.

"You're weaving all over the place," Tara remarked.

"Am I?" McLean queried, his words sluggish. "Must'va been something I ate."

"This isn't funny," Tara snapped as the big man maneuvered a turn using three lanes. "You're driving horribly."

"I can't understand..." he started to say before he struggled to focus on moving the accelerating minivan toward a center lane.

"For heaven's sake, slow down!" Tara yelled.

"Can't."

Tara stomped her foot on top of his. The Voyager didn't respond.

"I'm so woozy," McLean said softly.

Coral unsnapped her seat belt and leaned forward. "What do you mean?"

"Those bullets," McLean whispered. "Poisoned."

"What should we do?" Coral asked.

"A tourniquet," McLean said as his hand slipped off the wheel. The Voyager moved right across two lanes. Tara grabbed the wheel with one hand and shoved it up and away.

The next half mile was a straight stretch. In the ensuing fraction of a minute Tara held the wheel steady while she reached over with her injured arm and turned off the ignition.

"We'll lose control!" Coral objected as she saw her daughter turn the key.

"Hurry with that tourniquet!" Tara yelled, her panic rising.

Coral grabbed Banner, unsnapped his lead and crawled toward the open window to the left of McLean.

The Voyager lurched to the right and Coral who was threading the leather leash under Spencer McLean's arm was thrown against the side and when Tara jerked the wheel to correct the excessive reaction, Coral's broken finger fell against McLean's arm. A scream of agony escaped from her as pain shot through her like a jolt of electricity.

"My God!" she cried. It was an exclamation. Almost a vainglorious use of the precious name. But it was also a prayer uttered from deep within. Everything she held dear was in this car with her. Everything was speeding down the freeway toward oblivion.

Her hands pulled the ends of the leash together and tied them tight. Banner nudged her. She glanced back at him. In his mouth was her pen-sized flashlight.

"How did you know?" she whispered. She slipped it under the leather leash, twisted it several times and tucked it under the leather strap.

"We're going to drive onto the truck runaway ramp," Tara announced. "It's just around the next bend."

"Will it stop us?"

"Crouch down," Tara ordered.

Coral looked at the dogs. Banner was standing.

"Down," the older woman yelled and Banner folded his legs beneath him and laid down beside Sandy.

Tara struggled to keep the car in the right-hand lane, but the minivan drifted left. One arm–even a strong uninjured arm–maneuvering at an angle wasn't powerful enough. The off-ramp was only a quarter of a mile ahead.

Tara released the wheel and reached across it. Her fingers pulled the steering wheel position lever and the steering wheel moved upward. Then she scooted from her seat and squeezed onto McLean's lap. There was no need for her feet to reach the brakes. They weren't functioning.

She slid her injured arm close to the wheel and grabbed it with that hand. She grimaced as the pain from gripping the wheel shot through her body. With two hands on the wheel, Tara moved quickly back into the right lane.

Sitting on top of McLean raised her head so high that it brushed the ceiling. She dipped it forward to look out the windshield.

With the turnoff only a couple hundred yards ahead, Tara decided that she couldn't be this bent over on impact, so she reached down and released the seat lock. The seat didn't move. There was too much jammed on the floor behind it.

"Oh, God!" she breathed. "Help us please."

Coral, her hand still holding the flashlight pen in place, fearful of letting go because she wasn't certain it would hold, saw the speed with which the Voyager was approaching the turnoff and a surge of panic caused her to let go of the tourniquet and throw herself down beside her dogs. As she did so her knee sank into the space between two of the trophy boxes crushing the side of one and moving the other. At that moment, Tara tried again to push back on the seat. It gave way, moved backward and locked into the last notch.

The looming turnoff sucked Tara's thoughts away from the pain in her arm and dragged them deep into an undertow of fear. She jammed her feet down on McLean's boots and braced herself as she turned the wheel. Both arms responded as one and the dark green Voyager left the freeway and headed into an unlighted stretch of sand.

A spray of sand flew in through the open window and Tara, momentarily blinded, froze in place with the steering wheel still slightly turned. Her eyes smarted as they automatically teared to clear themselves. Tara fought the urge to let go of the wheel and rub the grit from her eyes.

Together the lack of power driving the tires, the loss of the momentum provided by the descending roadway and the lack of firmness in the sand slowed the spin of the tires. The drag of the sand on the undercarriage of the wide vehicle stopped it as swiftly as dirt does a sled at the end of an icy run down a hill.

Despite the fact that Tara was tightly wedged into the front seat, her head flew forward and, because she was so high, hit the padded sunshade above the windshield rather than the glass. It was a solid, albeit slightly softer, bump.

Spencer McLean's head followed the motion of Tara's body forward and his nose smashed into the base of her neck before being thrown backwards against the seat rest.

With the weight of the passengers on the left and the wheels cocked slightly to the right, the minivan's rear slid to the left shoving the sand before it as it plowed to a stop.

Tara let out sigh of relief. "We're stopped."

Coral thanked God aloud and sat up.

Tara pulled up on her door handle. She poked her head out the window. The sand had sealed it shut.

Undaunted, she pulled herself through the window. She wondered why the air bag hadn't engaged and then figured that it must've been because the van stopped at an angle. It hadn't run head on into anything.

She slid down to the ground, extending both hands in front of her to break her fall. The sand wasn't soft like mud and hitting it jolted her sore arm and the pain that stabbed her stunned her.

She sat up and looked out past the headlights into the darkness. Ahead she saw only sand and a huge concrete barrier.

"Glad we didn't run into that," she murmured.

"Are you alright?" Came a voice from inside the car.

Tara climbed into a wobbly stand and peered into the dark interior. She reached inside the window and turned on the inside lights.

In the back Coral was holding her hand with the broken finger above her head while the dogs scrambled to right themselves.

"How's Spencer?" Coral asked.

Tara looked down at him and her eyes focused on the two holes in his arm.

"Still out, Mom," Tara said. She squatted down and looked at the wounds.

"What is it?" Coral asked.

"They aren't bleeding right."

"What's right?"

"Give me my flashlight," Tara said. "And dig the tweezers out of my bag."

Coral leaned between the bucket seats and retrieved the flashlight, protesting as she did so that she hoped Tara wasn't planning to mess with Spencer's arm.

"He said poison, Mother," Tara replied.

"He's got a police radio," Coral said. "We can call for help."

Tara ignored her mother's suggestion and proceeded to explain the dilemma she perceived.

"The minute I release the tourniquet, more will flood his system."

"Taking out the bullet won't help that," Coral argued. "Whatever was on the tip has already been absorbed."

"Where's my tweezers?" Tara demanded.

"You could do permanent damage," Coral cautioned as she reached out to retrieve Tara's purse from the floor in front.

Tara's camera strap was tangled with the shoulder strap and Coral began to extract both when Tara asked, "Do we still have that snakebite kit?"

"It's in the map storage drawer," Coral puffed, her body sprawled across the passenger seat.

Tara directed the beam of the flashlight directly into the depression in McLean's arm. "I can see it, Mother!"

"Really.   It's that shallow?" Coral grunted reaching below the seat and opening the drawer tucked beneath it.

"Just a little cut and I can pull it out like a sliver," Tara said excitedly.

Coral took the kit from the drawer.  She pulled several clean plastic bags from the box nestled beside the kit and opened the one with plastic gloves inside.

"Here," she said, handing the disposable plastic gloves to her daughter.  "I never thought I'd use these for anything other than cleaning up after the dogs."

"I still need the tweezers," Tara said donning the gloves. She winced as she used her injured arm to pull the glove onto her other hand and added, "And I will need your help."

"I'm looking for the tweezers," Coral said, dragging Tara's purse and camera onto her lap.

"Mother, quick!   Hand me the knife.   And hold the flashlight so I can see."

Coral shoved the purse aside and opened the snakebite kit.  She handed Tara the small knife.

"Are you sure you can do this?" Coral asked as she held the light where Tara pointed. "You're right-handed like me."

"The tweezers, Mother!" Tara demanded.

Coral picked up the purse with the three working fingers of her injured hand and dumped its contents onto the seat beside her leg. She scattered the items, careful to keep the splint elevated. Banner gingerly rose and bent over the display. Coral brushed him away with her elbow. Sandy thrust his nose between her and the contents and she told him to 'leave it' and continued to toss aside irrelevant matter.

Coral tossed Tara's leather wallet to one side and Sandy nosed it. When Coral didn't tell him to leave it, he picked it up, squeezed his body down in the farthest corner away from Coral, put the wallet between his paws and thoughtfully began to chew on one corner. Banner took the leather covered checkbook as his prize, folded down in place and began licking it.

Coral was simply grateful that the dogs were occupied. Now was the wrong time for them to nudge her. Tara would have to deal with the damage later.

The next time Tara asked, Coral slapped the tweezers in her hand.

"Do you have a plastic bag, Mom?"

"Right here," Coral smiled. "I know he'll want to examine the bullet later."

She opened the bag with her three working fingers and held it out.

Tara dropped something solid inside. Coral began to draw the bag toward herself for a better look.

"Keep it there," Tara said. "There's one more."

"Two in the same hole," Coral exclaimed. "That's lucky."

"Two holes," Tara corrected. "One to go."

Coral gasped. "You're going to cut him twice?"

"Just like going after two slivers, Mom," Tara said. "Ever wonder why they didn't shoot him in the head?"

Before Coral could answer, Tara dropped a second pellet into the bag.

"Seal it, Mom. And hand me the spray bottle."

Coral zipped the bag shut and protested that the spray bottle only contained water.

"Bottled water, right?"

Coral set down the small plastic bag and reached beneath the blanket and grabbed hold of the handles of the cloth carrying bag and yanked it onto the seat beside her. She extracted the spray bottle used to mist the dogs' faces and tongues before taking them into the ring.

"It's not really sterile," Coral protested anew as she handed over the bottle. "And it is not an antiseptic."

Tara held open the wounds with her fingers and sprayed water into them until blood flowed out with the water.

"What are you doing?"

"Cleaning out the rest of the junk, I hope," Tara said.

"It's been absorbed," Coral reiterated.

"Look at what's in the bag," Tara said.

Coral lifted the small bag up into the light.

"Ice, Mom," Tara said. "He was shot with ice bullets. One hundred percent whatever poison they used."

"Why not just shoot him? Poison would show up on an autopsy as surely as any bullet," Coral said. Her voice trailed off as she began to put together the pieces.

"They didn't shoot him in the head," Coral began talking to no one in particular–she assumed that her daughter had already finished the puzzle, "because that would be murder and they wanted this to look like an accident. So they shot him in the arm with bullets that melt leaving two strange wounds that would remain unexplained if they were even noticed after we crashed."

"I agree they just wanted to knock him out," Tara added. "The car would go out of control and even if we managed to get control of the wheel, no brakes on the downhill side of the Grapevine is certain death."

"They had it all planned out," Coral said.

"But, we had help they didn't count on," Tara replied.

"So, are we safe?" Coral asked tentatively. She handed Tara the flashlight and scrunched over and extracted McLean's radio from his belt and proceeded to call for help.

When she finished, she sat high on her heels and said, "There, now I feel better."

"But I don't," Tara commented. "I feel worse."

"It's just that your body hasn't settled down," Coral told her daughter. "Your adrenaline is still pumping."

"It's not that. Quick, Mother, unbuckle McLean. We've got to get him out of the van."

"The paramedics can do it better than two one-armed women," Coral retorted, but Tara was already in front of the headlights heading for the other side.

Coral yanked a lead from the dog bag and snapped it on Banner's collar. Her daughter meant to open the door. She stuffed the plastic bag in the empty purse, then picked up the cell phone and dropped it in.

She looked at Banner who was happily chewing on Tara's leather checkbook. She held out her hand and Banner dropped his treasure into it. Then Coral reached for Sandy's leash.

Tara, who'd crossed in front of the headlights, was now searching the far side of the ledge they were perched on.

Coral bade the yellow dog to give up his treasure. Sandy did so with reluctance and Coral dropped the gooey leather wallet into the purse next to the checkbook.

The side door was pulled back and Tara leaned inside. "You'll have to help me."

The dogs crowded on either side of her, pushing to get out.

"Quick," Tara added. "Give me my purse and a couple of bumpers."

Coral reached on the shelf beside the crate and pulled out two yellow-green bumpers with purple rope attached and shoved them out the door. Tara threw open the door and both dogs leaped out. They followed her as she ran toward a huge rock outcropping. Tara set her purse and the camera whose strap was still intertwined with the purse strap on the ground near the rock. She ordered Banner and Sandy to lay down. Then she put down the bumpers and told the dogs to stay. Both heads went down.

Tara spun on her heel and bumped into her mother carrying a can of dog biscuits, Tara's laptop and a cardboard box.

Coral set the items down beside the purse.

"What was in the box?" Tara asked as the two ran back to the minivan.

"The Winner's trophy and the ribbons. If the car's going to explode...well..."

"Who said it was going to explode?"

"I thought that's what..."

"You think I would have left you?"

"Well, I didn't, that is I didn't think the car was going to explode so I thought I wouldn't waste a trip."

"You're making no sense. Waste a trip? What does that mean? I told you I'd be right back," Tara retorted as she bent down and scooped sand away from the bottom of the van door.

Coral squatted down to help her. "You never come back as quickly as you imagine you're going to."

The small scoops of sand Tara was brushing away flew into her mother's face.

"We're getting nowhere," Tara said. "What about that other trophy. Wasn't it a bowl?"

"You're not going to use the perpetual trophy to scoop sand," Coral gasped.

"Mom, why do you object to everything I want to do?" Tara grumbled.

Annoyed, Coral pulled the blanket off the back seat and threw it on the ground. She pulled out the box with the trophy in it. She took the trophy out and set it down and handed her daughter the cardboard box.

"Use this!" she ordered as she tucked the engraved trophy under her arm and started over toward the place where the dogs lay.

Tara shouted at the retreating figure. Her voice was full of alarm. "Where are you going?"

Coral set down the bowl halfway between the minivan and where the dogs lay watching and rushed back.

"Why are we panicking?"

"Because they have backup," Tara replied.

"Who has?"

Tara tugged at the front door on the passenger's side and it opened. The opening was too small to pull a man through.

Coral crawled through the side door and pushed Mclean down onto the passenger's seat in preparation for pulling him out. Tara set her feet on the running board and bracing her back against the door, pushed. The door gave slightly. She picked up the box and resumed scooping.

Coral moved farther back into the depths of the van, leaned over the driver's seat and turned off the headlights. The inside lights shone like a beacon. She turned them off as well.

Only the moonlight was left.

Tara stood up, positioned herself again inside the door and pushed. Again the door gave a little.

The sound of a helicopter approaching propelled Tara into using all her strength to push the door again.

Coral scrambled out of the car. "Help has arrived!" she shouted waving her flashlight.

Tara grabbed the flashlight and threw it into the car.

"Grab an arm!" she yelled. "They aren't the good guys."

The panic in Tara's voice was contagious. Coral ran around Tara and grabbed the big man's injured arm. Tara had already moved him so that his head hung out the door. The two pulled. The body was heavy but fear strengthened both women and McLean slid out onto the sand as the helicopter, its searchlight circling the canyon below, drew near.

"Hurry," Tara breathed. McLean's feet hit the sand and Tara reached behind her and slammed the side door shut. Following suit, Coral reached over and pushed the front door shut.

Unexpectedly, the helicopter turned away.

Coral stopped when the helicopter veered away.

"It's gone," she said. "Let's do this right."

"We have to hurry!" Tara shouted. "They'll be back!"

Coral picked up the blanket and spread it out next to McLean.

"This'll be faster," she stated firmly.

Tara decided not to argue.

Together they lifted McLean's shoulders onto the blanket and each picked up an end of the blanket and wrapped it around an arm. They hurried across the sand onto the hardpan at the edge. Both were breathing hard.

Coral stopped and Tara immediately worried that her mother's heart was acting up. Then Coral plucked the silver bowl from the rocky ground and set it upside down on McLean's chest and urged her daughter to get a move on.

As she did so, the helicopter turned and headed back. It homed in on the dim light of Coral's flashlight emanating from the interior of the darkened van.

"Behind that big rock," Tara urged, her fear rising.

As they passed the dogs, each woman simultaneously reached for the leash of her dog. Banner instantly gathered the two bumpers into his mouth while Sandy's eyes lit on the purse with the leather chews inside. He snatched it up as he passed. The camera came with it. The computer was brushed off the top of the other trophy box and fell behind it.

The light from above lit up the stalled car and slowly moved into the area around it. It picked up the torn cardboard box near it and another old box a dozen yards away alongside a big round can. The laptop lay in the shadow behind the box.

The women crouched low behind a wall of rock, each hugging a dog.  The light lit up the outer surface of the rock outcropping, leaving them in the dark shadow between it and the granite cliff wall.

Tara threw Sandy's lead over her mother's arm.  Coral grabbed it as Tara stood up, camera in hand.

"What are you doing?" Coral hissed.

Tara moved to the other side of the outer rock wall and when the chopper light moved past her location, she popped her head up, the camera at eye level, and snapped a picture.

The helicopter hovered over the minivan and Tara snapped another shot.  The moonlight revealed an open door and the shadow of a man sitting beside it.

As the helicopter wavered, the faint light from the moon touched the barrel of the rifle pointed down at the minivan. The glint caught Tara's eye and she snapped a picture.

The sharp crack of the rifle startled both women.  Tara's finger shot another picture.  Coral clutched both dogs tighter.

The shot from the helicopter was well placed.  As the siren from an approaching police car neared, the minivan exploded bathing the entire area in bright light.

The helicopter slowly moved away.

Coral sucked in a lungful of air and held it as the power of the explosion hurled flaming bits of debris in all directions.  Tara's finger recorded the entire sequence.

Metal fragments sailed toward the rock shield behind which the group huddled.  One piece hit the metal can of dog biscuits with such force, the top popped off and a shower of biscuits exploded onto the ground.

Banner and Sandy strained to reach them. Fear gave Coral the strength to restrain the dogs. It was still raining flaming debris.

A new noise caught Tara's attention and she turned from the mesmerizing fire consuming her car.

"Mom, Spencer's breathing has changed," Tara reported, her voice tightening with apprehension. They couldn't lose him now.

Her mother looked at the man lying tucked partway under the overhang of the rock outcropping. "It's deep and fast. Maybe he's coming around."

"It's happened before," Tara said. "Once when I was cutting his arm and once when we were pulling him out of the car. He didn't wake up either of those times. And he's gotten really cold and clammy."

"He's in shock," the older woman surmised.

Suddenly, Spencer stopped breathing. A siren announced the fast approach of a patrol car.

Tara reached down and tugged at the blanket. Coral guessed she wanted him in the light so she grabbed the other corner of the blanket. Together, they dragged the big man into the unshielded area on the other side of the rock.

The leashes slipped from Coral's hand as the squad's headlights lit up the back wall and the two dogs raced toward the scattered dog biscuits, hugging the inside edge of the huge boulder. The headlights swung toward the burning car as the dogs exited onto the open ground and rapidly began downing the scattered baked bones one after the other. Their movement was caught by the flashing lights but when the driver of the patrol car glanced back, with their heads and tails down, the dogs appeared to be merely a couple of large rocks.

He turned off the siren but left the flashers on. Then he climbed out of his car and put his headset to his ear.

At that moment, Tara lifted her head from McLean's chest and sighed. "He's breathing."

Coral looked around. "Where are the dogs?"

Tara pointed to the other side of the rock. "Where else?"

Coral hurried to fetch them as Tara made her way across the rocky slope toward the man in the tan uniform who was speaking into his headset. His words floated back to her.

"No way anyone's alive," he said.

Tara was about to shout a correction, when she heard him say something that stopped her cold.

"How many shell casings am I looking for?"

# Chapter 44

Stunned, Tara stopped dead in her tracks. Her camera continued to swing back and forth until she caught the strap in her hand. She was totally exposed, a mere twelve feet away, too far from the rock to seek shelter behind it, too close to be missed when the cop turned around.

Slowly, she sank into a squat, her good hand searching the ground for a loose rock as her eyes stayed focused on the tan uniform. The camera strap slipped from her shoulder and the camera slid to the ground.

The fist-sized rocks were imbedded in the hard clay. Her fingernails weren't strong enough to trowel any loose. She looked around. Her eyes were gone from the man but a few moments.

She pinned him with her ears.

She heard him close off his conversation with the helicopter and radio for the fire brigade. She heard a loud crackling sound which she realized was someone shouting at the officer. In the distance she heard the wail of the approaching fire engines. Someone had called them.

"It's contained," the man replied hastily. "I was looking for survivors. I didn't..."

As he spoke, he turned to survey the area again. His eyes swept past the fire to his right. He stopped turning when he saw Tara.

She looked up when he clicked off his radio mid-sentence. The hairs on the back of her neck told her she'd been spotted, so, as she lifted her head, she slowly rose. The camera strap traveled down her arm and she took hold of the end of it with her bare hand.

The man in the tan uniform unbuckled his holster as he moved slowly around the car. Tara's mouth went dry and the words stuck halfway between her mind and her lips. She watched him withdraw the gun from his holster and raise it.

Tara, having never looked down the barrel of a gun, froze, her words of protest still lodged in her throat. Her body gave her away.

"So you heard," he said. "I thought so."

The deep wail of the approaching fire engine told Tara she would be dead before it rounded the bend. Then he would kill her mother.

That thought catapulted her into action. The words burst from her throat.

"Banner, here!" she shouted.

The black dog bolted. The leash flew from Coral's grasp and the big black dog ran toward Tara.

The cop kept his gun leveled.

"Won't work," he chortled.

Then a high-pitched feminine voice shouted, "Sandy, back!"

The cop turned his head and saw two dogs racing toward him. He swung his gun around and fired a warning shot.

The bullet split the small rock it hit and sent pebbles flying. Undeterred, both dogs stayed on course.

As he raised his gun, Tara's left hand tightened its grip on the camera strap as her arm swung it back like a golf club. It was the forward motion and the twist of her body that made the camera hit the side of the cop's head with a force strong enough to break his jaw and knock him out. His finger squeezed the trigger as he went down and the bullet sailed over the heads of the two dogs and hit Coral dead center. The slender gray-haired woman clutched her chest and folded silently to the ground. Tara, whose attention was on the approaching dogs, missed the end result of the stray shot.

She checked the fallen cop and then praised her dogs. Quickly she took her camera out of its case and snapped pictures of the uniformed man lying on the ground, the gun still in his hand.

She snapped his face from several directions and then she stepped back to get a picture of the whole scene as the fire engine turned off the freeway and moved alongside the sand pit.

Tara scrambled back ordering her dogs to heel.

She picked up their leashes and she looked around for her mother. She saw Coral sitting against the rock wall, and with the dogs in tow, she moved toward her.

She's fainted, Tara concluded. She raised her camera and snapped a picture.

We'll laugh about this later, she thought.

Then something about her position sent a chill of fear down Tara's spine. Her stomach flipped and her heart began to race. She knew before she knelt down next to her exactly where that second bullet had wound up.

The fire engine roared to a stop and men began pouring out of it.

"Over here!" she shouted. "He shot my mother!"

A man was at her side by the time the last word was out of Tara's mouth.

The fire chief dispatched a man to check on the chief whom Tara pointed out and another to see to the patrolman. When the reports came in, the fire chief called for a helicopter. Tara, holding the two leashes tight in her hand, gave a quick explanation. "He first shot at my dogs. The first bullet is in the ground under your truck. He raised his gun to shoot again and I swung my camera and hit him and knocked him out. The gun went off at the same time and the bullet hit my mother."

"So it was an accident," the chief concluded.

Tara didn't want to tell the truth, the truth being that she had swung her purse to keep him from shooting her dogs and that the bullet had gone astray and hit her mother. Would a jury convict him of attempted murder if he claimed he was merely going to shoot a dog and her interference caused him to shoot a person? Would the fact that he had aimed the gun at her count at all?

"He was aiming in my mother's direction when I hit him," Tara said finally. "I can't say what he was trying to hit but it wasn't the ground."

"Did he see your mother?" the chief asked.

"She yelled and he looked over and that's when he started shooting."

A fireman interrupted them. "A helicopter's coming. He wants us to back up so he can land."

"I just called," the chief replied. "Must be reporters. Tell them to go away."

"He says he's the Granite County sheriff," the fireman reported.

"This isn't his county!" the fire chief exclaimed. "You tell him we're waiting for a chopper from the hospital with a medic on board."

"This woman needs to get to a hospital now!" the man attending her said. "How far away is the other chopper?"

"Ten minutes," came the answer from the man on the radio.

The man attending Coral spoke up, "She could be at the hospital in ten minutes!"

"Back up the truck!" the fire chief ordered. "And get those dogs out of here."

With Banner and Sandy in tow Tara ran behind the rock formation and huddled down. A fireman, hurrying toward McLean, kicked the silver trophy bowl aside. In the dim light, Tara saw all the things her mother had dragged from the minivan being knocked by the heavy boots of men hurrying from one victim to another.

She snatched up the discarded blanket, and as the chopper settled onto the ground reached out and snatched the silver bowl. Banner, straining at the leash rescued the bumpers while Sandy dragged the purse over. As Tara left the rock formation, she picked up her computer and the second trophy box and added them to the items stuffed in her makeshift blanket bag.

"What do you think you're doing?" the chief shouted as the helicopter settled on the ground. "Tie those dogs up. I'll call animal control."

"Leave the dogs?" Tara shouted. "No way! They're going with me."

"Then you're staying here."

The first man out of the chopper was the sheriff. He ducked his head and walked over to the group gathered behind the rock.

"How bad?" Sheriff Tolliver shouted.

"The woman's really bad," the fire chief said, motioning his men to load her into the chopper. "I don't know about the police chief."

"Haven't got enough room for everybody," Tolliver shouted.

"McLean can wait," Tara shouted. "I've got a sample of what poison is in his system in my purse. They can analyze it at the hospital and be ready to treat him when he arrives. The next helicopter is only minutes away. Leave your man to guard him and take our stuff."

The fire chief objected, "The police will want to question you."

"For heaven's sake," Tara shouted. "I'll be with the sheriff."

"Let's load up," Tolliver ordered tactically accepting Tara's plan.

Tara snatched up her purse and camera from the pile.

"Hey, you can't take those!" the fire chief yelled.

She thrust them at the sheriff.

"Sheriff Tolliver will have custody of them." Tara yelled above the noise of the whirling blades. Then putting her head down, she moved toward the door of the chopper, one dog at each side.

"Hey I told you. Animal Control takes the dogs," the fire chief shouted, running after her.

The chopper pilot turned around.

"No dogs," he said. "No room."

Sheriff Tolliver picked Banner up and plunked him down next to the stretcher. He looked at the two firemen. "One of you two get lost."

One of the firemen jumped out.

Tara climbed aboard. Sandy leaped up behind her. He stood on the quivering floor, shaking. Tara pulled the two dogs toward her and the sheriff clambered aboard and shut the door.

The helicopter rose immediately. Sandy climbed into Tara's lap and Banner crowded against her knee.

During the short ride, Tara started to tell the sheriff what had happened, but her curiosity stopped her after a few sentences.

"How did you get there so quick?"

"I was responding to your mother's call," Sheriff Tolliver said. "No matter what happened, I knew no one would believe you."

Banner rubbed against the sheriff's leg and he reached down and stroked the black head. "What are we going to do with you two when we reach the hospital?"

What indeed? Tara thought.

# Chapter 45

The solution turned out to be simpler than Tara dreamed it would be and Sheriff Tolliver came up with it automatically.

When they arrived at the helicopter pad on top of the hospital, while the medics were dashing out with a gurney, Tolliver jumped out, grabbed Banner by his midsection and lifted him down. Then stepping on the end of his leash, he scooped up Sandy and gave him a swift soft ride to the hospital roof top. He took both leads and led the dogs away from the noisy, windy area through the door. Tara watched her dogs march down the hospital corridor with the county sheriff whose demeanor brooked no questions. No one blocked his passage. Obviously, the police were removing the dogs from the hospital.

It wasn't until he was out of sight that Tara realized the sheriff had her camera and her purse. By that time she was scrambling out of the plane and racing to catch up to the gurney carrying her mother. It wasn't that her mind was on her purse or the clue to what poison had invaded McLean's body. Her mind was centered on her mother. She had been filling herself with busy work up until that moment, gathering the trophies her mother rescued from the fire, arguing with the fire chief, taking care of their dogs, fighting to stay free so she could help and here she was trailing after a team of doctors and nurses helpless to do anything that really mattered.

A nurse with a clipboard took her aside when they reached the treatment area and began asking questions and the question about insurance reminded that she didn't have her identification or her charge cards with her to guarantee payment for the treatment.

"She has a platinum card in her skirt pocket that will cover everything," Tara said.

"Not if she doesn't live to pay it," the nurse reminded her.

"She owns a house worth over a million," Tara said. "You will be paid."

"No insurance?"

"Her purse was stolen. I don't know the carrier."

"We need that information."

"I can write a check for ten thousand dollars," Tara said. "As soon as I get my checkbook from the sheriff."

"The one who confiscated your dogs?" the nurse asked.

"They weren't confiscated," Tara objected. "He's taking care of them."

The nurse raised an eyebrow.

"I'm not a criminal. I'm a reporter. I work for the Oakland Journal."

"Then she's covered on your insurance?"

"I'm not even covered on my insurance. That's why we paid cash this morning."

"She was here this morning?"

"Well, yes. She paid my hospital bill."

"Why didn't you pay your own bill if you had that much in your account?"

"Mother used her card. She insisted," Tara replied, and then abruptly switched the subject. "Is her treatment being delayed because I can't furnish proof of insurance?"

"Everything is being done..." the nurse began.

Tara tore herself away and burst through the doors of the treatment room. The medical team looked startled.

"Look I'm a reporter. I'm being given the runaround out there because the admitting nurse doesn't know us. You see we aren't from around here. My mother is rich enough to put a wing on this hospital and, if she dies, I'll be rich enough to take one off," Tara spat out. "But don't save her life because she can pay you, save her life because it needs saving."

The ensuing silence was profound.

Tara opened the door and held it open. "The operating room is ready, Gentlemen. Do your job."

"Let's go," a portly man said roughly. He turned to a nurse. "Call upstairs. Tell them we're on our way."

The admitting nurse protested. "You can't..."

Tara took her clipboard from her. "Where do I sign?"

After she scribbled her name on the line, she looked into the eyes of the portly doctor as the elevator doors closed. The last thing she saw was a wink.

"Now," she said to the admitting nurse, "how much money does the hospital require up front?"

"I couldn't possibly guess," the nurse stammered. "That's why we need the insurance information."

"The Ardilla police will get that for me," Tara said. "All I need is a phone."

"The police?"

"They're guarding my mother's house personally," Tara said with a smirk. Her mother was safe. Now she could play.

"The Ardilla police chief is being brought in... shit... I forgot. Where's the phone?"

She didn't wait for an answer but picked up a phone on the nearest desk and dialed the information operator who connected her with the sheriff's office.

"What do you mean he's still here?" Tara said. "I saw him leave with my dogs... Oh, the dogs are there... It's important I reach him. He has a packet... Oh, you know... Two analyzes? Why two...? Yes, I see. What was it...? Morphine...? Morphine can do that... It can? Really...? So, Sheriff Tolliver is here. And he knows... Thank God!"

Tara turned to the nurse. "It's morphine. He got an overdose of morphine." Her voice shook with anxiety.

"There is a treatment," the nurse counseled, a touch of kindness in her voice.

"Yes, I know," Tara replied. "Naloxone. But delay could be fatal. And I thought he could wait. Mother was bleeding. I thought she was going to die."

"He isn't even here yet," the nurse said. "How do they know it was morphine?"

Before Tara could explain, the elevator doors opened and Sheriff Tolliver burst into the admittance area.

"There you are," he boomed. "I heard you called. Here's your purse. My forensic team is going over the camera."

"My film!" Tara wailed.

"It's being developed," the sheriff said grinning. "I figured you took some snazzy photos considering how tightly you hung on to that camera."

"And my dogs are guarding the doors?" Tara teased suddenly relaxing.

"They're sound asleep under my desk," Tolliver said. "Aren't you going to ask about McLean?"

"Okay," Tara replied casually. "What about him?"

"I called the test results in and the doctors are meeting the chopper with a shot in hand. I thought you might want to be there. It could wake him up within a couple minutes they tell me."

The nurse cleared her throat.

"Oh, hi, Marina," Sheriff Tolliver said in response. "I know you have paperwork to complete, but let me steal Tara for a few minutes."

"You know better," Marina replied. "With no insurance..."

Tolliver looked at Tara with a raised brow.

"Proof of mother's insurance is at home," Tara said. "I was just going to call one of the men McLean has posted there and..."

The sheriff butted in. "You can do that later."

He took her hand and hurried toward the elevator. The nurse rushed after them protesting.

Tolliver stopped at the elevator doors and pressed the up button. "Do you know what this woman did?"

Flustered, the nurse stammered that she didn't.

"She dug two bullets out of a police chief's arm and saved his life," Tolliver said stepping inside the elevator and pulling Tara in with him.

"You're used to having people in custody, aren't you?" Tara quipped.

The sheriff immediately released her as he finished his explanation to the admitting nurse, "And she's not going to miss out of the pleasure of seeing him wake up."

"But the insurance," the nurse protested weakly.

"She'll get to it or else she'll just pay the whole thing in cash," the sheriff said. "These are very, very rich people, Marina. Very rich people."

After the doors closed, Tara said meekly. "There are richer."

The sheriff grinned. "Sometimes to make a point you have to exaggerate a little."

Tara blushed. "I told the doctors Mother could afford to put a wing on the hospital. I exaggerated a bit."

"Money does motivate people," Sheriff Tolliver said.

"I also threatened to take a wing off if they didn't get going."

"Oh, you did, did you?"

Tara grinned. "I'm not as nice as I seem."

The elevator doors opened and the two stepped out onto the roof. Waiting in the alcove near the elevator were two teams of medical personnel with gurneys. The sound of the approaching helicopter almost drowned out the sheriff's words.

"Tara, you are exactly who you seem to be."

Tara laughed. "I'm better than that."

"You do like the last word, don't you?"

The helicopter hovered briefly over their heads before descending.

"Yes," Tara said, "I do."

The noise prevented further repartee and the two waited as McLean was loaded onto the gurney. An IV had already been started. The first team ran with him toward the elevator. Sheriff Tolliver's deputy followed and inside the quiet of the descending elevator, the sheriff told the man to arrest the cop.

"Already did, Sir," the deputy said. "That's why I put him in the helicopter."

"Stay with him," Tolliver said. "I'll get some more men over here to help us guard McLean and Mrs. Svenson."

"Then she made it?" the deputy asked. He looked pleased.

"She's in surgery now," Tara said. "We won't know for a while."

And when she spoke the words, Tara's heart pounded a bit faster. She could lose her mother.

# Chapter 46

Two milligrams of naloxone were injected into the established IV tube every two minutes starting with the first shot given in the elevator until finally one of the series elicited a response. McLean opened his eyes as he was transferred from the gurney to the treatment table. When the doctor tried to put a tube down his throat, McLean objected. The doctor argued briefly, but McLean was adamant.

The doctor then walked the sheriff and Tara outside to talk. "He's still in danger. His system won't be rid of the last effects of the opiate for forty-eight hours although the more time that passes, the more likely he'll recover."

"But he's awake and breathing just fine," Tara protested.

"The drug we gave him has a half-life of thirty to eighty minutes. Do you know what that means?"

Tara nodded. "It means it will be at half strength in anywhere from thirty minutes to an hour and a half. But it's already done its job."

"It doesn't work quite like that," the doctor explained patiently. "He needs the naloxone in his system at a sufficient level to maintain the reversal of the respiratory depression. You see, the morphine keeps its strength longer than the naloxone and if the level of the naloxone drops too low, quite simply, he could go into respiratory arrest."

"Stop breathing," Tara murmured to clarify the situation to herself, "and die."

"In a nutshell, that's it," the doctor said nodding.

"Can you give him more naloxone to prevent that?" Tara asked.

"We can't give it in advance if that's what you're asking. We have to monitor his symptoms and respond with another injection when it becomes necessary."

"You mean when he stops breathing?" Tara charged.

The doctor put on his most persuasive smile. "We will, of course, monitor his breathing and respond at any sign of respiratory distress, but it is important to maintain ventilation. We need to control his breathing."

"By putting a tube down his throat."

"Correct."

"And you want us to persuade him."

"Correct."

"Will he be able to talk with that thing in his throat?" Sheriff Tolliver asked.

"No."

"That's not acceptable to him," Tara said. "That would be his worst nightmare come true."

The doctor grew stern. "We're trying to save his life!"

"And no one wants it saved more than I do," Tara said. "And we have no business discussing this out here as if Spencer McLean were a child."

"That wasn't what we were doing," the doctor protested.

"Weren't we?" Tara snapped pushing open the door and reentering the room. She marched up to McLean's bedside noting that the nurse had managed to strip him of his clothes and redress him. She refrained from commenting on the change and her mind snapped back to her primary focus as a soldier snaps to a general's order.

"They want to shove a tube down your throat so that when the drug they gave you begins to wear off and the morphine kicks in again, you won't stop breathing and die while they give you another shot and are waiting for it to take effect. That would take longer than your brain wants to be deprived of oxygen."

The sheriff stole a look at the doctor's face. The annoyance faded rapidly and was replaced by not only approval but a bit of admiration. She'd not only summarized and clarified his convoluted explanation but also understood more than he had expected and cut to the heart of the matter with all the skill of a surgeon.

"No!" McLean said adamantly.

"Are you willing to compromise?"

"No!" McLean said.

"You haven't even heard my compromise," Tara spit out. "Don't you dare assume I don't understand your need to be able to speak!"

McLean flushed and mumbled an apologetic, "Go on. I'm listening."

"You told me just before you lost consciousness that you felt woozy. Do you remember that feeling?"

McLean nodded.

Tara turned to the doctor, "Can we give him a shot when he begins to feel woozy?"

The doctor hesitated, "I..."

"You need to work with us here," Tara said. "You know that system they use so the patient can inject a dose of painkiller into his IV before the pain escalates. Before that system, twice as much morphine, or whatever, had to be used..."

The doctor finished the argument, "because the response time allowed the pain to rise to a higher level and it took a stronger dose to combat it."

"That's it," Tara agreed. "So why not let Chief McLean tell us when the morphine is beginning to get the upper hand."

"We have established monitoring methods," the doctor said.

"Which are slow in comparison to the patient's, wouldn't you agree?"

McLean dared not smile but the corner of his mouth twitched as he repressed it. It wasn't that the scene was funny, but rather that Tara was amazing in her ability to go straight to the core of the problem and willing to tackle even the most knowledgeable with her gut-level assessment.

"Patients are sometimes..." the doctor began.

"Intimidated by doctors who believe they know better? Afraid that they may be laughed at? Reluctant to share minor discomforts because they don't recognize their importance?"

The doctor nodded. "Exactly."

"That wasn't what you were going to say, was it?" Tara charged. "You were going to say that sick people are often unreliable because they're afraid."

"Well, er, yes. That's part of it."

"Well McLean isn't afraid. McLean's mind works fast. He saved his own life by telling me what to do."

The doctor's face registered shock.

"He told you to dig out the bullets?"

Tara flushed. "Well, I added that part myself."

McLean burst in.

"No wonder my arm hurts like hell."

"Live with it," Tara snapped. "I had to operate using a snake bite kit knife and my left hand. If you had subdued the cab driver properly, I'd have had the use of my right."

"No one asked you to jump on top of me."

"You needed saving."

"I was in control."

"In control of getting killed!"

The doctor coughed and Sheriff Tolliver laughed.

Tara pulled herself together and went on as if the verbal altercation had never taken place. "McLean will know instantly if the morphine is taking hold."

"We can't set up a drip for naloxone," the doctor protested. "The system doesn't work to accommodate such a proposal."

Tara turned to McLean. "Can you inject yourself?"

The doctor's protest was instantaneous and forceful. "We can't do that."

Tara turned to the white-coated man with horn rimmed glasses. "Does naloxone need refrigeration?"

She caught him off-guard again. He frowned.

"No. Why?"

"So you could have a series of needles ready right here."

"I told you, or at least I thought my protest, short though it was, told you that we can't allow our patients to inject themselves in the hospital."

"But if there were a nurse here and the drug was already in the syringe, the injection could be immediate."

"Well, nearly. She'd have to check..."

"That's why you need the tube, isn't it?" Tara argued, "So you can do all these checks and not lose the patient."

"They are necessary."

"Why?" Tara charged. "You know what his problem is. You know what the treatment is. Why are you waiting for signs of respiratory failure? Why not inject him when he feels woozy, or disoriented or funny? Why not inject him at the first symptom that the morphine is again in control instead of the second?"

"A nurse would have to be stationed at his side continuously," the doctor said. "That's not the way we do things."

"Sheriff, are any of your men married to a registered nurse?"

"I'm getting woozy," McLean said.

Tara looked at McLean and spat out an order. "Give him the shot now!"

The nurse looked at the doctor who nodded. She prepared the syringe and by the time she injected it, McLean's breathing had become labored.

"Get the next syringe ready," the doctor said. "And from now on, make sure one is always ready."

A second shot was given two minutes later and shortly afterward McLean's breathing settled down.

"You win," the doctor said. "It's only been twenty minutes. His system must be loaded. I'm surprised he's not dead."

"Clean living," Tara said.

"I'll get that nurse for you," the sheriff said and stepped outside.

The sheriff knew Tara had asked him for one of his deputies' wives because a delay in administering the shot could spell death for the chief. He called his wife.

"I'm not a nurse," she protested. "I'm a vet tech."

"You know how to give a shot."

"I could go to jail."

"I'm going to deputize you and assign you to work undercover."

"With the hospital's permission," she added.

"Of course," he said. "This is terribly important. If he dies, I'll be next."

"I'll be right there," she said. She knew he wouldn't tell anyone. He wasn't in a trusting mood. She'd step in until he could get someone else. Maybe her sister-in-law.

He had said she wasn't to leave McLean for any reason. That would excuse her from getting in over her head elsewhere. It could work. She'd make it work.

Following her husband's instructions, she poured what was left of the coffee in the pot into a thermos, grabbed the smock she wore at work and left. She didn't need to look like a nurse. She wasn't going to wander the halls. Andy would meet her and escort her to the room.

It would work. It had to.

# Chapter 47

By the time Adrienne Tolliver arrived and was met by her husband, Spencer McLean had been moved from the treatment room to a bed next to the intensive care unit, the charge nurse had been fully briefed and a dozen packaged syringes and a large bottle of naloxone had been placed in the room.

Sheriff Tolliver swore his wife in as a deputy in the elevator and pinned a badge on her tunic. This gesture caused her to beam all the way to the room.

The bespectacled doctor did a double take and stammered something about recognizing her but not being able to place her.

"I work in a clinic not too far from here," Adrienne said, not mentioning that it was an animal clinic.

The doctor gave her instructions and his beeper number. She was deferential out of habit and that trait reassured the doctor that she was a professional medical person. McLean lapsed as the doctor was preparing to leave and Adrienne immediately picked up the prepared syringe, held it up, tapped it and squeezed out a tiny bubble of air before injecting it into the IV tube. She did this with an obviously practiced hand.

She glanced at her watch and repeated the doctor's instructions as to the timing. She quickly noted the administration of the dose on the chart and then prepared a fresh syringe.

The doctor didn't leave until he was satisfied that the second dose had fully reversed McLean's respiratory distress.

He paused at the door. "I still have a feeling we know each other, Mrs. Tolliver."

Adrienne merely smiled.

When the door closed, she said, "He brings his dog to our clinic. He knows me as Adrienne. What do I do if he remembers?"

"You stay here. You've been deputized."

"Not as a nurse. It's one thing to administer a shot with a doctor standing by... Andy this isn't going to work," Adrienne said, fear turning her voice into a whine.

"Of course, it's going to work," the sheriff assured her. "McLean will make sure it works, won't you, Spencer?"

Adrienne wasn't going to let the matter rest with an assurance.

"I'm not equipped to handle a medical emergency. And they always come up, believe me," Adrienne insisted. "That much I've learned from the work I do."

"I need you here," the sheriff said. "I trust you."

"My sister-in-law is a nurse," Adrienne said. "We could call her."

"No," the sheriff said. "I trust you. McLean's greatest enemy is not within anymore. You have good instincts. You are used to reading subtle signals. You're perfect."

"But I'm scared."

"Just don't let anyone near McLean except the doctor you know. That's all I ask."

McLean butted in.

"That and giving me my shots when I need them. Believe me, I promise not to have any medical emergencies. I hope you brought your own coffee."

"So that's where that idea came from."

"I'll bring you both food myself," Sheriff Tolliver said.

McLean nodded. He looked at Adrienne and added, "The people we are up against are whizzes when it comes to drugs."

"What happened to your arm?" Adrienne asked picking up the chart and reading it. "I see they already gave you an antibiotic to ward off infection."

"Tara pulled out the fangs of the snake that bit me," McLean replied.

"He's speaking metaphorically," Tara put in. "I better leave while he tells his version. I never come off the heroine which I should be."

"Don't go," McLean pleaded. "I'll be nice."

"I've got a date with Marina. Then I've got to call home and get one of your men to hunt for Mother's insurance information. That won't be a problem, will it?"

"Call Lim," McLean said. "He'll arrange it."

"While Tara's gone, my wife can take down your statement," the sheriff said. "It'll keep you from pining." He smiled knowingly and winked at Tara.

"I need my computer, so I can write my news story," Tara said, ignoring the sheriff's allusion. "You can bring it here."

"I thought..." the sheriff started then paused, not knowing quite how to express his concern.

Tara guessed what was on his mind.

"You thought I'd want to spend time in the waiting room waiting for news of my mother," Tara commented. "That's the last place I want to be. Waiting is not something I do well and it won't help Mother one bit."

"They have a chapel," the sheriff suggested.

"I don't need a chapel to pray. God has been reading my deepest thoughts for hours. Afterward, after the operation, He and I will talk. Then I may use the chapel. But right now, He's up to date with what I want and, more than that, He knows what I need. Mother's life is in His hands. If I try to direct Him, I'll only mess things up."

"I'll have my deputy bring over your computer," the sheriff said.

"And how about a couple of those photos? I can use the hospital's fax machine."

Sheriff Tolliver looked at McLean, "Do we want to publicize the whole mess?"

"It's the only way," Tara said. "We have to keep this going until the truth emerges. Someone will get nervous and take his finger out of the dike."

"I'll still need an official statement," Tolliver said.

"When you bring me my computer, bring a tape recorder. We can retire to the waiting room and you can ask all the questions you want."

Sheriff Tolliver nodded perfunctorily.

"What's wrong?" Tara asked.

"It's your mother. It would be good if she could tell me what happened; but, I doubt that she'll remember much."

"Her memory's pretty good," Tara remarked, "except for names. She uses a cheat sheet for those."

"A cheat sheet?" Tolliver asked.

"Sure, like for a test. She doesn't remember what she hears as well as what she sees, so she writes the person's name down first chance she gets and studies it. Before a party where she knows who's going to be there, she studies the list. Then later she'll come home and add a note about what they talked about, you know important stuff like what kind of dog the person owns."

Tolliver chuckled, but McLean grew thoughtful. "Does she keep these lists?"

"Yeah, as a matter of fact she does. In her memory file."

"So that's what she meant," McLean commented, then added,

"Tell Lim to look for them. Our clue may be on one of her lists."

"I doubt it," Tara said. "I've seen the lists. She never describes the people and she never puts down titles or occupations or anything like that. She just picks a clue to remind her about their conversation. It's meaningless stuff."

"Still, tell Lim to fetch it," McLean said. "It's the only written material we have to go on."

"That's true. Except for her memory notes, she never took anything home. But I know she didn't write down anything important like who was connected to whom," Tara said.

"Stop apologizing," McLean said. "If she knew anything, she would have told us. The lists alone can help us since we can't get access to the governor's guest lists without a warrant and we have no grounds for one."

"Ah," Tara breathed. "I see."

"I'm still with you on the photograph being the reason we've been targeted. My guess is that the governor knows we recognized Cee Cee and that as soon as we return we'll investigate that scandal. That is, you and I will. You because you're a reporter. And me because I'm a cop."

"Why take out my mother? He has her promise."

"She's the link in the evidence chain."

"And because she would have nothing to gain by revealing the contents of the photograph, she'd be believed."

"Exactly."

"I still think there's more," Tara insisted. "One doesn't kill a fly with a cannon."

# Chapter 48

Immediately after Tara called, Lieutenant Lim arranged to have the officer guarding the Svenson house search for the insurance file and the memory file. The young cop choked on the latter term and was about to make a joke when the serious tone in his lieutenant's voice told him that would not sit well.

Lim himself perused the memory file and stopped on the notation beside the name Varrieur. He called Shawn Gallaghan in from the outer office and asked him about it.

Shawn didn't hesitate. "'The Purloined Letter' is one of Edgar Allen Poe's most famous stories."

"A story?" Lim retorted. "That's all? I thought maybe it meant a stolen letter."

"It's famous. Didn't you have to read the story in English Lit?"

"I took other courses," Lim replied stiffly.

"It's a story about how this guy hid a letter in plain sight. No one could find it because no one looked at the letter sitting in the holder on top of the desk in plain view."

Manuel Guado poked his head in the room. The former cabbie had been put on dispatch. Nights were generally slow but with so many men in the field Manuel was charged with keeping track of their check-ins. Other calls he transferred to a desk where someone was working and then he was instructed to listen and get a feel for how such a call was handled. Lim had a knack for instructing neophytes.

Manuel gave his message as soon as Lim looked at him.

"Drew Manning is stuck in the city with Stormy somebody. You ain't seeing him until the sun comes up."

"Ever heard of the Purloined Letter?" Lim asked without preamble.

"Yeah. That was this story about a letter that was supposed to be hid but was out where everybody could see it only nobody looked there. It was right under their noses."

Lim frowned.

"I got it wrong?" Manuel asked, worried.

"Does everyone know the story but me?" Lim quipped, annoyed.

"You want I should ask?" Manuel inquired softly.

Shawn laughed. "Find someone and Lim will probably promote you."

Manuel nodded and then continued his report. "Sage County Sheriff called. Varrieur croaked. The coroner is gonna pick up the body; but he put him in the back of the line. The sheriff said someone needs to light a fire under the coroner's butt."

"That means we've got a homicide," Lim observed. "Shawn, come with me. We're going to look for that purloined letter at Varrieur's place of business. Manuel, call whoever has the keys to the Quiet Rest Funeral Home in Manzanita and tell him to meet me there."

Manuel looked dismayed and Shawn whispered, "Look in the Yellow Pages. Call the number listed. They get most of their calls at night."

Manuel beamed his appreciation for the tip. These guys were really backing him up. Marie needed to hear about this. She was still skeptical. She said he was only a plug in because they were so short, but nobody was treating him that way.

He decided he would light a fire under the coroner's butt. First he called the funeral home; then he found the night time number for the coroner on McLean's desk and called him.

"I'm calling for my boss," he said, his accent pronounced.

"And who is that?"

"The guy what wants the autopsy on that funeral guy done right now," Manuel barked.

"Varrieur?"

"Yeah, the Frenchie," Manuel said roughly. "Move him to the head of the line."

"I've got others..."

"No, you ain't. You only got one at the head of the line and that's Frenchie. My boss don't forget favors."

"I guess I could move him up a bit," the coroner offered tentatively. He wasn't used to calls like this.

"It should be done good. He won't like it if it ain't," Manuel finished. "So do I tell him Frenchie's number one?"

"Tell him I'll get right on it," the coroner said.

Manuel hung up inordinately pleased with himself.

The coroner turned the conversation over in his mind. Someone hit someone with connections that he didn't want to think about. Fear motivated the coroner to move Varrieur's autopsy ahead of the others.

Meanwhile, Lieutenant Lim arrived at the Quiet Rest Funeral Home in Manzanita only to find Chattaway's marked car parked in front. The door opened as Lim and Gallaghan approached the huge white double doors under the columned portico.

Lieutenant Lim stepped onto the polished slate floor, wiped his feet on the carpet and moved toward the back, his footfall lost in the thick carpeting.

"Chief Chattaway and a private detective are in the back," the man offered.

Lim walked down the aisle way between several viewing rooms. Each room had only a faint light glowing. Two were occupied. The caskets were open and the still faces of the occupants in repose gave Shawn a chill. He paused outside the room with no floral arrangements crowding around the base of the coffin.

"He just arrived," Varrieur's assistant whispered. "The funeral for the other gentleman is tomorrow. He was the last one Mr. Varrieur did."

Shawn stepped into the room filled with flowers.

"What does that mean exactly?" Shawn queried.

"He oversaw every detail. He was always very particular about details," the assistant replied. "Excuse me, please. I hear an argument in the back. I may be needed."

Shawn didn't follow. Lim never moved unless he was on solid legal ground. From his friend's stories, he knew that Chattaway did. Shawn stood in the center of the room and slowly studied it.

Hidden in plain view, he reminded himself. That means not in the vases, not behind the pictures, not inside the coffin. In plain view. What the hell was in plain view?

"Waste of time," came a voice from behind him. "I searched the room good. Coffin ain't got no hidden pockets and there ain't nothing else."

"You're a new man, aren't you?" said a second voice. "What force did McLean steal you from?"

Shawn Gallaghan spun around to face a pot-bellied man with gray brows squeezed together over angry eyes.

"I applied," he said, "and was hired."

"Well, who put time and money into your training only to have the robber baron snatch you away just when you was learning things?"

"I graduated from Berkeley," Shawn replied politely.

"McLean don't hire rookies. He only hires whose got good training."

"Interesting choice of words," Shawn retorted nettled.

"What's that mean?" Chattaway bellowed.

"Sharp instincts," Shawn replied coldly. "You live up to your reputation."

Chattaway responded with a string of expletives that brought Lim from the back room.

"Why are you swearing at my officer?" Lim said.

"He insulted me," Chattaway said. "I demand an apology."

Lim looked at Shawn. The move was up to him.

"I apologize for saying that you have sharp instincts and that you live up to your reputation," Shawn said flatly.

"There!" Chattaway shouted. "He did it again."

"Those were my exact words," Shawn said.

"He says I got a reputation."

Lim looked the fat man in the eye and said, "Everyone has a reputation. Had Officer Gallaghan said the same words to me, I would have felt complimented."

"He didn't mean a compliment," Chattaway insisted.

"I cannot read a man's mind," Lieutenant Lim replied. "Nor can you. I suggest that you have taken your anger out on an innocent officer and projected feelings onto him that you have. Go home and see to your own house."

Lim turned as he finished and motioned to Gallaghan to follow him into the back. When they entered the back room, Lim said softly, "I did take several psychology courses."

Gallaghan grinned. "I noticed."

"The purloined letter," Lim said. "I'm certain the detective looked in all the hiding places, even the most repulsive ones."

"You mean like under the bodies and in the coffins?" Shawn asked. "Let me go back into the viewing room. It was the last one Varrieur prepared for burial."

"You mean he didn't prepare the man in the other room?"

"Right."

"Let's go," Lim said hurrying ahead of Shawn and turning into the room bare of flowers.

"Not that one," Shawn protested. "The other one."

Lim stood in the first room he entered. "We absorb what's here and then move across and see what Mr. Varrieur added."

"But the hiding place wouldn't be temporary," Shawn said.

"Wouldn't it?" Lim asked.

The first room seemed bare.  A pale green curtain hung behind the open casket, its soft folds muting the harshness of the stark plain room.  Couches and soft chairs dressed in light beige textured fabric lined the walls.  Wooden tables held stately lamps with their brass rods rising from thick crystal bases.  The focal point of the room was the shiny bronze casket with a white-haired gentleman lying in repose.

The second room was much like the first but with a pale blue curtain behind a silver and gray casket.  The man lying inside was younger, nearly bald and quite rotund.  Roses draped the lower half of the casket and the metal base was hidden behind a row of gladioli sprays.  Potted palms anchored each end of the floral display arched around the chairs set in rows facing the open casket.  Off to one side stood a slender wrought iron lectern holding a massive Bible opened to a middle page.  A tasseled bookmark marked the Twenty-Third Psalm.

"He said he searched the casket," Shawn commented. "He said there were no hidden drawers."

"Our clue is that it is in plain sight," Lim reminded Shawn. "So what is in plain sight?"

"Flowers," Shawn replied. "They're everywhere."

"Go on."

"The chairs. The casket. The dead guy."

"Your observation is not as keen as it needs to be," Lim commented.

"There isn't anything else."

"No?"

Shawn surveyed the room again. "Except the stand holding the Bible."

"Start there."

"Where?"

"With the lectern and the Bible."

"I can practically see through the lectern," Shawn said advancing toward it. "It's wrought iron. You can't hide anything inside wrought iron."

He moved closer and studied the Bible. He flipped the pages. There were no marks and nothing tucked between the pages. The cover was a heavy parchment reminiscent of books fashioned in the sixteenth century. The book had been handcrafted to lend a dignity to the setting.

"Nothing," he said as he set the tasseled bookmark back where he had found it.

"The tassel hung down," Lim said.

Shawn picked up the bookmark and adjusted it.

"How did it feel?" Lim asked.

"What?" Shawn queried looking down at the Bible with a puzzled expression.

"The film was in your hand," Lim said. "Twice."

Shawn's fingers picked up the bookmark. The tassel was several loops of gold upholstery fringe threaded through a hole in the top of the shimmering silk wrapped around a stiff, lightweight paper insert.

"It's cloth," Shawn announced. "And it's thin. There's no roll of negatives in here."

"How about a strip?"

Shawn brought the featherweight bookmark to his lieutenant who untied the tassel and tapped the end of the cardboard cover on the back of a nearby wooden folding chair. Gingerly he extracted the piece of film hidden inside. Shawn produced a plastic bag and Lim dropped the film into it.

"Mission complete?" Shawn asked. "Or do we look for more?"

"Let's continue now that we know how Varrieur's mind works."

"We know that?" Shawn asked. "All we've got is one piece of evidence."

"He hides it in plain view and yet it isn't."

"I guess he figured everybody has read `The Purloined Letter'," Shawn observed. He noticed that Lim's face remained passive and he was grateful. He hadn't meant it as a dig. He hoped that Lim's blank look meant that he didn't take it personally.

"Tell me where it isn't." Lim said.

"Not in the caskets. They get buried. The bookmark tells us he uses a permanent object but not something hidden," Shawn stated. "What are we looking for anyway?"

"Records."

"Maybe the records are hidden in back."

"I think not," Lim responded. "I believe the detective searched every nook back there."

"Then the other viewing room," Shawn said. "The one with all the furniture."

"You think it's in the furniture?" Lim asked with a bit of surprise tagging on the end of his query.

Shawn hastened to correct the erroneous conclusion. "No, of course not, that's the first place anyone would look."

Still the two moved into the other room.

"I can't get my eyes off the man in the casket," Shawn remarked.

"That's why I know the records are here," Lim said.

Shawn began a verbal survey of the room. "Not the wall. Too flat. Not the couch. Not the tables. Not the lamps..."

Lim broke in. "Why do you race through the possibilities so quickly?"

"That detective would have turned over every table and pulled out every drawer."

"And the lamps?" Lim said.

"The bases are glass," Shawn pointed out. "You can see right through them. The center is clear glass and the brass rods are thin as pencils."

"And the shades?"

Shawn looked underneath. "Parchment with a cloth overlay."

"And between those two?"

"A decorative insert of vertical lines."

"Fine print?"

Shawn unscrewed the brass knob at the top of the lamp and removed the shade. He slipped his knife between the cloth and the parchment, tugged on a sheet of paper lightly glued to the parchment and pulled it out.

"I can hardly read the words," Shawn said turning the paper so the lines were horizontal. "But it looks like an accounting ledger of some sort."

"Computer generated," Lim observed.

"So there's a computer somewhere we can use," Shawn responded.

"Not anymore."

"Why go to all this bother? Why not just make a disk?"

"Oh, there was a disk. And Mr. Varrieur hid it well. And our visiting detective found it."

"I heard an argument."

"I do not believe Chief Chattaway knew that the detective had found the disk."

"But he must have known the disk was a copy and the computer held the original data."

"He did."

"Then why aren't we using it?"

"The files are destroyed," Lim announced. "Chief Chattaway said that when he turned it on, he accidentally set loose a virus that destroyed its memory banks."

"Chattaway doesn't know anything about computers," Shawn said. "Drew used to do all the computer work for him."

"Ah," Lim said.

"I bet that that detective slipped a disk into the computer and told the P.I. they were going to copy the information on it, then sat Chattaway down to do it while he continued his search. That's why he could pocket the disk when he found it without Chattaway knowing."

"How did Chief Chattaway get in without the access code?"

"Varrieur probably kept his access code in his desk drawer, taped to the front panel and the chief found it. It was easy enough with the detective's prompting. And it kept Chattaway occupied."

"And the virus was on the disk?" Lim asked.

"That's my guess," Shawn said, then added. "But you already figured all this out, didn't you?"

"Varrieur knew the way the search would be conducted," Lim continued, nodding his acceptance of Shawn's conclusion. "The disk would be a true copy of the material on the computer. A perfect decoy."

"No, it wasn't," Shawn argued. "If we got here first, we would have found the computer. If someone had taken the computer, we would have found the disk; but, there is no way Varrieur could assume that the police would be smart enough to find this stuff. He didn't tell anyone that he'd hidden a hard copy."

"Ah, but he did. He told Coral Svenson."

# Chapter 49

When Lieutenant Lim and Shawn Gallaghan returned to the station, Manuel greeted him with a message.

"Drew Manning faxed us the ballistic report on the three bullets. He needs to talk to you right away."

"When did he call?"

"Just before you got here."

"Why didn't you call me?"

"I tried, but the man said you'd left after destroying every lamp in the place."

"That's where Varrieur hid his records," Shawn burst in, his delight at their success taking hold. "In the lamp shades! In plain sight!"

"You should have used the radio," Lim commented.

"Couldn't. We had visitors. Two guys from the governor's staff. Had to get rid of them first."

Manuel handed the lieutenant a slip of paper. "Manning's waiting by a public phone outside."

"A public phone?" Lim queried as he looked around. "Where are the visitors?"

"Manning don't want no one to hear what he says," Manuel replied. "I sent the guys over to the Sage County Sheriff's office. That's where the guy is that was arrested for attacking the Frenchie."

348

"And they went?"

"Yeah, I kinda told them that the sheriff was handling the investigation."

"You didn't tell them where I was?"

"They didn't ask me. They asked Chang and he didn't know."

"I can see why McLean hired you," Lim said with a touch of warmth. "You have good instincts."

Once in his office, Lim dialed the number on the scrap of paper and a worried Manning answered, explaining quickly that he wasn't up on proper procedures.

"I don't want to mess up again," Manning finished.

"Tell me what you want to do."

"I faxed the ballistic report to you," Manning began.

"That was proper."

"I want someone to check the report to see if those bullets have been fired in the commission of a crime. Can you do that?"

"That's standard operating procedure. You can do it there."

"That's just it," Drew Manning objected. "I got suspicions, but that's all. Stormy's jumpy enough and Kathy and Devin are gone. If you can do it from there, it'll appear routine–well, sort of. It's just that we don't want anyone to know we're here."

"You think he used a throw-away piece to produce the bullets?"

"Yeah. I've been thinking while Stormy's been working. Where would Volatis come up with the bullets? If he rolled them in the blood in the cab after he left Ardilla, which is what I think, he had to come up with the bullets fast.

He wouldn't use his own gun. He didn't have enough time to get one from any of his contacts in the city. That means he had a throwaway piece with him. I'm thinking in the car because the bullets were large caliber."

"You're making sense so far," Lim said. "You not only want to do a computer search, you also want to search his squad."

"Yeah."

"You can't without a warrant which you won't be able to get, but Officer Riley, as his partner, does not need permission."

"And if she finds a gun, what do we do?"

"Turn it in," Lim said.

"Can we do a ballistics test first?" Manning asked.

"I do not believe that a forensic workup would be out of order."

When Lieutenant Greg Lim finished his call to Drew Manning, he rose from his well-organized desk and walked into the outer office and laid the stash of papers taken from the lamp on Sergeant Randal Chang's equally neat desk.

"See what you can make of these," Lim said simply.

Chang looked at the tiny print.

"Make of them?" he exclaimed. "I can't even see them."

He paged through the sheets. "Are they in order?"

"Probably not," Lim said. "Ask for help."

Chang looked around. "Who here has the best eyesight?"

Rose Marcellis popped up. "I do."

"You're on this with me."

"Sorry, can't. I'm due to guard Alex next shift."

"Get a sub," Chang ordered. "I need your eyes."

"Hey, Lieutenant," Manuel called as Lim passed his station, "I took care of the coroner."

Lim stopped.

"You did what?"

"Got the guy off his duff. He said he'd do Varrieur right away."

"You ever seen an autopsy, Manuel?" Lim asked abruptly.

Manuel shook his head. "Ain't on my list."

"Shawn, you and Manuel go over to the coroner's. You need to start sometime."

"But the phones?" Manuel asked.

"Is this some sort of punishment?" Shawn put in.

Lim's lips twitched. "Actually, it is a reward."

"A reward?" the two chorused.

"I'm glad you see it as I do. We will get along well if this attitude is maintained."

The two men stared at each other, dumbfounded. Lim was serious.

On the drive to the coroner's, Shawn ventured an explanation. "Maybe it is his idea of a reward–giving us an experience we haven't had before."

"Maybe he figures we'll scare the coroner into doing a good job."

"Us?"

"You being six feet. Me talking like I do."

"We're cops!" Shawn said. "Not hoods."

"If you don't say nothing, I won't," Manuel said, then added, "it's a joke."

"At least, we have the guy who did it," Shawn said.

"No, we don't. Sheriff Hobbs called. He says the guy has an alibi for the time the car plowed into Varrieur."

"Well, he knows who did it."

"The guy said he weren't working for nobody. He says Frenchie got into his wife's pants."

"There was a nurse working with him," Shawn said. "Guys out for revenge usually go it alone."

"Seems he ain't married even."

"Hope they got him to fess up."

"Sure. He lays another whopper on them. Says he got paid by Varrieur's son to finish the old man off. Sort of a mercy killing thing."

"That could be true. Varrieur's got a son, doesn't he?"

"Yep. Five years old."

"Did the sheriff tell him to quit the bull shitting?"

"Sure. So he finally says he was contacted by this woman who says Frenchie charged her too much to bury her mother. Sheriff Hobbs thought he was onto something until the address turns out to be an empty lot."

"Wow!" Shawn breathed. "This guy's a real jokester."

"Yeah, but I don't think cops like it when a perp pulls their chain."

"What was his last story?"

"That LAITA told him to do it because Varrieur abused his dog."

"Does he even have a dog?"

"Who knows?" Manuel shrugged.

Shawn grew thoughtful. "Maybe the question we should be asking is who knew Varrieur was staying in town overnight?"

"Why do we wanna know that?"

"Because there was a second attempt. Someone wanted him dead. If the person hit him accidentally, he would want him to live, wouldn't he?"

"That makes sense."

"There's more." Shawn went on, "He stays overnight at a friend's house because he's too drunk to drive home and he borrows sweats and jogs the next morning with what must a been a hellava hangover. Whoever killed him knew he was a dedicated jogger."

"That Mrs. Svenson. She'd know," Manuel said. "Bet that's why she's a target."

# Chapter 50

Meanwhile at the San Francisco forensic lab, Drew Manning had someone else in his sights. He snubbed out his cigarette and went back inside the lab.

"Guns have histories," he said to Stormy who was adding notes to his original forensic report. "Do we know the history of the gun that fired these bullets?"

"Look, Man, I'm swamped. Even if we find out the gun had a history what good would that do? This isn't a serial killing we're dealing with here. And we don't have the gun. Or its owner for that matter."

"Suppose it was used before."

"Most guns are."

"And the cops got the gun."

"Then it would have been destroyed."

"Or gotten lost on the way to the evidence room."

"I don't like where you're going with this," Stormy growled. "And you're traveling this road alone."

"My department is checking on it," Drew said. He noted Stormy's sigh of relief, minute as it was. "But I need something from you. Some speculation."

"I only do facts, Man."

"You can arrange them," Drew pressed. "Hear me out. When a bullet is dug out of a victim and brought to you, do you usually find anything on the bullet?"

"Sometimes."

"Hell," Drew said. "I thought I had something."

Stormy was still scowling. "Maybe you do."

He opened the bag with the single squashed bullet. Drew pulled his chair up close and watched as Stormy dipped into the bag with a tweezers and extracted a hair which he placed under the microscope.

"It's a hair," Drew said. "The cab had passengers."

"This is animal hair," Stormy explained. "I figure that when Volatis extracted the bullet with his knife, he flipped it straight into the bag and this hair came along for the ride."

"So a dog rode in the cab."

"Or a person who owns dogs," Stormy said.

"Mrs. Svenson has dogs," Drew responded, his excitement beginning to bud.

"Dog hairs adhere to everything," Stormy said. "And they particularly like plastic."

"So?"

"If Volatis laid a plastic bag on the seat of the cab," Stormy said.

The conclusion was left unspoken. Stormy pulled the bag with the three bullets across the counter. "Can't get rid of them. Dog hairs cling like magnets."

With the tweezers, Stormy lifted a hair from the outside of the bag and put it on a slide and compared the two slides.

"A perfect match," Stormy said. "Both of these bags picked up a dog hair from the same dog."

"Mrs. Svenson has Labs."

"These are not from Labs. Wrong color for one.

"You sure?"

"A wire-haired breed, like a terrier."

"Hell, I was hoping we could tie the dog hair to Mrs. Svenson's presence in the cab."

"Maybe we don't need to tie it to Mrs. Svenson," Stormy suggested.

"Where are the cop's clothes?"

"We only have the shirt," Drew said sliding it down the counter.

Stormy spread it out face up and began his examination at the middle button. With a tweezers he plucked off a dog hair and stuck it on a slide. After her examined it under the microscope, he raised his head and smiled.

"You mean the dog hair came from Alex?" Drew queried. He didn't expect an answer. Puzzled, he stammered, "Alex doesn't own a dog."

"Well, he held one before he got in that cab. His shirt has a number of hairs imbedded in the fabric."

Drew went to the phone and called the hospital. After a brief conversation, he turned to Stormy. "You were right. Alex held a dog, a wire-haired dachshund just before he entered the cab."

"It won't sell to a jury," Stormy observed. "They don't like statistical probabilities. If there's any doubt, it's reasonable doubt. They want to hear that there was no chance; however, Internal Affairs works on suspicion and that we've got."

"Internal Affairs?" Kathy Riley asked holding the door for her partner.

"What's up?" Devin Simonton chimed in. "What did we miss?"

"Did you get the paramedic's clothes?"

"Too late. They're at the laundry."

"He gave us the shirt off his back though," Kathy said, then chuckled softly as she added, "Literally. Just in case."

Drew filled them in.

Kathy listened with a deeply furrowed brow.

"I know where Mark Volatis' car is," she said when he finished.

"We need a warrant," Drew said. "We gotta do this right."

"I shared it with him. I've got a key," Kathy said. "And I want to be sure. Sorry, Stormy, I believe you; but, I need something more solid than percentages to move against Mark."

"Kathy, let Internal Affairs handle this," Devin urged. "You're not alone in this. There are four of us that believe he tampered with the evidence. I.A. can get the gun and Stormy can test it. Volatis isn't supposed to have a throw away piece anyway."

"Drew can turn him in," Stormy added.

"Drew? On what grounds?" Kathy charged, the Korean half giving into Irish ire.

"It's coming through now," Drew said. The fax machine clicked on. Drew pulled out the sheet and waved it. "I'm ready."

"What's that?"

"Our three bullets match those in a gang shootout. Three guns were turned in. One group of bullets was unmatched. It was assumed that someone got away with that gun."

"That doesn't help," Kathy argued.

"The investigating officer was Sergeant Mark Volatis."

"You call Internal Affairs," Kathy said. "I'm going to get the gun."

Kathy spun around and charged out the door. Devin ran after her yelling at her to wait.

"She doesn't trust Internal Affairs?" Drew asked.

"Kathy is too smart to trust anyone," Stormy said. "My guess is that Volatis would say she knew the gun was there all along and take her down with him."

"Will she bring it back here?"

"You bet your ass she will!"

# Chapter 51

Tara Svenson's call from her cell phone to the Ardilla police station was picked up by the man sitting in a van parked in the hospital parking lot. Her second call to her editor was longer and even more informative.

She had pictures of the rifleman in the helicopter. She would fax them.

A call was made from the men in the van to a special number in northern California. The man receiving the call walked into the governor's office and closed the door.

The faint click of the lock woke the gray-haired man lying on the leather couch.

"What is it Brian?" he asked.

"They lead a charmed life," Harvath replied. "The earlier report was accurate up to a point. The van did explode only no one was in it. And Tara Svenson got pictures."

"I thought her camera was stolen."

"It was. And all her film."

The governor shrugged. That a reporter would unearth another camera didn't surprise him.

"So they are all alive and well?"

"Alive, yes. But not well."

"Oh?" The gray brows rose in hope.

"Coral Svenson was shot in the chest by the first cop to arrive. She is still in the operating room. Her chance of survival is slim. Chief McLean is in intensive care. If Tara Svenson hadn't operated on him the minute they stopped, he'd be dead."

The governor's jaw dropped. Harvath enjoyed the moment. Ordinarily, he couldn't indulge himself without feeling the man's wrath. He hurried to explain what happened, finishing by saying that McLean was under guard and still considered in serious condition.

"Is there more?"

"Tara will be faxing the story complete with photos to her editor sometime soon."

"Can we stop her?"

"We can. There is a plan."

"Doesn't the sheriff down there know what's going on?" Governor Atkins asked, obviously worried.

"The plan will take care of her and the evidence as well."

"And her mother?"

"That will be handled simultaneously."

"And McLean?"

"Will be taken care of as well."

"How?" the governor started, then stopped. "No, don't tell me. I just wish you had some good news."

"I do. The detective our friends hired, thanks to Chief Chattaway, had full and free access to Varrieur's place of business in Manzanita. He was just finishing up when the Ardilla cops arrived. He took care of the financial records, but didn't find the negatives. He assumes that the place is clean."

"I don't like it. That negative has got to be somewhere."

"The detective is still looking. Varrieur had ten funeral homes. He's dead, by the way. He never regained consciousness."

"Whoever did him in did me no favor," Atkins grumbled. "This is absolutely the wrong time for this to have happened."

"You do have an idea who did this, don't you?" Harvath ventured.

Whalen Atkins' look of surprise told Harvath that the governor had not been able to solve the puzzle.

"Not a clue. Why? Do you?" the governor asked staring straight into the steely eyes of his square-jawed, right hand man.

"You don't want to know," Harvath replied.

"You're right. I don't," Whalen Atkins confessed. "Just take care of it. And send in Cox."

Everett Cox, slightly disheveled, appeared at the door within minutes of being summoned. This was a night of crisis. Cat naps were all that were allowed. Harvath was on the younger man's heels.

"Everett, I need a speech. Short. Simple. Moving."

Cox nodded. "For what occasion?"

"Mrs. Svenson was shot a couple hours ago. The press will seek my reaction upon her death."

"You want a second statement?"

"Whatever for?"

Harvath stepped in and answered Cox, "The press isn't going to ask his reaction if she recovers."

"Get right on it," Atkins said. He turned to Harvath. "How much time have we got?"

Again Harvath recovered the fumble. "The report is that she probably won't last an hour."

"Where is she?" Cox asked.

"Why?" Harvath responded.

"I think it would be good to inquire periodically as to her condition," Cox replied disarmingly. "It would show the governor's concern."

Harvath scowled for a few moments, then his face brightened. He looked at Whalen Atkins who was waiting for him to decide. "It could work in your favor, Governor."

"Yes. Yes," Atkins said. "It would show concern for a volunteer who has been a strong supporter. Two supporters killed in a day. What a..."

"You can't say that," Harvath warned.

"What? That two of my staunchest supporters have been killed? Of course, I can say it!" Atkins declared. "I can use their deaths to mount a renewed commitment from their friends. People are angry when someone dies. I want them to channel that anger into support for me."

"When did Varrieur die?" Cox asked.

Harvath, who was focused on the governor, barely heard the question.

"Just happened," Atkins said.

"Shouldn't I be writing something about that?"

"We already did him," Atkins said coolly, "when he was hit. They won't ask about him, but include it in my statement about Mrs. Svenson." Whalen Atkins rubbed his chin thoughtfully. "I think I need a shave. Those TV cameras can be brutal." He moved toward his bathroom.

Cox frowned. "I don't think we should use her death for political gain."

Atkins paused. His chuckle had overtones of sarcasm. "He has a lot to learn, hasn't he, Brian?"

Harvath picked up the cue. "Everett, everything that happens has political consequences. It's our job to put a positive spin on it."

"Should I change shirts?" Atkins asked his chief political advisor.

"Yes," Harvath replied. "You don't want to appear as if you've been worrying. This comes as a shock, remember."

"I'll make the call to the hospital," Everett Cox murmured as he backed out of the office.

# Chapter 52

Tara Svenson was standing at the nurse's station asking about her mother when the call came through from Everett Cox. The nurse stammered when the governor's name was thrown at her and mumbled the standard line about the hospital not releasing information on any of its patients.

"Who is it?" Tara whispered.

"He says his name is Everett Cox," the nurse said. "Do you want to talk to him? He says he's calling from the governor's office."

Tara's first thought was to respond by giving him a piece of her mind–a big angry piece–and then slamming the phone down. But as she indicated to the nurse to hand over the phone, she realized that such a display would shut off communication with a potential source. For her story to have merit, she needed quotes from the governor. If she weaved them in artfully, her editor would print it all. She put the phone to her ear, grabbed a pen from the holder and waved it at the nurse who quickly fed her a piece of paper.

"Mr. Cox," Tara said politely. "This is Tara Svenson. I will be happy to answer your questions."

"Tara," Cox said. "How nice. Your mother has spoken often of you. I called because the governor just received word that your mother is... er... please tell me, how is your mother? I understand she was shot."

"In the chest."

"How did the operation go?"

"It's still in progress."

"Then there's still hope," Everett Cox said. His voice reflected genuine relief, and Tara was touched by it.

"You heard otherwise?" she asked.

"Well... er... yes. Our report was not as positive. I'm..."

"You were told she was dying?" Tara pressed.

"As a matter of fact," Cox said, recovering his equilibrium, "we were. I'm glad our source was in error."

"And who was your source?" Tara said. "And how did you know we were here? The press hasn't found us yet."

"I assumed it was your editor," Cox replied.

"That was fast," Tara said. "I just called him, but I don't remember telling him where I was calling from."

"He probably has a caller ID on his phone," Cox suggested.

"I used my cell phone."

"Then perhaps Chief McLean called someone," Cox suggested.

"There's no phone in his room."

"Then I'm at a loss," came the reply. "But it's obvious the source is not trustworthy. I am pleased he exaggerated."

"Your source is either on the fringe or at the heart. His information could have futuristic overtones," Tara pointed out. "Is the governor aware that there is going to be another attack on my mother? Has he been involved in planning one or ordering one?"

"You sound like a prosecuting attorney," Cox remarked. "The governor knows nothing about this attack on your mother."

"May I quote you?" Tara asked politely.

"Yes, of course."

"And these attacks have nothing to do with two of the governor's aides breaking into my mother's house late Friday night?"

"That problem has been resolved. The missing records have been returned."

Tara gulped back her desire to hammer him to the ground with his own admission and instead passed over it lightly. "So there is no reason why the governor would want my mother dead?"

"Of course not," Cox shot back. "Mrs. Svenson has been a valuable member of the governor's team."

"May I quote you on that?" Tara asked with seeming innocence.

"Yes," Cox replied. Then spurred on by Tara's positive response, he added, "The governor considers her a friend."

"A trusted friend?"

"Yes. He trusts her."

"Did he also consider Andre Varrieur a friend?"

Cox's voice reflected his relief at being led to safer ground. "Mr. Varrieur was a staunch supporter. A tireless worker in the governor's campaign."

"So he wouldn't want him dead?"

"Never!" Cox protested heatedly. "Mr. Varrieur was a major fund raiser for the governor's campaign."

"And the governor has others like Mr. Varrieur?"

"Many," Cox said.

"Do his supporters include the publisher of the Oakland Journal?"

Cox was surprised at the question. He answered it forthrightly. "Yes, your publisher is a supporter. That's common knowledge. He hosted a fund-raising dinner for the governor a few weeks ago."

"Was Mr. Huxley Zurich at that dinner?"

"I don't believe so," Everett Cox said. "I believe the first fund raiser Mr. Zurich attended, as a private citizen, was last Friday evening."

"And after his meeting with the governor, two of Governor Atkins' staunchest supporters are attacked. Do you see any connection?"

"None whatsoever!" Cos declared vehemently.

"But isn't Huxley Zurich the founder of the animal rights' group that advocates violence?"

"LAITA advocates animal rights," Cox replied stiffly.

"Do you believe Huxley Zurich targeted my mother because she shows dogs? LAITA is waging an all-out war against show people. Did you know that Varrieur was running the same route on the Country Club side of Ardilla that my mother runs every morning?"

"I wasn't aware of that," Cox replied. "But I don't believe that your mother was the target. If she were the second man would not have gone after Varrieur in the hospital. Varrieur was definitely the target."

"So you believe LAITA is not involved?" Tara pressed.

"If there is a connection," Cox declared. "The police will find it."

"The governor is a strong supporter of law and order, correct?"

"Absolutely," Cox came back firmly.

"He believes that the law should be the court of last resort, correct?"

"Absolutely," Cox reiterated staunchly.

"What does the governor say about the fact that a cop shot my mother?" Tara charged.

"A cop?" Cox stammered.

"You didn't know?" Tara queried. "A State cop–California Highway Patrol."

"He wasn't a real one," Cox declared. "The man who wore the uniform wasn't a real cop. Real cops don't shoot unarmed women."

Again Tara switched topics.

"Have you ordered a guard around the governor?"

Cox was ready this time.

"The Secret Service will supply protection once Governor Atkins declares his candidacy for the Presidency."

"So despite the fact that two of his supporters have been hit; the governor is not worried about himself or the rest of his staff." Tara concluded. "Any comments?"

"Yes," Cox replied with assurance. "The governor doesn't believe either 'hit,' as you put it, has anything to do with him. That he knows two victims of violent crimes is merely coincidence. He is, however, deeply disturbed that it happened and has resolved to include a tough-on-crime plank in his platform for the presidency."

Tara danced away.

"My mother likes you, you know," Tara commented disarmingly.

The sudden switch to the personal caught Everett Cox off guard.

"She trusts you," Tara went on. "She says you're a good man. Is she wrong?"

"I...I would like to think not," Cox replied, bewildered at the new tactic. "I like her too."

"But not enough to save her life."

"Save her life?" Cox gasped. "I'm not involved in a conspiracy, believe me."

"Actually, I do. Goodbye, Mr. Cox."

Everett Cox reviewed their conversation. Had he said anything that could be damaging to the campaign? He decided that he hadn't.

He pulled out a sheet of paper and began writing the governor's remarks.

# Chapter 53

Cox isn't part of the inner circle, Tara decided. Her mother would be glad. She liked the man. He knew their location but that fact told her that her pursuers did too. She had told Lieutenant Lim but not her editor and Cox had called the hospital less than ten minutes after she had called Lim from her cell phone.

Somewhere, somehow the men after her had tapped into her cell phone. She was sure of it. She glanced at the clock above the nurse's station. Her editor needed her copy soon.

She had been on her way to the waiting room on the surgical floor, her computer tucked under one arm along with copies of the photographs she had taken. The lab man had blown them up. She had taken them along because she needed to write a caption for the prize shot of the lot–the photo of the unidentified man leaning out of the helicopter side door, his rifle aimed straight down at her minivan as it burst into flames.

Until the call came, she was planning to sit in the waiting room and type her story. But now that seemed like a bad idea. It's where they would expect her to be. And it was empty. Only emergency surgeries were performed at this hour. She'd be the proverbial sitting duck.

Tara headed for the elevator and went down two floors. The hall was deserted. She walked down it hoping to meet a nurse so she could ask what floor she was on and where she might find a room. She saw a light on in a room and entered it. The curtain was drawn around the bed.

There was movement on the other side of the curtain.

"Excuse me," Tara said hesitantly. "I was hoping you could help me find a room."

The nurse pulled back the curtain.

"It's after visiting hours."

"Oh, it's okay. I'm supposed to be here. My mother..."

The nurse didn't let Tara finish. "Oh, you poor dear. I'm so sorry."

She stepped away from the figure on the bed. The sheet had been drawn up over the face.

"She's dead?" Tara stammered. "I was just told... But someone else told me she... Different people told me...when did it happen? Why wasn't I called? Did she ask for me?"

Her voice broke and tears gushed out. The nurse gently led her to a chair. "Take all the time you need. I'm sorry. We were having trouble reaching you."

"But I was right here in the hospital," Tara protested.

"So you got our message," the nurse said.

"What message?"

"We left one on your answering machine," the nurse said.

"I'm afraid there's been a mistake..." Tara began.

"There's no mistake," the nurse said. "You just sit here. No one will disturb you. Take as much time as you need."

And before Tara could straighten her out, the nurse left, closing the door behind her. Tara stared at the closed door and at the draped figure on the bed. She had wished for a sanctuary and God had provided one.

She bowed her head and prayed for the woman on the bed. The door opened and was immediately closed again.

She moved the chair toward the bed, put her laptop on her lap and began her story. Unlike news stories of old, the modern journalist didn't fit every fact in the first sentence. Perhaps it was because the television newscaster had already spewed forth the pertinent data thus stealing the standard opening lines. Newspapers, in order to compete, now opened with provocative statements to draw their readership deeper into the story they had had but a glimpse of on the TV news.

Fifty minutes later, Tara left the room. The hall was empty. She took the elevator back upstairs to the surgery floor. The nurse couldn't tell her when the operation would be completed. Tara left her cell phone number with the nurse and went up to where McLean lay in intensive care. She pushed her worry about her mother deep inside her. There were things that had to be done if they were ever to be safe.

She was greeted warmly by the three in the room.

"My mother's not out of surgery," Tara announced.

"We were worried about you," McLean said, "although I must admit you found a great hiding place."

"You knew where I was?"

"Andy went to get your statement. When he didn't find you in the waiting room, he asked the nurse. She remembered you'd gone down in the elevator and which floor it had stopped on."

"She was puzzled," the sheriff put in, "you know, as to why you left the waiting area."

McLean continued. "Andy took the elevator down to three and asked the floor nurse if she'd seen you and she told him where you were."

"I went to Room 307 and opened the door," Sheriff Tolliver said. "And you were praying."

"That was you?"

"I decided you were in good hands."

"It was weird. Sitting beside a dead woman writing a story about all the attacks on us."

"I would imagine it would be," the sheriff said. "Visions of it being your mother..."

"No, not that at all," Tara said. "Oh, maybe at first when I first thought it really was my mother. Part of me said it wasn't possible, but part of me was afraid it was, afraid I'd blanked out somewhere along the way and while I was out my worst fears were realized. Then I worried lest it be a prediction, God's way of preparing me. Sounds crazy, doesn't it?"

"Not with all that's happened," McLean said softly. "So, when did you know the truth?"

"Not until I was close to the end of my story."

The sheriff's intake of air was sharp and distinct. "You thought it was your mother and you wrote?"

Tara laughed lightly. "Sorry, Sheriff, you don't know the way my mind leaps about. I knew it wasn't my mother right away. Too tall."

"Then what?"

"I looked up from my writing several times and imagined that this white sheet was snow. Sounds crazy, doesn't it? But think about it. Something white covering something dead. It's not too big a leap, is it? That made me think that we might be accepting an illusion as reality. That we might be assuming that Atkins is in bed with the mob when actually he's in bed with greed."

"You lost me."

"Mother is a threat, right?" Tara said. "Mother is also naive. She wouldn't ever believe that the people she met were part of a new type of underworld. As far as she was concerned they were businessmen."

"You would have us believe that businessmen hired thugs to attack us?" the sheriff asked. Disbelief hung on every word.

Tara turned to McLean. "Think about it. Why weren't we just overpowered, taken somewhere and shot? That's the way the mob does it."

"Alex was pumped full of lead," McLean said.

"But not Manuel."

"Are you saying Manuel is a plant?"

"No," Tara said quickly. "I'm saying that the shooter made two mistakes. He didn't make sure Alex was dead and he didn't shoot Manuel. The mob doesn't leave witnesses."

"So he was a klutz," McLean said.

"He doesn't have the mob mentality. The mob doesn't use poison the way these guys do. It's as if they've all taken a course in it."

"So the signature is different."

"That's important," Tara went on, her excitement rising. "They're really into this accident thing."

"The mob uses accidents," Tolliver pointed out. "Trucks run people down. People drown."

"The mob would have gunned us down on the freeway," Tara said. "As close as we are to the truth, they wouldn't have played around."

"What are you saying?"

"Our pursuers are cops, that is, former cops. They know what's needed to wrap up a case. That's why the bullets disappeared. No bullets. No case."

"The bullets were supposedly picked up by a cop," McLean mused. "I'll bet SFPD never thought to run the description against those who've quit the force."

"And storming my headquarters," Tolliver went on. "To get the photographs. The mob would have blown the place up."

"We've been concentrating so hard on the possibility that this was all mob-connected we forgot that what drives the mob drives business as well," Tara said. "Old-fashioned greed."

"You're talking about big business. A business that wants something from the new president," McLean said. "Lend me your cell phone, Tara. I want to call Lim."

"I think they're tapping my cell phone," Tara said and then explained her reasoning.

"Tolliver believes his radio calls are being monitored," McLean said, "so he used the phone in the hall to call Lim for me. We can do it again."

"The pay phone?"

Sheriff Tolliver shook his head. "Two weren't working. That made me suspicious. I used the phone at the nurses' station and called Lieutenant Lim from there."

"Maybe that one's being tapped as well," Tara ventured.

"Might be by now," the sheriff agreed. "I guess we could call from headquarters."

McLean nodded. "Good idea. By the way, Tara, Lim says that thanks to your mother's notes, they found the negatives and Varrieur's financial records. He has Chang going through them."

"Tell them to look for oil companies and their subsidiaries," Tara said. "Write a note. We'll fax it from the sheriff's office."

"Why oil companies?"

"What's the biggest environmental issue we're facing today?"

"Logging?"

"The money's not there," Tara said decisively. "It has to be the desire to drill in Alaska. That's why cozying up to LAITA is so important. They are going to do a trade-off."

"You can't buy off animal rights groups," Tolliver stated flatly.

"Not real ones. But this Huxley that heads LAITA is an opportunist. He wants power. If he can win some major battles, he can probably be persuaded not to fight others," Tara said. "And there's money in oil, and with our economy so oil-dependent, there's power. Atkins listens to people with money and power."

"If we take him down, won't someone else just take his place?"

"Probably," Tara finished. "But fear of losing the war is a poor reason not to try to win a battle."

A quiet voice from the corner spoke up. "You're tackling such a big opponent."

"Like David and Goliath?" Tara asked.

"Only you don't have a slingshot," Adrienne Tolliver said.

"Oh, but I do," Tara replied. "I have a pen."

"But you can't print what you think, only what you know," Adrienne insisted. "And you'll be dead before you know enough."

"To protect my mother, all I need do is take out the man whose campaign she threatens," Tara said. "Before, when I thought he was in league with the mob, I didn't believe the photo was of any real consequence. It wouldn't faze them. But I don't believe businessmen would view such a sexual aberration with quite so cavalier an attitude as a bunch of mobsters."

"You have a plan?" McLean asked.

"Don't I wish!" Tara exclaimed.

"Well, I have the beginnings of one," McLean said. "By the time you bring back breakfast, I'll have it ready."

"We have to hurry," Tara said. "I have a deadline to make."

"I'll order breakfast and pick it up," Tolliver said. "We have a great place near headquarters."

"They do take-out?"

"One of their specialties," Tolliver chuckled. "I think my men keep them in business."

Outside in a van parked in the lot, one man turned to another. "You get that?"

"Every word," the second man said. "Told you. Men don't abandon patterns. Our plan is a go."

"What about McLean's proposed plan?"

"He'll never get to use it."

"How much time on the clock?"

"Hmm," the stocky man mused. "It'll take them ten to get to the station."

"It might take longer."

"She's in a hurry, remember? Add five minutes to that for everyone to gather. And five minute contingency factor. Twenty minutes from pick-up to explosion."

"She could have enough time to fax her newspaper.

"We have that end covered," Herb Guzman commented. "Are our men in place? We go in as soon as the place blows."

# Chapter 54

The white Styrofoam boxes were stacked one on top of the other in groups of five and tied with string. The one containing the C-4 explosive was at the bottom of the stack.

Someone would have to open it immediately upon its arrival for there to be time to do anything at all. And if they did open it and scatter, the men outside would take them out as they emerged from the building. It was as close to a bombing and strafing attack as one could get without an aircraft. It would be just as lethal.

Sheriff Tolliver parked directly in front of the entrance and Tara jumped out and ran up the few stairs to the glass walled entrance. She raced across the narrow reception area, through the half gate leading to the common desk area and into the room near the middle of the building where the fax machine was.

Her dogs bounded up from their sleeping place under the chief's desk as soon as they heard her footsteps and caught a whiff of her scent. They met her halfway. She greeted them both by name and rushed on.

They were about to follow her when the chief entered the front door laden with boxes of hot food. The Styrofoam boxes didn't hold back the scent from the dogs' keen noses and they ran toward him in anticipation. He set the boxes on the nearest empty desk and slipped off the string so he could open the top box.

"Breakfast!" he announced to the two men seated at desks upstairs.

One man ran downstairs to tell the men in the lab. The other disappeared into the washroom.

"You two been good dogs?" Tolliver asked his bright-eyed four-legged companions.

Both Banner and Sandy wagged their tails and perked their ears. The chief reached into the box and took out a sausage, bit into it and thoughtfully chewed it. The dogs remained in place as their tails wagged with greater fury. Sheriff Tolliver broke the remaining bit of sausage in two and gave each dog a piece.

Then he looked at his hands. "I'd better wash up," he said to the dogs. He took his open box and set it on the top of the file cabinet and peeked into the fax room. "How's it going?"

"I'm printing up the article. The photo and caption are going through the fax machine now," Tara said. "That is they'll go through as soon as the line is clear."

"Send the note to Lim first," the sheriff suggested. "Might get through to him right away and then we can leave the other in the machine."

"Good idea!" Tara said as she pressed some buttons that cancelled the first call. She added McLean's note and dialed a new number. The fax machine clicked and hummed in response.

"I'm gonna wash my hands," the sheriff said. "Will your dogs leave the food alone?"

"I'll watch them," Tara promised.

The sheriff hurried off and Tara turned her attention to gathering her article from the printer. She could have tried to e-mail it, but the FAX machine was a faster and surer method to get it in under the wire.

When the sheriff headed for the washroom, the two dogs headed back to the desk that held the food. They sniffed at the boxes and perked their ears at the tiny clicking sound coming from one of them.

Sandy jumped up, put his front paws on the desk and nosed the noisy box. The clicking was faint and steady, like a beating heart. He pawed at the boxes and the stack fell over. He hooked the bottom box with his claws and pulled it onto the floor. One of the other boxes was dragged along and fell open on top of it.

Tara, hearing a noise, peeked around the corner. She saw a stack of boxes untouched on the desk. Two individual boxes were separated but still on the desk top. She spotted the open box on top of the file cabinet and concluded that the sheriff had already dispensed some boxes. She didn't see the two on the floor behind the desk.

"Be good!" she warned the dogs and turned back to her task. She removed McLean's message, added the computer printout of her story to the photograph and set the pile on the plastic holder.

As she was doing this, Sandy was staring at the two open boxes at his feet. The food from the one box had spilled onto the contents of the clicking box. Banner dipped his head and snagged a sausage. Sandy, possessive of the clicking toy, chomped down on it and dragged it from the box and carried it to Tara. Banner, meanwhile, wolfed down two pancakes and a strip of bacon.

The big yellow Lab came in the door as Tara was looking around for the card with her editor's fax number on it.

Sandy stood waiting, his prize hanging from his mouth, his tail wagging excitedly.

"Just a minute, Sandy," she said without looking. "I need to send this."

She set the card with her editor's fax number next to the machine and glanced down at her dog.

Her finger, which was poised to set a new number, dropped on the send button and the fax machine purred as it clicked into gear, sending her news article to the police station in Ardilla.

Tara took no notice that the pages were being faxed because in front of her was a dog with a device in his mouth that had a digital clock counting down numbers. She put her hand beneath his jaw and took hold of the putty-like substance and said firmly, "Out!"

Sandy opened his mouth but the C-4 stuck to his teeth. Tara wrapped her fingers more firmly around the clay-like substance and tugged it loose. She told Sandy he was a good dog and yelled for someone to come.

Banner came on the run.

The C-4 was nearly bitten in two. Tara was staring at the numbers. She could see them, but she couldn't read them. Her mind refused to focus.

Sandy jumped up and grabbed the dangling plastic end. Automatically, Tara tightened her grip and held on. Sandy pulled. The plastique stretched but didn't separate.

Banner, seeing the long thin rubbery substance being tugged on by his two compatriots decided to join in. He clamped down on the substance near the middle and his teeth neatly chopped it in two.

Sheriff Tolliver was the first to appear at the fax room door. He assessed the problem with one glance. Two of his deputies nearly crashed into him in their rush to answer Tara's call.

"Looks like we have about four minutes," Tolliver said as he gently pried the block from Tara's fingers.

"Take it out and heave it," one deputy suggested.

"I say leave it and run!" a second voice said.

"No!" shouted Tara. "They'll have men out there to pick us off if we leave."

"She's right," the sheriff said. "Cole, you check to see if there's another one in any of those boxes. Bill, help me move the desks. Luke, Mike, take Tara and the dogs downstairs and break out the riot gear."

"Sandy has a wad in his mouth," Tara said as she reached down and scooped it out. She threw the plastic wad in a nearby wastebasket.

"That's why maybe we can contain it," Sheriff Tolliver said. "He tore off most of the C-4."

Cole was already ripping open boxes. Banner was watching with anticipation. Bill hurried to the desk the sheriff indicated and together they moved it toward the front of the building.

"Banner, come," Tara called. Banner perked his ears and looked at her, but, with boxes being ripped open in front of him, the aroma of freshly cooked bacon was too much.

Sandy pulled away from Tara and tore off in the direction of the food being carelessly tossed aside.

"Luke, Mike," Tara said, "go break out the riot gear. I'll be there. I just have to give my dogs a little incentive."

Luke ran out the door and down the stairs. Mike followed.

"You can't leave the C-4," Luke called back.

"Got it!" Tara yelled and turned. She hurried toward the wastebasket. The fax machine clicked off as she passed.

"Grab a dog," she heard the sheriff yell.

"I got the yellow!" Bill called at the same time Cole yelled that he had the black.

Tara looked at the card sitting on the fax machine. Her news article was still unsent.

She punched in the fax number for the newspaper then reset the material. She pressed "send" and the fax machine clicked on.

Tara grabbed the wastebasket and ran for the stairs. Sheriff Tolliver met her halfway, a helmet in one hand, and a vest in the other.

"Where were you?" he shouted. "Put these on."

Tara slipped into the vest and the sheriff clapped the helmet on her head and dragged her the rest of the way down the stairs and into the hall that led to the jail cells. She was still holding the wastebasket.

The men were donning riot gear while holding onto the dogs' collars. All were crowded against the concrete staircase wall. "How safe is that stuff?" Cole asked nodding at the basket.

"It needs a primer explosive to detonate," Luke replied, then seeing confusion on Cole's face, added, "Something has to explode inside it, like a blasting cap."

Tara squatted next to her dogs and hugged them.

384

"What about a piece of flying debris?" Cole persisted.

"Not even a bullet shot into it or..." The rest of his words were lost in the sound of the explosion.

The building rocked. Tiny bits of cement block dropped on the floor around them.

Upstairs, the power of the blast blew the huge desks across the room. One desk hit the file cabinet on one side which folded as if it had been gut-punched, the top drawers snapping their locking mechanisms and flying into the center of the room. Folders flew into the air and the papers inside sailed over the counter through the shattered glass-paneled wall in front and out onto the miniature patch of lawn on either side of the walkway.

The other desk rammed the water cooler and sent the heavy jar skyward. It came down intact, but, when it found its stand gone, it hit the floor, rolled, fell into a huge hole blasted in the middle of it and bounced on the hard clay beneath the front half of the building. The ceiling plaster showered the entire area with white chunks.

The sheriff issued orders and his four deputies armed with guns and wearing helmets ran up the stairs and took their positions. Two carried fire extinguishers although the sheriff expected more trouble from people than from fire. He told Tara to stay put.

Tara didn't like being exposed in the corner next to the jail cells. She wanted a place where she could close up the dogs and keep them out of harm's way.

The first door on her left was the evidence room; the second, the equipment room. She picked up the wastebasket and urged the dogs to follow her into the equipment room.

As she entered the room with the dogs at her heel, Banner stopped and growled at the outside door. It was a warning growl.

Tara's mind flashed back to the fact that when the first invasion took place, the men had entered through this door and stolen the film. Why wouldn't they come in from the back as well as the front?

The equipment room was stocked with guns, but she had no time to load one.

"Kennel!" she hissed and Banner entered the equipment room. Sandy was already inside investigating the stock. The smell of gun power excited him.

Tara set the basket with the C-4 on the counter, reached inside and took out the hunk of plastic explosive which had already been stretched by the tug of war with Sandy.

She rolled the C-4 between her hands into a long spaghetti-like strip. It was stickier than modeling clay and she couldn't pull it apart easily. She looked around the room for something to cut the strip with. She didn't want to use her teeth.

She saw what appeared to be the end of a knife handle on a high shelf. It had been there long enough for a spider to spin a web and catch a few flies. She brushed aside the web and grabbed the handle. When it tipped, it knocked a small box off the shelf and onto the counter. The box split on impact and out spilled a string of small firecrackers still attached by their wicks.

Tara remembered Luke's words. "...needs a primary detonator." Quickly she cut apart the firecrackers and picked up a fistful of them.

With the long strand of C-4 slung over her shoulder, she opened the door a crack and listened. She heard nothing.

Maybe Banner was reacting to men outside sneaking towards the front of the building. Maybe the sheriff had guessed right.

Still, she had to cover their backs. She stepped into the hall and cut a small strip of plastique, stuck a firecracker in it and set it on the floor.

The only sound she heard was the soft squeak of her own shoes on the tile floor. Her fear mounted in the silence and she laid down several more tiny strips between the door and the stairs.

She laid her knife on the fifth stair as she got ready to lay down the last strip. Then she heard the crackle of a radio. With trembling hands she shoved the remaining firecrackers into the plastique and dashed back toward the equipment room.

The knife lay nestled against the riser two steps above the plastique.

The sound of a key being inserted in the lock on the outside door made her jump. It was a tiny sound, one that wouldn't be heard upstairs, and one that she wouldn't have heard were she not so close. A tiny sound. It was followed by a whisper on the other side of the door. The click of the lock opening upgraded her fear. They were coming in. While she had planned for it, her mind had played a game telling her that if she prepared for them, they wouldn't come.

She froze in place and stared at the moving door handle. Suddenly, Banner barked.

Startled, Tara took three giant strides and grabbed the knob to the equipment room and turned it quietly. As the outside door opened, Tara slipped into the room and hissed at the dogs to be quiet.

She heard the soft shuffling of feet as she eased the door closed. She didn't realize how tightly she was gripping the knob until she felt pressure on it from the other side. Her reaction, born of fear, kept the knob rigid.

Tara glanced around the room. A few firecrackers lay still scattered on the counter. A box of roadside flares sat tucked against the wall. She couldn't see the knife anywhere. She grabbed two flares and lit one.

Tara could barely hear the scuffling of feet outside the door. She envisioned the lab door being thrown open next. They were checking for survivors.

Sandy and Banner were standing facing the equipment room door, hackles raised, deep rumblings coming from their throats. Tara's hand released the knob. No one upstairs would hear the approach of this force.

Suddenly, a spatter of gunfire shattered what glass remained at the front entrance. It was a noisy frontal assault meant to command attention.

The sheriff had prepared only one trap. And while he was springing it, another would be sprung on him.

Tara opened the equipment room door a crack. Three men were already at the staircase. They would wait until the shooting stopped so as not to get caught in the crossfire. It was now or never.

Flares in hand, Tara slipped through the door, shutting the dogs in the room. Banner barked his protest.

The men on the staircase turned. While they were dressed in black, their faces were uncovered. They planned to leave no witnesses alive.

Tara quickly slid along the wall hands held high. In one hand, she held a lit flare; in the other, an unlit one.

"Put down your guns!" Tara ordered. She meant to shout the command, but her voice cracked and it came out weak and soft. The barks of the locked up dogs were more forceful.

A voice from behind her chortled. "You scare me to death."

"I should," Tara said touching the tip of the lit flare to the unlit one in her other hand and subsequently holding two lit flares. "That stuff you have all over your shoes, the sticky stuff you stepped through is C-4."

The men on the stairs looked down at their feet. Bits of dough like substance were visible on the edges of their soles.

"Ignore her," the leader said. "C-4 doesn't explode when it's exposed to fire. The only danger down here are those dogs of hers and they're locked up."

"You want to bet your legs on that?" Tara spat back.

"You sure that she can't light us up?" one of the men on the stairs asked. Tara saw his face muscles tighten.

"I'm sure," the leader said. He turned to the man at the back door. "Drop her."

"If you do," Tara hissed, "I'll drop this flare right there at your feet where the firecrackers are. They'll detonate the C-4."

The leader looked down. The man behind him caught the momentary flash of fear in his leader's face.

"She's bluffing!" the leader shouted. "She'd go up with us."

Tara's arm came down and she stepped toward the speaker. "Try me!"

"Go ahead!" he challenged. She stared up into cold eyes that showed no fear.

"No!" shouted the man behind him. "Let me get outta the way. I ain't spending my life in a wheelchair to protect some sleazy politician."

The man behind him backed down the stairway as well. "Me neither!"

"Don't go too far," Tara said. "You won't want to miss the show."

"You're stalling," said the man with the cold eyes.

"This is for my mother," Tara said as she brought down the flare.

"Wait!" shouted the man standing near the back door. "You touch him and I'll shoot through this door."

Everyone could hear the barking and the scraping of the paws against the door. The dogs were flush against the panel. There was no guessing involved.

The man's gun swung toward the door.

Tara's throw was instantaneous. Laughing, he ducked sideways and a bit of the burning tip touched his sleeve. It glowed. When he went to brush it off, he pulled the trigger of his gun. The bullet sliced through his shoe, then the soft flesh between the bones and finally straight through the tough rubber sole. The firecracker caught in a ridge in the sole of his shoe was hit. It was a tiny explosion but it triggered the C-4 that clung to it. The man was thrown backwards out the door. His agonizing scream told the onlookers as much as the bits of bloody flesh that splattered the walls and doors.

He'd bet against Tara and he'd lost.

Deputies in riot gear appeared at the head of the stairs.

## The Puzzle

The invaders all carefully laid down their weapons.

# Chapter 55

The screaming sirens and the wail of the fire engines broadcast the magnitude of the incident. A man in a dark suit rushed into Chief McLean's hospital room and Adrienne immediately rose from her chair.

The man held out his hands. One held a badge; the other, was empty. "I'm here to take your place. Your husband is being brought to Emergency downstairs."

"Andy?" Adrienne gasped. Her face went pale. "What happened?"

"Someone blew up the sheriff's headquarters. I got the call on the radio from the ambulance. He asked for you."

"Someone needs to watch Chief McLean," Adrienne said. "He...he..."

She stopped and looked at McLean. His breathing appeared labored. "He needs a nurse right now. He's going into respiratory arrest."

"You go!" the man urged. "I'll take care of it."

Adrienne picked up the syringe. "He can't wait. He needs his shot."

She fumbled and the syringe dropped on the floor. Adrienne began to cry.

The man picked up a fresh syringe. "I can do this. Just tell me how much."

"Two milligrams," Adrienne said. "Hurry!"

"I've pressed the call button," the man said. "The nurse will be here any minute. Now go. You're not doing the chief any good. See to your husband. He might not have much time."

Adrienne saw that the man had the antidote in the syringe and had inserted the needle into the tube properly. She hurried out the door.

The dark-suited man looked over his shoulder. As soon as the door closed, he laid down the syringe. The chief sucked in a great gasp of air and then fell limp.

The man coolly pinched McLean's nose shut with the fingers of one hand and put the other hand over his mouth. There was no struggle, but the attacker was uncertain. After two minutes, he lowered his head to listen for a heartbeat.

McLean's hand came out from beneath the sheet. He pressed a gun against the man's ear and the man slowly released his fingers and put his hands over his head.

He started to speak, but McLean put a finger to his lips and motioned to the man to move toward the door. The man did so slowly.

McLean hopped out of bed and the man realized that McLean was without pants. The muscles on the police chief's thighs told him that the man under the flimsy gown could take him in a fight.

Before McLean reached him, the dark-suited man shoved the door open with one shoulder. McLean's sudden grip of his other shoulder surprised him. The big man was also fast.

"Take off your pants," McLean hissed.

"Out here?" the man asked him, his tone objecting. "Let's go back in the room."

"And warn your friends? No way!" McLean replied squeezing his assailant's shoulder. The gun was planted firmly in his back and the hold on his shoulder was solid.

"I know you're thinking about reaching for that gun under your arm or the one strapped to your ankle, but I wouldn't," McLean warned. "I'd love to just shoot you. And if you have a gun in your hand, I can."

The man unbuckled his belt and unzipped his zipper. McLean nudged him with the gun. The man lifted his left arm. He kept both his hands locked over his head as his pants fell around his ankles.

A nurse and an orderly rushed toward them.

"What are you doing?" the nurse cried.

"He's crazy!" the half-naked man said. "I'm a cop. I was sent here to protect him. He thinks I'm going to kill him."

"You," McLean said to the orderly. "Take his gun."

The man whose pants were around his ankles took the offense.

"Go down to the surgery floor. My partner's there. He'll tell you who I am."

The orderly hesitated. He looked at the nurse who nodded at him to go get the other cop. The orderly turned to leave.

"May I remind you who has the gun," McLean said coldly. The orderly stopped.

"First I gets the gun," the young black man said to the nurse.

Gingerly, he reached inside the man's jacket, unsnapped the holster and removed the gun.

"Throw it back inside the room," McLean said, holding the door open with his foot.

The orderly bent over and slid the gun through the door into the room behind McLean. He was still crouched down when McLean told him to remove the ankle gun. The orderly felt the legs of the man's pants bunched around his ankles.

A second nurse joined the first and whispered her query. The first nurse hissed orders and the second nurse turned to leave.

"Don't move," McLean said. "I know you don't understand this but trust me. His partner isn't a cop either."

"I can prove I'm a cop," the man said. "I have my badge in my pocket."

"Pull it out," McLean said to the orderly.

The orderly produced it at once. McLean nodded and he handed it to the nurses.

"Now his wallet," McLean said.

The orderly searched the pants on the floor, eyeing the hairy legs warily. He produced the wallet within seconds.

"Hand it to the nurse," McLean said. "While they look at that you find his handcuffs."

"He don't have none. I knows that already."

"Strange," McLean said. "A cop with no handcuffs."

"Yeah!" the orderly said.

"The names don't match," one of the nurses said.

"Suspicious, wouldn't you say?"

"I was undercover," the man put in hastily. "I was called away. There's been a terrible explosion at the sheriff's headquarters. My partner will verify this."

"Where's my room?" McLean asked.

"Down the hall," the head nurse said pointing toward the nurses' station. Her finger trembled slightly.

"You're lying!" McLean decided aloud.

"It's this way," the orderly said walking in the opposite direction.

"You two come with me," McLean said. He waved his gun and the two nurses preceded him down the hall. The man, a gun pressed to his neck, hobbled behind them.

Once inside the door, McLean said, "In my stuff, there should be handcuffs."

It took the orderly only seconds to find them.

"Strip!" McLean ordered the man.

"Why?" a nurse objected. "You've got your own clothes right here. You don't need his."

In a few minutes, the man stood naked, his clothes and shoes at his feet. McLean kicked them under the bed, then tore off his hospital gown and threw it at the naked would-be-assassin.

"This is inhumane," the man yelled as he donned the gown.

"I agree," McLean said stepping into his own pants. "Cuff him."

McLean yanked his shirt from its hanger. "Let's go."

"Go?" the man objected. "Go where?"

"Bring him," McLean ordered looking at the orderly as he held the door for the two nurses.

"I need an empty room," McLean said.

"511's empty," the orderly volunteered. The head nurse threw him a dirty look.

McLean herded the group into 511. The elevator at the far end of the hall opened and Adrienne stepped out and hurried to catch up. She held the door for the women. They saw the deputy's badge on her chest and their fear began to fade.

"He lied!" Adrienne burst out, glaring at the naked man.

"I figured," McLean said.

"I'm so sorry, I panicked," Adrienne said her voice catching.

"What did you find out?"

"The man they brought in had his legs blown off. The whole station is a mess, but everyone else is okay," Adrienne reported. "Why are these nurses here?"

"They want to sound an alarm and we've got the rest of the crew at the hospital to round up. Mrs. Svenson is still a target."

"Why is he naked?" Adrienne said nodding at the cuffed man in the gown that was too short to cover him completely.

"Because he probably had a tracking device or a radio transmitter in his clothes."

"Cool, Man," the orderly commented. "I be thinking this be TV stuff."

"I'm glad you never had to get out of bed," Adrienne commented.

"Oh, but I did," McLean smiled. "And I knew I would which is why I let you go."

"You let the nurses see you," Adrienne huffed. "I could have handled it."

"You're used to dogs and cats," McLean huffed back. "Now go get my medicine."

He turned to the two nurses. "The people after us are very dangerous. They just blew up the sheriff's station. They would have no trouble quietly strangling a couple of nurses and stuffing them in a closet if they appeared to know too much. You are not their primary target. Keep it that way."

The nurses' faces drained of color. He was getting his message across.

"Because they took out the sheriff's headquarters, I can't call him."

"I can..." the lead nurse began.

McLean waved off the suggestion. "Too risky. He will be here. He's bringing me breakfast. He knows how cranky I get when I get hungry."

Properly warned, the nurses left.

McLean chatted with the orderly until Adrienne reappeared with the medicine, her thermos and the guns she found on the floor.

"Now what do we do?" she asked.

McLean hopped up on the bed.

"We wait."

The orderly rushed out.

# Chapter 56

The two men slid into the room, guns drawn, silencers elongating the barrels. Each man plastered himself against the wall in the short hallway made up by the closet on one side and the bathroom on the other.

Herb Guzman had chosen this assignment for himself. McLean had frustrated him one too many times. The man with him wasn't Eddie, but it didn't matter because he too had incentive. McLean had escaped death from his morphine-loaded ice pellets and was a blot on Jack Anello's otherwise perfect record.

The room was empty except for the man in the bed at the far end of the room.

"Not me!" the man in the bed shouted. "He's in the bathroom."

Simultaneously, Herb Guzman and his partner swung in between the two beds, faced the closet and pumped bullets through the closed sliding doors. The pattern guaranteed a hit no matter what part of the closet the man had chosen to hide in. The silencers kept the noise level from the guns to a minimum but the smashing of the bullets through the plywood door announced to the floor nurses that shots were being fired. Neither nurse left her station. They had been warned.

"Drop them!" Came a strong voice from the open bathroom doorway.

Neither Herb Guzman nor Jack Anello obeyed. The two simultaneously whirled around, fingers still on the triggers of their automatic weapons. The first rounds from McLean's guns hit their targets.

Guzman took his in the shoulder. His hand numbed by the bullet hitting a nerve, released the gun. It dropped on the bed its last few rounds tattooing the wall up to the bathroom door. As Herb collapsed to the floor, his left hand reached across to his back and pulled out a second gun.

Anello felt McLean's first shot bury itself in his arm. Steeling himself against the pain, he held on to his gun and let it also spatter the paint from the wall as it traveled to the doorway where McLean stood.

Without even a millisecond hesitation, McLean squeezed the triggers of his two hand guns. It was hard to believe he had time to aim. But he did.

As Herb had dropped to the ground, McLean's right hand gun had followed him down. Its bullet shattered his other shoulder. The one round Guzman managed to get off from his pistol grazed McLean's ear.

The bullet from the gun in McLean's left hand buried itself in Anello's chest before the man's spray of bullets passed the doorframe. As Jack went down, his finger squeezed the trigger one last time. The last round hit the mark.

McLean felt a stinging pain in his thigh and his knee buckled. Herb Guzman, crouching on the floor, a bullet in each shoulder, managed to tip his gun upwards toward the falling police chief. He would finish this.

"I wouldn't," McLean said, his voice like a clap of thunder.

Herb looked into the eyes of the man who'd successfully evaded death at his hands and saw a resolve there that matched his own. He knew that even if he got off a shot, he was beaten. He let the gun drop out of his hand.

Running footsteps in the hall told McLean the nurses could ignore the gunfire no longer.

"Adrienne," he yelled, "guard the door."

The plump middle-aged lady emerged from the shower. Herb Guzman saw a shiny gold badge on her chest and almost laughed. What the hell did this guy need back-up for?

The woman stepped through the door and immediately barked orders. "We need three gurneys and a medical team for each."

Adrienne's presence announced the victor.

# Chapter 57

With the police, fire engines and ambulances came the TV crews and other reporters. They swarmed around the outside perimeter facing the sheriff's compound and filmed the loading of the man with mangled legs into the first ambulance.

The police strung a yellow ribbon across the wide entryway as the sheriff told the fire chief about the C-4 on the back stairs.

The cameras caught the men exiting the building by the side entrance untying and kicking off their boots as soon as they hit the parking lot.

Sheriff's deputies accompanied each shoeless suspect shoved into a patrol car and refused to comment as they did so.

Tara, a blanket thrown over her shoulders, sat on the running board of a fire engine, her dogs beside her, watching as the men who had threatened her life were systematically arrested, handcuffed and loaded into patrol cars.

Her mind was busy with the fact that this was but one unit. An enemy force as large as the one pursuing them would simply call up another company of men. She had won but a skirmish.

Her plan to fly home, confront the governor and have him cave-in to the pressure of media exposure seemed more like a fantasy than a reality. She and her mother and Chief McLean would never make it home at all. She would expose no one. She'd be dead by nightfall.

The men arrested would one by one slither out of serious jail time. None of them would fold. She'd looked into the eyes of the man on the stairway. There had been no fear there. That his legs weren't blown off wasn't due to the fact that he had backed down. Another had posed more of a threat.

As she thought about the confrontation with the men on the stairs, Tara decided to make a trade–the story of the year for her mother's life. She stood up and walked over to Sheriff Tolliver. Their conversation was brief.

The sheriff announced that he would have a statement in two minutes. The word was passed along the fence and crews and reporters scrambled to position themselves at the front gate.

The sheriff was handed a microphone, politely asked if everyone could hear and, after an affirmation, he held up his hand for silence. He then began to outline the happenings of that morning and introduced Tara Svenson who would complete the story.

"She is the reason none of us were injured. I leave it to her to tell you that part of the story."

Tara began with her dog delivering the bomb to her as if it were a duck. The cameras dropped to take in the dogs sitting beside her.

She finished with the laying of the C-4 on the floor and the subsequent stand-off. She left out not one word of the exchange between her and the four men, not emphasizing any of the lines spoken more than any other. It was a factual report down to the throwing of the flare and the man's gun discharging into the firecracker buried in the plastique under his shoe. It was a freak explosion.

"Any questions?" she asked.

"So the men were taking off their boots because there was C-4 stuck on them, not acid?"

Tara had heard the whispered speculation of the reporters who could only see the frantic discarding of the boots by the three men exiting the building. Several reporters had seen her carry out both her dogs and hand them to a deputy and then kick off a pair of oversized galoshes. The reporters assumed correctly that there was more than broken glass on the floor. Acid had been their first guess.

Questions about the throwing of the torch came next.

"You aimed high," one reporter queried. "Why?"

Tara laughed. "It was automatic. When I throw for my dogs I always throw high."

"So you weren't trying to blow him up."

"I was trying to stop him from shooting my dogs."

"But would you have blown up the man on the stair?" another reporter pressed.

"I don't know," Tara replied.

"Sure you know," came a heavily sarcastic response. "You're covering your ass."

Tara sought out the face that went with the voice. "You weren't there. I was. There were five armed men upstairs and after the initial blasting of what remained of the front windows, no shots had been fired. The men on the stairs thought that meant that everyone upstairs was dead. I hoped it meant that the sheriff and his men had managed to surprise the intruders and take them without firing a shot. I don't know what I would have done if the man at the door hadn't threatened my dogs."

Another reporter burst in, "You said that one of the intruders said and I quote, 'It's not worth losing my legs over some sleazy politician.' What politician was he talking about?"

"I can only guess," Tara said. The murmurs increased in volume. "But I can give you several facts and let you draw your own conclusions."

The group grew silent, expectant.

"Fact one, of course, is that the man made the statement under duress; however, as I wasn't asking a question, his statement was purely voluntary.

"Fact two, before my mother left the campaign office of Governor Whalen Atkins, she took a shredded photo after seeing the governor himself shred it. We put the photo together and saw the picture of the governor committing an act of sexual perversion. My mother promised the governor she would return the photo and say nothing out of respect for the family of the other party involved."

"Do you have the photo?" shouted a reporter.

"No. It was stolen when..." Tara started.

"Was that what was taken out of the cab when the cop was shot?"

"No," Tara said. "That was something else. The photo was snatched at the hospital when I was..."

"So you don't have it?" yelled a reporter. "So you can't prove your allegations against the governor, can you?"

"Let her finish," yelled another.

"I'm a reporter," Tara announced. "I deal in facts; not suppositions."

"What paper?" a man taunted. "The Little Town Weekly."

"<u>The Oakland Daily Journal</u>," came a voice from the back. "She's got a by-line. And I wouldn't mess with her."

The group grew silent. That fact alone commanded respect.

"We don't have the original photo which was snatched from the hospital where I was having a bullet taken out of this arm." Tara pointed to her arm, again encased in a sling. "But, we do have the negative."

The crowd murmured at this bit of news.

"There's more," Tara said. Quiet descended.

"The man who took the photograph and was blackmailing the governor was Andre Varrieur. My mother spoke with him at a party and with her help the Ardilla police were able to locate the negative."

The murmurs began again.

"There's more," Tara said.

"Your paper won't like you giving us everything," a reporter near the front commented quietly.

"My paper has a terrific front page story right now. This is an update."

"Are you going to publish the picture?"

"No, we aren't," Tara said.

"Surely, your mother doesn't owe the governor?"

"She respects the family of the other person," Tara said. "But I promised more. The evidence taken from the cab when Lieutenant Alex Caribou was shot was not sexual, but financial."

The shouted questions multiplied.

"Is Governor Atkins being backed by the mob?"

"Did the governor have anything to do with the death of Varrieur?"

"Do you have any proof?"

Tara held up her hand. The reporters fell silent. "I know of no connection between the governor and the mob. And I don't believe the governor was involved directly or indirectly with Varrieur's death. Varrieur was a valuable asset with his own agenda. But he was connected to a group with another agenda. And yes, I have proof–that is, the Ardilla police have proof. Following my mother's lead, they uncovered hidden financial records. Financial records in Varrieur's computer had been destroyed prior to the arrival of the Ardilla police by the Manzanita Police Chief Dick Chattaway himself. He possibly allowed a copy to walk away with a detective hired by the major group funding Governor Atkins' campaign."

"You can prove this?" charged a reporter.

"Chief Chattaway admitted destroying the computer files. He told Acting Chief Greg Lim of the Ardilla Police that he did it accidentally," Tara said. "The presence of the detective is a verifiable fact."

"Who's funding the governor's campaign?"

Tara was quiet.

"Do you know?" the reporter pressed.

"Yes, I do," Tara said and then smiled. "But as you said, I have to save something for my readers."

"That's it?" queried one of the group.

"This much I'll say," Tara replied. "And then I'm done. The forces at work here are bigger than the governor. He's like a captain in an army. Above him, making the decisions, far removed from the fray, are the generals. Today we took captive a handful of foot soldiers. The war goes on."

"Are you saying the military are behind this?" charged a newsman.

"I was speaking metaphorically," Tara shot back. "Most of you understood that I'm certain, but for those of you who slept through English, let me speak plainly." A titter of laughter greeted this observation. It soon died down, and Tara continued, "The motivating force behind all this is greed. These men aren't spurred on by love of country but by exactly the opposite. They would destroy our country if it meant they would gain financially. You hunger for a better look at one man's perversion, but it is the obsession of the rich man for more wealth that is obscene."

The respectful silence lasted a mere second before the questions began anew.

Tara turned to the sheriff and whispered, "Take me to the hospital."

"Are you ill?" Sheriff Tolliver whispered.

"I don't feel right," Tara said. "I feel faint."

Sheriff Tolliver put his arm around her and called for a paramedic. The men from the second ambulance responded immediately.

By the time they reached her, Tara was trembling and unable to stand unaided. Her dogs were crowded next to her.

"What a silly thing to do," she murmured.

"Delayed shock reaction," one of the paramedics ventured. "Did your head hit the wall when the explosion occurred?"

"Which one?" Tara replied waving away the gurney. The sheriff led her to the ambulance. Her hand gripped the two leashes. It wasn't necessary. Banner and Sandy were not about to leave her side.

"You could have a concussion," the paramedic said. "But I need to check you out."

"Your sling has blood on it," one of the paramedics noted. "Were you hit?"

"Sheriff, the dogs," Tara murmured just before she slipped into unconsciousness.

The paramedics quickly loaded Tara into the ambulance. Reporters crowded around ready to suck up any tidbit of information. The cameras continued rolling.

The sheriff attempted to board with the dogs but was blocked by one of the paramedics. "The dogs stay."

"Don't waste precious time," Sheriff Tolliver said. "If she wakes up, she's going to see her dogs. And that's how it's going to be, boys."

Cole and Luke stepped up and each grabbed an arm and hoisted the paramedic away from the door.

Banner and Sandy scrambled inside and thrust their noses on Tara's stomach. Sheriff Tolliver grabbed their leashes and hauled them away from the paramedic who was on the radio giving the hospital Tara's vital signs.

He turned. "We are going nowhere until those dogs are gone," he snapped.

Sheriff Tolliver leaned out the open door. "Boys, get us there."

Luke slammed the back door shut. A second later the key was turned in the ignition and, with sirens blaring, the ambulance sped toward the hospital. Squad cars fell in line lights flashing, sirens screaming. Cars dove toward the sidelines as the ambulance approached.

Tolliver radioed McLean. "I'm coming in right now with Tara. Your breakfast blew up. I have my men with me. Stay in bed. We'll come to you."

He didn't mention that the "we" didn't include Tara.

That the dogs were tethered on the end of leashes was due to Cole's foresight. When he'd hidden in the sheriff's office after the blast, during the few seconds he was waiting, he was squatting next to the trophy box on which the leashes had been dropped. He'd stuffed them in his pocket and later he'd been the deputy who'd snapped a lead on Banner and been left holding the tethered dog while Tara dashed back and carried out a second. When Sandy had been secured, he told her the trophies were safe. The plaster from the ceiling had fallen on the table they were tucked under.

Now, Cole exploded from the driver's seat full of apology. "She carried out both dogs. I didn't see her carry out Banner, so I didn't know she had until a reporter shouted at me. Then it was too late. She was already inside. I didn't think she'd carry out Sandy, with that injured arm and all. It's her arm, isn't it? That's what did her in, isn't it?"

Tolliver shoved the dog leashes into Cole's hands. "Guard these two with your life," he ordered. "You know how important they are to her."

"Yes, Sir!" Cole snapped.

"And Cole," the sheriff added, "just so you know. No one could have stopped her."

# Chapter 58

When Tara woke up, she stared at the white ceiling of a hospital room. The lights were on. She heard the murmur of voices. She turned her head.

"It's about time," her mother said. "It took you longer to wake up from arm surgery than it took me to wake up from chest surgery."

A chair scraped as it was pulled closer. The smiling face of Spencer McLean came into her field of vision. "It seems that throwing that flare and then carrying both dogs out of the building was a bit hard on your arm."

"You broke a blood vessel," her mother put in. "They had to operate and repair the damage."

McLean grinned. "I, of course, have been a model patient which is why I'm up and about."

"Don't believe a word he says," the sheriff put in. "He arm wrestled one man and shot two more. He just got lucky."

"So I was losing blood?" Tara asked. "I mean I had a real reason for fainting?"

"As good as they come," the sheriff replied.

"How long have I been asleep?"

"Hours," everyone chorused.

"We had breakfast," McLean said. "We were discussing lunch."

"Discussing?" Tara looked puzzled. "Is the hospital giving us a choice?"

"Nope," McLean replied. "Andy's favorite chef is feeling guilty. We get whatever we want forever or until we leave whichever comes first. I figure we'll be ready in a couple of days."

"Mother can't travel," Tara exclaimed.

"Private plane," Coral said. "I can manage that in a couple of days the doctor says. Ambulances will take me to and from the airport. I'll hire a nurse and stay in bed."

"Will that be safe?" Tara asked. "And why am I here? Why aren't I in a recovery room? Are we still in danger, is that why?"

McLean grinned.

"You made all the newscasts. We've been enjoying your performance," he said. "The governor pulled out of the presidential race and resigned."

"He resigned?"

"Lim gave him a private showing of the photos reproduced from the negatives," McLean explained. "He decided to fade out of sight gracefully while he still could."

"Wow!" Tara breathed. "What else did I sleep through?"

"Your friend Sergeant Kathy Riley brought Volatis' throw away gun to the forensics lab in San Francisco while Drew Manning was there. It turned out to be the gun that fired the bullets Volatis turned in as those that were taken from Alex's body at the hospital."

"Is he in jail?"

"Wait, it gets better. Drew Manning, who didn't have much else to do in San Francisco but think, suggested that if Volatis had thrown away the original bullets, he would have thrown away the bag they were in; but, since he didn't and since, in fact, he had it with him when he doctored the phony bullets, the original bullets from Landecker's gun must also be in the car. Kathy had already called her captain and asked for a warrant when Drew and Devin began tossing around where one would hide bullets in a car. Drew's attention was drawn to the throwaway piece and they talked about what Volatis probably planned to do with it. They concluded that he would definitely dispose of it. Then Drew asked, 'Why not the bullets with it?' And that's where they found them. In the chamber of the throwaway gun."

"Did you find any of Alex's blood on any of them?"

"You want everything, don't you?" McLean commented. "No. No blood. And a pretty weak chain of evidence without Sergeant Volatis' testimony."

"So?"

"He decided to cooperate."

"Did we need him? There was the tape."

"He promised more."

"What more?"

"He gave us Brian Harvath."

"Not the governor?"

"Governor Atkins claims he didn't know anything about the police cover-up," McLean explained.

"He'd leave that to Brian," Coral added.

"Anyone else implicated?" Tara asked.

"Harvath says he handled the whole thing himself."

"And you believe him?" Tara charged.

Coral broke in. "I told him that that's how things worked around there. I honestly don't think Everett Cox knew what was going on but I can't say the same for Frank Whiting and Caleb Brinson."

"It was Cox who hinted that you might be a target," Tara countered. "He knew something."

"He suspected," her mother put in. "He's a good man."

"Mother, you aren't still trying to pair me up with him, are you? After all this?"

"I was a part of that group up until two days ago," Coral sniffed. "You could do worse."

"I can do better!" Tara shot back. "Let's change the subject. Sheriff, how is that guy whose legs got blown off?"

"He survived," Tolliver said. "They saved a piece of one leg. He lost the other."

"I'm sorry," Tara said sadly. "That's a terrible thing for anyone to have to deal with."

"You do remember that he shot himself in the foot," McLean put in. "You do remember that he was going to shoot Banner and Sandy. They're safe and in good hands, by the way. I've got more news from home. You want to hear it? It's really good news.

Tara nodded half-heartedly.

"The Manzanita mayor fired Chief Chattaway. They offered Lim his job."

"You consider Lim leaving good news?"

"Lim doesn't want the job," McLean went on good-naturedly. "He says he likes where he's at. He doesn't have to fight for respect. And he says he's too old to take on the task of cleaning up Chattaway's mess all alone."

"So he turned it down?"

"He told the mayor he'd consider the offer. He wants to talk it over with me."

"And you're going to tell him to take it, right?"

"And lose a great officer? No way. Lim and I are going to persuade the three mayors to consider an independent police force servicing all three towns. Lim will head up the Manzanita station, Alex will take over Newell and I'll promote a couple sergeants to lieutenant and be able to take time off to pursue my new hobby."

Tara's half-scowl was replaced by curiosity.

"What new hobby?"

"Making babies and watching them grow."

Tara's mouth dropped open in astonishment. Disappointment clouded her tone. "I didn't know you were married.

"I'm not–yet."

"Or engaged for that matter," Tara added, trying to swallow her feelings.

"I'm not–yet. But I've found the girl, a youngster really," McLean said a twinkle in his eye. "Her mother says she's almost old enough to get married."

"Almost old enough!" Tara spat out. Her feelings escaped in anger. "You're disgusting, McLean. You should be looking for a woman with your level of maturity."

"But I like this one."

Tara abruptly changed the subject. "Exactly where are my dogs?"

"In good hands," McLean said. "Don't you want to know more about...?"

"What, in your opinion, are good hands?"

Coral butted in.

"Joyce Webb has them. She came over as soon as she saw them on the news. She was afraid that they'd get lost in the shuffle. They're in her kitchen playing with Sweetie."

"And what's Talker think about that?" Tara charged, too much anger built up to take a softer tone with her mother. "You can't mix mature males like puppies."

"Talker left for a circuit with a handler right after Sunday's all-breed show," Coral said. "He took the Breed, got a Group Two by the way. Now is his time to be specialed."

Tara harrumphed her approval.

McLean dove back into the fray. "Your editor called. He said your article was great. He said your photo is spread over three columns and your story has a double column next to it. All front page. He's anxious for your next installment."

"I was scooped by every news media in the state."

"They don't know everything that happened," McLean said.

"Sure they do," Tara protested. "I told them everything."

"Your editor picked all that up off the wire," McLean went on. "He wants more."

Tara, however, was still depressed. "There is no more."

"Sure, there is," McLean said. "There's this wonderful story about how this brave police chief fought off three assailants."

"No one knows about that?" Tara asked, with a spark of interest.

McLean smiled. "You had to have something to tell your readers, so we saved you some good stuff."

"We?" Tara asked looking around.

"I was in the shower during the shootout," Adrienne offered. "I haven't talked to any reporters yet."

"And we have pictures of the damage to my headquarters," Andy Tolliver said. "Nobody's been inside but my men."

Tara's eyes began to come alive.

Coral spoke softly. "And with McLean's help I zeroed in on the conversation I had with Andre Varrieur when we were talking about jogging. Remember I told you his gift was getting people to talk about their hobbies. Well, he had me describe the trail around the Country Club in detail. I remember his interest warming me. Cox was there. So was Huxley. McLean has filled in Lieutenant Lim and you've got a heads-up on this one."

"Is my computer safe?" Tara asked.

Sheriff Tolliver nodded. "It never even slid off the table. Of course, the fact that half the ceiling fell on it might have been the reason. But it survived."

"And finally there's my impending marriage," McLean put in. "That's got to be news. I can see the headline. `Cop Hero To Be Wed.'

"How old is this child?" Tara spat out.

McLean raised his eyebrow. "I don't know."

"Fifteen, sixteen, seventeen?"

"Double the first number," McLean replied.

"Thirty?" Tara gasped. "That's no child! That's a woman!"

"Well, sometimes she is. When she dug the bullets out of my arm, she was a woman. When she stood face to face with a bunch of armed men and bluffed them with a couple of roadside flares, she was a woman. When she gave up an exclusive story to save her mother's life, then she was truly a woman, the finest kind."

Tara blushed. She brushed her discomfiture aside and dove into battle. "When was she a child?"

"When she scrambled up my back and got shot."

"I was trying to help!" Tara protested.

McLean laughed. "Okay, I'll give you that one. Now can we talk about making babies?"

"In front of my mother?"

"She says I should ask you if you want children."

"Of course I want children. What a silly question."

"How many?"

"I haven't thought about it."

"Sure you have. You have an opinion on everything."

"I don't know. One. Maybe two."

"We'll aim for five."

"Five? Where'd that number come from?"

"A boy and girl you for, a boy and girl for me and pick of the litter for your mother–five."

"We can share our boy and girl and mother can take pick puppy from Biscuit's litter."

"That sounds good to me," McLean said affably.

Tara smiled. The smile widened into a grin. "You win."

"What do I win?"

"Me," she said. "You win me."

"Then that's settled."

"And being contentious is not childish."

"You always want the last word?"

"Always," Tara said firmly.

And McLean simply smiled.

www.ingramcontent.com/pod-product-compliance
Lightning Source LLC
Chambersburg PA
CBHW050858250626
47155CB00001B/20